MW00896248

Elizabeth's Destiny
Written by Jolynn Raymond
Edited by Rachel Scott
Copyright November 2012
Written 2007
All rights reserved

This book is a work of fiction. Names, characters, places, and incidents either are the product of the author's imagination or are used fictitiously, and any resemblance to actual persons, living or dead, event, or locals is entirely coincidental.

Other books by Jolynn Raymond:

Lessons of Love: A Historical Romance
Sweet Agony: A Collection of BDSM Erotica
Dining In: A Taste of Erotic Food Play

Coming out next:
Jolynn Raymond's Dark Obsessions: A Collection of
Lesbian BDSM Erotica

India 1816

Elizabeth Thornton gazed longingly at the barely clad children milling around her in the market. The heat of the day was stifling, especially in her long, high-necked gown. She was an oddity to be sure, with sleeves that reached her wrists and sturdy boots that covered her feet instead of the cooler sandals and brightly colored cloths worn by the native people. Elizabeth couldn't even indulge in the relief of fanning herself because one arm was hooked through a heavy basket full of her purchases, and the other hand held a much needed parasol to block out the scorching rays of the sun. Her skin was still milky white, and she intended for it to stay that way, even here in this God forsaken land.

It had been a month now that she'd lived in India, sent here by her mother and the elders of their church, to be a missionary with the Baptist Mission Society. Almost all of the women in the society were wives of the men who spread the gospel, but they had made an exception in Elizabeth's case.

There had been trouble back at home, and she'd been packed off like a shameful secret. Her refusal to marry the rich Baron Von Sheffield, and then a subsequent scandal involving a young British soldier who had escorted her home without a chaperone when her carriage had broken a wheel, were all it took to set the tongues of the town's matrons wagging. The rumors were false of course, and the Baron an old pig, but her mother had been humiliated, and had shipped Elizabeth off to India in a heartbeat when the elders had proposed this solution to her delicate problem.

So now here she was, shopping in an open market, haggling in a language she barely understood for the items she needed, and hating every minute of it. It wasn't really the actual task she despised so much, being away from the mission grounds gave her a sense of freedom she rarely felt any longer. It was the fact that the market was dusty and blazing hot, and she had to go about in her proper garb regardless of the fact that she felt faint and uncomfortable. If only she could loosen her stays and actually breathe.

She was planning on doing just that as soon as she returned to her cramped little room. She would lock the door and indulge in a cool bath, and she wouldn't give a care about all the water she used. It was her only day free of bible studies, training, and church duties, and nothing was going to spoil it. Oh she was sure to get a scolding from Pastor Dawson for leaving the mission's grounds, even if she didn't have obligations, but it would be well worth the old goat's tongue lashing.

The rebellious nature that landed her in India to begin with hadn't been dampened by a change of location. This simple act of disobedience combined with the thought of a decadent bath, were enough to lift her spirits, and the fact that she hadn't been deemed subservient enough to actually spread the gospel to the women of India yet was also a plus in Elizabeth's mind. She wasn't looking forward to the day when she would be given the task of preaching about God day in and day out. It wasn't that she didn't believe in God, but she wasn't particularly pious either.

The practice of harems was barbaric, and in her mind all of the women of the country were oppressed no matter their caste, but speaking to them wouldn't change anything. It was the men who ruled them that needed to change. Granted her view was seen as scandalous so Elizabeth kept it to herself, but nothing she had been taught since arriving in Haldia had changed her opinions.

Deciding she had everything she needed, Elizabeth started for home. She wasn't looking forward to the walk, but she also didn't want to waste the last of her money on a hired carriage. The Society's mission was located at the outskirts of town, and it was a considerable distance from the market, but she preferred to come and go under her own power. She found their carriage driver rude and intrusive, and hated the way his eyes raked over her every time they spoke. He wore the trappings of the rest of the pious men of the church, but the man was no gentleman. Elizabeth had doubts about the purity of his thoughts. If the price of avoiding him was a long walk in the blazing sun, then she would pay it.

Unbeknownst to Elizabeth, she was being followed, again, and her decision to walk home would have life altering consequences. Maxwell Harrison was watching her every move like he had since he'd spotted the lovely English woman three weeks ago. First thing he'd done was to look for a wedding band on her delicate hand, and after seeing none, his mind had begun to develop a plan. He made it a firm practice to stay away from the married women, their husbands were bound to kick up a fuss, but the unwed girls were a whole different story. This one was enchanting, and she made it a habit of going out unescorted. If she disappeared, the men and women at the mission would place the blame on this beauty's shoulders, and most likely decide she got what was coming to her.

Her face was like that of a porcelain doll. Perfect, with a unique little nose, made cute by a tiny bump on the bridge. Her eyes were vivid, green in color and large as a frightened doe's, and her mouth was as sweet as a cherub's, yet very sensuous and kissable. Her hair, though almost always entirely concealed by a bonnet or sun hat, was the shade of burnished gold. Just once he'd seen two long curls cascading down her back like a waterfall of silk. The one time had made him long to run his fingers through it, and wrap it tight in his fist as he kissed her into submission.

The fact that her body was one a man would die for couldn't be hidden beneath the folds of her full skirt or long sleeves, nor by the high lace collar. There were some things a man just knew would be delectable, even without removing the gift wrap, and this English woman was one of them. She was also a tiny little thing, but he'd seen her haggle with the best of them in the market place, her green eyes flashing in anger when the merchants tried to take advantage of her because she was foreign. It showed him the girl had spunk, and that was very important for what he had planned for her future.

Maxwell worked for a powerful Indian man named Jeeval, who collected beautiful women like some men collected objects of art. Jeeval was the nephew of the Emperor Akbar Shah II, but had no taste for family politics. He'd moved from Delhi to Haldia to get away from the madness, so he could live his life of decadence in peace on a grand estate just outside of the city.

His birthright and riches granted him leave to take as many wives and concubines as he saw fit. Some were bought as slaves, some presented as gifts from fathers seeking to win favor with the royal family, and some, like the woman before him, were stolen from the streets. Jeeval's royal blood all but ensured a blind eye would be turned if his wives and concubines were the result of kidnapping, still, Max knew it was wise to be cautious.

Jeeval had very unusual tastes, and the whispered secrets of the harem, or the means by which most of the women were acquired, were things best kept quiet. Jeeval's women were sexual slaves, like many women who lived in harems, but there were differences as well. There were eunuchs who guarded the women's quarters to be sure, but there were also men among them, ones whose sole purpose was to school them in the art of erotic and sadistic pleasures. It was a rare happenstance that a virgin would be summoned to Jeeval's bed. He had very distinct preferences, and wanted his women to be trained to please. They needed to have fire, but also the proper amount of submissiveness for the wicked games he loved to play. Weeping maidens or wildcats who still had all their claws, held no appeal.

When they were brought to Jeeval's estate, they were carefully groomed in the style of his liking, taught how to perform to his expectations, and punished if they didn't do as they were told. They were also kept aroused night and day, and always in need of bedding. Wet, waiting, and continuously ready for him to take his pleasure, was how their lives were lived. He had no use for a concubine who had no idea how to please a man, nor ones whose body hadn't been trained to become sexually aroused from pain. Jeeval relished those who put up some resistance, it added to the thrill of the taking, just as seeing a beautiful woman naked and showing submission by kissing his feet made his cock swell with lust, but his trained men assured there would be no ice maidens or insolent women in his bed.

Max had met Jeeval while at a formal function, and the two had hit it off well, talking as men do, and boasting of sexual conquests. He'd invited Maxwell back to his estate, and gave him free-rein for the night with his stable of women. The very act would be unheard of in any other harem, but Jeeval had ulterior motives for showing Max how his specially trained slaves behaved. Maxwell Harrison seemed the type who could charm any maiden, but also would have an adept hand when it came to igniting just the right amount of fire in those brought to his estate in the future.

The women's submissiveness and desire to be dominated both with the lash and sexually, had aroused Max immensely, and come morning, Jeeval had offered him a job as a trainer for his newly acquired beauties. Now Maxwell had his eye on Elizabeth, and he couldn't wait to begin her lessons in passion. He had no compunctions about taking a virgin to bed. He would gladly deflower this sweet young thing before him, the thought of burying himself between the delectable thighs he knew were hidden beneath her long skirts, made his cock jump and swell.

Dropping his hand and readjusting his suddenly tight breeches, Max set his plan in motion. It was time to capture this little dove. He reached down and slipped a rupee into the hand of a waiting boy.

Chapter Two

"That one, the English woman. Steal the basket and knock her to the ground."

"Yes Sir." The boy beamed up at him and quickly put the coin in the pocket of his tattered pants. He hurried after Elizabeth, and waited until she was past the busiest of streets, then swooped in on her. He slammed into her from behind, full force, and grabbed the heavy basket. Elizabeth cried out in shock, flying forward into the dust as the basket was torn from her hands. She landed hard, chin bumping the dirt road, cutting it open, hands scraping across the small stones, then lay still, stunned by the attack.

Maxwell, watched with delight then ran a hand over his face to turn his smirk into a grimace of disgust, and rushed to the lady's aid. No one else was close enough to have seen the assault, and therefore only he was aware of her peril. He raced forward, past Elizabeth, as if he were contemplating chasing the thief, but then turned back to her and knelt by her side. "Here now, Miss. Are you hurt? Let me help you."

Elizabeth tried to push herself up but winced when her injured palms touched the ground. Max put a hand under her elbow and steadied her, helping her into a kneeling position.

Looking at her like this, his mouth no more than a foot from hers, took his breath away. He'd known she was beautiful; he'd been close enough to see the color of her eyes before as she stood in the shade of a market stall bargaining for fruit, but he'd never been this close, never close enough to kiss her. He felt her body begin to tremble, and watched as her eyes filled with tears, her lower lip starting to quiver.

"There, there now luv. It's all right. I'm here to help you."

"I... He... I never saw him coming. My things, oh he took all my things."

Elizabeth knelt there in the dirt, her mind in a whirlwind because of the attack and the nearness of the stranger who'd come to her aid. His soothing English accent and gorgeous blue eyes were both mesmerizing and comforting. She studied his face in silence, admiring the sharp sensuous cheekbones and full lips. His hair was so blonde it was almost white, and some curls had escaped the leather tie that held it back in a tight ponytail. She imagined some would call him beautiful if the term was used for a man. The sight and nearness of him addled her wits.

She dropped her eyes, unable to meet his gaze, only to take in the broad expanse of his chest and muscular arms. She shook herself mentally as she gawked at him. What was the matter with her? Here she was, sprawled in the dirt, and all she could do was gape at her savior, her heart pounding like a bird trapped in a cage.

She brought a tiny hand up to rub at a painful spot on her chin, and gasped when it came away red with blood. The combination of the heat, the excitement, Maxwell's nearness, and the sight of her blood made Elizabeth's head spin. She closed her eyes, moaning, feeling as if she were about to faint.

"Here now luv, you need to get out of the hot sun. I'll take care of you, sweet. Don't fret about your chin. It's still pretty as ever. I'll fix you right up."

Maxwell scooped her up in his strong arms and Elizabeth didn't protest. He gazed down at the beauty he held close, stunned by the ease with which her abduction was going to take place.

"Ah, I see some shade down this street Miss. Let's find you a place to rest before you faint. Then I'll tend to your chin and hands."

Maxwell carried her down the deserted alley to a wooden crate in the shade. He set her upon it gently, and Elizabeth tried to give him a little smile, but her lip quivered again.

"There, there pigeon, it's okay. What's your name luv?"

"Elizabeth Thornton. I'm from the Baptist Mission. I... I was headed home from the market and... Oh I simply hate taking a carriage, so I decided to walk. I've been so foolish and look where it has gotten me."

She gazed into those gorgeous blue eyes again then bit her lip as she lowered her own. That also proved to be a bad move because the sight of his muscular thighs encased in his tight breeches only made things worse. Her heart skipped a beat, and she drew in a quick breath. Elizabeth was finding her rescuer's presence to be extremely unnerving. Maxwell saw a hint of a blush tint her cheeks and had to hold off a wicked grin. Miss Prim and Proper liked what she saw.

"Maxwell Harrison at your service, Miss Thornton, but everyone calls me Max. I'm with the British East India Trading Company, been here about three years give or take. I must say it's a good thing too, or I wouldn't have been here to tend you after that little scallywag's attack. As for you being foolish, I disagree, luv. The fact that you like to walk shows me you're independent. You aren't one of those simpering ninny's who can't lift a finger to fend for themselves. I prefer my women to have spirit."

Elizabeth's chin and eyebrows shot up at this declaration, her cheeks flushing with anger, and she made to get off the crate, but Max quickly dropped to his knee before her, damning himself for forgetting a lady would take offense at such talk.

"Forgive me Miss Thornton. I didn't mean to insult you. Please believe me when I tell you I am only here to help. I won't do anything to tarnish your virtue, nor make any improper advances. You have my solemn word. Will you allow me to clean your wounds and escort you home?"

Elizabeth eyed Maxwell carefully. What should she do? On one hand, it was this type of situation that had gotten her into trouble back home in England, on the other, her knees and hands were scraped up and her chin was bleeding. She was also frightened and quite shaken up. Elizabeth couldn't deny the trembling that still gripped her body. She would be terrified walking home alone, afraid of every noise, jumping at her own shadow.

"I will, as long as you promise to conduct yourself like a gentleman. I do have spirit Mr. Harrison, and I have also been told I have a fiery temper. Don't get any ideas about me being your kind of woman. I am a lady, and as such you will treat me that way and refrain from further undignified comments."

The fire that flashed in her green eyes and the proud way she held up her bleeding chin made it impossible for Maxwell not to admire her spunk. The woman had sass all right, and it led him to believe she would be a spitfire in bed. Right now her breasts were heaving as she fought to control her anger, and her cheeks were flushed the prettiest shade of pink. Max very much wanted to kiss her senseless, but those activities would have to be saved for later. Right now it was time to get her safely back to Jeeval's estate.

"I promise to be nothing but a gentleman, Miss Thornton." Maxwell pulled a handkerchief soaked in ether from his back pocket before she could say anything else, and moved to wipe the blood from Elizabeth's chin. He tilted her head back then slipped his hand around behind it to hold her steady.

"This will sting, luv. Close your eyes. I promise to be gentle." Elizabeth did as he asked, and Maxwell moved in for the kill, pressing the drug soaked cloth to her nose and mouth and sliding his hand under her sunhat so he could wrap a fist in her hair. Elizabeth began to struggle immediately when he covered both her nose and mouth, but Maxwell held tight, and before long she was forced to take a breath of the ether. Once she was unconscious he pulled the cloth away and wiped the blood from her chin before bending down and brushing his lips over hers.

"So sweet. I'm going to greatly enjoy your lessons, luv. Such a beauty and all mine, at least for the time being. You're going to show me every bit of that sass and fire pet, and I'm going to teach you how to put it to good use with a little help from my riding crop." That said Maxwell scooped her up and carried her to the other end of the alley where his closed carriage was waiting. He set Elizabeth inside and climbed in after her then knocked on the roof to tell the driver he was ready. Their next stop would be Jeeval's estate, and Miss Elizabeth Thornton would find out that her world had changed forever.

Chapter Three

When they arrived at the estate, Max carried Elizabeth to his portion of the estate. He had been given very elaborate quarters in which to do his work. His rooms were filled with exquisite items, a brass candelabra and ornate oil lamps lit every corner of the rooms, marble floors gleamed underfoot, the best crystal and silver adorned his table, stunning tapestries and oil painting covered the walls, and an enormous marble bath, the size of a small pool, part of which extended outdoors into a meticulously kept garden graced one end of the main room.

His bed chamber held a huge four poster bed, with silk sheets, down pillows, and crystal oil lamps that lit the skin of the women who graced it with a golden glow. Many a woman had lain in said bed both willingly and with protest. He wondered absently how long it would take sweet Elizabeth Thornton to get over her virginal shyness and give in to her inner desires.

His set of rooms also held a special chamber for women who refused to cooperate. It wasn't anything barbaric, but it lacked the comforts they would find if they were obedient. Maxwell hoped he wouldn't have to imprison Elizabeth for long, but thought the feisty wench would probably spend some time behind the locked door. He thought taming her with carefully applied pain and pleasure would be much more effective, but impudence couldn't be tolerated, not anymore. If she proved to be an uppity insolent shrew then she would be locked away until she decided to be sweet and do as she was told.

Maxwell deposited Elizabeth on the floor amid a mound of satin pillows, then stood back to admire his catch. He congratulated himself on the ease with which he'd kidnaped her and marveled once again at her beauty. She was young, probably no more than eighteen, but he couldn't imagine why she hadn't been snatched up by some wealthy baron or duke back in England. Her manners and decorum spoke of good breeding, and her dress, while modest, indicated she came from a family of higher class. Why hadn't she married? Why had she been sent to India? She certainly didn't seem the missionary type. Most of the women he'd seen from the Baptist Mission traveled in a pack and were well chaperoned. They seemed at home in their drab matronly gowns, and seemed so pious and

Red.

serious. Elizabeth was as different from them as night and day.

Well, it didn't matter, and it certainly made things easier. He imagined the mission would look for her for a time, but things would die down quickly. This was India and young women disappeared on a fairly frequent basis. Elizabeth was obviously cut from a different cloth than most of the other women, and therefore would shoulder the blame. It wasn't politically correct to question the Emperor's nephew, or other rich and powerful men about these matters.

Maxwell was pulled from his musings by a little sigh made by Elizabeth. He knelt down beside her and removed her boots, loving how tiny her feet were. He then loosened the ties of her sunhat, pulling it free and exposing her hair in all its glory for the first time. Yes, he'd seen a bit of it, but the beauty of her gilded locks, shiny and soft as silk, made him catch his breath. Maxwell ran his fingers through her tresses, loosening the pins so it fell in a cascade of gold around her shoulders and over her breasts. It was long, magnificently long, and Maxwell couldn't wait to see her wearing only her golden hair.

"Beautiful luv, simply exquisite, and I haven't even had a peek under that smothering gown. Jeeval is going to love you once you're properly trained." Maxwell moved his hand around the back of her neck and began to expertly unfasten the long row of buttons that kept Elizabeth's body from is gaze.

Elizabeth fought through the cotton that seemed to fill her head, trying to open her eyes and place a face with the voice she heard. Hands were in her hair, pulling her pins loose and unfastening her dress! What was happening? Her eyes fluttered open, and she looked at Maxwell in confusion, and then shocked fear as the events of the day came back to her. Elizabeth tried to sit up, but the sudden motion made her head spin, and she feared for a moment she would vomit. Crying out, she pressed a hand to her mouth and looked at Maxwell with huge green eyes.

"Here now, kitten. It's all right. I'll get you some water, don't try to move." Maxwell quickly returned with a goblet of cool water and helped Elizabeth sit up. She eyed him warily, remembering his hands in her hair and along the back of her neck, but accepted the refreshing liquid all the same. There was a horrid bitter taste in her mouth, and her throat was dry as a bone. After a few sips she pushed his hand away and turned steely eyes upon Maxwell.

"Where am I, and what am I doing here? How dare you touch me?"

"Now pet, don't you want to rest a bit more before we get down to the nasties of business? Just lay back and relax." Elizabeth pushed up on the pillows, intending to rise and run but Maxwell caught her around the waist and pulled her into his lap. She slapped his face, eyes flashing with rage at being manhandled, and then began to pound her fists against his chest.

"Let me go! What are you doing? Get your filthy hands off of me, you beast! I'll scream. Let me go or I'll scream until the roof falls in." Elizabeth continued to beat upon his chest as Maxwell tightened his arms around her. One hand crept up her back to entangle itself in her hair while the other held her like a band of steel around her waist. He pulled her head back, and then held it still as he swooped down for a kiss to silence her cries.

Elizabeth went wild in his arms, but Maxwell crushed her to him, effectively stilling her hands as his mouth began to work its magic over her lips. She set her mouth in a grim line, refusing to open to him, refusing to give in, but Maxwell had met with resistance before. He moved his mouth over hers gently, while his hands held her like steel. He backed off just an inch, knowing what she would do, and Elizabeth fell right into his plan. Opening her mouth to lash out at him, to berate him, to scream, he quickly silenced her by swooping down again, this time upon her open mouth.

Elizabeth froze in his arms as his tongue swept across hers and explored her mouth, the heat of him could melt butter, and she moaned as he caressed her cheeks and tangled with her tongue. Smiling into the kiss at her reaction, Maxwell pulled back and nibbled at her lips, tasting, teasing, little licks and tiny nips that drove her to distraction and caused a heat to spring up deep in her belly that she didn't understand.

The heat began to build with every thrust of his tongue and it frightened her. She looked into his eyes and saw triumph and smug satisfaction in their blue depths and it broke the spell. Giving a cry she pushed against him and resumed her fight, thrashing and clawing like an alley cat. Fighting until he had a wild hellion in his arms. Maxwell let her go and she sprung away, head whipping back and forth, not knowing where to go. She ran towards the garden, his mocking laugh ringing in her ears.

"Nowhere to go out there, luv, but go ahead and have a look. You're a trapped little dove now, a thing of pleasure, a woman who's owned, a priceless piece of art in a vast collection. There will be no escape."

His words sent a shiver of shocked fear through her body, panic rushed through her veins as she ran. Down a winding path lined with marble statues she went until she came to a tall brick wall. Turning, she ran along the wall only to find herself trapped in a corner. Elizabeth whirled again, intending to flee or find a way over it, but came face to face with Maxwell instead. Spinning again, she began to scream, slapping her palms against the brick in desperation.

"Help me, somebody help me! I've been kidnaped. Please, can anyone hear me? Help me!"

"There's no one there pet. All you're doing is wearin' yourself out. Come back inside. There is no escape. You're here and this is where you're going to stay." His voice was lazy and soft, like he didn't have a care in the world and it infuriated her. She turned on him, eyes wild, hair whipping around her, ready to spring if he got any closer.

"But... but why? Why me? Please let me go. *Let me go!*"

"Sorry luv, I can't do that. As for why, you're here to be used for pleasure, that's why. Jeeval is gonna love you after I have you trained to please him. You're really a beauty, kitten. That hair, those eyes, that cute little nose. You were made for lovin' sweet. Now be a good girl and come back inside." Elizabeth tried to dart around him but Maxwell caught her around the waist and hoisted her over his shoulder. "Have it your way, pet. You're about to get your first lesson in obedience. The women in this house do as they're told when they're told, and you'd do best to learn that soon."

He carried her, fists pounding against his back, feet kicking uselessly in the air, back into the estate and sat down on a straight backed chair. Lifting her up and over his shoulder, Maxwell positioned the screaming and wiggling Elizabeth over his lap, pushing up her many layers of skirts and trapping her kicking legs between his. He loosened the ribbon on her knickers, and tugged the two sides apart, effectively baring her bottom.

Elizabeth froze. Her screams silenced by stunned disbelief. He wouldn't. He couldn't possibly mean to spank her? She felt her skirts being pushed further up her back, and then his cool hand sliding over the skin of her naked bottom, and that was all it took to set the fireworks off again.

"How dare you, you beast. Get your hands off me. Stop it! Don't touch me. You're a vile creature who should be horse whipped. Damn you, you heathen!"

"My, my, such language from a lady. How dare I? I will dare to do anything I want luv. Your body now belongs to me to do with as I please, and right now it pleases me to turn your pretty little bum a nice shade of crimson. Let this be your first lesson, pet. You are to do as you're told or suffer the consequences."

Maxwell hand came down in a hard smack upon Elizabeth's creamy white bottom. She gasped and he paused for a moment to admire the bright red print his hand had left in its wake. "So beautiful, pretty little bum, I knew you'd be exquisite." That said, Maxwell began a relentless series of stinging spanks that had Elizabeth gasping and whimpering.

"You are never to tell me no. You are to do as you're told the instant I tell you. Your body now belongs to me, and I will do anything I like to it. Is that understood Elizabeth?"

Each phrase of reprimand was punctuated by a series of stinging spanks. Elizabeth was sniffling and whimpering, never had she been so manhandled before. Her bottom was on fire and there was that funny tingling she didn't particularly like squirming in her belly again. He had ceased, but his hand resumed the spanks at her silence.

"I asked you a question woman."

"Yes, yes I understand. Please stop. Please."

"That's a good girl. Let's see if you truly did learn something." Maxwell moved his hand over her blazing bottom, stroking, squeezing gently, sliding his fingers between her bum cheeks, grazing the hot smooth flesh. Elizabeth hissed in a shocked breath but didn't move. He pushed her thighs apart and skimmed his hand over the downy soft curls of her sex, and smiled when his fingers felt the dampness there.

Just as he thought, this one would take to submission like a duck to water, once she learned her place. Pushing slowly, Maxwell moved his finger between her cunny lips, up and down he slid in her wetness, pausing to stroke her clit, tickling the little nub of pleasure until Elizabeth gasped. He then moved lower and pushed his finger into her virgin opening. Elizabeth bucked on his lap and Maxwell put a stilling hand on her back.

"Easy, luv."

He went back to stroking her sensitive nub until she lay like a rag doll over his lap. She'd never felt anything like this before and the sensation was both scary and wonderful, but heaven help her she didn't want him to stop. Just as her body was quivering on the brink of release, Maxwell slid a finger from his other hand into her virgin cunny. Elizabeth stiffened again, but Maxwell didn't pull back. He pressed onward until he felt the barrier of her maidenhead, then eased out.

That's all he wanted to know. Yes she was virginal, just like he'd thought. He would have the pleasure of deflowering Miss Elizabeth Thornton in the very near future. The thought made his cock swell with hot blood, but he ignored his desires for now. There were other matters to tend to first.

Elizabeth moaned on his lap, bringing Maxwell out of his musing and he wrapped an arm around her waist, holding her securely as his fingers went to work on her clit. He rolled it between them then rubbed, faster and faster until she was quaking and whimpering and rocking her hips.

"Remember this, pet. I can deliver pain or pleasure to your sweet little body. The choice is yours." That said,

Maxwell pinched her quick, causing a brief bite of pain in her nubbin before rubbing her to orgasm.

Never had Elizabeth felt anything like the sensations rushing through her as Maxwell's fingers moved over her clit in a blur of motion. Liquid gold fire soared through her veins and straight to her core. She cried out, eyes wide in wonder as her climax roared through her. Up, up, up, the feeling took her until she fell over the precipice, tumbling down into a sea of physical bliss. When it was over Maxwell rocked her on his lap for a moment, stroking her cunny softly as her breathing slowed, then pulled her up into his arms.

"See there, kitten, good girls get good things. Tell me sweet, did your mum have a nickname for you? Somethin' cute as you are? Tell me."

Elizabeth grimaced, but at this point she could deny him nothing. "She called me Beth when I was little. I dislike it. It makes me sound like a child."

"Beth. I like it, much better than stuffy Elizabeth. No one here will mistake you for a child no matter your name. You will be my Beth. Get up now and turn 'round. Let me get at those buttons. Never again will you wear such smothering gowns. Your body will always be on display whether it be for me or Jeeval. You are a sensuous creature who must be open, visible, and available for our desires."

His horrid words snapped her out of her dreamy haze, and Elizabeth leapt off his lap, backing away. He caught her wrist and tugged hard, growling at her behavior.

"Have you forgotten your lesson so soon, Beth? In need of another spankin' are you? Let me tell you, luv, that my hand won't be the only thing used to discipline your pretty bum and body. Defy me and you'll regret it, that's a promise."

Chapter Four

His eyes had turned a dark stormy shade of blue and there was no warmth to be found in them as Maxwell spoke of another spanking. All of the wonderful feelings from a moment ago fled, and in their wake Elizabeth was filled with disgust, disgust at him for touching her in that way, and disgust at herself for liking it. She was no better than a harlot.

Standing firm and still as stone, Beth stared right back at Maxwell, making no move to turn and offer up the buttons on her dress. He snarled at her and ripped the bodice of her gown from prim lace collar to waist and then gave another mighty tug to tear it to the hem. Beth cried out, wanting to bolt, but he held her wrist tight and quickly removed the rest of her gown, petticoats, and chemise, until she was bare before him.

"Get in the bath, Beth, your body needs to be properly prepared." Her eyes widened big as saucers and she shook her head defiantly in defiance.

"No!"

"Beth, I'm warning you, get your sweet little body in that bath before I take a riding crop to your pretty little tits."

Beth paled at his words, her heart pounding with fear. What kind of monster was he? Before she could do as he told her, Maxwell scooped her up in his arms and carried her to the radiant pool, he dropped her unceremoniously in the warm water and laughed as she sputtered and kicked, then he looked her straight in the eyes and began to unbutton his breeches.

Elizabeth sputtered and coughed as she pushed her dripping hair from her eyes. She stood for a moment, outraged, temper flaring, ready to curse her tormentor. Looking up, her gaze settled on Maxwell who was grinning at her from the edge of the pool, drinking in her naked form. Elizabeth immediately fell to her knees in the water, crossing her arms over her breasts in a futile attempt at modesty. Maxwell simply stood and looked down on her, totally enchanted.

Her hair floated around her like a dark golden rose, its petals open in full bloom. Her green eyes flashed with anger but her cheeks were flushed with embarrassment. Her adorable little mouth was turned down in a pout. He just wanted to catch her lip between his teeth and nibble until she lay panting with need in his arms. She began to back away and Maxwell turned his cocky grin into a scowl.

"You are never to hide your body from me, luv. That is strictly forbidden and will bring a harsh punishment.

Uncross your arms and stand up. I wish to look at my new toy."

"I... your... toy! How dare you? I will not stand up, you filthy beast. Get out of here and leave me be. Haven't you done enough?"

"I'm only getting started, pigeon. I have many things planned for today before I take you to bed, sweet. Is your bottom so recovered from your spanking that you are ready to defy me again so soon? Stand up, woman, so I may look upon your body."

The last was said in a low chilling tone that sent a shiver down Elizabeth's spine. No, she hadn't forgotten about her spanking. Her bottom was still on fire from his cruel hand, but what he was asking of her was unthinkable.

"No."

"While I admire your spirit luv, I detest your disobedience. If you will not cooperate at will, you will be forced. Have it your way. I will find my pleasure whatever your decision."

Elizabeth gasped, her mouth opening and closing like a fish out of water, but no words came out. She backed away towards the far end of the pool, but Maxwell simply followed her around as he unbuttoned his shirt. Shedding it, he stopped, sneering at her attempt to avoid him.

"You're like a dove trapped in a gilded cage, pet, and I'm the one who holds the key. You belong to me now, and here you will stay. Accept it and your life will be easier."

"Accept you? Never!" She paddled backwards and Maxwell simply watched, knowing she had nowhere to go. His hand moved again to his breeches as he kicked off his boots, then slowly, as he held her gaze, Maxwell unfastened the buttons restraining his hard shaft.

"Have you ever set eyes on a naked man, Beth? Ever seen a man when he's aroused and ready to take a woman? Do you know what lies beneath my breeches?"

She looked down, blushing an adorable shade of scarlet. "Did your mother ever tell you what goes on between a man and a woman behind closed doors? How a woman must satisfy her husband in the marriage bed? Have you ever seen animals rut and mate, pet?"

His taunting questions horrified her and made her head spin with confusion.

"Stop it. You're disgusting!"

His laughter rang in her ears and she brought her hands up to cover them, the movement exposing the tops of her creamy white breasts to Maxwell's hungry gaze. He licked his lips slowly, wanting to nibble the delectable pink nipples that lay just under the surface, made hard as pebbles by the water.

"I didn't think so. So innocent my sweet, but you won't be that way for long. Look at me, Beth."

"No!"

"I said, look at me, woman. It was an order, not a request. Look at me this instant, or I'll use a strap between those sweet thighs where my hand gave you such a delightful feeling just a minute ago. Pain or pleasure, Beth, the choice is yours, but be assured, I will whip that delicate cunny of yours until you scream if you defy me."

Maxwell watched her body tense up at the suggestion. Fear making goosebumps rise on her flesh. Her bottom lip began to tremble but Beth raised her eyes and looked at Maxwell. His eyes were full of mocking merriment at her predicament, the anger that had turned them stormy, gone as quick as it had come. He arched his eyebrows and wiggled his tongue at her lewdly, then yanked down his breeches.

Maxwell's cock sprang forth and Beth gasped. Her hand flew over her mouth to stifle the sound of shock but her eyes remained fixated on his shaft, unable to tear her gaze away. Maxwell bent and stripped off his breeches, then stood before her bold and proud, as Beth took in the sight of an aroused male for the first time in her life. Her eyes traveled up to his broad shoulders, taking in his strong arms and perfect form, then lower to his abdomen. His muscles were hard and rippled there, and part of her longed to brush her fingers over his stomach, longed to discover if he felt as wonderful as he looked, but it was what lay just beyond that had her mesmerized the moment she allowed her gaze to slip even lower once again.

Beth looked down and couldn't help but stare. His cock was huge, rising from a patch of curly hair between his legs. It stood straight up and was so big that Beth didn't understand how on earth he had fit the thing in his breeches. She knew nothing of men or mating. Her father had died when she was young and her mother never said a word about anything concerning her body or its changes. She had been shocked when her menses had begun; being completely unaware that it was a natural occurrence. Her mother had simply shoved a ball of rags in her arms and mumbled that it would happen every month.

When her body had begun to attract the stares of men, her mother had simply had the servant girl bring her the appropriate undergarments so she would be dressed properly. Never was one word said about her becoming a woman or what it meant. So now here she was, trapped in a room with a mad man, staring at his naked form, and knowing nothing about what he planned to do to her.

Maxwell's hand dropped to his shaft and he began to stroke it, curling his fingers around it and moving up and down, stopping to squeeze and pull back the foreskin to expose the head. It glistened with a drop of precum, and Maxwell rubbed the slippery fluid around the bulbous tip, making it wet and shiny. He stroked again, up and down, and still, all Beth could do was stare. Her eyes huge as dinner plates, her mouth, slightly agape.

"Do you know where I will put my cock when I take you to bed, Beth? When I play with my new toy?"

Up and down, stroking, circling the head, up and down, rubbing his thumb across the tip. Beth gulped and shook her head, a little squeak of fright emitting from her constricted throat, as terror pressed in on her, making it hard to breathe.

"I'm going to put it in your sweet little mouth, between your thighs where I slid in my finger, and even in your tight little bottom. What do you think of that pet?"

Beth panicked at his words and began to paddle backwards frantically, a little cry of horror escaping her. That? He was going to put that huge thing inside her? It would never fit. His finger had caused her pain. Surely that thing would tear her apart!

Maxwell stalked around the edge of the pool like a panther, sleek body moving with cat like grace, ready to spring on his prey. Everywhere Beth turned, he cut off her escape, quickly and efficiently by merely walking around and around. She went to the center, knowing she was trapped, shaking her head, splashing water at him in desperation.

Maxwell sneered at her futile attempts to fend him off, and scooped up a sponge and some soap. He jumped in, ignoring the water she splashed his way, dropping the things he carried so he could wrap his arms around her and crush her body to his.

Maxwell managed to get one arm around her before she turned into a wildcat in his embrace. Now Beth was the predator and Maxwell the prey, she was on the attack. She kicked and clawed and fought his touch, snarling as a shriek of outrage tore from her throat.

"NO! LEAVE ME ALONE. I WON'T LET YOU TOUCH ME!" Her fists beat down on his chest and arms, her legs kicking out over and over ineffectually under the water. Maxwell let out a growl of pure fury and grabbed both of Beth's arms in a punishing grip, shaking her until her teeth snapped together.

"That's enough! Stop it you little bitch. Beth, stop it right this minute." He easily hoisted her over his shoulder and began to rain slap after slap down upon her wet bottom and thighs, holding nothing back in his anger. She struggled and screamed, her legs kicking wildly as the sting of his spanks shot through her entire body. The pain was magnified because of the wetness of her skin, and the fact that she had just been spanked.

Down his hand came over and over, until her screams turned to pleas, and her pleas to whimpers that could barely be heard above the stinging wet slaps upon her bottom.

"Damn it woman! You are not to fight me." Slap after slap made her bottom burn. "I own you now, and you will learn to obey me!" He spanked her hard, determined to make her obey, then harder still, determine to make her submit. "Do you understand? You belong to me and you will do as you're told."

His hand rose and fell in a relentless rhythm without mercy. Maxwell could feel the flesh on her bottom quiver as he slapped her, her body jerking in shock and pain after every blow but he didn't care. Beth's skin was hot and tight and his cock swelled with each smack of his palm. He'd teach the little hellion a lesson in obedience she wouldn't forget.

Maxwell spanked her until she lay limp over his shoulder, all resistance long gone, then spanked her some more. He'd be damned if this uppity bundle of fire was going to get the best of him. Beth would remember who controlled her fate every time she sat down for a good long while. When her whimpers turned to sobs, and the heat of her skin burned his hand, Maxwell finally relented and shifted Beth, so she was lying in his arms.

Beth's eyes were squeezed tightly shut, and her lower lip trembled as she fought back the last of her sobs. Maxwell bent down and kissed her tear streaked face, then began to place small kisses on each nipple, licking quickly and softly, and then suckling until they turned into hard little buttons under the laving of his tongue.

Beth fought the sensations running through her, but in the end, arched her back and moaned. Her body was in turmoil, filled with both pleasure and agony. Her bottom was on fire, but the burning deep within her had returned as well, along with the stinging pain. Maxwell's mouth on her bare breast felt wonderful, and she was dizzy from the feelings rushing from her nipples to her very core. She could feel his hard shaft beneath her body, its tip pressing into her bottom. What was happening to her?

"So full of fire my little luv. Why must you be so naughty? If I were to touch your sweet little cunny it would be wet and ready for love, yet you fight me like a wildcat. I'm going to put you down on your feet and you're going to stand like a good girl and let me wash you. I don't want to hear a single word of sass out of you Beth. I've let you off easy so far, kitten. Trust me when I say there are many other more painful ways I can make your body pay for your rebellion."

Maxwell brushed his lips over hers in the gentlest of kisses then kissed her aching nipples once more, eliciting a moan from Beth. Her body quivered in his arms and

Maxwell smiled down at her. She would be a good pet when properly trained. He set her on her feet and Beth stood obediently just as he'd told her. Maxwell grinned his approval at her surrender.

"That's my good girl. Why must you fight me, pigeon?"

"Because ... Because I have to. This isn't right. I... I'm so ashamed. I.. Oh..." Beth gave a little cry, her hands moving up to cover her face but Maxwell quickly pushed them back down. "I am a lady and ladies don't... they wouldn't ..."

Maxwell felt a moment of tenderness for the woman before him. She was no bigger than a child in some aspects and damn well looked like one right this moment with her head hung low and a mournful pout on her lips. A feeling he refused to identify swept over him, but Maxwell pushed it away and turned gruff once more.

"Spread your legs." The harshness in his voice made her cringe, and Maxwell grit his teeth, not liking how Beth was making him feel. This job was no place for emotions. He had to play the heartless bastard in order to break her spirit. However, his voice softened, she'd suffered enough and was being obedient. "Spread your legs, luv, I won't hurt you."

Keeping her head down, her hands at her side, letting Maxwell move her like a puppet, Beth did as she was told. Her bottom burned and her body yearned from and for his touch, but she would never ask him for it. Never! What he did to her and the way it made her feel was shameful.

His hands and the sponge moved over her skin, shoulder to fingertips, neck to waist, up and down, stimulating, caressing, stroking. Beth bit her lip as his soapy hands kneaded her breasts and teased her nipples. They were hard as stone under his ministrations, and she had to fight back a moan as he pinched and rubbed them over and over, his palms lying flat, moving over the buds as his fingers stroked the sides of her breasts.

His hands were everywhere, belly, hips, and thighs. He coaxed her legs apart further and began his journey upward. Beth tensed but Maxwell persisted, knowing she would never misbehave after the spanking she'd just had. His fingers found her cunny and her woman's dew flowed from between her lips, making his fingers slippery in the water. He stroked her and washed her with slick hands, lathering her sore bottom as one hand teased her clit and slid over and over again between her cunny lips. Beth had stood still as stone through it all, but this was too much. She knew she would disgrace herself if he didn't stop.

"Please."

"Please what, kitten?"

"Please stop. I don't like that." Her voice was breathless and lacked conviction.

"Oh but I think you do, luv. Your body gives you away. Your quim is wet and wanting. It tells of your desire." He slipped a finger into her tight virginal opening and she cried out, the sensation shocking and pleasurable. He was right. She did like it. She wanted more, but it was wrong.

"No, please, please don't." Tears filled her eyes and her voice shook with them. Maxwell heard her distress and tilted her head up. Beth closed her eyes, her cheeks red with shame. Why was her body betraying her yet again? She hated him and what he was doing to her. It was dirty and disgusting.

"Beth, luv, you don't need to be ashamed of how you feel. It's why you're here, for your pleasure and mine. I will teach you to need, want, and take great pleasure from the things I can do to your body. Look at me, sweet." One arm wrapped around her, holding her close. Beth felt his hard cock pressing into her belly, and trembled with a mixture of fear and desire. His other hand held the back of her head, wrapped in her hair, forcing her to meet his eyes. "Do not disobey me. Open your eyes, Beth."

She did and found herself drowning in his deep blue pools of promise. Maxwell lowered his mouth to hers and captured her lips. It wasn't a kiss meant to punish, but one meant to bring forth pleasure and longing. He brushed his lips over Beth's and teased her mouth open, slipping in his talented tongue so it could dance across hers. The kiss deepened as Maxwell moved his mouth slowly over hers, his tongue darting, caressing, stroking her cheeks and tongue, igniting a fire in Beth until she melted like butter in his arms. When she was breathless, he relented and pulled back, delighted by her response.

Feeling her go limp, Maxwell picked her up and sat her on a pedestal in the middle of the pool. Water lapped at her cunny as his body created little ripples around. "Lay back my pretty dove, and don't move."

Chapter Five

Maxwell walked away from Beth and she did as she was told, laying back upon the pedestal and closing her eyes. He returned, and Beth again felt the ripples of warm water caused by his body splashing her bottom and cunny. Everything that touched her there sent a bolt of pleasure to her core and she shivered. Maxwell slipped a cushion under her head and kissed her softly, gently, like a tender lover. He wanted to keep Beth relaxed and submissive.

"Such a good girl. Good girls get rewards Beth. Remember that. Now it's very important that you don't move and don't fight me kitten. This will be done with or without your consent. Let yourself enjoy the feel of my hands on your delicate skin."

Her eyes flew open at his words as did her mouth, but Maxwell silenced her with a kiss. "Just relax pet. I won't hurt you." Beth felt Maxwell's hands moving up and down one leg, lathering her up, slipping and sliding from ankle to thigh. He rinsed his hands in the water and picked up a straight razor.

"Lay very still luv," Maxwell quickly skimmed the blade over one leg then the other, and then deftly removed the hair from under each arm. When he was done, he began to lather the curls between her legs. Beth whimpered and closed her thighs an inch or so.

"Why?"

"The women within these walls must be smooth as satin over every inch of their bodies. In a few days I will use a special sticky substance and strips of cloth to remove what grows back. Your cunny will be soft to the touch, silky to the mouth, and open to the eyes, your needy little pearl peeping out as a testament of your arousal."

Beth gasped and tried to sit up but Maxwell placed a hand on her belly. "Need I remind you of the consequences for disobedience, Beth?" She shook her head quickly, not ready to risk another spanking. "Good girl. Open your legs for me sweet, and don't move."

Beth did as she was told and tried to still her quivering body as Maxwell's hands lathered the soap between her legs. He quickly removed the curls that crowned her cunny, neatly wielding the straight razor with astonishing speed and a steady hand, and then slipped his fingers under one of her tender lips.

"Please."

"I'll be gentle as a lamb, luv. You won't be hurt."

Beth squeezed her eyes shut as Maxwell dragged the wicked blade carefully over her delicate cunny lips. One side then the other, then down lower, making sure every inch of her quim was bare. Beth found the whole thing strangely erotic and cursed the burst of fire that ignited once more in her core from his touch.

Maxwell was very aware of her body's reaction, and it pleased him immensely. This woman had been a good choice. She was full of fire and passion, and her spirit would be tamed in time. Her flame of disobedience would be turned into a burning desire to please her Master.

Maxwell rinsed off the last of the soap and looked down at his handiwork. Her cunny was pink, smooth, and very delectable. The lips of her quim folded over her secret opening like an orchid touched with dew. Maxwell folded back one glistening petal, and gazed upon her engorged clit. It was standing up, swollen and bold, not shy like its mistress, ready for loving. Her opening was tight and wet and he slid a finger into her depths once more. This time Beth didn't tense and Maxwell felt the unmistakable quivering in her walls of her cunny as it grasped his finger. She was getting used to being touched here, liking it in fact.

Maxwell pulled out and added another finger, twisting slowly, gently, opening them up, opening her up, and was rewarded with another rush of moisture and a sigh from Beth. He pumped his fingers in and out slowly, carefully, wanting her to experience only pleasure.

"Pull your knees up, pet." Beth did and Maxwell increased his pace, his fingers sliding in and out smoothly. Beth rocked with the rhythm; little mewls of pleasure escaping from her lips. Maxwell reached inside and tried to curl his fingers up, tried to stroke her sweet spot, but he encountered her virginal barrier. Should he tear it away now when she was so relaxed and willing, or should he wait for the pleasure of feeling her body succumb to his as he buried his cock between her thighs? Beth's moan and slight shifting of her hips pulled him from his thoughts.

"We better wait on that luv. It's not quite time for that lesson. Feels good doesn't it sweet? Do you like the way I pet your sweet quim? I can make you feel so good, kitten. Tell me you like it, Beth."

Maxwell pressed the pad of his thumb against her swollen clit and rubbed back and forth, over and over as Beth bit her lip and arched her back. He increased the pressure and the rhythm then stopped when she refused to speak.

"Tell me, Beth. Tell me you like it when I touch your cunny."

Beth shook her head and moaned, both from denial and the loss of stimulation. Her body was on the precipice of orgasm, and fire roared through her veins. She heard Maxwell chuckle at her stubbornness but kept her eyes squeezed shut. He pulled his fingers from her cunny and she made a small sound of anger.

"Now, now, kitten. All you have to do is say. 'I like it when you touch my quim.' Say it."

Beth still remained mute but Maxwell would have none of it. She would yield to him. He bent down and held open the puffy lips of her cunny then darted out his tongue to lick the hard little button buried beneath them.

Beth cried out in shock at the touch of his hot tongue between her legs. She slapped her palms down hard upon the stone pedestal and arched her back.

"Feels good doesn't it, pet." He lashed his tongue over her clit again and again until he felt her stomach muscled clenching, ready to explode. Maxwell knew she was incredibly close to cumming.

"Say it, Beth. Tell me, 'I like it when you lick my quim.' Say it and I'll make it feel oh so good."

Beth was tossing her head, legs pulled up tight to her chest, dying for the touch of his tongue between her thighs but her pride burned deep. Maxwell slapped her bottom hard, one, two, three times, and then laved the flat of his tongue across her hypersensitive nub.

"Say it, Beth. Don't be ashamed. We both know you like it. Want me to get a paddle and go to work on that bottom again? Pain or pleasure, luv? It's your choice. Just tell me."

Maxwell pressed his tongue between her legs once more and held still, the heat of his breath teasing her, the tip of his tongue moving oh so slightly on her clit. He let out a little chuckle and the vibrations tickled her in a way she'd never been tickled before, then Maxwell upped the ante by sliding a finger into her hot quim once more.

Beth's stomach quivered uncontrollably. Her whole body was on fire. Her blood was roaring through her veins as she clawed at the stone beneath her. Why? Why did she have to like this? Why did her body betray her? God help her, but she wanted him to lick her, wanted him to suckle and taste and do everything to her quim that he'd done to her mouth and her breasts with that talented tongue. Maxwell made a deep purring sound and the vibration broke the rest of Beth's resolve.

"I like it when you lick my quim. God forgive me, I like it. Please, please do it. Lick me there."

Beth's hands flew up to cover her face as she blushed scarlet. Maxwell grinned in triumph and dove in like a man starved. He swirled his tongue around her nub then thrust it into her incredibly tight opening, faster and faster, then out to lap at her clit. Sliding a finger into her cunny, and latching his top lip over her nub, Maxwell suckled and wiggled his finger in and out until Beth's world exploded.

Her hips came off the pedestal and Maxwell threw his arm over her to still her movements, a loud wail tore from Beth as Maxwell relentlessly suckled her clit. He quickly switched, moving his hand to her nub and thrusting his tongue deep inside, not wanting to risk tearing her maidenhead as he made her orgasm go on and on.

Beth squealed and cried, never had she felt like this. It was so intense, too intense; her entire being was centered on the heat erupting between her legs. Each time she came down Maxwell would increase his pace and her body would fly over the edge again. The stone beneath her rubbed her sore bottom, mixing pain with her pleasure as she thrashed under his assault, even Maxwell's strong arm thrown over her hips couldn't contain all her wild movement. When finally he slowed, she was left quivering and in shock, a boneless bundle of nerves, trembling in the wake of his touch.

Beth made a little mewling sound as Maxwell moved away from her body and ran his hands up and over her belly and breasts.

"Such a good girl. So good. Did you like that luv? I can do so many wonderful things if you'll just stop fighting me, kitten. Look at me, Beth. Open your eyes, luv, I want to see the pleasure there."

He stroked her like a cat, gentle sweeps of his hands over and over as she regained her senses. Beth opened her eyes and met Maxwell's, ashamed at how she'd reacted, but too satiated to fight the feelings he instilled in her anymore. Maxwell smiled and kissed her nose, forehead, and lips, and Beth marveled at how he could be so tender with her now, and yet so cruel when angered. The pain that still burned in her bottom was a vivid reminder of his harshness. Maxwell had beaten her without the slightest thought. He had spanked her until she was begging and crying. How could she respond to him now with such abandon?

Pain and pleasure, he said. Pain and pleasure were the two things he'd told her he could provide. The thought made Beth shiver. Yes, he certainly could and had. How could she like it when he touched her so intimately? It was disgraceful and oh so wrong, and yet right at this moment, Beth wouldn't have wanted to be anywhere else in the world, laying here while he smiled down at her and slowly ran his hands over her body.

Chapter Six

Maxwell stroked her cheek and gazed at the beauty of his new captive, totally consumed by her loveliness and naiveté. She was laying before him, sprawled out like a harlot, hair in a wild tangled mass, body spent from passion, eyes smoldering with sexual satisfaction, lips swollen from his kisses, yet her innocence still shone through. The mix of qualities was so enchanting it made the feelings of tenderness rise up inside him again, regardless of the fact that he refused to recognize them for what they were. "My Elizabeth, my sweet, sweet, Beth."

She smiled shyly and a blush stained her cheeks once again, one that Maxwell thought was most enchanting. His answering grin made her turn away in embarrassment, but made her heart flutter at the same time. Damn this man. He was always making her blush. She felt his arms slip under her body, and was suddenly lifted up and pressed against Maxwell's strong chest. The feel of his hard body and the masculine scent of him were comforting, and she suddenly had the urge to nuzzle into him. The thought made her stiffen. What was she thinking?

"Easy luv. It's all right. Nothing to fear now." The heat of Beth's body was pressed against the head of his cock and Maxwell had to stifle a groan. He would have to make a decision soon. Would he bed her tonight, teach her other things to ease his desire, or simply pleasure himself and allow her to adjust slowly to her new world? For some reason he wanted to give her time. He didn't want her to be frightened of him. Maxwell didn't like the idea of forcing himself on her. He wanted her to give her innocence to him freely, but how long would that take? Could he possibly wait that long? He was already hard as nails.

Maxwell carried Beth to a long table covered with a cushion and a sheet. He laid her down and positioned her arms at her sides.

"Am I to be sacrificed?" Her question stunned him until his gaze met hers and he saw the teasing glint in her eyes.

"No you little minx. Only a fool would waste beauty and sensuality such as yours. You shall be alive for a good long time, my dove. I have oils and scents to rub into your skin. Close your eyes and relax, let my hands do their work. You will enjoy this."

Beth closed her eyes; her body was heavy and satisfied, floating in the afterglow of sexual bliss. She couldn't have fought him at that moment even if she'd wanted to. The urgent need to flee had melted away, at least for now.

Maxwell rolled her over onto her stomach. She felt the drizzle of warm oil upon her back and then his wonderfully strong hands kneading her muscles. Every stroke made her relax even more. It felt so delicious to have his hands sliding over her skin.

He got to her bottom and his touch became gentle as he danced his fingers over her crimson cheeks. He stroked the faint hand prints left there tenderly, with delight, and then traced them with a bit more pressure. His touch a gentle reminder of what was and would be. Maxwell knew Beth wouldn't have bruises, but she would feel the effects of the two spankings she'd gotten for a few hours.

He ran his fingers over her reddened cheeks again, and Beth shivered at his touch, his hands caused a mixed sensation of pleasure and pain, and the memory of his hard hand spanking her bottom brought a renewed rush of moisture between her thighs. Her reaction to the memory shocked and shamed her. Beth shivered as the unwelcome emotion stirred inside.

"Easy luv. It's okay. Okay to feel, okay to want." Maxwell continued to stroke her sore bottom, applying enough pressure to remind her of the sting, while sliding a finger between her legs to find her hard little nub. He gave her a few slow circles there until she relaxed and moved in time with his hand. Pain and pleasure, pleasure and pain, he wanted the two to meld in her very core. She must be taught to crave both, as well as give her submission, and from the way Beth was reacting, the lessons were working.

Little moans of bliss escaped her, try as she might to remain silent, and Maxwell grinned as he worked. Yes this one was full of sensuality and passion. He couldn't wait to bed her. His cock was demanding he do something soon. Down her legs his hands went, rubbing and kneading her thighs and calves, then circling his thumbs on the bottoms of her feet until she was wiggling from his feather light touch. He gave her a little slap on her bottom then flipped her over again.

"Almost done luv. How does that feel?"

Beth smiled, her eyes hooded with lazy passion. She felt wonderful, pampered and cared for. Maxwell poured more oil on her belly and began his task once again, working up to her breasts until she was mewling and arching under his palms.

"Born for pleasure you were, luv. Made for a man's touch." He indulged her by teasing and roughly playing with her nipples until she was whimpering then moved back downward to her now bare mound. Beth automatically spread her legs beneath his touch, which ~~and the~~ ~~act~~ pleased him greatly.

"That's right, pet, open up for me." Maxwell rubbed in the oil, once more igniting the fire deep within Beth, but this time he stopped before she was sated.

"It's time for you to give me pleasure, pet. Do you want me to feel as good as I make you feel?"

Beth drew in a sharp breath, her eyes grew big, her thighs snapped shut, and she bit her lip. "It won't hurt one bit precious, I promise. Give me your hand."   Beth complied, holding out her shaking hand, and Maxwell took it. He rubbed her tiny one in his, oiling up her palm, then brought her hand to his shaft and encircled her fingers around it. Beth could feel his cock throbbing in her hand. Hard as marble, yet velvety soft and alive. Moving in a steady rhythm, Maxwell began to guide her hand up and down slowly as he gazed directly into her eyes.

"That's a good girl, now squeeze and pump, up and down, that's right, kitten, you're gonna make me feel real good."

Beth blushed yet again, but smiled and tightened her fingers around his shaft as she began to pump her oil slick hand up and down on her own accord, learning yet a new lesson in the art of love. This one giving her a slight feeling of power, as Maxwell moaned with pleasure, his eyes closing as his hard shaft pulsed with hot blood in her hand.

Beth watched Maxwell's face intently as her hand moved up and down on his hard cock, the oil on her palm making the movements smooth and fluid as she established an age old rhythm. Each time she saw the muscles in his hard stomach ripple, or an expression of intense pleasure cross his face, Beth would continue the action to gauge his response, then experiment some more, until she had a small set of movements she knew he liked. She kept going from one to the other then back to the pumping motion as he grit his teeth and threw his head back. Her hand slid up and she rubbed her palm over the head of his cock, making Maxwell moan, then ran her fingers along the ridge under the tip and made a gentle twisting motion, smiling when he hissed in pleasure. Beth tentatively reached out with her hand and grasped his shaft low, while the other continued to make small, quick strokes over the bulbous tip. Maxwell's hips jerked in approval, his eyes turning a deep blue, darkening with desire as Beth grasped him tighter.

The fingers of her lower hand grazed his balls and Maxwell moaned again. Curious, Beth moved lower and cupped the sack in her hand, cradling it gently, and softly caressing it with her fingers. Maxwell moaned again and looked as lost as she had felt when he'd been pleasuring her. Elizabeth made the realization that there was power here if she chose to use it. She wasn't quite as helpless as she'd thought.

"That's it pet. So good, stroke me now, both hands, squeeze a bit harder." Beth did what he asked and again held his cock low in one hand as she circled his pulsing shaft tightly with the other. "Up and down now Beth. Faster, so good pet. Faster now."

The look on his face was one of pure rapture as Beth's small hand pumped and squeezed, sliding up, running her palm over the head, and sliding back down. Maxwell covered her hand with his and began to thrust his hips forward in time with her strokes. "That's it, kitten, so good, oh, Beth, that's it. So good, pet, that's right. That's right, oh, God, Beth!"

Her hands moved up and down, up and down, as the muscles in Maxwell's abdomen began to clench. He threw back his head and growled out his pleasure as Beth's hand moved over his shaft. Blood boiling, fire roaring through him, his cock exploded with the intensity of the sensations and he came hard and long.

Beth cried out in shock as the milky strands of his semen erupted from the tip of his cock but Maxwell held her hand tightly and continued the rhythm they'd begun until he was spent, rubbing his cum over the head of his shaft and mixing it with the slippery oils as the last of the pleasure tore through his body. Finally his orgasm was over, and it left Maxwell weak kneed and in shock at the intensity of it. What had this woman done to him? A simple hand wank had made him cum harder than he had in a long, long time.

Catching his breath, aftershocks coursing through him, he looked down at Beth who was staring at him with a bewitching little grin on her face. Yes, the sudden eruption of semen had shocked her, but the shock had been quickly replaced by pleasure as she'd watched Maxwell's face and seen the ecstasy there. She had made him feel as good as he'd made her feel, and it made her proud, proud and empowered. A feeling of satisfaction filled Beth and she smiled shyly up at Maxwell, quite pleased with herself.

Beth felt Maxwell's shaft begin to soften in her hand and looked down. Now she understood how he'd gotten the monstrous thing in his breeches.

"A man grows hard and big when he desires a woman, when he is sexually excited, pet. Now that you have satisfied me, my cock will stay like that for a while. I don't imagine it will be long though kitten, I find you delectable and very arousing. Now you will know when I want you and need to be pleasured just like your woman's dew is a telltale sign of your own arousal." Beth blushed at the mention of her body's reaction to him, but a flood of moisture wet her thighs none the less at his words.

Maxwell smiled at the now all too familiar coloring of her cheeks, and ran a hand down her body, stopping to slip a finger between her cunny lips. He grinned when he found her very wet and wanting, her clit standing up, ready to be teased and pleased, but she would be made to wait this time. Not only was she responding to his touch, but she became aroused from pleasuring him. Both those things were as they should be, but denying her was a lesson to be learned as well. She would soon find out that the ache between her legs would be her near constant companion.

Chapter Seven

Beth arched up into his touch and spread her legs wider but Maxwell pulled his hand away after a few small strokes. The women here were to be kept in a state of constant arousal, always ready to be taken, always needing to cum. It made them obedient and sensual.

"You must wait now, kitten" Elizabeth mewled her displeasure and Maxwell gave her a tiny pinch on her clit. "No pouting allowed, pigeon. I want you full of desire, always wanting to be loved, always ready for my touch. Come now, it's time to dress you."

Maxwell sat her up and helped her from the high table, stopping a moment to pull her into his arms and brush his lips over hers. Beth sighed and pressed into him, and her actions filled him with intense pleasure. She was warm, sweet, and supple, and her skin smelled of flowers and spice.

"Such a good girl. Do you feel nice and tingly inside, luv? Do you want me to touch you?" Beth bowed her head but nodded in spite of her embarrassment and pride. Yes she wanted him to touch her. God forgive her but she did. Those feelings, those incredible feelings he caused deep in her belly made all rational thought flee from her mind.

"Later, Beth. I'll give you just what you need in a little while. Good girls get rewards. Come now."

Maxwell led her to the center of the room and told her to stay put. Beth did, and watched him as he went into another chamber and returned with his arms full of shimmering green cloth threaded with strands of gold. She'd never seen such beautiful material. It was sheer, incredibly sheer, but glistened in the light of the lamps as if made of precious metal and jewels. Maxwell set the cloth on a small table and grasped the end of one piece, unfurling it. It was long and wide and shone as he shook it out. Maxwell held the material before him and Beth could clearly see his outline through it. "This matches your eyes perfectly pet, my little green eyed kitten."

Grasping the long piece in his hand and gathering it up, Maxwell approached Beth. He put the center of the cloth behind her neck the pulled each side forward over her shoulders. He crossed them over her chest, then quickly turned her around and tied the ends behind her back. Beth looked down in dismay. Yes the cloth covered her breasts, but it was so sheer that her dusky nipples could clearly be seen, and her stomach and shoulders were bare as was her back. She turned and looked at

Maxwell, shaking her head, her eyebrows draw together showing her displeasure, ready to protest, but he held a finger up to her lips to silence her.

"Bad girls get punished, good girls get pleasure Beth."

Maxwell went back the table, and picked up more of the shimmering cloth and a wooden chest. Moving towards her, he held up the garments in his hands. It was similar to pants in that it had material panels for her legs, but was it slit down the middle and joined only with small chains, and each of the legs was slit from top to bottom. Maxwell unhooked the waist chain and put it around Beth's middle. It hung low on her hips, revealing her belly button. He then bent and fastened smaller chains around each ankle. These held the billowy pieces of the 'pants' in place. Without the chains, the material would have fallen to the floor in a shimmering green puddle.

Maxwell began to make adjustment, pushing the gathered material around on the waist chain so it fell down over her hips and legs and came somewhat together in front and back. He did not however, pull it firmly closed, her cunny would be very accessible to the eyes, and one had only to slide the fabric apart to bare her bottom.

Beth had never felt more exposed in her life. The so called clothes barely concealed her. The cloth was too sheer and too skimpy, not to mention the fact that one tug would untie the top and all that was needed to bare the rest of her was a simple pull to open the pants.

"Are you mad? I... I can't wear this. Please. It's obscene. I feel ... " What should she say? Horribly exposed, open and accessible, vulnerable? He would laugh at her and tell her that was exactly how she was meant to be.

"Now, now kitten. Pull in your claws. You need to try and accept your new way of life. You may wear this or go naked. The choice is yours, sweet."

Beth's eyebrows drew together and her forehead creased in a frown as her bottom lip stuck out in a trembling pout. She wanted to run but there was nowhere to go. She wanted to fight him but she had felt the strength in his body and hands. She wanted to scream and kick and cry, but knew it would do her no good, and just merit another painful punishment. Anger burned hotly in Beth's cheeks. She shook her head, eyes flashing, wanting to slap that infuriating smirk off his face and choke him with his sweet words.

"I ... You ... Oh!" Beth threw up her hands and turned her back on him. She knew there was nothing she could do or say to change anything. Her dress was in ruins and if she wanted any type of clothing at all, this would be it. Damn him! Damn this place!

Maxwell looked at her, and raked his gaze down her body. She was bare expect for the loop of cloth behind her neck and where he tied the ends across her lower back. The sheer silk pants sat very low on her hips. They covered the sweet curve of her bottom, but did little to actually conceal it, the fabric being too thin to really hide her body from his eyes. His gaze kept going down her shapely legs to her trim ankles and tiny feet. Perfect as a little doll she was.

"Aw luv, don't be like that. You look breathtaking pet and lookey here, I have something else for you. Something pretty for my beautiful girl."

Beth stamped her foot in irritation and stood her ground, refusing to give in to his charms. Maxwell smiled at her antics, not able to resist the adorable sight she made. The feeling of delight rather than irritation surprised him. He was being much more lenient with Beth than he usually was with the women he trained.

"Pretty baubles for my pretty dove. Come on pigeon, don't you want to see what I have?"

Beth put her hands on her hips and spun around. "You're impossible!"

"Ah, so you do want to see." Beth pouted and looked at Maxwell from under her lashes. "No playing the coy little minx. I know you want to see. Come here Beth."

She maintained her pout but went forward none the less, when Maxwell opened the wooden box once again. Curious, she tried to peer around his broad shoulder.

"Ah, ah, ah. You just wait princess. Close your eyes and hold out your hands."

Beth did as he requested, and felt Maxwell slip a ring on the middle finger of her left hand then fasten something around her wrist. He did the same with her right. She opened her eyes without being told, and gazed down at the unusual bracelets. Each started where her finger met her hand in a ring and went up over her hands in a mesh of gold and tiny emeralds that then formed a bracelet around each wrist. They were stunning. Beth had never seen anything like them, and had no idea the bracelets were reserved for slaves only.

"They're beautiful." Her voice was a mere whisper as she held her hands up to the light and watched the jewels glisten. She'd never had beautiful things growing up. Unfashionable gowns were what her strict mother had insisted on. They were good quality of course, to be anything other would have made it look like they lived in poverty, but pretty or elaborate they were not, and jewelry was frowned upon. It brought attention to one's self, and was frivolous.

"Not as beautiful as you pet. There's more."

Maxwell took out a matching necklace that fastened like a collar around her neck and dipped low between her breasts in a cascade of gold strands dotted with green gems. Cuffs of the same style as the bracelets, that went from a toe ring to her fasten around her ankle were the last thing to come out of the chest. When he had adorned her with all the jewels, Maxwell gathered up her long golden hair and pulled it over one shoulder, running his hands through it to smooth out the silken locks. He made a final adjustment to the split pants, sliding the material over her cunny aside so the bare pink lips were exposed and stood back to admire his handiwork.

"Now then, one last thing, and I don't want to hear a bit of sass kitten or I shall have to redden that delicious bottom of yours again. Your status in this household requires you to wear certain jewelry and wear it you shall." Beth looked at him dubiously, her delight at the pretty necklace, bracelets, and anklets fading quickly as she wondered about this 'other' adornment he had planned for her.

Maxwell opened another smaller box and held up a U shaped jeweled clip, quite similar to a hair pin. "This luv goes over your cunny lips. The gem will hang down and dangle on your sweet little nub, keeping you aroused and ready."

Beth looked at him and started to step back, but Maxwell's eyes flashed a warning in no uncertain terms, so she held her ground. Submit or feel his wrath.

He slid his hands between her legs and opened the outer lips of her smooth pink cunny, then the inner, teasing her clit so it stood out. When it became swollen with need and he was satisfied the 'special' jewelry would do its job, he slowly slid the clip down over her labia so the emerald dangled right on Beth's prominent little nub. She slapped at his hands and jumped at the sensation, causing the jewel to dance, stroking her hypersensitive nubbin, making her moan and cry out.

"No please. I can't."

Maxwell grabbed her wrist to keep her from yanking the thing off and hissed a warning at her, eyes becoming cold and cruel.

"Beth. It is this pretty bauble on your sweet cunny or the riding crop. One tickles with pleasure while the other bites with fire. I promise you this is the better of the two choices. Do not try my patience further. Are you going to obey me?"

Beth squeezed her eyes shut and stood stone still to quiet the rush of pleasure the dangling jewel clip caused with every move she made. She felt both incredibly aroused and horribly shamed but nodded none the less. The thought of him spreading her wide and whipping her between the legs made the blood in her veins turn to ice.

"Good girl. We're done. It's all right now, you'll adjust. Now you're a perfect little toy all wrapped up for

Christmas. Simply delectable, kitten. Want me to unwrap you so we can play?"

Maxwell was looking at her, his eyes hooded with lust and an infuriating smirk on his face. His words and his expression were just the thing to light Beth's fuse. Her delight with the jewelry, the first jewelry, had evaporated in a flash with his words and the lewd addition, and anger exploded deep inside her. Maxwell may have thought he'd tamed her, but he wasn't even close.

"You ... You're nothing but an ill-mannered, uncouth, heathen! The day I want to play with you is the day it snows in this God forsaken country. I am not your toy nor am I a Christmas present, and if you think... "

Her fists lashed out at him, striking his hard chest ineffectually, as her foot connected with his shin. Maxwell let out a fierce growl of rage and came at her. Beth brought her hands up again, ready to fight to the death, to claw at him, to break their little truce and show him what she thought of him and his vile ways. He grabbed her wrists before she could act out her wishes, and pinned her arms behind her back, then slapped her bottom sharply over and over as she twisted in his iron grip, before wrapping an arm around her thighs to crush her to him.

"You are a toy, luv. My toy, and I'm going to get great joy out of playing with you. Now it's up to you whether you enjoy it or not. At this point I don't much care. I've had enough of that sharp tongue of yours so I suggest you shut your mouth before you find yourself over my knee again."

He continued to hold both her wrists in one hand and then snake his other down and squeeze the very cheeks he was threatening to spank even more. Beth flinched at his harsh treatment of her sore bottom and he laughed, his face composed in a mocking sneer, containing none of the warmth from a moment ago. His mouth came down to claim hers, but Beth turned her head. Maxwell snarled, his eyes flashing, as his hand moved up to entwine in her hair, holding her head immobile, his lips coming down with bruising intensity, claiming, taming, possessing.

Beth stiffened and kicked out at him, fighting the cruel kiss, but Maxwell continued to kiss her hard, making her whimper with the intensity of it, punishing her lips as he forced them apart and entwined his tongue with hers. He let her hands go and they beat upon his back as he refused to stop the onslaught of her mouth.

Maxwell wrapped his arm around her waist, grabbing her tight, forcing her against him so she could feel his need for her. Looking down at Beth, Maxwell saw tears trickling from the corners of her tightly closed eyes. The sight of them made him relent and stop the punishment of her mouth. He loosened his hold and she shoved him away, angry and confused as she swiped at her bruised lips with the back of her hand and backed away. Her breast heaved as she fought for composure, and her eyes shone with new, as yet unshed tears.

"Why? Why must you make everything so beautiful, and then make me feel like ... like a whore? I'm not a plaything. I'm a woman, a human being. I have feelings, damn you. I've a heart and a soul. Why must you crush them?"

"Beth" Maxwell moved to take her in his arms. He felt the need to comfort her, to make things right again, but she shrank back from his touch.

"NO! Leave me be. I hate you. *I hate you!*"

The tenderness Maxwell had been feeling melted away with the heat of her cruel words. Hurt and anger replaced it. "You don't have to like me luv, in fact you can feel anything you damn well please. It doesn't matter to me one way or the other Beth, but you had better get back over here if you know what's good for you."

Beth stood her ground, green eyes flashing, cheeks flushed red with indignant rage.

"That wasn't a suggestion, Elizabeth. Move now or be punished." Still she didn't move towards him. Maxwell had to grit his teeth to fight back his fury as her chin rose an inch higher in a display of haughty disdain.

"So quick to turn into the bitch again aren't you? Well I know better. You may stand there and act all high and mighty, pretend you're a lady whose virtue has been plundered, but I know what lies beneath those highbrow ways and scornful words. You were sprawled before me like a whore, begging me to lick your quim and nothing can change that. You're no more a lady that the prostitutes who sell their bodies in the gutters."

His words bit into her like a whip, and a flinch of pain cracked her angry facade. Maxwell saw it and went in for the kill, he was done being the doting, caring idiot. The feelings she inspired in him made him confused, angry and resentful. She was a slave and a sexual toy like all the rest, nothing more, nothing less.

"You think you're so special? Think that you don't bloody belong here? Well guess what? None of the women behind these walls thought they did. Now every one of them is an obedient little whore who begs for the chance to be touched, and you will be too.

"I tried to be gentle, tried to be patient, well guess what sweetheart, I'm done caring. You will do whatever I want you to do when I want you to do it. You will be my plaything, my servant, and my slave, in and out of my bed, and you will kiss the ground I walk on by the time I'm through with you. You'll bloody well lick it if I tell you to Beth, or you'll feel more pain than you've ever felt in your life. Now shut your mouth and get over here. This conversation is over."

With those final words, Maxwell stalked to a table and picked up the riding crop. His eyes flashed with rage and he swished it through the air, and brought it down with a deafening crack upon his palm. Beth jumped, fear rising inside her. He could and probably would whip her to shreds with that thing. No one had ever laid a hand on her in all her life. She'd been born and bred a gentlewoman, a lady, and to be here now, confronted with pain, punishment, and captivity was terrifying, and went against everything she'd ever known.

The look on Maxwell's face broached no room for defiance. Beth had seen it before, right before he spanked her so hard her bottom was on fire, and she knew he meant to use the crop this time if she didn't do as he told her.

With her heart laying heavy in her chest and a lump of hot tears burning in her throat, Beth lowered her head and went to stand before him. Maxwell grasped her chin and tilted her head up. Beth winced, not from pain, but because she didn't want to see the cold look of hate in his eyes. She couldn't bare it, not after how he'd held her and made her feel so incredible and cared for, and especially not after he'd thrown all those horrid words in her face. She was a whore, a harlot, a Jezebel and she couldn't deny it. Shame filled her, and she whimpered fighting to hold back her tears, to hold on to at least that one little shred of dignity she had left. God, she couldn't let him know that what he thought of her, hurt.

"Look at me Beth." Beth steeled herself to gaze into those incredible blue eyes and opened her own. She swallowed hard. His were stormy, full of anger and cold dominance.

"You've been a very bad girl, and you will be punished for it, but lucky for you we have something else we must attend to first. Your sweet bottom has earned five lashes for your insolence and shrewish ways. One more word and it will be ten. Do you understand pet?"

Beth gave a tiny nod, and Maxwell smiled, his face softening instantly at her acceptance, the storm in his eyes turning calm. "Good girl. Come with me."

Chapter Eight

Maxwell took Beth's arm and led her towards the huge set of doors that exited his chambers. Beth felt a surge of hope at the prospect of leaving the confines of her prison, but then her heart sank. She knew he would never take her anywhere escape could be possible. There was also the fact that her outfit barely covered her body, and the parts that were covered, were done so with material that was almost transparent. The 'special' jewelry on her cunny gave her a most disturbing feeling too. She felt so vulnerable and yes, aroused in spite of her anger and fear. She hung back, digging in her heels.

"Please no. I'm ..." Beth's eyes swept down over her clothing and the familiar blush of shame colored her cheeks.

Anger flared up once more inside Maxwell, but one look at Beth's stricken face shattered any impatience he was feeling. She was terrified by the prospect of leaving his quarters. "It's all right sweet. No one will see you or touch you tonight. You and I will remain hidden from inquisitive eyes. You're not ready for the likes of them yet. I'll keep you safe."

The thought of Beth being bedded and disciplined by Jeeval or used and abused by one of his many, often brutal guests, made Maxwell's stomach clench. A feeling of protectiveness swelled up in his chest, but the feeling again caused irritation. Damn this little bit of a thing with her porcelain doll face and pleading eyes.

He clenched his jaw and shook his head to rid himself of those dangerous thoughts, and allowed his eyes to travel lower over Beth's body. If anything could keep his mind on his task, the sight of her curves and delectable bare quim certainly could. It was puffy and damp, her clit swollen with desire from the constant stimulation from the tiny emerald dancing upon it.

Beth shut her eyes at his frank appraisal. She could feel the heat of his stare as it traveled over her barely concealed breasts, down her exposed stomach, lingered on her smooth cunny, and took in each perfectly shaped leg. She shivered as if his stare was actually stroking her skin.

Maxwell clucked his tongue and drew in a sharp breath. "Perfect, my little dove. Pretty as a rose in full bloom, sweet and ready to be picked. Come on then, I've something to show you."

Instead of going through the doors, Maxwell walked her straight up to one of the ornate panels beside them. He turned her away from him and covered her eyes, then ran his hand over the panel and pressed down on the figure of an elephant. It was one of many and very small, but Maxwell's fingers never erred. He pushed quickly and firmly, and the panel swung open to reveal a long dark tunnel. Maxwell spun her in his arms and Beth gasped when she saw the secret passage.

"It extends throughout the palace along each hallway and borders every room. We shall travel in here my sweet dove, and no one will be the wiser. Stay close now, the floor is smooth, you won't trip but it's dark and makes many turns. And Beth, if I ever catch you near this wall I will flay the skin off your back. Understand?"

Beth shivered against him and nodded her head, but her mind was already working over this new bit of information. If he was forbidding her to go near the wall, it must mean the tunnel exited the estate somewhere. She would keep her eyes and ears open and pray for a chance to escape.

Maxwell held her close against his side, and started down the secret passage. They went forward, winding around, turning this way and that until Beth had no sense of direction at all. The only light came from small rectangular slits in the walls, no bigger than her hand. They didn't illuminate much of the passage at all, and did nothing to help Beth keep track of where she was. If Maxwell had left her then and there, she would be hopelessly lost with no idea how to get back to his chambers let alone out of the estate.

They finally stopped before a wall containing several of the tiny windows, all at different heights. Maxwell moved her to a place where she was eye level with one and pulled her close against his body. He bent over her shoulder, so he too could watch what was going on behind the wall, and whispered in her ear.

"Quiet as a little mouse now kitten. You are to watch and learn. This is what you are being trained for. The man is Jeeval, master of this estate, and the woman his favorite pet, Siri. One day you will pleasure him in the same way."

Maxwell's arm held her tightly around the waist as his other hand tilted her head up so her face was in front of the window. Beth stiffened in his arms at his words and tried to back away, but Maxwell would have none of it. He gripped her chin, forcing her to do as he said and hissed in her ear.

"I said look." Beth peered through, gasped loudly, and squeezed her eyes shut.

"Hush Beth. Open your eyes and look at them. Watch what you will someday do." She tried to twist in his arms but Maxwell was too strong. He held her fast and grasped her chin harder. Beth gave in and opened her eyes to the scene before her. Siri, the woman, was at Jeeval feet, bent over with her forehead pressed to the floor. She was nude, as was Jeeval, and her bottom was crimson in color with welts crisscrossing her flesh. It was clear she had been punished quite recently.

Her legs were spread and Beth could see her wet and puffy quim glistening in the lamp light. It was shaved bare just like her own. Jeeval brought the leather flogger he was holding down upon her bottom again, grazing Siri's tender cunny in the process. Beth jumped in Maxwell's arms but the other woman didn't move a muscle. Beth watched in silent shock and listened as Siri spoke to her Master, her voice coming out in breathy little pants, on edge and full of longing.

"Thank you Sir, may I please have another?" Jeeval brought the leather strips down again, the tips lashing across the center of her bottom cheeks. Siri leaned forward and kissed his feet, then thanked him and asked him to please strike her again. The only show of emotion was a slight quivering of her flesh, and the trickle of woman's dew dampening her thighs with each strike.

"No my little whore, it is time for you to pleasure me. Take my cock in your mouth Siri."

Siri scrambled to do her Master's bidding and enveloped Jeeval's cock in her lips. She wet it then pulled back to bathe the thick shaft with tiny licks. Beth watched in fascination as her little pink tongue darted out again and again, washing Jeeval's shaft as it grew to its full size and hardness before she took it between her lips once more and tilted her head back. Jeeval wrapped his fingers in Siri's hair and began a steady rhythm as Siri's cheeks hollowed, sucking him hard as he thrust into her mouth, using her hard and fast. One of his hands still held the flogger and he flicked it up and down between her bottom cheeks, lashing her in a place Beth couldn't believe, and tickling the lips of her cunny with the leather strips, in time to rocking of his hips.

Beth's hand flew up to her mouth. She was both repulsed and stimulated by the scene before her. Maxwell reached up and took her hand in one of his. He held it as he encircled her waist again, then took his other and slid one finger into Beth's mouth. "Suck it pet, swirl your tongue around my finger and suck it as I move it in and out." Beth shook her head and Maxwell growled deeply in her ear and nipped her neck at her refusal.

"Do it!" He briefly brought a hand down and squeezed the still tender flesh of her bottom, promising more of where that came from if she disobeyed. "You already have five lashes with my belt coming, pet. I will gladly make it more. Now do as you're told."

Beth could feel his hot breath tickle her skin as Maxwell hissed his commands in her ear. His cock was growing hard again. She could feel it pressed against her bottom. The heat of him burned her as surely as any fire, and she wanted to both wiggle against him and run away.

The yearning deep inside her core was building hot and fast once more as she watched the disturbing yet erotic scene, and felt Maxwell's finger slide in and out of her mouth. The lady in her screamed that this was all so very wrong, but the newly awakened woman was filled with passion and desire. Maxwell's finger slid over her tongue as he whispered his command yet again, then came out and traced her lips before being thrust back in her mouth.

"Suck it like a good girl and watch how a woman pleasures a man with her mouth. Be a good girl and suck my finger."

Beth did as he told her, emulating Siri, whose head was bobbing back and forth as she suckled and licked Jeeval's cock. She swirled her tongue around Maxwell's finger as he thrust it in and out with the same rhythm Jeeval kept.

Beth's actions stirred a fire in him as did the feel of her soft bottom on his cock. Maxwell released her hand, ordering her to put it at her side, and toyed with one nipple then the other. Her thin top did nothing to block out the heat of his hand. He took turns back and forth, circling the hard pebbles, running the flat of his palm over them, rolling them between his fingers, tugging and teasing until Beth moaned. She arched her back, thrusting her breasts forward toward the heaven of his fingers, and pushed her bottom back against his now rock hard cock, sucking his finger as she did so and watching in fascination as Siri sucked her master to orgasm.

Jeeval thrust forward into Siri's mouth and held her head still as he erupted down her throat, roaring with satisfaction as he came. Siri swallowed fast, her cheeks sucking in and out, eyes closed, concentrating on her task, knowing she dare not spill a drop as she drank. When he was spent she pulled back and gently cradled his cock in her hands, cleaning him of all traces of semen with her tongue before once again taking position at his feet with her forehead pressed to the floor. Jeeval snapped his fingers and Siri rose, crawling quickly across the floor to kneel under a set of shackles that hung from two pillars.

"Up." Siri stood at Jeeval's command, holding up her arms and balancing on her toes. Jeeval strode forward and quickly cuffed the beautiful woman. He ran his hands roughly over her body, pinching and kneading, twisting her nipples and kicking her legs further apart. Siri strained to maintain the position, barely able to keep her feet on the floor.

Jeeval ran his hands over her inner thighs, and then pinched the tender skin there before slapping her once on her bare cunny. His hand made a wet sound as it landed on her quim, and Siri threw her head back, moaning. Jeeval smiled and thrust two fingers deep inside her, pumping, twisting, and rubbing his thumb over her clit, before abruptly yanking his hand away.

"Punish me, Master. Please."

Chapter Nine

Beth froze as she watched the woman, hardly able to believe what she'd heard. Her eyes assessed Siri, taking in her sultry exotic beauty, and Beth couldn't help but compared it to her own looks. Maxwell told her she was beautiful but Beth felt she paled in comparison to the other woman.

Siri's skin was the shade of coffee with cream, her eyes dark and almond shaped with thick glossy lashes that swept over her cheeks when she lowered them in deference to her Master. Her long hair was thick and black as midnight. It flowed down her back like a silken waterfall, grazing the top of her bottom. Her breasts were large and full, and her nipples dusky rose in color. Her waist was trim and her hips curved gently, her legs were long and lean. Beth could see Siri was slippery wet between her legs, her cunny was puffy and moist and she knew she should turn away in embarrassment or shock, but she couldn't take her eyes away from the scene.

Jeeval picked up a coiled, single tail whip and approached Siri, and Beth let out a little cry. Maxwell pulled his finger from between her lips and put his hand over her mouth to silence her. If either of the participants in the erotic act before them had heard her, neither showed any sign. Jeeval walked around Siri, flicking her lightly with a practiced hand, teasing her nipples, sliding it over her bottom, running it up and down each thigh until Siri was moaning and pleading with him to punish her. Her words shocked Beth to the core. How could Siri want the pain she was sure the whip would inflict?

Jeeval did as Siri begged, and began to lash her. He struck her belly and breasts, hard and fast, leaving angry red stripes, then moved behind her. He gathered her hair and put it over her shoulder to bare the smooth canvas of her back. Raising the whip Jeeval began to lightly flick her back and bottom as Siri called out and begged for more. Harder and harder his strokes became, until she was arching her back with each lash and gasping with each blow, but still she begged him to hit her once again.

Beth watched, horrified, and she began to twist in Maxwell's arms, but a sharp slap on her bottom and his arms of steel kept her from running away.

"I can easily trade my belt for a whip just like that my dove. Would you like a taste of something so fiery so soon?"

Jeeval's cock grew hard once again as he punished his slave, and soon he unbound her, ready for a new game. She dropped to her knees and kissed his feet, thanking him for each lash, rubbing her cheek against his foot lovingly. Glancing over his shoulder towards the wall Beth and Maxwell hid behind, Jeeval pulled Siri up to her feet by her hair and led her to a padded bench. Siri immediately took her place bent on the bench, kneeling, legs spread wide, and every inch of her on display. Her bare mound was wet and shiny between her splayed well whipped thighs, ample evidence of her need. How, Beth wondered, how could she become aroused from such brutal treatment?

Jeeval poured some oil on his hands and Beth thought he was going to massage the welts the whip had left but she was very mistaken. He moved behind Siri, but stood off to the side so the visitors he knew were hiding behind the wall would have a clear view of his actions. Jeeval enjoyed these performances, and taking Siri hard and fast in her sweet bottom would make any new captive think twice about her new lot in life. He oiled up his hand and spread Siri's cheeks apart, exposing her tight little anus. Pressing a finger against it, Jeeval slowly slid it in, making Siri gasp.

As Jeeval began to prepare Siri's body to take his cock, Maxwell's hands worked their own magic on Beth's body. One went back to playing with her breasts while the other slid her pants further open to gain more access to her cunny and bottom. He coaxed her legs apart, whispering sweet words against her skin in the darkness, and brought his hand to her bare quim, stroking her clit, flicking the small jewel to make it dance over her aroused nub, spreading her wetness, making her slippery from the top of her cunny to the start of her bottom. Back and forth his hand slid along the groove between her cheeks and legs, pausing to gently thrust inside her to gather more wetness to spread around every few passes. Over and over again his hand went cunny to bottom and back again until Beth was dizzy with desire. It was too much, the darkness, his nearness, his scent, his touch, the erotic yet horrid scene before her. Her body was on fire and filled with a riot of emotions.

"Please"

"Relax kitten. Relax and learn."

As Beth's breathing sped up, Maxwell focused on her sensitive nub, teasing the tiny bundle of nerves as he licked and suckled her neck and rolled her nipples between his fingers, his hard cock pressing against her bum cheeks all the while. Beth moaned, all her resistance melting away from the heat of his touch. She put her head back, baring her throat to his nibbles and licks, mewling, trembling, offering herself up to him. She quivered against him and turned her head, seeking his lips but Maxwell's hand came up immediately and turned her head back. She was to watch Jeeval and Siri.

"No luv, watch, listen, and learn." Maxwell knew what Jeeval was up to and he wanted Beth to see this act of passion. Beth stared at the couple before her once more and listened intently to Jeeval's words, as her body trembled with desire. It shocked her to see Jeeval putting his finger in Siri's bottom, but that shock was joined by a jolt of arousal. She couldn't deny that watching Jeeval and Siri was causing tingles of desire to spread through her belly.

Jeeval pressed his finger further into Siri's bottom and she moaned. "That's right my little pet, tonight your bottom will be used to satisfy my needs. Relax and push back." She did and Jeeval thrust his finger in and out, twisting and wiggling it, before adding a second. Siri tightened again, and he slapped her bottom hard. "You will be open to me woman. Let me in."

Siri did as commanded and wiggled back onto his fingers. Soon Jeeval was thrusting them in and out, twisting fast, crossing them over, pulsating and spreading her open, stretching her, relaxing the oh so tight muscles of her bottom, preparing Siri's body for what was to come. After adding a third finger to her tight little rosebud, Jeeval knew she was ready to accept his shaft. He stroked his hard cock, covering it in oil, then spread more oil on Siri's opening. Jeeval glanced back towards where Beth and Maxwell were hidden once more, before placing the bulbous head of his cock at her tightest entrance and pressing forward.

Siri gave a little cry of pain as her body worked to accept the size of his cock, and Jeeval grasped her hips, his fingers digging in as he held her still. There was no warmth in this man, he took what he wanted, whatever it was, in whatever fashion pleased him. Beth squeaked at his actions, hearing Siri moan and pant, watching her thighs quivers as Jeeval sank his cock into her bottom. Beth was frozen, enthralled and in shock, but that shock was nothing compared to what she felt when Maxwell slipped his finger out of her cunny, quickly moving to her rosebud, and pressed his finger into her bottom. Her breath came out in a whoosh of surprise, and she bucked back against him hard, and then shot up and away, struggling against his arms.

"*NO!*" The word came forth, loud and clear, echoing in the long passageway, and Jeeval looked over his shoulder at them, a frown of disapproval on his face before resuming his hard thrusts into Siri's bottom. Siri too had turned at the disturbance, eyes wide in shock, women in the estate never said no, to do so would bring swift and severe punishment. Jeeval slapped her bottom, hissing at her to turn away.

Beth twisted and fought Maxwell but he growled in her ear and held her tight. "Would you like a taste of the whip like Siri just had Beth?" Beth shook her head.

"Then be still and shut up. He is your Master now, and you aren't to disturb him. He will punish you and take you however he likes, so you better learn well my sweet."

The mention of the whip and the thought of the barbaric man who had wielded it sent ice water flowing through her veins, but Maxwell's finger thrusting in and out of her bottom was too much to take. She couldn't stand this latest affront to her dignity. It was simply too much. As Maxwell moved his other hand to Beth's quim to try and subdue her with pleasure, she wrenched out of his arms. Maxwell lunged for her and caught her around the waist, hauling her back against him and clamping his hand over her mouth.

"Enough." The word was a quiet hiss but it was delivered with deadly menace. Beth thrashed and wiggled, kicking back and making solid contact with his shin and driving her elbow into his stomach. She bit the hand that covered her mouth, and Maxwell let out a string of curses as he shook his wounded palm. Jeeval again stopped to gaze at the wall and shook his head. It sounded as if the new slave had much to learn. He would have to find out more about her, but now was not the time. He gave Siri's bottom a few playful spanks and resumed his rutting as she moaned and wiggled in front of him. The disturbance was the very reason he let

Maxwell break the captives in. Jeeval wanted nothing to do with willful women.

When Maxwell released her to shake his wounded hand, Beth charged off into the passageway, running frantically, having no idea where she was going, blinded by the darkness and her tears. She slammed into a wall, crying out in shock and pain, and Maxwell was on her in an instant. Beth turned on him, wild and terrified. She was in a panic, surrounded by blackness and being hauled to her feet by a very angry man. She lashed out at Maxwell, catching his cheek with her fingernails, and leaving a deep scratch.

"Bloody hell woman! Stop it. Stop it Beth." Maxwell threw her over his shoulder, ignoring her ineffectual fists pounding on his back, and rained slap after slap down on her bottom as they wound through the passageway in the darkness. Beth screamed out her frustration, letting loose a litany of curses that would have made a sailor blush, and fought Maxwell every step of the way.

When they finally arrived back at his chambers, Maxwell marched into the small punishment room and dumped her unceremoniously onto the small bed. He straddled her quickly and held her hands over her head in a death grip, his weight pressing her down into the mattress, making it impossible for her to get free. Beth screamed and cursed some more as Maxwell quickly bound her wrists to the headboard then spun and did the same to her ankles.

He quickly unfastened the chains that held her pants together around her ankles and waist leaving her bare, before reaching under her and tugging the bow of her top free, pulling it from her body. Maxwell stood back, his nostrils flaring, eyes flashing with rage, chest heaving as he fought to control himself. He ground his teeth as he looked down at her, sprawled upon her back, spread eagle, unable to move, totally bare, trying to decide what her punishment should be.

"I'm beginning to think you're more trouble than you're worth Elizabeth."

The way he used her full name and the icy tone in which he said it left no doubt in Beth's mind that Maxwell was in a rage. What would her do to her now? She was totally helpless, trussed up like a Christmas goose. He could do anything to her, anything. The thought terrified her but she shut her eyes and turned away, dismissing him. She would never beg him for mercy.

Maxwell watched as she snubbed him yet again, his hands curling into fists at his sides. Part of him wanted to flay her alive, but he had a better idea. Little Miss Elizabeth had an overabundance of pride, and it was time to take her down a notch or two.

"So high and mighty aren't you princess? Well you

won't be for long. Think you won't be begging and performing like Siri? Think you're too good to kiss Jeeval's feet and suck his cock? You're wrong pet, very, very wrong. You're going to do all that and more. Before I'm done, you will beg me to punish that bottom inside and out, beg me to hurt those tender nipples and thrust my cock in your mouth. You're going to want me Beth, and I'm going to take you, over and over, anytime and anywhere I like, and all you're going to say is "Please Master, and thank you." Without another word Maxwell knelt on the bed and settled himself between Beth's spread legs.

"No damn you, not that."

"Oh yes luv, exactly this." He lowered his mouth and began to lick her sweet quim, lashing his tongue across her nub over and over, and then thrusting it inside her tight passage as he rubbed his upper lip over her clit. Suckling and teasing, darting in and out, smiling through his work as her juices began to flow over his tongue, building the wonderful sensations in her core.

Maxwell brought her to a peak over and over, and then backed off each time she was ready to explode. His hands found her breasts as his mouth brought her to near ecstasy, and Beth squirmed as much as she could in her bindings, raising her hips to his talented tongue, her pride chased away by the pleasure only he could give her. When he had brought her to the brink of orgasm for the fifth time he got up from the bed and wiped his mouth with the back of his hand, leaving her hot and needy.

"Goodnight pet. Hope you sleep well. I told you that bad girls get punished. I imagine it will be a long night. Just remember who brought you to this point, and never forget that if you'd been good I wouldn't have stopped. You'd probably be cumming and screaming right now. Sweet dreams, kitten."

Beth's eyes went wide and she made a little mewling noise of protest before her mouth fell open in disbelief. He couldn't mean to leave her like this. He wouldn't. She moaned in frustration as the unquenchable fire burned deeply in her core and her wetness trickled down between her legs. Maxwell smirked, licked his lips, and clucked his tongue, then turned and shut the door, leaving her alone in the dark with every nerve in her body focused on the need between her legs.

Chapter Ten

Beth lay on the bed in a frenzied heat, her wetness pooling under her bottom onto the sheets beneath her. Her cunny was throbbing and swollen with need, her tender nipples dying to be touched by the very man who's name she was cursing. She fought her bonds and bucked her hips, but could find no relief, nor way to quench the fire between her legs. Still, Beth refused to cry out and she refused to beg. Damn that beast with his talented hands and mouth, damn her traitorous body, and damn herself for being such a little fool as to get herself into a situation such as this in the first place.

Tears stung the back of Beth's eyes but she defied her pain and anger. Her emotions were in turmoil, her body was crazed with need and she was exhausted from the long, terrifying ordeal of the day. Finally, she slipped into a fitful sleep, one where her dreams were invaded by a blue eyed devil of a man who haunted her with his handsome face, sweet words and sensuous lips, then turned and mocked her at every turn with his caustic words. One moment he was as charming and gallant as a prince, the next he was sinister and foreboding, yet still even in her dreams, her body yearned for him.

She awoke as the sky outside the tiny window was turning pink with the coming dawn, covered in a sheen of sweat, still wet and swollen between her legs, still cursing Maxwell, yet still needing him desperately.

As for Maxwell, he had been up most of the night, watching his little caged bird from the doorway as Beth fought her bonds and struggled with her raging desire as the darkness wore on.

His need and desire for her had grown steadily throughout the night, as did the tender feelings he held for her inside him. It was because of this, that he never once considered going in and taking what he so desperately needed. Those feelings and the act of restraint were still something that he steadfastly refused to acknowledge. Heartless rouges who kidnaped innocent young girls didn't and couldn't give a wit about them.

Maxwell could admit he was relieved that he hadn't gone along with his first impulse and whipped the girl senseless in his fit of rage, but the reason why he was pleased by his untoward gentleness must not be questioned. It was simply a matter that hurting her would have done nothing but cause fear and mistrust in Beth and that was something Maxwell knew he didn't want. Yes she had to be broken, she must always hold a small bit of fearful respect for the men in this house, but Miss Elizabeth Thornton was a delicate treasure whose spirit needed to be nurtured and tamed, not crushed. He wanted her to blossom and open under his skillful touch, not wither and die.

No, Maxwell would not examine his feelings of tenderness for the girl sleeping in the small, prison like room. He pushed them aside and told himself that each captive was different. That was all it was, and therefore they must be handled as such. Beth needed to be tended and taught with a special, gentler, hand. Passion would tame the fiery hellion better than force, and it had nothing at all to do with how she felt about him after a punishment or while he readied her for Jeeval. Not that he was ruling out a good hard paddling, or strapping, discipline definitely had its place, and Beth had to be taught to crave the pain along with the pleasure. It was required.

Besides, the little wench had gotten wet between her thighs when he'd spanked her anyway, which showed she was partial to the sexual games that went on in the estate. Jeeval wouldn't have it any other way whether Little Miss Beth liked it or not. The fact that her lithe body sent a raging bolt of desire roaring through him whenever he had her over his lap was also a bonus, one he couldn't and wouldn't deny. He liked smacking the smooth ivory skin of her soft bottom until it was a delicious shade of crimson and hot under his touch. Hell, he loved it, the act made his cock hard as granite.

Maxwell smirked as he allowed himself to think of all the delightful games he would teach Beth, but then his mind drifted to why he was doing so and he remembered Jeeval. Cruel, ruthless, heavy-handed, Jeeval. The thought of the man touching Beth and taking the crop or whip to her, or even bedding her for that matter also caused a riot of emotions to rise up inside of him, just as thoughts of the little wench herself did, but he shoved these aside as well. Pure foolishness was what that was. She had caught his fancy was all, with her little porcelain doll face, unique little nose, and huge green eyes, but she was simply another slave to be added to Jeeval's harem, a delicate piece of finery to be used for pleasure.

She was an uppity bitch full of too much sass to be honest, who'd given him nothing but willful disobedience. Didn't lasts night's rebellion and the painful scratch on his face prove she was an insolent, willful brat? When the day came to present her to the master of the house, he would send her on her way with a swat on her pretty bum and not a second thought. There was no room for sentimental drabble in this business. The women here were toys, slaves, objects of delight. Besides, there were a million other Beth's out there. She'd be gone from his mind the minute she walked out his door, and he'd go fetch another pretty bauble to play with.

With those thoughts firmly in place, Maxwell decided to take a walk in the gardens and leave the little minx to her own doings, but when he heard Beth moan, Maxwell went quickly to the open door of the chamber. She turned at the sound of his footsteps, green eyes flashing anger and fear before turning away. Would he beat her or torture her with more of his lewd games this morning? All she wanted was to disappear, to be left alone, to be able to escape his piercing blue eyes and mocking sneer. He would know exactly how her body had felt throughout the night, how it still felt, and he would use it to his advantage, despicable creature that he was.

"I see you've still got your claws out, kitten. Perhaps you ought to think twice about your behavior and temperament this morning. Haven't you learned your lesson, pet? Is your attitude still in need of correction? I'll be happy to oblige sweet. There are many ways to tame you my wild little hellion." Maxwell smirked at her as he delivered his threats, but when Beth looked back at him, Maxwell saw tears shimmering in her eyes. He wasn't sure if they were from anger, despair, or regret but they made the smirk disappear none the less.

"Please untie me. I... I hurt all over. My body needs to move." The whispered request burned in her throat. Asking anything of him was a bitter pill to swallow.

Beth's eyes clearly conveyed her pain and distress, both physical and emotional, and Maxwell's heart lurched in his chest as he gazed into those luminous pools of emeralds. It was clear she was fighting tooth and nail to maintain her composure.

Maxwell moved to the bed and sat on its edge. It was narrow and his hip pressed against Beth's as he did so. The contact caused an immediate spark to jump between them, the heat of him burning her as surely as the hottest flame. Beth tried to move away and Maxwell clucked his tongue.

"Here luv. None of that. Be a good girl for me now." Maxwell slowly drew his hand down between Beth's breasts and over her mound to slide his finger between her cunny lips, smiling upon finding her still very wet.

"Did you have pleasant dreams, pigeon?"

Oh that smirk! How Beth was coming to hate that smirk that always adorned his face. How could he look so angelically beautiful yet so wickedly evil at the same time? She didn't answer at once, and he raised one eyebrow then stroked her cunny once more, circling her needy swollen nub.

Beth grit her teeth against the pleasure soaring through her veins at his touch. His shirt hung open and she closed her eyes. The last thing she needed was the sight of his hard naked chest just inches from her breasts. Her body remembered how it had felt to be crushed against those rippled muscles and kissed until she was dizzy. Her blood was heating to a boil and her body yearned for release.

"Don't... please. I'm sorry about last night. I am sorry. I'll be good. Just don't." The words burned her pride, but having her body respond to his touch would shame her far more.

"Beth you have to stop denying your desire. It's why you're here luv. It's also what got you into trouble last night. If you had simply allowed me to touch you as was required, as I wished to, if you had simply allowed yourself to feel the pleasure I can give you and learn what must be taught, none of that unpleasantness would have happened. It's all about desire, sweet. Arousal and passion Beth. You're full of fire, kitten. Why must you try to deprive yourself and me?"

"NO! You... That was disgusting. Jeeval is a wicked, evil... I ... He hurt her! "

"Siri was a very willing participant my love. Yes he hurt her, but Siri's pleas for more were not lies. I hurt you my sweet and you liked it just a little didn't you? You liked my hand spanking your delicious bum and the special tingle that shot through your body with each stinging slap. That oh so confusing mixture of pain and pleasure. Admit it pigeon. Your body didn't lie, Beth. Your quim was wet even as your bottom was burning."

"NO! No... I didn't. I didn't like it!"

Maxwell bent down and gently kissed her into silence. His lips grazed her lightly with just a hint of pressure, but it was all that was needed for Beth to respond. She opened her mouth, allowing his tongue free rein to dance across hers. He swept it from side to side, teasing, tantalizing, reminding her of what he could do with his talented mouth if he so wished. Her body, strung tight as a violin string, molten passion still raging through her from the way Maxwell had repeatedly brought her to the edge then deserted her the night before, almost exploded from the kiss alone, and she pulled on her bonds and moaned into his mouth.

"Yes Beth, you did, and you were punished for denying me access to your body, for refusing to give into the pleasure I was making you feel, for not doing as you were told, and for this." Maxwell's hand ran across the deep scratch on his cheek and Beth winced, her heart flooding with guilt.

Why did it bother her that she had hurt him? He had deserved it and so much more, yet here she was, gazing into his blue eyes, apology ready to spill from her lips so he would forgive her and kiss her again. Her heart gave a little flutter in her breast that had nothing to do with the ache between her legs. The thought of Maxwell being angry, displeased, or disappointed in her, caused a deep sadness inside her that Beth didn't want to acknowledge. He was her captor! Why should she care if she had injured him? Beth didn't know why, but she did. Oh she was so very confused. What was it about this man?

"I'm sorry I hurt you." The words came out in a soft little voice, very much like that of a little girl truly full of remorse. "But I'm not sorry about the other things." This was said with much more force and her eyes once again flashed in defiance. "It... it was disgusting."

"It was an act your body will learn to crave kitten. I will touch you in many places luv, with my hands, my mouth, and my hard cock, and you will enjoy each and every one of them. You simply need to trust me."

His words were like a gentle caress, mesmerizing her, and Beth found herself becoming lost in the sea of his blue eyes even as she tried to maintain her outrage. Maxwell couldn't help but smile at her. She was his Beth, an intriguing, beguiling mix of innocence and fire. His Beth? Where had that come from? She wasn't his, not now, and never would be. He was preparing her for Jeeval just like all the rest. Maxwell suddenly growled and shook his head, running his hand back through his hair, making Beth look at him quizzically. One minute he was smiling, the next scowling. She never knew what to make of him.

"Just tell me luv, are you going to be a good girl? I can easily do a repeat performance of last night if you think that particular lesson hasn't sunk in yet. Or we can make the sweet skin on your bottom burn before I bury my tongue between your legs." Maxwell stuck out the tip of his tongue and waggled it at her in a way that made all of her blood rush to her core. Beth blushed scarlet and lowered her lashes.

"You are to obey me and do as you're told. Is that understood?" Maxwell cupped her chin in his hand and forced her to look up at him, and then once more his hand trailed down between Beth's breasts, pausing to stop and circle each nipple before proceeding further and reaching the open lips of her sweet sex. He stroked her with one finger, lightly teasing, and Beth bit her lip to stifle a moan. She closed her eyes again and nodded her head.

"Oh no pigeon, that won't do. I want to hear your passion and see it in your eyes."

Chapter Eleven

The talented finger continued to stroke across Beth's swollen nub, and then was exchanged for his rougher, larger thumb, and she couldn't stop her hips from moving in time to his rhythm. "That's it pet. Open your eyes." Beth did and found herself drowning in the depths of his stormy blue orbs that were full of lust and tenderness.

"Tell me how it feels kitten. Purr for me sweet Beth." Again and again his thumb stroked across her nubbin and then he slowly slid a finger inside her tight virgin cunny. Beth gasped and moaned in pleasure, the feeling was so foreign yet she craved it, wanted him to touch her in that very intimate way, to stroke her there and never stop. Tossing her head from side to side, Beth let out a little cry of pleasure. "That's my girl. Now tell me luv. Are you going to be good? Have you learned your lesson?"

"Yes. Oh yes please. Please untie me. I... Oh." Beth blushed the now familiar shade of pink as a flush of a very different sort crept up her body. Maxwell quickly undid her bonds and paused to massage each wrist and ankle with the utmost care, kissing and rubbing them until the blood returned and the stiffness was gone. His mouth then traveled from hands to breasts as his hands seemed to travel everywhere. Teasing, tickling, caressing, stroking, kneading her breasts as he suckled, then moved his mouth and hands lower, igniting a fire deep in her womb.

Beth was in a state of arousal she couldn't deny. She wrapped her arms around Maxwell and pressed her body to his, needing him close, needing his heat, hating the clothes keeping him from her touch. She was so close, so hot, had been on the precipice of cumming all night long and nothing mattered but the man who lay atop her. Maxwell's hands and mouth were everywhere as he whispered naughty nasties and sweet words of tenderness alternately in her ear and against her skin.

"Please, please... "

"Please what my little dove?" His hand found the folds of her womanhood and began to stroke her again. The dew of her desire wet his fingers as they slid back and forth and performed their magic. She was slick and swollen, molten hot and ready to be loved. Maybe it was time to take her. Maybe it was time to deflower his beautiful rose.

Beth's small hand closed over the bulge in Maxwell's breeches as she explored his manhood with her limited but very arousing skills, and his decision was made for him. Maxwell needed to bury himself inside her. He needed to feel the hot velvet grip of Beth's cunny squeezing him as he mounted her, and pressed deep within. It was time to initiate his little love bird into the world of true passion.

"Please... Maxwell." The sound of his given named whispered in a breathy plea sent his head and heart in a spin. Maxwell closed his eyes and grit his teeth, trying to keep himself together. He had to go slow, had to be gentle. He couldn't hurt his precious angel, wouldn't force her either. Beth had to be sure. There could be no regrets. Maxwell knew he couldn't stand it if she ever looked at him with accusing hate filled eyes.

"Do you want me to make you feel good kitten? Want me to send you to the stars? I can make it oh so good my luv. Make you feel things you never dreamed possible. There will be a bit of pain at first, but it will be over quickly, and I will make your body sing. I promise kitten."

Maxwell covered her small hand with his and encouraged her stroking of his cock as it swelled in is breeches. He thrust his hips forward in time with the movement of his fingers over her cunny and clit driving her almost over the edge. Beth cried out and squeezed him with just enough pressure to send Maxwell into a whirl, fire shooting through his vein. What was this little minx doing to him with a simple touch? He had to have her and it had to be now.

"Tell me Beth. Can I take you as a man takes a woman? Can I take you here? Bury my cock inside you?" He slid a finger deep enough into her tight passage to cause just a hint of pain so she would know what was coming, hoping against hope that she wouldn't turn scared. "Tell me luv."

Beth mewled and Maxwell quickly rubbed her clit to ease the pain his finger had caused. She immediately arched up into his hand, eyes wide; yearning, needing more, hair in wild disarray, cheeks flushed, and nodded a silent yes.

Maxwell scooped her up to carry her to his bed, crossing the chamber quickly, lips descending on Beth's open swollen ones, heedless of anything around him. Just as he reached the door of his bed chamber the ornate secret panel swung open and Jeeval strolled in, frowning as he saw the couple in a seemingly blissful, loving embrace. He moved in behind them, unbeknownst to Maxwell and Beth who only had eyes for each other. Jeeval then listened to the exchange of dialogue between his hired man and the new slave and scowled in grave disapproval.

"Gonna send you to the stars kitten. Gonna be so good my little luv, you'll see. Make your body soar, make my girl so happy. That's what good girls get. You're my good Beth. My sweet little tiger. I'll be so gentle."

Beth melted against Maxwell, her arms encircling his neck, sighing as she drew his head down for another deep kiss. Her body yearned for him, needed him, she was filled with a passion so strong it was sweeping her away. Beth didn't care what he was going to do to get her to those stars; she just wanted to get there as soon as she could. There was no fear; all that filled her was desire and trust for the man who held her in his arms.

"It's going to be wonderful my sweet. My precious dove."

"Please." Maxwell began to kiss her again, lovingly. Little kisses across her cheeks and nose, on her forehead, light and gentle then more demanding as he found her lips once more, a growl of passion rising from deep in his throat.

"My Beth."

Maxwell froze in shock when Jeeval cleared his throat not five feet from where he stood holding Beth in his arms. He turned, instinctively pulling her close, and met his stone cold eyes. Beth cried out and brought her arms down to try and cover herself, then tried to twist out of Maxwell's embrace to flee, and Jeeval's eyes turned colder still. His anger and disapproval all too clear.

"You aren't to move or cover yourself in my presence unless told to do so my little bitch. Put her down." Maxwell hesitated. He could feel Beth trembling in his arms. Jeeval's eyebrows rose inquisitively. Was Maxwell protecting the new whore?

"Is there a problem with my command?"

"No, of course not. You surprised us is all. Not knocking these days, Jeeval?"

"Forgive my manners." His words were pleasant enough but the tone was caustic. "I do tend to forget, seeing as it is my home. I've come to check on the status of this slave who dared to be so intrusive and disobedient last night. I assume she's been properly disciplined. I will not tolerate being interrupted at my games. The cost of her disobedience was taken out of her tender skin was it not?"

Maxwell had put Beth down, but she was pressed up against him, seeking the comfort he desperately wanted to give. The urge to push her behind him was strong, and he had to grit his teeth to keep from shielding her with his body. He knew Jeeval would find the action unthinkable. Instead, he moved his hands to restrain Beth's arms, to keep her from covering up her nakedness, an action that made Beth tense and let loose a little sound of rage and distress but Maxwell refused to let go. If she covered her body in addition to her obvious show of anger, Jeeval would beat her bloody. Hiding what he considered his property was a sin not soon forgiven in Jeeval's eyes. Maxwell also knew that if Beth did not do as she was supposed to, if she didn't behave as a proper slave, Jeeval might well take her away and give her to someone else to train.

When Maxwell didn't answer, Jeeval asked his question again, this time with a hint of menace. "Has she been disciplined for her intolerable behavior? I must say she doesn't appear to be very obedient this morning." At his words about discipline, Jeeval's hand moved to the coiled whip hanging from his belt, and Beth pressed back even further into Maxwell, turning pale. She remembered well the way he had mercilessly lashed Siri over and over.

"Her disrespect has been dealt with, and I can assure you she won't ever cause a scene again." Jeeval's eyes raked over Beth then took in the scratch on Maxwell's face.

"And what of that? How many lashes did she receive for daring to attack you?" Again, Maxwell didn't answer, Jeeval wouldn't understand why he hadn't whipped the life out of Beth. Jeeval raised his eyebrows at Maxwell's silence and he knew he had to say something.

"As many as I saw fit." The answer would have to do. He wouldn't explain himself to Jeeval, besides, it was the truth.

"Come here whore." Beth blanched even whiter at his tone and the insulting term, and remained motionless, her mouth open, ready to let loose a string of curses. Yes she was terrified, but he was depraved and vulgar and disgusting, and needed to be told so. In the end, common sense stilled her tongue. At her lack of instant obedience, Jeeval began to unfasten the whip from his belt, ready to teach the new slave proper manners.

Instinctively, Beth jumped then took a step forward out of self-preservation. The look of cold evil was clearly evident in the despicable man's eyes, and Beth knew he would show her no mercy.

"Closer! Do not toy with me. I am your Master."

Chapter Twelve

Beth moved closer, biting her lip, refusing to give in to her tears. She felt horribly exposed and it only added to her terror. How could she face him or stand up to him with nothing to cover her body? It shamed her for him to see her like this, and put her at a disadvantage. She wanted to kick him, fight him, and claw his eyes out, but then where would she go? Would Maxwell protect her? Could he even if he wanted to? This man would catch her and do horrible unthinkable things to her body if she tried to lay a hand on him. He could chain her up and do anything he pleased. Better to do as she was told for now and pray for a way to escape.

Her legs trembled from fear, but Beth closed her eyes and set her lips in a grim line of determination before opening them again, forcing herself to ignore the screaming inside her head that told her to run. She had to obey Jeeval. There was no choice. This was the man whom she'd seen beat Siri with the cruel whip, and now he was looking at her with fury in his eyes. Well she couldn't escape, but she wouldn't be weak either. She willed herself to be strong and looked up, facing him determined not to show her terror.

"Lower your eyes when you are in my presence, insolent bitch." Before Beth could react, Jeeval's hand lashed out and he slapped her across the face. She staggered back, stunned by the blow, but Jeeval caught her by the wrist and pulled her forward out of Maxwell's reaching arms. Jeeval scowled at Maxwell's uncommon show of leniency and compassion, and again raised his eyebrows at his hired man. Was Maxwell getting soft with this one? He couldn't allow that. For good measure he slapped Beth again, just to prove a point to both of them. The woman was his to do with as he liked, and to be trained as he ordered.

Beth fell to her knees, head reeling after the second blow. Never had she been struck before, and she was in shock. She tasted blood in her mouth and had to fight with every ounce of courage she possessed to hold back her tears, yet even then, in pain and full of fear, a flicker of potent rage burned inside her. She reined in her anger and dared to look up and face the man who was tormenting her. She looked briefly into his eyes in complete defiance, and then cast hers down to prevent a more severe beating. Beth wasn't a fool, she had simply wanted to make a point, not incite him to whip the life out of her.

Maxwell's nostrils were flaring with unspent rage. His eyes narrowed, and his fists were balled tightly at his sides. This man, his longtime friend, was abusing Beth and it made his blood boil, but Maxwell knew the situation had to be handled delicately. They were in Jeeval's estate, surrounded by Jeeval's men.

"Jeeval, she's only been here one night. Give the girl time to learn. That's why I'm here right? So you don't need to be bothered while she's still disobedient and willful. She doesn't know what's expected of her."

"After what she did last night she ought to be kissing my feet, not staring me in the eye."

Jeeval pulled Beth up by her hair and slowly circled her, taking in her smooth unmarked skin, touching her here and there, pinching her nipples, slapping her breasts, and roughly shoving her legs apart. Through it all Beth kept her eyes lowered and stood still, though her mind was demanding she fight back or run. The rational part of her brain told her in no uncertain terms that if she displeased this man he would hurt her severely. She also wanted to turn and look back at Maxwell, but knew that wasn't to be done either. Why was he allowing this? In truth she knew, still, it was hard to face the cold facts. He was saying nothing, doing nothing to stop Jeeval from molesting her, because his job was to ready her for this very thing, for the sexual attentions of this hideous man.

When Jeeval's fingers began to probe between her legs Beth had to bite back a scream. He wasn't hurting her per say because she was still wet from her arousal only moments ago, but his touch made her ill. Ice water replaced the fire that had so recently run through her veins as his finger slid deep inside her cunny. She closed her eyes and fought back her tears of humiliation and disgust. Bile rose in her throat as Jeeval probed deeply then found the proof of Beth's virginity and yanked his hand away.

"So tell me Maxwell, if she hasn't been bedded and she hasn't been beaten, exactly how did you correct her disobedience last night. I would have dragged her back here, whipped her until she was begging me to let her live, then rutted between those sweet thighs without regard to her wishes. Instead I find her unmarked and intact."

"Whose job is it to train the new slaves?" The edge in Maxwell's voice made his displeasure very clear. He didn't like to be questioned, especially about Beth, and he didn't like seeing her hurt and touched by Jeeval.

"It's what I pay you for. " The last of the words were said with a cold hiss, making it clear that Jeeval felt Maxwell was overstepping his bounds.

Maxwell fought with everything inside him to keep his tone casual. "I suppose raping and whipping her would have been one method, but I preferred something more subtle, something that actually left her with a long time to think over her actions and focus on her needs and desires. You want women who crave the whip and the passion, not ones who fear it, isn't that right?"

"Don't question me. You know damn well what I want, and this insolent slut isn't it."

Maxwell wasn't about to back down or give in yet he still tried to be somewhat respectful. Jeeval simply couldn't take Beth from him. "My way left her wet and wanting, not cowering in terror."

"Your way left her disrespectful and useless."

Beth had had just about enough, punishment be damned. They were talking as if she weren't even in the room and about things as personal as her virginity, as if they were speaking of the weather. Whip or no whip, she was about to lose control of her temper. Her chest was heaving as she fought to bite back a caustic comment, and her small hands tightened into fists.

Maxwell saw her body tense, saw how she was reacting, knew his kitten was extending her claws, and wanted desperately to stop her, but if he defended Beth, then Jeeval might toss her to one of his guests to be beaten and raped. He couldn't lose her.

He wouldn't think about why or about how seeing Jeeval touch Beth had enraged him, but right at that moment, Maxwell knew he couldn't lose his beautiful angel. He quickly stepped forwards and grabbed her arms a bit roughly for show, pulling her back, willing her to keep her mouth shut, hoping she would know this was for the best. Right now, all he wanted was to get Jeeval out of his chambers without Beth being hurt any worse than she already had.

"Look Jeeval. I admit she's a willful, uppity little bit of a thing, but just give me time. Have I ever let you down before? I'll teach her right, and when she's presented, she'll be a fine gift. Just leave this one to me. She may take a while longer but I promise she'll be ready to service you soon. I've never let you down before. As for the whipping and raping, sometimes you need to take a different approach. Don't want me to take all the fire out of them do you? I'm the one with the expertise in taming them right? You've always said I was your best man. It's why you pay me. Let me take care of this one. I'll mold her into a perfect little pet."

Beth bristled at his words but thankfully kept her mouth shut much to Maxwell's relief. He had to resist the urge to slip his arm around her and hold her close. Everything inside him was screaming for him to protect Beth from Jeeval, to comfort her and sooth her hackles, so she was happy and loving again, and to hell with the reasons why.

Jeeval sneered again as he raked his eyes over Beth. "The only fire I want to see in *my* women are when they are responding to passion or pain. There is no room for anything else. Remember that. I expect total submission. Don't forget whom you work for Maxwell. Everything you have is mine. All of it, including this little bitch here. This whore is mine, this estate is mine, and your very comfortable way of life is mine. All of it is mine to give or take. She deserves to be whipped bloody for disturbing me during last night, but I'll settle for five strikes, and another ten for daring to attack you. It's up to you who will give her the first taste of the lash, Maxwell. I'll be more than happy to met out her punishment."

Once again Jeeval's hand stroked the coiled whip on his belt. It was obvious to all present that he was dying to punish Beth. In his eyes her behavior had been intolerable, and Maxwell's seemingly lack of discipline, unthinkable. Only Maxwell's long time, prosperous dealings with him, was saving Beth from Jeeval's cruel hand, and that stay wouldn't last but a few for moments.

"That won't be necessary. I'll take care of her. Like you said, it's my job."

The two men stared each other down for a moment, had they been predators in the jungle they would have been circling, waiting to fight over their prey, but finally Jeeval nodded. Maxwell had been a very good employee. Trustworthy, loyal, and he always brought in the best women. This new one wasn't an exception. Once she was broken, she would be a delight. She was stunning.

"Very well. You take care of her. I will be back tomorrow, and I expect to find her properly marked and rid of that maidenhead. Undisciplined slaves and blushing virgins have no place in this household. Fifteen Maxwell, a hard fifteen. I will count each one."

Jeeval stormed out, and Beth made to bolt, but Maxwell caught her about the waist. She sagged backwards into him, her entire body trembling, a sob escaping from deep within, all of the pent up terror, rage, and humiliation rushing out. He turned her in is arms and pressed Beth's face to his chest, hushing her as he gave Jeeval time to move out of earshot. When he felt it was safe, he tilted her chin so her eyes met his. The fear in Beth's gaze made him half crazed.

"Do you have to hurt me?"

"Yes kitten, I do. It's that or he'll take you away."

"But I'm sorry. Tell him I'm sorry. Oh please Maxwell just let me go. Please. Can't you just let me go? Please don't hurt me."

"I can't Beth. I can't allow you to leave. Once you've entered these walls, you can't ever go back to the outside world again. I'm sorry luv. I promise I'll go easy on you, baby. I promise. I won't even use the bloody whip like he said. There are other things that leave marks that won't be as painful kitten. I'll build up the pleasure with the pain, and it will be all right." Beth shook her head no, still not ready to accept his answer.

She looked up at him, her green eyes so frightened yet still full of hope. Just maybe... "But you can Maxwell. Please. You can take me away from here. Please. Take me away. I ... I want you to take me away and stay with me Maxwell. Please. I want to leave this place, but I don't want to leave you. We could get away if we went together and you could stay with me. I wouldn't tell. I hate the men at the mission. I won't tell a soul. I swear. Please." Her words spilled out in a rush of terror. She was shaking her head frantically and a sob caught in her throat.

Maxwell looked down at the woman in his arms and his heart ached at her fear and pain. Did she really want him, or did she just want a way out? His heart wanted to believe her. Either way, was he really willing to risk his very life for her? Jeeval would hunt him down and have him killed for daring to take what was his, never mind that Maxwell was the one who'd brought Beth inside the estate walls to begin with. It didn't matter. To remove her now would be unforgivable treason.

He gazed into Beth's deep green eyes that were shimmering with unshed tears and tried to sort through the warring emotions inside. What was he to do? Could he believe her? Could he, Maxwell, the man who had kidnaped and terrorized so many innocent women find love in the arms of one so sweet?

"Please." Beth whispered the plea again, her soft lips moving against his chest as she clung to him. Could he find salvation in her arms? Did he dare to hope?

"Please. Please Maxwell, please save me."

Chapter Thirteen

"Beth it isn't that easy luv. We can't just walk out of here. Jeeval... "

"No! I hate you. Everything you say is a lie. All your sweet words, all your gentle touches, everything. All you want is for me to obey and be some... hideous, docile, toy you can present to that disgusting man. How could I ever have thought you cared about me? All you care about is your own pleasure and making that monster happy. Let me go. LET ME GO!"

Beth pushed away from Maxwell with a strength borne of terror and rage and went racing to the intricately carved panel by the double doors. Her fingers grasped and clawed at the ornamental decorations, trying to spring the secret latch, trying desperately to find freedom, but there was none to be had. Maxwell watched her frantic fumbling and his heart broke for her pain.

He went to her and tried to place his hands on her shoulders, tried to turn her and pull her close, to shush her and calm her fears, but Beth wouldn't have it. She lashed out at him and slapped his cheek with all her might, then sprung back, away from her captor, falling on her bottom as she lost her balance. She righted herself before a stunned Maxwell could move. He watched her go, fleeing him and the comfort he wanted to give her, a cry of pain stifled behind his tightly clenched teeth. There was no growl of anger at her attack upon him, only sorrow that the bond that had been forming between them had been shattered.

Beth ran past the bathing pool and into the garden, tears blinding her vision as she went, nothing mattered but getting away, knowing she'd tear Maxwell apart if he tried to stop her. She raced down pathway after pathway only to be met by a high stone wall at every turn. Beth had done this dance before, but her heart wouldn't let her give up.

Through it all, Maxwell stood at the edge of the garden and watched her mad flight, waiting for her to expend her energy. There was no sense in chasing her and trying to subdue her. Nothing would be gained by that, she would simply fight him. She had to give up on her own. Beth was clearly beyond reason. Besides, what could he say? Nothing she truly wanted to hear right now. Finally, when Beth had reached a corner of the wall and was pounding upon it with her fists, her shoulders shaking as she sobbed uncontrollably, Maxwell went forward to try and ease her pain. He couldn't allow her to hurt herself.

He sank down on his knees next to her, but Beth didn't acknowledge his presence. She continued to beat upon the wall with slow but steady blows that were bruising and scraping her hands. Her anguish crushed him, sent a knife through his heart, and Maxwell knew he had to make this better. He took off his shirt and wrapped it tightly around Beth's shoulders, covering her nakedness and trying to give her a sense of security, then took her injured hands in his and held them to his lips, kissing them gently. Beth didn't fight him, but she remained rigid and refused to look at him.

"Listen to me luv. We can't just leave. Now I'm not saying I don't want to. I... you've done something to me woman, something I can't explain, and I can't stand the thought of you being hurt or touched by Jeeval, but getting away would be next too impossible. There are estate guards everywhere, pet. I can't just waltz out of here with you in my arms telling everyone to have a nice day. We'd never make it past the front gate let alone off the grounds. Even if we did, Jeeval would hunt me down until the end of time. He wouldn't rest until I was dead and you were back in his possession. He's a man who's used to getting everything he wants sweet, and right now that includes you."

"Only because you brought me here!" She finally looked at him, and the accusations and pain in her eyes was just the thing Maxwell had told himself he never wanted to see again. "Damn you. Damn you for what you did to me. I had a life. It wasn't a great life but I wasn't a captive whore. Damn you. I hate you. I hate you. I hate you!"

She tried to tug her hands from his grasp but Maxwell held them gently but firmly. Beth balled them up, her nails cutting little crescents into her palms. Maxwell scowled in frustration, not because she wouldn't obey, but because he was failing miserably in his effort to calm and comfort her. His words were falling on deaf ears and it certainly wasn't the time to try and subdue her with passion.

"I'm sorry for that kitten. So sorry, but it can't be undone now. I... I had no right to take that from you. I... " How could he explain the complicated choices that had led him down this path in life and molded him into the man he was? More important, how could he make her realize now that he was changing? Changing for her and because of her. "All I can do is to try and protect you and try to make your life here better."

"How can you say that? A better life? Here? You said yourself that I'm a bird trapped in a cage. I'm being held against my will like a thing with no feelings. Trapped in an ornate prison to be used and abused by a hideous man after you manage to beat enough life from my soul to suit him. Do you know how I felt when he touched me, Maxwell? I felt ill. I wanted to retch, but I didn't dare because I knew I'd be whipped. I have come to understand what you've been telling me all along. I understand it far too well. Nothing I want or say matters."

"It matters to me, kitten. I... I care Beth." The words were a shocking admission to him. To care was unthinkable. To care was pure foolishness. To care was dangerous and would only lead to trouble he didn't need, but damn it, he did care. He cared about this beautiful woman before him, this little bit of a thing that had stolen his heart. He cared for her like he'd care for nothing else ever in his life.

"Caring won't help me Maxwell." Her words were whispered, but stung all the same.

"I'm sorry." He was. So very, very sorry. He wanted to whisk her away from here and keep her with him forever. Keep her safe and happy; keep her so content that she'd never want to leave his arms. He wanted to turn back time to before he'd abducted her from the market and go about courting her properly, but that couldn't be. Both of them were trapped in this life. Jeeval would vigorously protest Maxwell's leaving as much as he would Beth's. Maxwell knew too much about the intricate dealings of the estate and the women housed here. There were secrets that had to be kept, secrets that were more deadly than where the women came from, ones that involved the deaths of those who were used too hard. Those were secrets worth killing for.

"Sorry won't save me from that beast. Sorry won't keep you from hurting me when you are told to. *Sorry won't keep me from becoming a plaything for that sadistic monster!!* You say you don't want him to touch me but you won't do anything about it. He is going to touch me unless you stop him. You have to stand up to him.

"He's going to come back Maxwell. He's going to come back and inspect me, and touch me as if I were a thing. He'll be back tomorrow, and if you don't do as he said, then he'll take me away and do unspeakable things. How can you let that happen? How? You called me your Beth. *YOUR BETH*!! Was that just another lie to lull me into being docile and obedient? You... How can you say you care?"

Her voice cracked as she said the last of her words, the question a whispered plea. She wanted to believe in him, wanted him to really, truly care, because her own heart was telling her she cared too. Beth didn't know how she could be falling in love with this man who had done so many horrid things to her, but it was happening. It was happening no matter what her head told her. Her heart was pounding a mile a minute in her chest and it wasn't simply from fear and anger. She felt something for Maxwell, something very real.

Beth's lips were parted in the most enticing way as she made little gasps for breath, trying to get herself under control. She gazed at Maxwell, her heart on her sleeve, her eyes full of pain, longing and hope, as he searched her face, his own eyes pleading for understanding. Beth had to fight the urge to run her fingers over the beautiful lines of his cheeks. He looked so sincerely sorry and saddened, so lost and confused.

"Oh kitten." Those eyes. Damn those eyes of hers. They cut to his very soul and made his heart pound in his chest in a way he'd never felt before. What had she done to him? Was this what love felt like? Had the little minx stolen his heart? He didn't want Jeeval to touch her. Hell no! Never! The very thought made him insane. She was his. His to cherish, his to protect, his to... love. His Beth, his sweet, sweet angel, and he'd fight Jeeval and his army of guards to the death before that happened, but they needed time, time and a plan.

Maxwell looked cautiously around the gardens to make sure none of the eunuchs were tending the flowers before speaking again. What he was about to say would put both of them in jeopardy if they were found out. Jeeval would storm Maxwell's chamber with his men and yank Beth from his arms before he could blink, let alone fend them off. Hell, he'd do it if he even suspected what Maxwell was up to.

"Listen to me, kitten. I am going to save you. I will, but you have to trust me, and you have to be patient. We need to make a plan. I have to get you real clothes, set up a safe place for us to hide, and secure a way out of the city. There's ships coming and going from the docks, night and day, but most wouldn't be safe. Jeeval is the most powerful man here. He has eyes and ears everywhere.

"I have to find a safe way to take you out of the palace too. When we leave here, we can't stay in India. I need to talk to some of the men. Feel them out, see if I can trust anyone, because this will be almost impossible to do alone. There are one or two who seem to have a few morals left, but mostly everyone is satisfied with the way Jeeval does things. He's very rich and powerful, Beth. He's related to the Emperor. The timing has to be just right or our escape will never work. I swear on my life that I will keep you safe Beth, but you have to give me time. Do you trust me?"

"Will I have to go to him?"

"No! I swear kitten, he won't touch you."

"But you will. You have to punish me."

Maxwell's jaw clenched together and his nostrils flared as he tried to control his raging emotions. Beth's gaze had changed to a bold, intense stare, looking right into his soul, and he felt so raw and vulnerable. He figured it served him right, probably how all the women he'd brought to this place felt. Now the shoe was on the other foot and he was finding it a very tight fit. Maxwell reached out and brushed a lock of hair back behind Beth's ear then leaned forward and kissed her forehead. Joy filled him when she didn't flinch or back away.

"Yes luv. It will take a few days before we can escape and as you said yourself, Jeeval will be back tomorrow to inspect you. I swear to you, sweet. I will do everything I can to bring you pleasure with the pain. There are ways Beth. It's what the sexual games in this estate are all about. Siri really wasn't pretending when she was asking for more Beth. I'm telling you the truth. You saw the evidence of her desire. Her body yearns for the exquisite torment. It will hurt when I punish you, but I will bring you pleasure too. The two can mix as one and make the experience that much more intense. Can you trust me, luv? We have to keep you out of Jeeval's hands. He can't have a reason to take you away."

Chapter Fourteen

Beth pulled her hands from his and Maxwell's heart lurched in his chest. She was going to reject him. Instead, she stood and pushed his shirt from her shoulders, baring her beauty before his eyes, offering herself up to him. Maxwell's breath caught in his throat. She was exquisite; so regal, yet tiny, and so passionate and fierce. His Beth. He stood and moved to take her in his arms and Beth went willingly. She wrapped hers around his neck and Maxwell scooped her up, kissing her hard as he carried her into the estate.

He paused before setting her on his bed, nibbling, kissing, and tasting her sweetness. His tongue swept over hers again and again, lighting a fire inside her core, driving away the memory of Jeeval's touch and the terror of the past hour. She arched her back with need, and then nuzzled closer to his heat. Maxwell's chest was hard as marble, and Beth longed to run her hands over every inch of him. His kissed her long and hard, so long that her head began to spin as the fire roared through her veins and everything else disappeared. Her nipples were hard as little pebbles aching to be touched and the feel of his arms supporting her, burned her naked skin.

When he was done, she lay panting in his arms, weak as a kitten, mewling, dizzy with desire.

Maxwell let out a growl of pleasure and need as he released her and set her on his bed, then moved his hand to his breeches to quickly unfasten the button. His cock sprang forth and Beth smiled. Maxwell grinned back, incredibly please by her eagerness. Little minx was made for loving. He guided her willing hand to his shaft and she grasped him tightly, circling the head, rubbing the satiny smooth skin there until he moaned.

A bead of precum formed on the tip and she slid her thumb through it, spreading the silky liquid, and teasing the top of his cock. Maxwell grit his teeth, her hand was so hot and tight, but he had to resist the urge to allow her to pleasure him, it wasn't time. He put his hand over hers and stopped her movements. Beth looked up; eyes full of questions, and Maxwell shook his head, then stripped off his breeches, and sat on the bed next to her.

"No luv, you didn't do anything wrong. It was just right, too right. That's enough of that for now though. Come on, over my lap with you. I'll go easy baby, I swear. Warm you up nice and proper, get you all tingly. I can make it good pet. It's what I do."

Beth hesitated but only for a moment before crawling and kneeling next to him. He pulled her in for a kiss, his hand coming up to tease her nipples, gently at first with his palm, rubbing in soft circles, then harder, rougher, with his thumb and forefinger. The sensation caused a mixture of feelings in Beth, none of them unpleasant. The pain was sharp but brief, the caresses sweet and teasing, and she longed for his touch in whatever form it came. Gentle then rough, gentle then rough, Maxwell's hand moved over her breasts and nipples, back and forth until Beth was moaning.

"Such a beautiful gift from the heavens you are my sweet. Soft as a kitten but full of fire. Gonna make you feel so good, my love. Do you like that? Like it when I play with your pretty tits? Little pinches and sweet caresses. Hard and soft kitten, pleasure and pain. Are they really so different?"

One hand slipped around and cupped her bottom, squeezing her cheeks then giving her a sharp slap without warning. Beth made to move into position, thinking it was what he wanted, but he held her where she was. "Not yet luv." He squeezed her bottom then slapped it sharply, squeezed and slapped, squeezed and slapped, and then he added rubbing to the mix. So many sensations. Soon it was a few sharp slaps followed by a soft rub to ease the sting and to test the heat of her skin. These warm ups had to be done slowly so as to increase the desire with the pain and desensitize the skin just a bit.

Beth was wiggling at his side, her thighs quivering. One of Maxwell's hands was still pleasuring her breasts while the other was doing wicked things to her bottom, and he was kissing her senseless all the while, murmuring whispered words of desire against her lips. Finally, she began to sway, her legs not able to support her. There were too many feelings rushing through her. She was weak with pleasure and need. Maxwell lifted Beth under her arms, kissed her gently then looked deeply into her eyes.

"Trust me baby?"

"Yes" And she did.

He lay Beth over his lap and positioned her comfortably. She could feel his hard shaft pulsing against her belly and wondered briefly if it was the heat and nearness of her body or the act that was about to take place that had him so aroused. Her emotions were in turmoil, part of her yearned for his touch in whatever form it took, but part of her, the innocent girl of yesterday, was terrified by the pain that was to come and of how she would respond to it. Could he really make her body crave the sensation like Siri had?

"Easy now, kitten. Let yourself feel. Let the passion rise and mix with the pain. They can and will become one if you let them. Don't fight it Beth. I'm gonna go easy luv. Nice and easy to start with. Gonna warm up this sweet bottom of yours." Maxwell began to stroke Beth in the small of her back. Slow, lazy circles until he felt her relax. Round and round, feather light touches designed to make her feel at ease with his touch again. She had tensed up in this new vulnerable position, and he had to soothe her fears. If she were tense, the pleasure wouldn't build as it should. He used his other hand to hold her securely. Wrapping his arm around her bottom, not to restrain, but to comfort. "I've got you kitten, it's okay."

Little by little the circles he made dipped lower, grazing her creamy cheeks, touching the top of her bottom, making her want more. "So sweet, so perfect, my little dove." Lower and lower his talented hand went, side to side, up and down, and sometimes in the pattern of slow circles. At times he would graze her swollen needy cunny, making her yearn, making her need. He'd start one rhythm then change it, just as she began to move in time, keeping her wanting more. Beth mewled as his practiced fingers grazed over her hard little clit, touching it oh so lightly, then sighed in frustration when he moved on again.

"That's right precious, that's where you need Maxwell to touch you. I'll give you what you need and desire my love. I know just what my girl needs."

Maxwell eased Beth's thighs apart, moved his arm so it securely encased her waist, then slid a finger gently into her virginal opening. "Christ pet, so tight and hot you are." He did it with practiced ease, like a thousand times before, but somehow, this time was different. It had to be done just right. Just enough pressure, no pain within. He wasn't trying to prepare her body for his cock yet, that would come later, all he was doing was trying to get her aroused and relaxed.

Maxwell pressed forward with the utmost caution so as not to break her maidenhead. She had to trust him for what was about to take place, and that would be too much of a shock. His little dove knew nothing of the carnal dealings between a man and woman. Maxwell slid his finger out then pushed his thumb into her opening, while moving two fingers over her cunny to form a V around her swollen clit. This time Beth's moan was one of pure pleasure and Maxwell smiled.

"That's a girl. Purr for me kitten. Maxwell's gonna make it good luv. Do you like that?" He rubbed the tender sensitive flesh until she squirmed on his lap and he pinched her clit gently as he scissored his fingers opened and closed. It was slippery and swollen and so very needy and Beth arched her back like a cat, lifting her hips then pressing down into the heaven Maxwell's fingers were creating between her legs. When she was moaning and panting and on the verge of an orgasm, Maxwell gently slid his arms under her and moved them so he was leaning against the headboard and she was draped over his lap. He wanted Beth to be as comfortable as possible for what was to come next.

Maxwell spread her out, stroking her back and bottom and once again Beth stretched like a feline, toes pointing then curling as she made herself comfortable, wiggling, loving the feel of his hand gliding over her skin. Her legs were spread eagerly, hair in wild abandon, arms outstretched, and her hands holding the silk coverlet tightly in her fists.

Maxwell teased her cunny for a few more precious moments, feeling the ample evidence of her need flowing over his fingers and decided she was ready. How he longed to bury his face between her thighs and take her to heaven, but there were other matters to be attended to. He would drink of her sweetness later. Adjusting Beth so her legs were spread in a way that allowed his hard thigh to put pressure on her sensitive clit, he wrapped his arm around her waist and delivered the first spank without warning. This one was harder than any of the others had been, but still not overly harsh. Beth jumped in his arms and cried out, not from pain, but from surprise.

"It'll be all right kitten. I'll start out nice and slow. Get you all warm and tingly. Get this sweet bottom used to the feeling of my hand. Just let the feelings flow in pet and I promise to make my good girl cum. Promise to make it oh so good angel. Just let yourself feel everything and it will blend together. Gonna make it good, sweet."

That said Maxwell began a volley of light spanks upon Beth's upturned bottom. He started slow with a steady rhythm, almost caressing her skin with his fingertips after each strike. Back and forth, top to bottom, no part of her bottom was spared. He did a thorough job, turning her once porcelain skin a lovely shade of pink.

"Such pretty color you have, kitten. All pink and soft like the inside of a seashell. Crimson and cream, my delicate girl, so lovely. Your bum simply glows Beth, makes me crazy with need. Feel me under you? Can you feel my cock pressing into your belly? You're beautiful Beth and I want you. Pretty little bum. Beautiful baby."

Maxwell continued his litany of praise as he began to spank her harder. He spanked and spanked as her once creamy flesh turned from pink to rosy red, loving the sight before him. The way her soft bottom jiggled under his hand, the way she was spread out all willing and needy, the way her hair floated around her like a golden cloud. How he needed this woman, how he … cared. His heart skipped a beat at the thought, and Maxwell knew this time it wasn't pure lust that was driving him on and sending a torrent of hot blood pounding through his veins.

As Maxwell spanked her harder and harder, he was very careful to watch for her reaction. This had to be done just right. There could be no fear. Not where his

Beth was concerned. Every time Beth showed signs of pain, if she whimpered the wrong way, or tried to wiggle in his grasp, Maxwell would pause and resume his ministrations between her legs. The fact that she was wet as a river didn't escape him one bit, and it did wonders to reassure him that things were progressing as planned. After a few more minutes, he left his fingers pressed against her swollen cunny as he increased the sharpness of his spanks, knowing by this time that Beth would do nothing to move from his lap.

His action brought forth a few cries of protest from Beth at first, but his talented fingers soon overcame them. As for Beth, her body was a mass of tingling, riotous emotions that stemmed mostly from her very core. Every stinging slap caused her cunny and clit to press against Maxwell's fingers. She was dying for the pressure whenever it let up and was actively seeking his hard hand on her bottom. The sting in her bum sent strange tingles to her womb and the duel means of stimulation left her breathless and on the edge of ecstasy.

Maxwell could sense this, knew how close she was, and also knew it wasn't time yet. He knew she felt the most pressure on her clit when he spanked her gorgeous bum so he began to vary the slaps. He spaced them out until Beth was bucking up in an effort to make contact with his hand and then grinding down to find the delicious pleasure she desperately needed but Maxwell wouldn't oblige for long enough to let her go over the edge. She needed the spanks, she was desperate for them, and this was exactly what he wanted.

"Oh no my little minx. I control what you feel and how this shall be done. Soon I will give you what you want kitten, and it will be worth it."

Beth was delirious with need. She tossed her head back and forth and emitted little mewls and pleas. Her legs were spread wide, hips rocking, her bottom a fetching shade of scarlet, her thighs glistened with the evidence of her desire and Maxwell thought she'd never looked more enticing. It was time for the real punishment to begin. She was so far gone that the pain and pleasure would meld together. With barely a pause, he picked up a leather paddle from the table near the bed, and brought it down with a loud crack on Beth's upturned bottom. She cried out in shock, and twisted on his lap, but Maxwell quickly moved his hand from her cunny to hold her tightly around the waist.

"It's okay kitten. This will leave the marks Jeeval wants to see. Just relax and breathe. Feel the burn. I'll take care of your need. Promise me you'll stay over my lap and I'll put my fingers right back where you want them to be, sweet."

Beth nodded and Maxwell took a moment to rub her back and bottom, cooing words of encouragement and telling her she was a good girl, telling her she was strong and could take this punishment and that he would take her straight to heaven when he was done. He moved his hand between her soft folds, and slid his fingers up and down, up and down in her slippery dew, then found her swollen nub and traced lazy circles around the hard little bump until Beth thought she'd go mad with longing and was jerking in his arms for an entirely different reason.

"That's a girl, that's it Beth." Soon he added the sting of the paddle to the delicious torment his fingers were building between her legs and she was lost. Again and again the paddle came down and again and again Maxwell pressed on her clit. Each strike brought the pressure she craved. Pain and pleasure, pleasure and pain. There was no difference anymore. Both sensations went straight to her very core and boiled like molten lava there, waiting to erupt and flow through her veins.

"Oh God."

Her body was trembling; her mind in a whirlwind, her bottom was burning, and her very center on fire. Spanking, rubbing, spanking, rubbing, spanking, rubbing. Each blow brought her closer to bliss. Maxwell timed them so she needed each strike. Without the paddle, without the pain, there was no pressure on her clit. He increased the strength of his blows; these had to leave the marks ordered by Jeeval. They wouldn't be from a whip, but hopefully dark bruising would satisfy his order as well. Harder Maxwell spanked and faster he rubbed until her bottom was on fire. The blaze within matched the one on her bottom, and Beth was too lost to feel the difference. She moved into them, rising to meet the sting of the paddle. Needing, craving, wanting, and demanding. So close, so close.

"Please, please, please, please."

"That's a girl, come on baby, come on Beth. I know you feel it, let it happen kitten, come on Beth, that's it baby. Cum for me Beth, let yourself go."

Down, down, down the paddle came on her bottom. Center, side, tops, where her thighs met her cheeks, and even over her cunny. It was these that drove her beyond all reason. Maxwell's fingers moved like a blur over her slippery nub every time the paddle came down, until Beth was like a wild wanton thing in his arms.

"That's it Beth, that's my girl. Come on. Do it for Maxwell now. Let yourself feel it kitten. It's okay. Come on baby." And she did. With a cry that was torn from deep within her, her orgasm, one of burning fire mixed with liquid gold ecstasy soared through every nerve and Beth's body exploded. She stiffened and bucked and wailed as Maxwell continued to spank her crimson bottom and pleasure her aching clit. He slid two fingers inside as her cunny spasmed. Stroking her sweet spot, adding a new sensation as he eased off on the paddle and Beth came again, gasping and quivering and near tears, as her body tried to come back to earth and she fought to make her world stop spinning.

When she was spent and exhausted, Maxwell pulled her up into his arms, kissing her face, her neck, brushing back her hair, nibbling her ear, whispering sweet soft words over and over. Beth nuzzled his hard chest, relishing in the feel of his strong arms holding her. She felt strangely safe and secure, blissfully protected. Beth knew Maxwell would never let anything happen to her. Yes her bottom hurt like hell, but it was a pleasurable sensation as well. Maxwell had been good to his word. It throbbed, but it was in time to the aftershocks still coursing through her, she sighed, utterly content.

She felt lazy, languid, totally satisfied and strangely at peace, at least for now. There were massive obstacles for them to overcome, trials to endure, dangerous roads ahead, but they would be together. Beth knew that Maxwell would keep her safe until his last breath. Yes he had spanked her, delivered a harsh paddling, but it had been a strangely delicious feeling. He had made it good, just like he'd promised, and she didn't regret it one bit, in fact, the memory of being over his lap caused a tremor of renewed longing to shoot through her. She boldly looked up and brought his mouth down for a kiss, then smiled at him, eyes full of love. Beth gazed at him as if in a dream and Maxwell felt as if he was drowning in her eyes, but then those eyes clouded over.

"What is it baby? Was it too much? I have a special cream. Ways of taking the sting away."

"No, it's not that. That was... it was ..." Beth bit her lip and looked down as she blushed. Even now, after everything, the shy virgin came though at times. "That was wonderful Maxwell. You made me feel so good, it was everything you promised it would be, but... was... you didn't use the whip. That cruel beast wanted me whipped and you didn't do it. He said he'd count the marks. I don't want him to try and take me away. I.. I can be strong if we aren't done. Just tell me."

"Kitten what I did will mark you good and proper. It will be enough. I'll not take a whip to your delicate skin. You're not ready for that yet. As it is your sweet bum will be black and blue. It will have to do."

The thought of leaving crimson trails of fire upon Beth's skin made Maxwell ill. Siri may crave that kind of pain, but Beth was very far from being able to find pleasure in it. He wouldn't hurt her like that. On the other hand, how would they feel and what would happen to her if Jeeval stormed his rooms and dragged her away because he wasn't happy with what he saw when he inspected Beth tomorrow? Perhaps they could compromise, but that would come later.

"Listen kitten, I'll take the strap to you, lash you up just a little if I must, but I won't go at you with the whip. I'll not chance it. You're not ready, precious. It's too harsh. The strap won't be easy, you don't crave the pain enough yet, but it will be easier."

"I told you when we met that I wasn't a simpering ninny. I have spirit Maxwell. Can you make it... like before? Make it so I... so it feels ..." Beth blushed again, as scarlet as her bottom, and Maxwell grinned and kissed the tip of her nose.

"Yes luv. The strap will be harsh, but I will give you pleasure as well, just like before. But there is something else we are going to do first. We have all night. I want to make love to you Beth. I want to take you and pleasure you in all the ways a man can. I want to take you to those stars I promised."

With those words Maxwell's lips descended upon hers, and all thoughts of punishment were forgotten. The time had come for two to become one.

Chapter Fifteen

Maxwell held Beth close to his chest. He could feel the heat of her recently punished bottom and the wetness of her pleasured cunny pressing against his thigh and it was driving him wild. He knew he had to have her and soon, but it had to be done with great care. Maxwell had ripped away the innocence of many a virgin in this very bed, but none were like his Beth. He'd never cared about their cries. The initial time hurt, and that was that. There was time to give pleasure and rebuild passion later, all that mattered then was the exquisitely tight feeling of thrusting into an untried woman for the first time and sheathing himself in her scorching satiny depths as her virgin walls quivered around him, but not anymore, not today, not with this woman. This was his Beth.

Maxwell kissed her lips, nibbling and teasing until Beth was panting and open to him. He darted his tongue in to dance with hers and the taste of her was so sweet and incredibly intoxicating he got lost in the passion of the simple act. He kissed her gentle then hard, teasingly then firmly, soft as a breeze then ravishingly over and over. Beth mewled and made little sounds of delight and her hands began to explore his hard chest as she wiggled in a very enticing way on his lap. Then in a very bold move, one arm slid around his neck and held his head down possessively.

She kissed him back with wild abandon, opening her eyes to stare into his, and the emotions he saw there stole his heart away. Was that love in those deep emerald pools gazing at him? Could it be love? There was passion. It was there without a doubt and trust, she had given herself over completely, but the two were mixed with something Maxwell had never seen before. It was a look of complete blissful happiness. A tenderness that said you're mine and I'm yours and I'll never want to leave you. A look that told him there was no place she'd rather be than in his arms. He pulled back and stared at her, his eyes full of questions, his heart pounding.

"Beth? Kitten I... Oh my love. Do you know I how feel for you sweet? Can you feel my heart beating?" He took her tiny hand and placed it over his heart and held it there as he looked at her with wonder. "It's beating for you my love. Only for you my sweet, sweet Beth. You've stolen it away and it's yours forever. I've never felt like this before."

Beth pulled his head down for another kiss then pressed her lips over his pounding heart. She murmured little words against his skin, things Maxwell couldn't make out. He tilted her chin up and gazed into her eyes. "What kitten?"

"I... I've never felt like this before either Maxwell. My heart is so full and I'm so happy, even here and now, even in this horrid place. How can that be? It makes no sense, but I am happy because I'm wrapped up in your arms. Love me Maxwell. Love me please, for I truly believe I am in love with you."

"Oh Beth. I do kitten. I do love you." Maxwell pulled her around so she straddled his waist and wrapped his arms around her like a vice. This was his woman. The woman he loved beyond reason and no one would hurt her or take her away. His lips met hers with a fierce intensity, and she answered back with a passion borne of love and need. Their hands explored each other's backs, stroking, feeling, getting to know every inch of burning skin, lighting a fire deep inside. Beth's hot wet quim was pressed tight to Maxwell hard shaft and he moved his hands down and grasped her well paddled bottom, then brought her hips up and down to rub her against him.

She was silky wet and the contact made them both moan and gasp. He could feel her slippery heat sucking the sensitive skin of his cock, as she slid the length of it, needing him inside her, though she didn't quite understand. He lifted her up and brought her down over and over. Sliding so soft and wet, her heat pressing on his aching cock and stimulating her needy clit.

Beth's legs wrapped around his waist and she pressed forward eagerly, picking up his rhythm and wiggling against him. He felt delicious. So hard and yet smooth as silk. Her movements were fluid and all Maxwell could think about was the molten heat of her cunny, and how much he wanted to bury himself in the depths of her womanhood, but she had to be made ready. He was determined that her first time would be full of pleasure, not just pain.

Maxwell squeezed her sore bottom again and Beth wiggled and giggled into his kiss. He moved his lips to her neck, nipping, then to her ear. "Naughty minx."

Moving quickly he pressed forward with Beth in his arms and moved her so she was spread out under him, head at the foot of the bed, his weight pressing her down into the soft mattress. To Beth it was the most secure feeling in the world. Maxwell lay atop her and slid his body back and forth; cock riding in the groove between her cunny lips until she cried out with need, then nudged her thighs apart with his knees. He knelt there and rose up so he could pay proper homage to her breasts. Suckling and nibbling he began to work back and forth using his talented tongue in a way he'd perfected.

"Oohhh!" Beth cried out as his lips pulled her aching nipple into his mouth and he began to draw upon it. The sensation shot straight down to her womb making her arch her back as her eyes flew open wide. Maxwell moved a hand to hold the other breast, making little circles on the nipple then cradling the soft mound gently as he rubbed the tender tip between his fingers and continued to tantalize her other breast with his lips and tongue.

"Like that pigeon? Such perfect little berries. So sweet, so ripe. Mine for the eating luv, mine for the tasting. Gonna eat you up my love."

Back and forth he went, hands, fingers, mouth and tongue, driving her wild. She arched up over and over, trying to find friction against his body for her aching nub but Maxwell denied her for a bit. He wanted her crazed with need when he took her.

After what seemed like an eternity to Beth, Maxwell began to nibble his way down to the center of her womanhood. She cried out in anticipation, lifting her hips, her thighs wet with dew, her body flushed and raging with fire. The memory of his talented tongue doing wonderful things to her cunny flashed through her mind and sent bolts of promised pleasure to her core. Maxwell settled himself between her splayed legs and gripped her bottom tightly then lowered his mouth to her aching quim.

"Maxwell!"

"That's it kitten. That's right luv. Maxwell's gonna take you to the stars my angel. Take you to heaven."

He lowered his mouth and slid his tongue between her folds, relishing the taste of her juices as they flowed over his tongue. Up and down he went so very slowly, teasing, building the heat, making her ready to explode. Up and down then darting in and out of her tight virginal opening his tongue went deeper and deeper inside, then flicking back and forth within her walls as they spasmed around him.

She flowed like a river and he drank it all in, loving the taste and proof of her desire. Maxwell drank of Beth's sweetness and waggled his tongue deep in her passage until she was screaming and on the verge of orgasm, then he pulled out and gently blew on her hypersensitive cunny.

Beth groaned and boldly reached for his head, trying to push it back down, wanting the pleasure to never end. He moved his hands from her bottom to her thighs and stroked her there with his thumbs, letting her come down a bit, then bent forward and gently sucked her clit between his lips.

"AARGGGGGGGHHHHHHH"

"That's right kitten, tell me how good it feels. I love to hear your passion. Tell Maxwell what you like. Does it feel good, sweet?"

In response, Beth shoved his head back down into the heat of her quim and Maxwell chuckled, the vibrations adding a new sensation. He went back to suckling her sensitive bundle of nerves then slowly slid a finger into her very core. Beth arched up off the bed. There was no pain, only pleasure, and the need to be filled. Maxwell worked his finger in and out slowly, twirling it around, stroking the walls of her cunny, pulling out, and then adding another. He scissored the two, slowly spreading her wider, relaxing her muscles, preparing her body of the girth of his cock. Maxwell knew his cock was large, and he had to make her as ready as possible.

He twisted and pulsated his fingers, spreading, opening his sweet little virgin, but always careful not to rip away her maidenhead. It would be best done in one hard thrust with his cock. He added a third finger and Beth moaned in discomfort. Maxwell held his fingers still and increased the suckling of her clit. When she was wiggling beneath him again, he pumped his fingers in and out, in and out, until she was craving the rhythm, loving the feeling of his fingers thrusting inside her, and finally decided he could wait no more. Beth was as ready as she would ever be and his cock demanded release. Maxwell kissed her beautiful quim one last time then knelt above her between her legs and gazed at the woman he loved.

God she was a sight, beautiful beyond words. Glowing like an angel. Hair wild, body flushed, lips swollen from his kisses, nipples hard as pebbles. Her eyes opened and the need in them did him in. It was definitely time.

"Gonna be a bit of pain kitten, but I'll do what I can to make it easy on you. You have to trust me and not fight me okay luv? Just trust me Beth, and let your body accept me."

Her eyes had opened wide at his words and she gazed at his huge shaft with fear mixed with longing. She did trust him but still wondered how? How could that fit inside her? Beth bit her lip and nodded her consent.

"That's a girl. Just trust me and it will be okay precious. Hold on tight."

He gathered her back into his arms and to Beth's surprise moved them backwards so they were leaning against the headboard again. Maxwell pulled her close and kissed her, then moved his hands to her hips and lifted her forward and up. He resumed the riding rhythm they had begun before in this position, her silky wet cunny sliding along his hard shaft over and over. The tip grazing her clit as her body rose and fell. Finally he held her up and still, the tip of his cock pressing against her opening.

The heat of her burned him even now. Would he be able to control himself or would he disgrace himself like a schoolboy the moment he was buried in her depths? He held her, poised above him, the tip of his shaft just brushing her entrance, and moved her just a little, rubbing her clit just a tiny bit more, his cock head teasing, making her want, then he lowered her slowly just an inch.

The feel of his bulbous head pressing into her shocked Beth and her eyes grew wide again. She felt a stretching that bordered on pain. He was so big. Maxwell lowered her another inch then pulled her back up and lowered her again, up and down a bit at a time, slowly opening her passage. Beth whimpered and her hands balled into fists as she fought the urge to try and twist away. Maxwell held perfectly still, a quarter of his cock buried in heaven.

"Easy kitten, easy now, it's okay Beth." He spanned his hand so his fingers could graze her clit and rubbed in an effort to ease the pain, but Beth was too focused on the splitting sensation in between her thighs. She shook her head and looked at him, tears ready to spill over her lashes and Maxwell made his decision. He had to do it now and do it fast.

He moved his lips to her ear and whispered "I love you", and then with one smooth motion, he lifted her up and brought her down hard, tearing through her maidenhead and plunging deep inside her core. Beth screeched, her nails digging into his shoulder as she twisted and fought him. She felt as if he'd penetrated her very womb. Gone was the pleasure, gone was the languid feeling of floating in bliss. Now all there was only pain.

Chapter Sixteen

"No. No! It hurts!! Stop, oh stop. Please Maxwell. Let me go. I don't like this."

"Beth hold still and it will pass. I swear it will pass. Just hold still and relax baby."

He stroked her back and kissed her tear stained face, whispering again that he loved her. Over and over his hands stroked and caressed as grit his teeth to stop himself from moving. Her heat was incredible, liquid fire, squeezing and surrounding his cock. Her struggles had made the walls of her womanhood spasm, driving him to the edge. She felt like heaven and he was dying to move within her. His body was demanding he seek his pleasure, but Maxwell remained still for his love.

Finally, her shaking stopped and her body relaxed against his. Maxwell kissed her again and again then moved a hand to her swollen nub. He stroked gently and built up the pleasure. He could feel her cunny tremble and grip him as the new waves of pleasure coursed through her, just as Beth could feel each pulsating throb of his cock.

When she began to make little movements on her own, Maxwell laid her down on the bed beneath him, never breaking their bond, and began to slowly take her. He slid ever so gently into this woman he loved, careful to listen for any noise of distress, but heard only mewls of pleasure.

"That's a girl, let it feel good. It can be so good kitten. It will be."

His mouth found hers and they were completely joined as they began the age old dance of love. Maxwell moved over her again and again, slowly and carefully, angling his hips so his cock hit her sweet spot, and Beth's eyes flew open in shocked pleasure. Maxwell smiled down at her and moved into her again and Beth arched up, wanting more. He took her slowly, letting the passion and fire build deep inside her. There would be no rushing headlong into bliss for him. His would come when it was time, when the woman in his arms found the ultimate ecstasy.

Little by little Maxwell increased his pace and Beth responded in kind. He stroked her skin, teased her breasts, kissed her hard, and then cupped her bottom with one hand to tilt up her hips, as he moved his other hand to her swollen clit. Her nubbin was a fat little button of need and Maxwell rubbed it hard and fast and urged Beth on to heaven, as his hips began to pump up and down, his cock sliding deeply in and out, in and out of her molten core.

Beth cried out at all the sensations, her body was in a spin, she was lightheaded and her blood was roaring through her veins, her very core was throbbing to an ancient primal beat. Maxwell rubbed her clit and thrust into her depths over and over and over and Beth's cunny gripped him like a vice, she was liquid fire surrounding his shaft, caressing, burning, stealing his breath away, but still he held back, waiting for her. It had to be perfect for his Beth.

"Come on, pigeon. Come on Beth, let it come, baby. Feel it, feel the pleasure. Let yourself go. Gonna take you to our stars."

"Oh!"

"That's right, come on kitten."

Beth was mewling and throwing back her head. His hands, his hard hot body, his lips, his cock. The feelings were rushing at her, making her dizzy with desire and longing, something was building deep inside her, something stronger than anything that had come before. This was different, this was... bliss, Heaven and stars and ecstasy, all swelling in her core. She felt her womb begin to spasm, felt his hand blurring over her clit, felt his lips pressed against her ear urging her on. In and out, in and out. Thrusting, pounding, and demanding. Oh he was hot and hard and strong. Over her, on her, in her, surrounding her. In and out, in and out, commanding her body to submit and respond. She was on the brink of something incredible. Before it had been wonderful but this, oh this. In and out, in and out.

"Oh God, Oh Maxwell!"

Beth cried out, her walls grasping and clenching his cock in her molten heat as liquid gold fire burned through her very core. She was panting and twisting and meeting his every thrust, bouncing on his lap, hands fisted on his shoulders, pushing herself up and down in time, and her orgasm overtook her. Light exploded behind her eyes as flames tore through her center and she clung to Maxwell for dear life. Before had been good, before had been wonderful, but this, this was deeper, primal, raw and sensual. She cried out again, a mixture of a sobbing and screaming in pleasure was torn from deep inside as she let herself go. Beth slammed her hips forward, grinding against Maxwell and squeezing his cock with all her might as her orgasm went on and on. Clinging, riding, twisting, writhing, feeling every nerve sizzle with pure rapture.

Maxwell roared and snarled in shock at Beth's wild abandon and her incredible gripping heat. He felt his cock spasm as his balls constricted, ready to explode. There was no more restraint. Maxwell wrapped his arms around Beth and thrust deep inside her, then leaned forward so he was once more laying on top of her, pressing her body down into the soft bed, as he pounded into her core. She clung to him, feeling his pulsating shaft entering her over and over, knowing instinctively that he was almost there. She squeezed her inner muscles and wrapped her legs around his waist and Maxwell roared again, his orgasm overcoming him like a runaway train.

It was sudden and fierce, white hot pleasure erupting from every nerve. He'd been holding back for so long, too long. It tore through him, stealing his breath, making him crazed, and he plunged into Beth again and again. So hot, so tight, her walls squeezed his shaft until he thought he would die from the intensity of the sensations. He continued to thrust with all his being as every muscle in his body convulsed.

His cock burned in her depths and he buried himself as far as he could, up to the hilt, deep in heaven, as he came and came and came. Finally, he jerked and thrust forward one last time, a scream of pleasure filling the room as he emptied the last of his seed into her satiny depths.

"Beth, Beth, Beth, oh my sweet Beth." Pumping lightly, quivering with aftershocks, trying to regain control, Maxwell clung to Beth as his blood pounded in his veins and love spilled from his heart.

They lay trembling in the wake of their passion, wrapped in each other's arms, both trying to control their wildly beating hearts. Maxwell kissed her face over and over, professing his love, telling her how beautiful she was, how wonderful, how perfect. He swore he would protect her for always and never let her go, that he would make her happy for the rest of her life.

Beth lay beneath him, relishing in the weight of his body, listening to his words and whispering her own vows of love. Nothing else mattered right now except the man in her arms. She loved him fiercely, and knew they could get through whatever the future held together. She trusted him with her entire being.

Maxwell finally rolled onto his side, keeping her tightly encased in his arms, and pressed her head to his strong, comforting chest. Beth lay silent, listening to the sound of his heartbeat and letting her breathing slow gradually until they had the same measured tempo. She nuzzled into him, loving his scent, the feel of his skin, the taste of him that still lingered on her tongue. They were truly one, in heart, body, and soul, and no one would ever tear them apart. Maxwell stroked her back and kissed her temple over and over until each drifted off into a bliss filled sleep.

Chapter Seventeen

Beth and Maxwell were roused by a sharp rapping on the huge double doors. Maxwell opened one eye and saw Beth curled up next to him, still lost in dream land. She looked all soft, sweet and cuddly, but then the knocking came again, louder this time, and her serene look vanished in an instant. Her eyes flew open and she tensed in his arms, and then moaned, her body sore from the aftermath of her first night of loving. The insistent knock came again and she jumped, causing Maxwell to let out a curse.

"Bloody hell. What time is it and who the hell is that?" Again the knock came, this time it was akin to pounding. Maxwell answered his own question with a scowl on his face. "Jeeval."

At the mention of the hated man's name, Beth made to scramble from the comfort of their bed but Maxwell wrapped her up tight. He moved so he was lying on top of her, body pressing hers to the bed, and gazed down into her eyes.

"Look at me, Beth. I'll protect you kitten. You know in your heart that I will. Just follow my lead and be the docile creature he wants you to be. We... you have to endure him touching you luv, but just think of how much I love you and remember that we'll be out of here soon. If things get too bad, if he tries to take you away, I'll fight him to the death."

"But the marks, Maxwell! I don't have the whip marks. We fell asleep." It was true, although her bottom was painted various hues of blues and purples, there wasn't a lash mark on her. They had repeatedly dozed and awakened to make love, but Maxwell had never brought up the issue of the strap, not even being able to think of laying it upon her tender skin.

"I'll think of something, baby. Just do as I say and trust me. I... I may have to say things you won't like. I don't mean them kitten. I swear I don't. You know I love you right?"

Beth nodded, and he kissed her fiercely. There had been many whispered declarations of love during their heated night of passion by both of them. Neither doubted the way the other felt. Their hearts had truly bonded. Once again the pounding sounded and Beth bit her lip to stop from crying out.

"I swear kitten, he won't harm you."

With one last kiss Maxwell rose from the bed and strode over to the double doors. Beth couldn't help but admire his long sleek legs, couldn't help but notice how muscular his thighs were, or the perfection of his bum. He was truly magnificent. She sat up in bed and pulled the silk coverlet to her chin but then remembered the fury such action had brought forth from the evil beast who was even now demanding entrance into their quarters. Well she wouldn't cover herself, but she sure as hell wouldn't rise to meet him until she had to.

Maxwell grumbled under his breath as he slid the latch that secured his chambers. Jeeval shoved the door open with an angry show of force and strode in, stopping to look around for Beth. He looked Maxwell up and down, taking in his naked state, and raised an eyebrow.

"Seems as if you've been fulfilling one of my commands, has the other been carried out too? Where is the little bitch?"

Maxwell yawned lazily, not at all impressed by Jeeval's show of bluster or embarrassed by his own nudity. "Thanks for knocking Jeeval, but did you have to wake the dead?"

"As I said yesterday, it is my house. I go where I please, when I please. Where is the new slave?" Jeeval strode forward into Maxwell's chamber and to the door of the bedroom. He scowled when he saw Beth sitting all comfy in the huge bed. "My, doesn't she look all content."

"Would you have me rut with her on the floor just for her discomfort? I have a stake in this too you know."

"No, but she should have been tossed into the prison chamber when you were through."

"I wasn't through." Maxwell's words were taunting and caustic, clearly annoyed but also amused to be baiting Jeeval just a bit. His pride wouldn't let him get walked upon, and he needed to develop this attitude before it came time to fight for Beth. An abrupt change in his tone or mannerism would make Jeeval suspicious.

Jeeval turned, nostrils flaring, eyes full of rage. He'd never seen Maxwell like this, full of contradictions and anger. Well he'd had enough. If this little whore was going to have that kind of effect on his best hired man, then she had to be removed from his care immediately.

"Come here whore."

As before, Beth took grave offense at his tone and term. She held her head high, but was careful not to look the bastard in the eye as she got out of bed. She walked until she was standing within arm's reach, and bowed her head. Everything inside her screamed to look up and spit in his face, but sanity won out. Let Maxwell handle this. All she needed to do was get through the next few moments. If she behaved, maybe he would be satisfied and accept the bruises in place of the whip marks.

The first thing Jeeval did was to slap her thighs apart. "Women here are to always stand with their legs spread when they are before me. I wish to look at what is mine.

Tell me my little bitch, did Maxwell rut between those sweet thighs? Did he dispose of your virginity? Are fit for my bed?"

Beth had to fight with every ounce of restraint she could pull from within not to scream at Jeeval. 'I'll never be fit for you bed!' Her mind screamed, but she remained silent. Oh how he made it all sound so vulgar and cold. But it wasn't, she had to remember that. No matter what happened now, last night had been beautiful.

When Beth didn't answer but bit her lip to stifle her anger instead, Jeeval lifted the riding crop he held in his hand and lashed Beth across the breasts forward and back. She let out a little wail of pain and shock and turned to run but he caught her by the hair.

"One more step and you shall feel this crop a dozen times over. I asked you a question. Did he mate with you? Did he take you? Did he shove his cock deep inside your tight virgin cunt until you screamed and kicked and cried? Did it hurt as he tore you up inside?" This last question was said with such a sadistic smile that Beth had to ball her hands into tight little fists to keep from striking out at him in fury and disgust.

Maxwell stood, just a few feet away, his own hands fisted, legs slightly spread to brace himself. It took every drop of sheer willpower he possessed not to kill Jeeval with his bare hands for daring to hurt Beth, but he simply couldn't, they'd never escape. They needed time and a plan. He and Beth had to get through this, and then he would make it up to her. He'd love her so much that Jeeval would be but a distant memory that never came back to haunt her.

"Answer me woman."

God he was a sick bastard, he wanted all the details, well Beth knew she had to play along. She couldn't very well tell him it had been beautiful, and that Maxwell had been oh so gentle and caring and had taken her to the stars. Couldn't tell him how Maxwell had carried her to the bathing pool and washed the virgin blood from her thighs and rubbed numbing cream on her bottom before carrying her back to bed and making love to her again.

"Yes M...Master. He did as you told him. I am no longer pure. He... oh..." Beth let out a little sob praying her little dramatic act of horror would convince this sick man that she had truly endure a terrifying, repulsive experience at Maxwell's hands. Before she knew it, Jeeval was slapping her legs apart again and shoving his fingers deep inside her again. He probed and prodded and Beth gagged. She couldn't help it.

Maxwell saw her turn deathly pale at the touch of his employer, and again had to fight not to react. 'Say something you bloody fool', his mind screamed. Make him stop. Beth eyes were staring into his, pleading, begging, for help, but they both knew Maxwell shouldn't react.

"No maidenhead there Jeeval, she's broke in, in that sense. Have lots to work on in other ways but we're getting there. Give me time and she'll..."

"Silence." He abruptly pulled his hand from between her legs, much to Beth's relief but then he spun her around and bent her over, tapping her thighs with the crop so she spread them.

"Hold your ankles. Why doesn't she know any of this Maxwell? She knows no proper slave positions, doesn't respond immediately to my questions. She should have kissed my feet when I came in but instead she stood. Have you even taught her the techniques to please a man in bed or did you simply allow her to be pleasured?

"She made no move to satisfy me with her mouth when I was clearly angry. And this," Jeeval ran the crop over Beth's very colorful but un-welted bottom, "This gives me even more reason to doubt that you're doing a proper job with this one. I told you she needs a heavier hand and yet you have defied me. Explain yourself."

"I imagine she's too frightened of you to suck your cock just now Jeeval, but she'll be taught well. Besides, a good slave waits for permission. I paddled her good and proper, spanked her till she was bawling and pleading like a baby, made her cum from it too just to show her who controls her body, then spent the rest of the night showing her who's her Master by bedding her over and over even though she pleaded with me to stop. I was planning on taking the lash to her as an early morning reminder after I raped her again, but we were interrupted. Blame my cock. It had other priorities."

"I am your main priority. And this, this thing." He motioned at Beth and Maxwell nearly lost all sense of reason. "This bitch was to be presented at the banquet tonight, trained and prepared. I have important guests coming for dinner and entertainment, and she was to be part of the fun. I am torn between tossing her in the dungeon to rot for a few days and giving her to Raspian for some proper lessons in hopes of getting her ready in the next few hours."

Both Maxwell and Beth had to stifle their panic at his words. He was going to take her away. Maxwell swallowed hard and forced himself to breath normally, he couldn't show his true emotions, not now.

"Come on Jeeval, I don't see what all the fuss is about. I've kept the new ones longer than this before. You're just upset because she caused a little ruckus when you were playing with Siri. What's the hurry? Give me another day, better yet, make it two, and I'll wrap her up all pretty and spread her out all nice on your bed to do as you please."

"I wanted her at the banquet tonight. You know I enjoy showing off my new toys. She is unique with her golden hair, a true trophy. I would be envied. As for what the fuss is, I simply can't allow a woman to continue to feel that she has any place in my home except at my feet or in my bed. This one has too much pride. It is unthinkable and I won't tolerate it. Raspian will have her broke in an hour."

"He'll have her turned into a cowering terrified thing that will give you no pleasure. Would you rather take a fiery passionate woman, or a limp cold rag who's too afraid to move? I'm training her well Jeeval. The paddling and the bedding, all of it, is enjoyable to her. Her body is full of a desire she can't control.

She wanted the pain Jeeval, came as I spanked that sweet bum of hers, and she sure as hell wanted me to bed her. A few more days, and she'll lose the scrap of pride she's clinging to and simply be filled with the desire to please so she can find the release only you can give her. Just think of her willing and begging to be punished and taken. Then, she *will* be a true trophy."

Jeeval raised his eyebrows during Maxwell's speech. "So now you want a few days when before it was one or two. How long do you intend to keep her Maxwell? She doesn't belong to you."

"Do you want a woman who begs for your whip and cock, or a skittish ice maiden who shies from your touch?"

Jeeval dismissed Maxwell's question and returned his attention to Beth. He circled her like he'd done the previous day, running his hands up her legs, feeling them, her belly, her breasts, as if she were a horse at an auction. Through it all Beth kept up a mantra in her head to preserve her sanity, telling herself it would be over soon. 'Be strong and it will be over soon.'

Her strategy was working until Jeeval stepped forward and pulled her in for a kiss. She gasped in surprise and his thick hot tongue slid into her mouth. Beth gagged, bile rising in her throat, and Jeeval pushed her away in disgust as she gagged again, her stomach lurching.

Maxwell couldn't hide his smile. Her reaction had been perfect, just what had been needed to get Jeeval to back off, though Maxwell knew it hadn't been contrived and poor Beth was truly suffering.

"Told you she wasn't ready. She needs time to learn to appreciate you. Let me keep her, rough her up a bit, teach her what rebellion brings, and how sweetly the pain and pleasure can mix when she does as she's told."

Jeeval looked livid but he nodded his assent. "She still comes to the banquet tonight." With that he snapped his fingers and a tiny old woman whom neither of them had known had been hovering outside the doorway, entered the room carrying a wooden box. The happiness Maxwell had been feeling a moment ago vanished. He'd been hoping Jeeval wouldn't do what he was about to do before he and Beth escaped.

Jeeval turned to the old woman and lifted the lid of the chest, and removed a gleaming brass circle. It looked just like a ring, seemingly one piece, but it was much too large for that. He turned back towards Beth, and walked to where she stood, and pulled a small key from his pocket. Jeeval used the key to remove a tiny bolt from the ring and it opened up. He raised his hands towards Beth's neck and she suddenly realized what the thing was. A collar! He was going to put a collar on her and she wouldn't be able to remove it.

Her eyes flashed angrily and she shook her head almost imperceptibly but then heard Maxwell's low warning growl. Do as you're told or suffer, rang loud and clear through the chamber. Follow the script Beth, or we'll never escape with our lives. Beth stood stone still, and Jeeval put the collar around her neck, replacing the bolt and securing it with the miniature key.

"This shall be melted down and your collar never removed again. You are now my slave. I hope that is understood. You have three days Maxwell. Three days in which to prepare her for my delightful company. I shall see you both at the banquet tonight.

"Oh and Maxwell, I have an errand for you to run. Siead Kapur will be coming for a visit in a few days and you know how he likes young virgins. You are to find a girl this afternoon." Jeeval shifted his eyes from Maxwell back to Beth, and stroked the whip coiled on his belt as he gave his orders.

"This one needs to be taught and prepared. You said so yourself. Send someone else."

"I'm sending you. You have three days with the whore before me, and as you said, you're the best I have."

Everything in Maxwell screamed at him to refuse. He couldn't leave Beth unprotected, and he sure as hell wanted nothing to do with abducting another woman, but he had gained such a big victory in getting Jeeval to allow him more time with Beth. It would be very unwise to push his luck.

"I'll go, but I won't promise you a girl today. You know it must be done delicately. Perfect little doves take time to capture. I also have to make sure they have no one to come asking of their whereabouts. You are free to do as you please, but your uncle prefers it if you keep from upsetting too many families, unless of course you know of a father who is seeking to make a gift of his daughter to win your favor."

"If I did, I wouldn't be sending you out. Had I known of Siead's visit, I would have saved this one's virgin cunt for him. Word arrived too late, so you must do what you can today. As long as you look for one, it will be enough. I don't need her for three days' time."

That said, Jeeval fingered the brass collar around Beth neck, and smiled. "I'll be waiting for you pretty one. You have the wrong kind of fire right now little whore, but soon you shall welcome and beg for my touch. You and I will become great friends."

Beth fought back her revulsion and caustic remarks, choosing to dare a brief stare into his eyes instead. She cast her gaze upon him, eyes full of hate and revulsion, and then quickly looked down. If it earned her a slap, then so be it. To her surprise, Jeeval did nothing, but then she realized how deadly her mistake was when his hand shifted again to the coiled whip hanging from his belt.

"I want you to leave within the hour Maxwell." That said, he snapped his fingers at the old woman and the two of them left the chamber.

As soon as the door closed Beth sank to her knees. What had she done? "Oh God, Oh God, Oh God! Maxwell, he's going to come and hurt me while you're gone. Did you see that? He's planning on coming back after you leave. Why did I have to defy him and stare into his eyes?"

Maxwell rushed to her side and scooped Beth up into his arms. "Shhh... It's okay kitten. You did it because you have spirit my love, a fierce inner strength he could never understand. It's one of the things I love about you. I won't let him hurt you baby. I promised remember? I'll simply lock you in the prison chamber and take the key with me. He won't be able to get to you.

"There will be hell to pay when I come back, but we'll worry about that then, when were together. Besides kitten, this gives me a chance to check out which ships will be leaving port."

Truth be told, Maxwell was more worried about the collar Jeeval had placed on Beth's neck. It would be incredibly difficult if not impossible to remove. Anyone who saw it would know she had been a concubine in a harem someplace. It clearly branded her as an escaped slave. Having it around her neck now was a very, very bad thing.

"Are you sure he doesn't have a key? Maxwell, this is his estate, he must have keys for everything."

"Not for that door, kitten. I had some trouble once upon a time and the lock was broken. It was fixed but I never gave Jeeval a new key. He has no idea his doesn't fit.

"Come on now, let's get you dressed. We had a long night, and the banquet this evening will last until dawn. You might as well get some rest. Later on you can have a bath and we can make love again. Would you like that, sweet?"

Beth's green eyes turned dark with passion as she pulled Maxwell's head down to capture his lips in response to his question. "Always Maxwell, always with you. Promise me you'll hurry home?"

"I promise kitten. Promise me you won't be scared when Jeeval comes banging on the door? He can't get in there. I swear. Just keep your mouth shut luv, don't say a word. He'll think you're bound and gagged and will eventually leave in a fit."

"Can he break it down?"

"No. The doors here are solid through, meant to keep precious things locked up."

Beth stiffened in his arms at his words, and Maxwell cursed under his breath. "That was in the past Beth. I'm a changed man. No more captives, no more force. I was wrong kitten. I was so wrong until you showed me the light. Never again will I harm a woman Beth. Never again, I swear."

His eyes were so full of remorse for his past deeds that Beth couldn't help but forgive him. She believed Maxwell when he said he'd changed. She trusted him and loved him and she knew his promise was as good as gold.

"I know Maxwell, I believe you." Her whispered words of trust went straight to his heart, and Maxwell kissed her with all the love and passion he felt inside as he carried her to his bed. Jeeval's orders could wait a while. His woman needed to be loved and comforted, he wouldn't have her being afraid while he was gone and he had to erase the memory of Jeeval's filthy touch.

Chapter Eighteen

Beth rose from the bed in the tiny cell like room and paced the short length of it. The shirt Maxwell had given her to wear was falling to her knees in a white billow of silk. Her hair, which he had plated into one long braid, hung down her back, swinging like a golden pendulum as she walked. Her stride was purposeful even though she had nowhere to go. She needed to burn off tension, and pacing the tiny room was the only thing she could do.

She had tried to lie down and rest when Maxwell had first left, but it was no use. She was frightened and tense. Jeeval would be coming for her, of that she was certain, but the question was when. She dreaded his arrival, but the wait was killing her. She walked back and forth, back and forth, then sighed in frustration and returned to the bed, plopping down and running her hand over the cover of the book Maxwell had left her to look at.

They had made love again before he had gone his whispered words and feather light touches driving away the memory of that beast Jeeval until she was crying out with pleasure under his practiced touch and clinging to him as she tumbled into bliss. Afterwards, he had held her close and told her what to do.

She was to stay behind the locked door and keep silent at all times. It was best for Jeeval to think Maxwell had tied and gagged her before he left. Say nothing to incite him, Maxwell had told her over and over. He will be mad enough to find himself locked out, without thinking she was whiling away her time in splendor. That said Maxwell had brought her one of his shirts so she wouldn't feel as vulnerable. The scanty harem garb would be saved for the banquet that night, though Maxwell hadn't told her that.

After plaiting her hair and kissing over and over, promising things would be okay, he'd led her to the punishment room and then given her the book that was now lying on the bed with a wink and a cocky grin, telling her that it would certainly keep her mind occupied, and teach her something too.

Now Beth looked at the cover again as she ran her fingers over the leather bound volume and blushed scarlet as she remembered what she had seen when she had opened the book the first time. What she had been expecting was something interesting to read while she was locked away, what he'd given her was something altogether different. She'd flipped the book open to find her eyes filled with the image of a man and a woman making love. The woman's legs were over his shoulders, crossed behind his neck, her hands tied to the bed, while he thrust inside. His huge member, partway withdrawn, her cunny vividly illustrated swollen and stretched wide, tinted pink.

Beth had slammed the book shut with a gasp, shot to her feet, and the pacing had begun, but the image had remained. Now, here she was, back to the book again, and it called out to her. Her newly awakened body wanted to know these things. It wanted to be stimulated. She could already feel the trickle of moisture between her thighs from just that one peek at its pages, and the thought of Maxwell mounting her in the same way.

Beth opened the book again and began to slowly page through it, marveling at the illustrations, her eyes wide as she took them in and read the captions under each one. There were so many ways a man and woman could make love. So many positions, so many places their bodies could join. There were even pictures of a woman being taken by two men at the same time and vice versa. As she paged through the book, Beth's cheeks flushed for an entirely different reason. She curled her foot up underneath her and pressed her heel into her now soaking wet cunny. Her nipples ached and she wiggled on her foot, needing relief for the fire that had built up in her womb.

Page after page of erotic images flooded her mind, and in each one she saw herself and Maxwell. How would it feel to have his mouth consuming her cunny as he thrust a phallus into her bottom. The woman's face in the picture showed ecstasy. Beth remembered Jeeval's taking of Siri there and the feel of Maxwell's finger in her own puckered hole. It all seemed so... so desirable now, and somehow less lewd. Looking at the book made her want to have the things done to her because she knew Maxwell would make them feel oh so good. She wanted to pleasure him in the ways the women were too. There were so many things she had yet to try, things she needed to learn. When Maxwell got home, she would surprise him by taking his cock into her mouth and learning how to satisfy him in that way.

Beth came to the section of the book that held the pictures of punishment and pleasure. She blushed anew at both the sights and her remembered feelings, but her cunny heated up just the same and her hand snuck down to rub herself just a bit. She refused to think about what she was doing. Proper ladies would NEVER touch themselves 'down there', but at this point, Beth couldn't help herself. She was so hot, her nerve endings tingled as she remembered being over Maxwell's lap.

The steady slap of his hand, the caressing touch of it as it slid over her burning cheeks, the pressure that had hit her clit in just the right way every time his hand landed on her bottom, all of it filled her mind again. She thought about how he had rubbed her cunny and mixed the burning pain with the intense pleasure, coaxing her legs open wider and wider. The sensations mixing as the paddle came down, her cunny flowing and rubbing and needing contact with every hard, stinging smack. The memories had her rubbing herself furiously.

Beth flung her head back and pinched her sensitive nipples through Maxwell's shirt. She could smell his scent lingering on it, and it was both comforting and erotic. Her legs were splayed wide as one hand worked on her swollen needy clit and one stroked her breasts. A moan escaped her as she rubbed faster and faster. "Oh Maxwell, I need you Maxwell." She was almost there, almost to heaven, when cruel laughter rang out from the other side of the door.

"Perhaps Maxwell is turning you into the obedient whore you need to be. Hands off you little slut, that activity is strictly forbidden, and it's time for you to learn a lesson from your true Master."

Beth froze, her heart in her throat, Maxwell's words admonishing her to be silent when Jeeval came, ringing in her ears. He had heard her. Jeeval had heard her. What had she done?

Beth heard Jeeval insert a key into the lock then turn the doorknob. It went back and forth a bit, but not enough to gain him entry. Jeeval rattled the knob, and then cursed in frustration.

"So he has locked his precious little treasure away has he? He thinks that will keep me out. There are other ways besides keys to reach you my golden dove. Your body has yet to receive the pain it deserves, and I can assure you no locked door is going to prevent this punishment. Count the minutes of your reprieve because I shall return in due haste with the tools to do away with this door.

Think about it, my new little toy. In just a few minutes this door will be tinder, and you shall be dragged from your safe little cell to feel the fire of my lash as you should have the first time I laid eyes on you. There shall be an extra punishment for daring to pleasure yourself too, my whore. Women here do not touch themselves, ever. Maxwell has been remiss in teaching you my ways and rules, but I assure you that will all change soon."

Beth had held her breath throughout Jeeval's little speech, her heart pounding in fear. He now knew she wasn't bound and gagged, and he knew what she had been doing. That was all she needed, yet another reason for him to punish her. The sadistic bastard seemed to find opportunity at every turn didn't he? Well she wasn't about to respond and goad him on.

Beth bit her lip and silently slid back to the far corner of the bed, pulling the huge shirt down around her knees, totally covering her body. Did she stay here in the corner, meekly going out to accept her punishment, or go at him, claws bared when he came through that door? It was simply too much to hope that Maxwell would come home in time to save her.

On the other hand, Maxwell had said the door was solid through, so it would take Jeeval's men a long time to batter it down. Unfortunately, Maxwell had also believed that Jeeval wouldn't go so far as to force it open. He thought that there was a certain amount of respect between them, but he was apparently very mistaken. Jeeval did and took what he wanted, regardless of who it might offend.

"I'll be back, and you shall feel my wrath slave, then you will know who you must answer to. If I were you pet, I would be very afraid."

Beth heard his footsteps as he strode away and cursed herself for being so absorbed in pleasuring herself that she'd missed his arrival. If she's been silent and Jeeval had thought she was trussed up like a Christmas goose, being punished, he may very well have left her be for today thinking Maxwell was doing his job. She put her head in her hands and allowed herself a moment of self-pity then tried to focus on her predicament again. What should she do when that beast broke down the door?

Chapter Nineteen

When Maxwell had left the palace, his mind was full of thoughts of Beth, and his heart ached at the thought of leaving her in danger. Rage rose up inside him every time he thought of Jeeval laying a filthy hand on his girl. He wanted to rush straight to the docks and search for a ship that would carry them away, but Maxwell knew he had to make a pretense of looking for a girl for Siead Kapur's visit .

How could he even think of capturing some other innocent now? Beth's plight and love had opened his eyes to the fact that these women had feelings. He had shut his ears to their cries in the past, but no more. They were living, feeling, beings, with hearts and souls, and they didn't deserve to be captured like animals.

If Maxwell had his way, he would free every one of the women in Jeeval's estate, but he knew that could never be. As it was, when he and Beth escaped, their lives would be in danger, and he would be a hunted man for the rest of his life.

He had committed serious crimes here in Haldia. If his past were found out he would be taken to jail and hung where ever they decided to settle. The kidnapping of young women might be overlooked for the most part here in India, but in England, it would be a different story. His taking Beth with him now that she was a collared slave who belonged to the grandnephew of the Emperor would place a bounty on his head even if the facts surrounding Elizabeth's and some of the other women's abductions were swept under the rug. He was about to steal one of Jeeval's prized possession, and that would not be allowed.

His heart felt a pang at the thought of Beth being tied to a wanted criminal all her life, but the thought of losing her overrode the pain. Guilt flooded him, but there was no way on earth he would give up his Beth unless she wanted to be free of him. Would she wake up one day with her eyes opened wide to his hideous past, or had her heart truly melted to all he had done? She said she loved him and trusted him, and Maxwell believed it was true, but would life on the run make her weary of him? Only time would tell.

After wandering around the markets for as long as he could bear, and finding a suitable gown for her to wear when they escaped, Maxwell made his way to the docks to find a ship on which they could book passage. He hoped to find a ship that would take them on without too many questions. One headed for England would be best, but Maxwell would take anything he could get as long as he felt it would be safe for Beth.

His plan had been to present her as his wife, and say they were a couple from the Baptist Mission in need of traveling back to England for an urgent family matter. That story had been jeopardized by the fact that Beth now wore the brass circle collar of an owned concubine. The women from the mission were part of the Zenana mission that allowed the women of the church into the harems, but that wouldn't explain her slave collar.

It was possible that a British military ship, or one from his old company would be the safe for them because many of the men who captained such vessels viewed such slavery as detestable, but one couldn't be certain. It would be far too late after someone had seen Beth's collar to find out their views. It was just as possible that the captain or one of the military personnel would arrest him, and give Beth back to Jeeval to maintain good standings with the Emperor.

Maxwell reached down and held the bag of silver tied to his belt as strode down the wooden planks. He had brought enough to encourage even the most unwilling Captain to turn a blind eye when it came to details about his passengers. Money talked, and tended to make people see things his way.

Perhaps he could buy their way onto a ship, perhaps not, all he could do was try. If it cost him a fortune in gold to secure Beth safe passage, then he would pay it. A ship bound down the Yamuna River, and then out to open sea would be the quickest way to freedom. Traveling on land across India would be much more dangerous. Either way, they had to put distance between themselves and Jeeval as soon as they made their escape from the estate.

There ended up being two navy ships bound for England, but even the offer of a bag full of money wouldn't buy them passage. Ships full of soldiers were no place for women he was told. The commanders refused to listen as he explained, reasoned and bargained, stating over and over that he only wanted to ensure quick passage because his wife needed to return home to tend her sick mother.

After being refused over and over by the military and reputable captains, Maxwell finally gave up and went in search of a ship carrying cargo whose captain might be more agreeable because of the prospect of riches. The men might be less reputable, but he was nearing a state of desperation. No matter who commanded the vessel, Maxwell knew he would do anything it took to keep Beth safe.

He walked slowly through the clutter on the dock, winding his way past the various tall ships until he found one being loaded with silks and spices. It was a precious cargo to be sure, but not one that would attract pirates like a ship loaded with guns or gold. He strode onto the deck and walked straight up to the Captain, toying with the bag of coins so they jingled as he went. The man's eyebrows went up and he paused in his orders to his crew, surveying Maxwell up and down, taking him for a rich aristocrat who wanted nothing but to waste his time.

"What do you want? I'm busy here."

"I'm looking to book passage."

"I only take on men willing to work. No leisure passengers, it's bad for moral."

"It's for my wife and I. I hardly think you want her swabbing the decks."

"I don't take women. They're bad luck at sea, and cause too much of a stir with the men. They lead to fighting and the like. I won't have it."

"They can't fight over a woman who is already taken. She's not some maiden, unattached and waiting to be wooed. She's a missionary and my wife, and she'll be confined to our quarters. I promise you I will see to her. You won't even know she's on the ship. We need passage. Her mum's sick and she needs to get home."

The Captain eyed Maxwell suspiciously, and he knew he'd just made a mistake. Should he walk away or push ahead. His choice of passage was down to one more ship, and escape was mandatory. The other had a crew that looked far too unsavory for his Beth to be around. The Captain narrowed his eyes and looked Maxwell up and down. "Funny how you never even asked me where

I was headed. If her mum's ill, shouldn't you need to know where you're off to? Sounds like you simply need to get away. You wouldn't be running from the law now would you? I don't need trouble."

"I heard you from the dock. British accent same as mine. Figured you were headed home with a ship full of cargo for England or thereabouts. We can book passage on another ship or travel by land once we get back to Europe if your destination's not the same as ours."

Would he buy it? Just because the man was English didn't mean a thing. The lie was flimsy at best and they both knew it. Maxwell reached down and toyed with the bag of gold again. Would the idea of riches make the Captain overlook the fact that Maxwell and Beth may be fugitives?

"I'll pay a high amount. The missus really needs to get to her mum. Been cryin' her eyes out since the letter arrived, won't let me rest."

The Captain looked him over again, then eyed the sack of silver and finally nodded. "Aye, you have your passage. We set sail for England in two days time. Pay now and be here at dawn. The woman goes straight to the cabin. I don't need any trouble on my ship."

"Oh she won't be any trouble at all. Meek little bit of a thing. She does as she's told."

Maxwell had to force back a smile as he said the words; Beth was far from that description. His little hellion would be spitting fire if she heard him talk about her that way, but it was for her safety.

"Thank you Captain, I'm much obliged. We'll be here." Maxwell untied the sack of coins and handed it to the man. The captain hefted in his hand then opened it up, grinning. What were two extra passengers compared to the fortune he'd just received? If the woman was an eyesore, she'd be kept below. If she was a pretty little thing, she'd grace his table whether the husband liked it or not. His word was law on the ship, especially when they were at sea. There was something funny going on here with this man and his 'wife', and the Captain began to think he could work it to his advantage.

"See you're not late or we sail without you, and keep your baggage to a minimum."

"Dawn, two days hence. We'll be here and we we'll travel light."

Maxwell didn't know how he was going to get Beth out of the estate, but he knew they were going to be on this ship when it left the dock. They were going to sail to freedom even if he had to cut a bloody path through the estate to do it.

Maxwell nodded his thanks and goodbye, and strode quickly away. It was time to return to Beth. He wondered what Jeeval was up to even now. How far had he gone to get at the toy that had been denied him, and how angry would he be at Maxwell for thwarting his plans?

Chapter Twenty

Beth cringed when she heard the chamber doors slam open. Jeeval hadn't returned as soon as she thought he would, and Beth had begun to hope he'd changed his mind. Apparently he just wanted her to wait in fear for a while. His footsteps came directly to the locked chamber and stopped, and then there was silence.

Beth could just see him out there. Dark eyes glowing with sadistic light, hair pulled back, arms crossed, or more likely fingers toying with that horrid whip. His chiseled features were probably drawn up in an evil grin as he pictured her hiding in fear. Well yes she felt fear, but she had also decided that she was going to fight for her life when the bastard came through that door. If he was going to punish her, then she'd damn well give him something to punish her for. She'd claw his hateful eyes out!

Beth pressed her back against the far wall and waited, hands curled, nails ready, she was going to spring the moment he came at her. She reckoned that none of his other meek little slaves had ever dared to defy him in that way. Well she would be the first, and it very well could be the last thing she did on this earth if Maxwell didn't hurry and get back soon. The fact that Jeeval might take her away had been considered when she'd made her decision, but in the end, Beth settled on defending herself. She wouldn't, couldn't go meekly like a lamb to slaughter and allow him to hurt her and defile her body. She belonged to her love, body and soul and this sick animal would never touch her.

"Are you frightened my little whore? You should be. There are so many things to punish you for. You have been very willful, but your time of disobedience has come to an end. You will learn to submit golden one. By tonight your body will burn with my rage, my mark will cover every inch of your skin, and the feel of my cock piercing your mouth, cunt, and bottom will linger into your nightmares. I will not go gentle with you bitch. You are mine to hurt and to take my pleasure from, and I will not wait any more. Already my cock is filled with blood at the thought of whipping you until you beg and scream, then rutting you senseless."

Nausea rose up in Beth's throat at his words. If Maxwell didn't come soon, her life would be a living hell in a matter of minutes. Yes she could fight him, but it wouldn't last. He towered over her, and would be able to subdue her in moments. She doubted he would kill her in a rage. That would be too easy. No, this one wanted her blood and pain and intended to take it slowly. Still, she would fight him; she simply couldn't roll over and allow him to abuse her.

Oh how she wished Maxwell had given her a knife, but he'd said they couldn't chance it. If it were found, or if she used it on Jeeval, Maxwell knew she'd be killed before she could blink, and he couldn't let that happen. She had argued that death was better than being touched by Jeeval, but Maxwell had paled at the suggestion. He firmly said no again. It would expose their plan and put her in danger. She couldn't use it and flee the estate without being caught and put to death immediately. So here she was, about to be raped and beaten by the monster on the other side of the door with nothing but her teeth, nails, feet and fists to defend herself.

Beth jumped as the sound of the ax bit into the thick wooden door for the first time. It didn't penetrate the door, but she had little doubt it wouldn't take long. Again the sound came and she pressed her fist against her mouth to stifle a scream. Yes she was tough and she would fight, but she was still a woman, one facing horrible abuse, and she was very afraid.

"Harder, you imbecile. Put some muscle into it. I want that door open." The splitting came again, this time the very tip of the ax blade pierced the interior wood of the door. Beth's eyes filled with tears at the sight, but she swiped them away. This was no time to fall apart. She began to pull on the bed, sliding it away from the wall, and then pushing it up against the door. Beth wished desperately for another piece of furniture, something, anything, bigger, but shook that thought away too. This wasn't the time for wishes. The bed wasn't much, they could climb right over it, but it would keep the door closed a minute longer if the man went straight for smashing the lock first. As if reading her mind, the knob rattled as the ax struck it.

"No you fool. Didn't you hear what she did? She moved the bed. Breaking the lock is useless. Chop down that door."

The man went to work with renewed effort and soon there was a hole the size of a fist in the center of the wood and it was growing fast. Time after time the ax came down until there was a gaping hole where a solid door used to be. Jeeval stopped the man and peered through. He looked Beth up and down, saw her fighting stance. She was ready to spring with her claws extended.

"So you wish to fight little one? So be it, but be warned, I will win. Bring her out."

The man cleared a few splintered pieces from around the gaping hole and leaned over to shove the bed away. Beth rushed forward and pushed on the far end to hold it in place, making the man growl in outrage. He stopped that tactic and simply climbed through and made a grab for her. Beth went at him, fists, nails, feet, flying. It wasn't this man's fault for what Jeeval had ordered, but he was the one who was going to deliver her to the devil.

Beth fought him for all she was worth, clawing and kicking, lashing out, but he managed to get both hands in a tight grasp and yank them up behind her back. Pain seared her shoulders and he slapped her hard, eyes flashing.

"Stop it you little bitch. Your Master is waiting."

Beth kicked out and the man jerked her arms higher, the pain made her dizzy and her knees sagged.

"I'll snap them like twigs. Be still." He pressed her up against him and used a foot to push the bed aside. Using his other hand he unlocked the door and pushed her out, making her stumble and land at Jeeval's feet.

The haze of bright red pain began to fade, and Beth looked up into the grinning face of evil itself. She narrowed her eyes and fixed a look of pure hate on her face to hide her fear as she began to rise. Jeeval lifted his foot and brought it down on her still throbbing shoulder, pressing her back to her knees at the same time unsnapping his beloved whip from his belt.

"You will rise when I tell you to whore. I see you are still full of pathetic willfulness. That won't be tolerated here. I will break you my spitfire and it will be a pleasure doing so. Raheem, tie her to the columns."

That said Jeeval pushed his foot against Beth's shoulder and sent her sprawling backward. Before she could collect herself, Raheem was on her again. Beth twisted in his grasp and began to fight him, but Jeeval called him off.

"Leave her be. I will whip her on the floor like a dog until she is ready to crawl to the columns herself."

"Never." Beth was shaking, her heart pounding so hard she could barely catch her breath, fear threatened to close her throat, but she wouldn't give up, she wouldn't submit. Instead she raised her chin higher to glare at her tormenter as she spat out her decree. "Never!"

"Such fire only has its place in my bed, little bitch. Passion is the only emotion you are allowed here. All others will be beaten out of you."

He walked to where she knelt and grasped the collar of her shirt, tearing it off her, exposing the flawless skin of her back, then stepped back, ready to begin his sadistic work.

Raising the whip, Jeeval brought it cracking down across Beth's back. She bit her lip, holding back a scream as fire erupted where the whip had left its welt. Again Jeeval raised the whip, he flung it back, intending to strike with all his might, but was suddenly jerked backwards. Jeeval snapped his head around in stunned shock, eyes blazing as they landed on Maxwell.

"You have no right to interfere here, Maxwell."

Maxwell had entered just as the first lash had struck Beth. His rage nearly blinded him, but he fought for control. His first instinct was to take Jeeval's whip and strangle the man with it, but if there were any way possible to get out of this situation he had to do it. Their ship didn't sail for two days. There was no way they could hide in the city for that long. A white British couple would be easily found, especially if gold greased the palms of those being asked.

Maxwell yanked hard enough to make Jeeval unbalanced so he'd have to keep his attention off Beth. He wanted to become the man's target. He'd do anything, including take the whipping himself, to save her. How could he have been such a fool as to think Jeeval would allow a door to keep him from what he wanted?

"Has the wench done something? Did she escape? I locked her up tight. What's the problem?" He would act as though he was oblivious to the fact that Jeeval had made a number of unsubtle hints insinuating he intended to come back and punish Beth himself while Maxwell was gone.

Jeeval seemed a bit taken aback by Maxwell's innocent attitude and questions. He'd expected rage, but Maxwell was carefully concealing his. This course of action was their only hope. Instead of answering

Maxwell's questions however, he posed some of his own.

"I have questions of my own. Why was I unable to open this door, and why was the bitch moaning in pleasure and touching herself when I arrived? Why is she wearing your shirt of all things? And better yet, why would she attack my man when I came to punish her? She dared to fight him, Maxwell, how can that be? You give her far too many liberties. She should have been bound, naked, and available for whatever I wished to do, not locked away. I am the one who owns her Maxwell. Have you forgotten that fact?"

"Well I haven't had much of a chance to tame her further since our last conversation, now have I, Jeeval? You send me off to do your biding and expect me to beat the fire out of this one at the same time. I told you I needed to stay here and work on her but you told me to go, and tend to her later. Make up your mind old friend. Which do you want?

"As for the door, the lock stuck one day, I broke it, then had it replaced. I must have forgotten to give you the key. I offer my apologies. As to why was she rubbing her cunny, simple, I have turned her into the whore you desire her to be. I should think it would please you to know her passion has been awakened, even if the act is forbidden. As for the shirt, well I thought she looked fetching, what can I say?"

Beth peeked up at Maxwell as he spoke to Jeeval. She wanted nothing more than to hide and curl up in a ball. His caustic words hurt even though she knew he didn't mean a word of it. They spoke of her as if she was a thing, not a woman. The pain in her back was excruciating, as was the pain in her heart. And as if that weren't enough to make her wish to be any place else but sprawled at the feet of the man who thought he owned her, Raheem was leering at her naked body with undisguised lust. She'd been left with not a scrap of clothing, nor shred of dignity.

Maxwell made quick eye contact, scowling for dramatic effect, and then looked away. "Leave us whore, you have displeased me greatly. Your sweet body shall pay for your misdeeds when I am through trying to soothe your master's ire. Go to my bed chamber and think of all I will do to punish you for this newest bit of insolence. You are to kneel, forehead to the floor, ass raised, cunny exposed, just as you have been taught while you wait for my wrath."

Jeeval's first instinct was to stop Beth, but he let her go. He had told Maxwell he had plenty of time to break Beth and insisted the man go out. What could he say now? Jeeval knew Maxwell was well aware he'd planned to come back for the girl, but why throw it in his face? Maxwell would just play dumb, and Jeeval would appear to be an impatient fool who didn't stand by his word. All was not right here, but he'd told Maxwell he could have a few more days to tame the slut. It was best to let it go... for now, but he would put a double watch on the pair.

"Very well, perhaps I am impatient for this one. She is a beauty, her hair calls for a man to wrap his fist in it, and her skin is like fine porcelain. It will make a lovely canvas for my whip marks. Prepare her well, for she shall pleasure me soon Maxwell, and make sure she is properly adorned for the banquet tonight. I wish to show off my newest pet."

"I will, Jeeval. We'll be there, and all your guests will all be jealous of the wondrous treasures you possess. She shall be chastised, decorated, and ready to show. You have my word."

Jeeval nodded and strode out the door, motioning for Raheem, who cast an ominous glace at Maxwell. He felt the man was making a fool of his boss, and didn't care for it one bit. The uppity new slut had dared to attack him and should at that very moment be laying in a quivering heap with stripes of red running across her back, bottom, and thighs. Raheem vowed to personally keep an eye on Maxwell. There was something afoot here. He could feel it.

The chamber door to Maxwell's quarters closed, and Beth let out a sob. Maxwell quickly rushed to forward to lock it then, turned back to Beth.

"Shhh angel, I'm here. He can't hurt you now luv. I'm here baby and he's gone. Oh kitten, I'm so sorry he hurt you. Come here luv. Come here."

Maxwell gathered Beth into his arms and held her close as she told him of her ordeal. He whispered that he was so very proud of his little tigress, and that he understood why she had to fight. He told her she was brave and how much he loved her, then he told her of their ship.

"We'll be free soon, kitten. You'll be a good girl at the party tonight, and everything will be fine. It will be hard, and I know you'll be mortified at being exposed to everyone, but no one will touch you, you'll still be under my protection. Just endure a few more days of this Beth, and we'll be free. No man will ever look at you again, my love. You are my girl and I love you, Beth. Just hang on a little longer."

Chapter Twenty-One

Evening came far too soon for them both, but Maxwell knew what had to be done. He was determined to please Jeeval by making Beth into a stunningly beautiful toy. He stood back and admired his handiwork. Beth looked exquisite. He'd arranged her hair in a cascade of curls flowing down one side of her neck with a few stray ones gracing the other, just to emphasize the slenderness of the ivory column. He wanted nothing more than to take a nibble, and had in fact done just that many times as he'd put her golden locks up, but now he resisted, it was time to endure the night's activities.

He'd lined Beth's eyes with dark kohl and painted the lids a green that brought out their emerald hue, and tinted her lashes as well. Her lips were darkened with berry juice as were her nipples, and her cheeks held just a hint of blush. Maxwell knew not much was needed, for he was sure those cheeks would be stained by her natural color either from embarrassment or outrage many times throughout their ordeal. All through his preparations he'd kept admonishing her on the importance of being good and doing as she was told no matter what happened. He just hoped her inner fire would be tamed by her knowledge of their fate should they be found out.

"Beth you look absolutely ravishing. The men will be falling at your feet, but you must ignore every one of them no matter what they say. They will make lewd remarks, calling you a pet and a whore, and tell Jeeval what they would like to do to you, but you must be silent. You are forbidden to speak or make eye contact unless instructed to by me or Jeeval."

Beth opened her mouth to once again declare the orders undignified but Maxwell held up his hand. "I mean it kitten, do not show your claws. If you misbehave tonight, Jeeval shall punish you in front of all his guests. Do you want to have your pretty little bottom bared for all to see and be spanked as they grin and rub their cocks? Chances are he won't mar his toy with his whip, but he will surely find a way to humiliate you."

Beth stamped her foot in frustration. The evening she was about to endure went against everything inside her. Every shred of dignity would be stretched to the limit. "I'll do it Maxwell, for us, but I won't like it."

"That's a good girl. I promise you a special reward when we get back here, okay luv?" Maxwell moved forward and pulled her close, burying his face in her neck. She smelled so sweet and her skin was soft as silk. He breathed in deeply and allowed himself a few caresses as she snuggled up against him, wiggling her body close.

"I... I have a surprise for you too. There's something I want to do for you, Maxwell."

"Is there now you little minx? Something from the book perhaps? Maybe the something that got you rubbing that sweet cunny of yours?"

Beth blushed scarlet at the mention of 'that' activity, and she tried to push away, but Maxwell held her fast and tilted her chin up. "It's alright to feel that need sweet, and I have no problem with you pleasuring your body, although I would prefer to be the one who enjoys that task. In the beginning, instilling passion and the talents of love is why you were brought here. Now I want you to continue to have all that same fire for me.

"Just because you aren't being trained to be a concubine anymore, doesn't mean I want you to be a lady in the bedroom. You are my wild temptress. I want you full of lust."

He kissed her hard, igniting that very fire he spoke of, until her knees weakened, and she clung to him from the magic his tongue created. Beth pressed her naked breasts to his hard chest, but Maxwell forced himself to pull away. Jeeval would never forgive him if they were late. It would be a huge affront to his dignity.

"Enough of that, my love. Time to get you dressed. Now I'm warning you kitten, you won't like what you must wear, but keep those claws pulled in. I promised to present you properly and that means a special gown and the proper jewelry."

Maxwell moved to the wardrobe and pulled out a sari made of the sheerest of green silk. She could clearly see him through it, right down to the clasp on his breeches. The sari had long sleeve like panels at the shoulders and would go from her neck to her toes, but the material left nothing to the imagination. She shook her head, backing away, and Maxwell scowled.

"Beth we have to get you ready. I know you don't like this kitten. I don't like it either. Do you think I want those men ogling you? Just remember they can't touch you, you are just for show."

He turned, dismissing her and her protests, enraging Beth, and went to the jewelry box, removing the hated clit clip, a set of tiny bells each on a small wire loop, a long thin gold chain, and a heavy looking metal object shaped like a small egg on a little stand. As Maxwell picked it up and turned back to her, she saw it had an emerald set into the bottom of the stand, and Beth searched her imagination for where on earth she could wear the thing.

"Now then, you know where this goes." He held up the clit clip. "These are for you nipples." He held the bells out for her to see. "And this goes in your bottom." Maxwell was moving forward fast as he said the last words, knowing he was going to have to catch her quick if he intended to put the proper adornments on her and he fully intended to do so.

"I want no argument, Beth. You will do as you are told. You are smart enough to know we have to present you properly. Any sign of resistance will be taken as an affront to Jeeval. Stand still. It won't be so bad."

Beth scoffed at his words, eyes flashing. "Have you ever worn that thing in your bottom and those degrading little bells on your nipples? I am not a horse who wears bells on its harness to announce its arrival, and I certainly won't wear that... that thing in... there!" She shoved him hard and batted at his hands, twisting free and backing away in a fury, her rage overriding her common sense.

"Damn it Beth, we don't have time for games! I don't like this either but it has to be done. Please baby, think about what you're doing. After tonight you will never have to do this again, but tonight we must put on a show."

Maxwell was trying hard to be reasonable, but his old self was rushing to the forefront. Dominant ways die hard, and Beth's refusal to do as she was told went against everything he had believed in for years. Even away from this place, a proper wife should submit to her husband's wishes, and in this matter, this matter of their safety, this matter of life and death, she should do as she was told without fuss and question.

"I mean it Beth. Get... over... here... now."

Maxwell's voice had dropped to a low hiss and Beth could see the anger in his eyes, but then she looked at the hideous jewelry and the revealing gown again.

"No."

Maxwell moved forward in a flash and grabbed her by the waist, hoisting her up and carrying her to a bench where he sat and positioned her over his lap.

"Just because I love you kitten, doesn't mean I will allow you to be reckless and disobedient in things that will endanger us. I will be your husband soon, and you will listen to me in this matter. I know what is best when dealing with Jeeval, and I will do whatever it takes to keep you safe, including punishing this bottom until you see things my way."

As his words came out his hand came down, smacking the still tender flesh in a flurry of spanks. Back and forth, up and down, side to side, he covered her bottom cheeks with stinging slaps, and Beth howled in protest. Her feet kicking as she tried to get up time and again, but Maxwell held her fast. He moved her so her legs were pinned between his, and raised her bottom higher as he spread her legs and rained spanks upon her thighs and now exposed cunny. Those particular blows sent jolts of sensation to her very core.

Beth shrieked as his hand grazed her cunny and clit but Maxwell spanked on, pausing to rub her bottom and stroke her between her now moist netherlips during his lecture until she was moaning. He teased her there, sliding a finger, then two, in and out, in and out, and then circled her swollen clit until she was grinding down on his hard thigh and then he began to spank her bottom again. Each blow sent a burst of stinging pain through her, but it also made her nub rub his leg. Over and over her slapped her now crimson bottom, telling her she would damn well listen to him, landing the occasion spank on her hypersensitive cunny until Beth was mewling and shaking.

"Will you be a good girl tonight? Will you listen to me in this matter?" His voice was a throaty growl, anger mixed with passion. "I know it isn't what you want. You're my proud girl and I love you for it. I know it tears you up inside but you must obey me in this. Tell me you will do as I say, Beth." The spanks had lessened, becoming gentler, well placed, pleasure inducing slaps mixed with mind numbing strokes between her cunny lips. Beth nodded her head and whispered a quiet yes.

Maxwell reached out and picked up the silver rosebud for her bottom. He dipped his fingers into her wet cunny then spread her juices upward, sliding his fingers around her puckered hole, teasing it, tickling. Beth tensed and he whispered and cooed, then slid his fingers inside her cunny for more moisture before moving upward again to her tightest passage.

Pressing slowly, Maxwell entered her bottom and Beth gasped. It felt so odd, not horrid, but so different. She remembered the pictures in the book and forced herself to relax.

"That's a good girl. Let yourself feel." Maxwell pressed deeper and Beth moaned, he pulled out and pushed in again. "Push back kitten and let me in. It will feel good, I promise." Beth did and soon his finger was buried deep in her flaming bottom.

"Oh!"

Maxwell smiled and began to move his finger in and out, stroking her inner walls until she was moving her hips in time, then he pulled out and was very satisfied when she let out a little sigh at her loss.

"Later kitten, there's no time. Now be good and take what has to come next." Maxwell spread more of her dew from her cunny to her bottom and quickly slid the cold metal rosebud deep into her bottom until just the jeweled base was showing. It glittered in the lamplight from between her crimson cheeks and Maxwell thought it looked delightful, though he knew Beth would die of shame if she could see it.

"That's a girl, that's my Beth. Thank you, baby."

That said, Maxwell gave her what she needed. He took his other hand and curled his fingers up, deep inside her, stroking her sweet spot then began to move them in and out, in and out, while his thumb found her needy clit. Beth bucked her hips at the triple sensation and rocked in rhythm to his ministration, her bottom was tingling and full, her cunny walls clutching his fingers, her swollen clit was aching, and her body erupted as she climaxed. It was powerful and all consuming, and her body tensed as her orgasm rushed through her, making every muscle contract, and in its wake a flood of tears came.

Maxwell gently pulled her up into his lap and cuddled her close. "Hush now baby. It's all right. Please understand why I did that. It's okay. Let the hurt and anger out. I know how hard this is for you. Let it out. I hope you understand why I did that kitten. Oh Beth I simply have to keep you safe, my love, and that fiery temper of yours won't allow it. I promise to never spank you unless it's because of something that put you in danger... or unless you want me too okay?"

His last statement, produce a smile from Beth who looked up at him through her lashes. "I know why you did it and its okay Maxwell. You're not like Jeeval. You don't spank me just to hurt me, or just to get your pleasure. You did it because I was being stubborn. I know we have to do this; it's just going to be hard. I'll do whatever you say. Promise. I do love you, my Maxwell."

And she did. Her bottom was sore but his words about being her husband echoed in her ears, and there was that delicious feeling of release still tingling deep in her belly. Funny how a spanking added a whole different sense of pleasure when she came, and the feeling of having something 'back there' was new, but not unpleasant. She was way too embarrassed to say it out loud, but she and Maxwell both knew that spanking wasn't an altogether bad thing, in fact, just the thought of being over her man's lap sent a new zing of sensations flooding through her.

"You ready now kitten?"

"Yes."

Maxwell set her on her feet and put the rest of the jewelry in place, smiling when Beth didn't fuss, even when he clipped the slim gold chain onto her collar. It dangled between her breasts but she didn't say a word. He then pulled the green silk sari around her and fastened it in place, standing back to admire his masterpiece and declaring her perfect.

"Alright then, just keep your eyes down and ignore them. We'll be out of here soon my love. You can do this baby. I know you can."

"I know I can, Maxwell. I can for us." With those words she strode towards the chamber doors, flinging the 'leash' over her shoulder at him. He watched her go, ready to take on the world, strong and proud and burning with her own fierce light.

Chapter Twenty-two

Maxwell unlocked the chamber doors and held his arm out for Beth. She took it, staring into his eyes with a fierce determination that he found very heartening. Despite their situation, he couldn't help but grin at her. "That's my girl. Strong as always. Be my little tigress inside love, but keep those claws where they can't be seen."

He opened the double doors and they strode into a wide hallway. It was the first time Beth had been out of Maxwell's rooms in this manner. The polished marble floor gleamed and the walls held wall sconces and oil paintings in gilded frames. When Beth looked at them, she gasped at what they portrayed. Each and every one was a scene of what should only take place in the bedchamber, but here they were for all to see. Nude bodies were wrapped together in a myriad of poses, engaging in a multitude of sexual acts, some were like what she'd seen in the book Maxwell had given her, and some were even more scandalous.

Beth blushed scarlet as they walked and painting after painting was revealed to her still somewhat innocent gaze. Some were of couples, but others held a multitude of people doing 'things' to each other in the same room at the same time! The floor, the couches, even the tables were occupied by men and women in various sexual acts. To be loved by Maxwell was wonderful, but to become a toy to Jeeval to be used in such a fashion would be revolting.

Beth wondered if the banquet tonight would have people doing things like this in front of each other and her stomach turned sour. She could take being spoken to in a demeaning way, could even withstand being prodded and pawed by Jeeval, but this, these scenes of people rutting like animals everywhere one looked, well how on earth could she cope with that?

"Maxwell?" Her voice wavered as did her step.

"Don't worry kitten, you won't endure that tonight. That kind of thing only takes place at Jeeval's very special parties. This is not one of those."

What he didn't tell her though, was that there would be one of 'those' types of parties, one of Jeeval's infamous orgies, the day after they were to set sail on the ship. Jeeval's friend Siead was scheduled to arrive then, and if they didn't successfully escape, Maxwell was sure Beth would be punished by being the main attraction at the gala. If that were to happen, Beth would be used in every way possible by numerous men and then sent to bed with Siead for the remainder of his stay. Maxwell had seen the after effects of being a toy to Siead, and they weren't pretty.

As they moved towards the center of the estate, statues began to appear in the hallway as well. These were not just any statues either, they were of nude couples engaged in sex, and all of the males had swollen oversized cocks that jutted up and out from their bodies. Beth couldn't believe her eyes. First the book, then the paintings, and now the sculptures, what else would the night have in store? She'd thought Jeeval depraved before, now his taste in 'art' made her wonder if he had risen straight from Hell. The sexual organs of the sculptured pieces were so disproportionate they would have been comical if they hadn't been so obscene. Beth tensed at Maxwell's side at these affronts to her virtue but Maxwell led her on.

As they neared a set of huge double doors, Beth spied what she thought to be another grotesque piece of art, this one of a man taking a woman from behind. As she moved forward, Maxwell pulled his arm from hers and slipped it around her waist, knowing what was really ahead. He cursed to himself as he did so. This was something Beth didn't need to see.

"Oh! Oh God, Maxwell. It's... It can't be. Oh Maxwell that is a real woman. What are they doing to her? Why?"

Beth stared in shocked horror at the slave before her. The woman's arms were bound behind her, held in place by ropes that ran over her shoulders and to the arms of the statue. She was gagged as well but it didn't silence her moans of anguish. The worst part of all though, was she was impaled on the phallus of the statue that stood behind her. Just the tips of her toes touched the ground, and the little bells attached to her nipples jingled with every struggling movement she made.

As Beth's eyes were drawn to the woman's breasts by the sound of the bells, Beth saw that her breasts were crisscrossed with welts, undoubtedly made by a whip, as were her thighs and belly. It was too much. The image was obscene and disturbing, and Beth wanted nothing more but to help her. No one should ever suffer such a fate.

She tried to pull away from Maxwell but he held her back, even as the guard standing next to the poor unfortunate concubine placed a hand on his coiled whip and made a growl deep in his throat. Beth backed off but let out a little mewl of anguish as her eyes met the captives. Her heart went out to the woman whose fate had been dictated by the sadistic Jeeval. Had the woman done something to displease him, so or was this just another twisted spectacle to satisfy his sick sexual desires?

Maxwell turned gruff in the face of the guard and yanked on Beth's leash, jerking her away from the woman. All Beth could do was follow after him despite what her mind screamed at her to do. The harshness of Maxwell's actions reminded Beth of how she must behave whether she liked it or not, and the words that followed did so as well.

"That's what happens to women who misbehave, my little bitch. There she will stay to be humiliated and abused by all who pass tonight. I could force her to orgasm if you'd like a demonstration."

Beth shook her head mutely, and had to force down the bile that rose in her throat.

"See that you do as you're told, or you'll find yourself in the same situation as that one."

She spared one last glance at the woman then hurried after Maxwell, not caring to be dragged along by her chain. The fate of the poor woman sickened her, but there was nothing to be done. To be a woman within these walls was to be completely helpless.

As Maxwell opened the doors of the banquet room, the sound of music, laughter, and loud conversation immediately flowed over them, as did the tempting aromas of the delicious delicacies that adorned the lavishly set tables. Beth's stomach growled in spite of her nervousness. She's been too uneasy to eat earlier despite Maxwell's urgings, and though she didn't think she could actually swallow a single morsel, the food smelled scrumptious.

Beth chanced a quick glance around and took in a huge room filled with glowing oil lamps, fragrant bowls and vases of flowers, tables laden with delicacies, long, padded benches, and a floor strewn with huge pillows. There were people everywhere, and for the most part, the men were dressed, and the women were not. Some had clothes on to be sure, but their outfits were like hers or were even more revealing. A few were completely bare. Some danced, some served food and wine on trays, some sat at the feet of the guests, some sat on laps or even lay over them, and were being fondled outright.

She turned her head to take in her surroundings, forgetting Maxwell's admonishment to keep her eyes down, and then made a squeak of shock when she looked more closely at the food tables. A few of them not only held food, but held naked women lain out and covered with food as well!

There were men plucking berries off their bellies and mounds, and as she watched, one nibbled a grape from around a woman's breast then bit her nipple, making the poor woman jump. One of the guards came forward and took hold of both her nipples roughly, bending low with a scowl on his face, no doubt chastising her for reacting. He stayed there pinching the slave's nipples until Beth could see the glimmer of tears trickling from the unfortunate woman's eyes, then laughed cruelly and retreated, apparently satisfied that she'd learned her lesson.

Along one long wall was a row of scantily clad women all kneeling with their hands clasped behind their necks. They were held in a stringent upright position by a gold collar and chain very much like hers that was attached to the wall behind them. The position made their bellies taunt, and their backs arch, showing off their breasts. Each one had their eyes downcast and was completely immobile. Beth was embarrassed for them all, for surely they felt the humiliation she did, and a blush of shame and anger stained her cheeks.

Maxwell heard her breath catch, and slid his hand up the chain till he held it close to her neck, pulling her ear to his lips.

"Those women are the ones chosen to be given to the guests tonight. Any man may take them to a private room. You will not be placed along that wall, kitten. Remember, this is just for a while. It will be okay. Eyes down, mouth shut, do as you're told."

A booming burst of laughter rang out from the far side of the room, one which Beth recognized immediately. She shivered at the sound of the hated Jeeval, but then drew in a deep breath and pulled herself up tall.

"That's my girl. Let's go."

Chapter Twenty-three

Maxwell led her to where Jeeval sat. He lounged against a huge mound of pillows, bare chested, wearing a pair of loose white silk pants, looking for all the world like the lord of his kingdom. A woman knelt at each side, ready to do his bidding. He was talking with much animation to a gentleman to his right, as he toyed with the nipple of one of his concubines and laughed heartily again at something his companion said. When he caught sight of them approaching, his words died on his lips as he took in the enticing sight Beth made as she was led across the room.

"Ah, there they are. This is my best slave trainer and my newest toy." Maxwell walked within a foot of Jeeval who didn't rise to meet them, and gave a slight nod of his head in respect. He then handed Beth's leash over to Jeeval. She had to fight back a surge of panic at his action, but managed to keep quiet. It would be okay. Maxwell said he'd be with her all night, right by her side. Jeeval yanked on the leash and Beth dropped to her knees as was expected. This action of obedience pleased Jeeval greatly.

"She's perfect Maxwell, just as you promised. Absolutely breathtaking."

"Well I wouldn't go that far. She may look perfect, but she's still got a long way to go. I had to take her in hand yet again this afternoon for not doing as she was told. This one has a fiery temper. I promise she'll be ready soon. I must say she certainly looks like a treasure. She's learning what's expected in bed so she can be your best whore. A natural little wanton she is, with the right persuasion. I still need to work on making her obedience something she does without thought. Right now she needs a harsh hand to remind her but she'll come around. I know you want them to have a whore's passion without the fire of insolence. This one will do me proud once I'm finished."

"I have no doubt you will get the job done to perfection, Maxwell. Palo, this is Maxwell, and this is Beth, my latest acquisition. Isn't she exquisite?"

Palo rose, he stood over Beth, looking down at where she knelt. "May I?" The man held his hand out for her leash, and Jeeval handed it over with casual nonchalance. His actions made Maxwell bristle with rage, but he displayed an outward calm he didn't feel. Palo pulled Beth to her feet then dropped the gold chain so it dangled between her breasts and slowly began to circle her, taking in every inch. His eyes raked over her, and Beth's skin crawled. She swore she could feel his fat fingers actually touching her, and she knew damn well what was going through his head.

"Spread and bend girl." Beth hesitated; this wasn't Jeeval or Maxwell doing the ordering. Was she to obey any man within these walls? She was 'owned' by Jeeval.

"Do as you're told Beth. You may obey him." Jeeval actually seemed pleased that she'd hesitated. Beth supposed it was because he thought she felt some loyalty to him, and was taking pride in his ownership. Little did he know that his days of so called ownership were numbered and her heart was filled with the vilest of hate whenever she thought of him. She belonged to no man, not even Maxwell. To Maxwell she gave herself willingly.

Beth took a deep breath and glanced over at Maxwell out of the corner of her eye. His face was calm, as if the whole scene meant nothing to him, but she knew that wasn't true. She spread her legs as wide as possible within the material of the sari, knowing to do less would gain her punishment, and bent over.

Palo made a guttural grunt of appreciation as he once again circled her and stopped directly behind her. Beth was becoming more horrified by the second, and didn't know how much longer she could carry out this farce.

Though she was dressed, the thin material of her sari did nothing to conceal her womanly charms. She knew her bare cunny and still bruised bottom were completely on display to this horrid man, but she fought back her revulsion. As she stood on trembling legs, Palo reached out his hand to stroke between the legs, leering, his thick tongue darting out to wet his lips in anticipation. Quick as lightening Maxwell's hand came up and snatched the man around the wrist, preventing any contact with his love's vulnerable flesh.

"See here now, it's look but don't touch. She doesn't belong to you. Hasn't even been had by your host yet. Sorry but this one is off limits. There are plenty of others for the taking. Beth be a good girl and go to your Master."

Beth quickly stood and then knelt at Jeeval feet. She hadn't seen Palo's actions, but from Maxwell's words, she knew she had just barely avoided being molested yet again. Jeeval was bad enough, to have to endure the groping of this pig eyed; greasy, bloated man would make her vomit.

She lowered her forehead and pressed it to the floor, not as the show of respect that it seemed, but because the coolness of the marble helped keep her head from spinning and her expression of revulsion from being seen.

Palo jerked his hand away from Maxwell, deeply offended, but said nothing. He'd been to visit Jeeval before, and knew he must do as his host wished if he wanted to continue to receive invitations in the future. He nodded to Jeeval and walked away to find an available slave he could take to a private room to relieve the painful bulge between his legs, but thoughts of the delicious Beth remained imprinted on his mind.

"Stand before me woman."

Beth rose and stood in front of Jeeval, eyes carefully kept lowered so as not to offend him. She took a step closer and spread her feet apart in the expected pose. She could see Jeeval's lean muscular legs and his hard, naked stomach from this viewpoint, but the sight of his sculpted body did nothing but turn her stomach. Beth was thankful she couldn't see his eyes because she knew evil dwelled there.

His hand reached out to her and Beth stood stone still. He traced down the inside of her thighs reaching the hem of her sari then sliding back upwards, the material caught in his fingers, raising it and exposing her naked skin. Beth bit her trembling lip but held still. She heard Maxwell's deep steady breathing as he tried to remain calm, and focused on the soothing sound, shutting out the actions of the beast before her.

When his hand reached her cunny, Jeeval toyed with her for a moment, and then let the fabric fall, back in place, seemingly satisfied with her obedience.

"Kneel at my feet facing my guest, so all may see my new pet." Beth did as he asked, then felt him pick up her leash and clip it to a pillar next to his mound of pillows. She was well and truly chained like a dog at her Master's feet. Her nostrils flared, and her cheeks flushed an angry red, but Beth remained subservient. This was necessary in order for them to survive, but how long would the banquet last?

Maxwell took up position next to Jeeval, arms crossed, guarding, watching, wondering as well when he could make excuses for them to leave. He stood and watched as Jeeval let down Beth hair and played with her golden tresses, toying with her silken curls, and stroking her shoulders, sliding the sheer fabric of the sari off one, so her breast was exposed.

To remain silent was pure agony. No one should be touching his Beth. He could gleefully strangle Jeeval for daring to lay a hand on his girl, but Maxwell knew he had to remain impassive. His only saving grace was the pride he was feeling for his girl. She was doing so well resisting the urge to bolt or rip Jeeval to shreds. He knew it was taking every ounce of self-control she possessed not to slap Jeeval's hands away and tell him what she really thought of him. His tigress was keeping her claws in check.

"Why don't you go and partake in some food and entertainment, Maxwell? You're not needed here anymore. There are many women to choose from, and you must be hungry. Surely you're tired of being around this willful little bitch. Have a woman who is soft and willing."

Beth visibly tensed at Jeeval's words.

"If it's all the same to you, I'd rather stay. To tell the truth, the little thing has me worn out. Besides, it's still my job to see to her behavior. I can't correct her later unless I watch her every move now. I want to know what areas still need work. The food and wine can be brought to me."

"Suit yourself. Mari, bring some refreshments for Maxwell." With a snap of his fingers the slave girl rose and scurried away, not wanting to risk the wrath of her Master. She soon returned and set a tray of food and wine on the floor next to Maxwell then pressed her lips to Maxwell's boots.

A deep pang of guilt surged up inside Maxwell at Mari's actions. He had been the one to break her when she first arrived, and had taken the skin off her precious bottom on many occasions until the woman had learned to be a proper slave. She'd been a gift from a wealthy father who preferred money more than his daughters. She'd been thrust into a life of subservience and sex on demand, and it had been a very hard transition for the young girl. Now here she was not a year later, the perfect little concubine.

Maxwell stroked her hair briefly and quickly told her to rise, motioning her back. As he sat, she again came forward, her job wasn't simply to serve, it was also to sit and be toyed with, or to please in any way, however or whatever a man wished.

"No Mari. That will be all. I need to keep a close eye on this one." Maxwell nodded towards Beth, and he could see her looking at him beneath lowered lashes. She'd been watching the entire scene from the corner of her eye.

Beth was very relieved when Maxwell rebuffed the woman. The jealousy that welled up inside her when Mari placed a kiss on Maxwell's boot took her aback. That, along with the anger over the girl's situation were making her half crazed, but she did her best to hide it. Beth's thoughts were immediately drawn back to Jeeval however when he pinched her nipple sharply.

"Too tired or too smitten with this one Maxwell? I'm thinking it's the later. Just remember that you now only have two days before Beth is delivered to me. After that I doubt you'll see much of her for a good long while. I plan to make good use of my new whore's talents. It might take me a month to get my fill. Tell me Maxwell, is her cunt extra tight? She's so tiny, I'll be it's a real tight fit."

"She's so tight I nearly lost control like a schoolboy. You'll not find her lacking there or anywhere else once I'm through."

"That's what I pay you for Maxwell. Just don't forget this is a job. You'll be moving on to a new wench soon."

"I enjoy variety, Jeeval, and wouldn't want it any other way. The only way I could have a harem such as yours is to be rich. With you I get my choice of blushing virgins to tame, and then get to move on before I tire of them. I'd say it's a perfect arrangement for us both."

Maxwell hoped his words hadn't given Beth any reason to doubt him. They were harsh indeed, but he had to act as if he didn't care one bit for her. He studied her carefully but could tell nothing by her body stance, and she wasn't glancing at him any longer since Jeeval has pinched her.

As he and Jeeval continued with their dinner, Palo approached once again. Jeeval, bastard that he was, slid the fabric of Beth's sari off her other shoulder to expose her to the hungry man's eyes from the waist down, baring both breasts. Jeeval knew damn well that Palo wanted his newest play thing, and he was going to take full advantage of his superiority in the situation.

"Palo, why are you back so soon? Surely there are other women to satisfy your needs. My selection is large and they are all quite willing."

Palo's eyes raked over Beth. She dared not look up, but her skin crawled at his nearness, so she knew she was being examined. She could feel his appraisal of her, could feel his eyes linger on her nipples as Jeeval pinched and played with them back and forth, making them harden in protest to his painful touch.

Jeeval grazed his fingers over her belly and the fabric of the sari slid even lower. It caught precariously on her hip bones, and just needed one more touch for her to be bare where she knelt. Palo drew in his breath then let it out with a low whistle.

"Your women are all beautiful Jeeval. No complaints there, never, but I have come to a decision. I want this one. Her unusual coloring has me quite smitten."

Maxwell stood up quickly. If there was to be trouble, he was going to be ready. No one was touching Beth, and Jeeval sure as hell wasn't going to give her to this foul man. He was known to be a particularly sadistic bastard, outdoing even Jeeval. The women he used always bore the worst lash marks and bruises, and were often torn up inside as well.

"You were told she's not for the taking. I suggest you find your pleasure elsewhere or leave before you offend your host further."

Jeeval raised his hand indicating that Maxwell should back off a bit. He could handle this. "My man speaks the truth Palo. You know I don't share my playthings until I have had my fill of them. Beth hasn't graced my bed yet. Surely you don't expect me to allow you to have her before I have had that pleasure myself."

"No Jeeval, you misunderstand me. I'm not suggesting I use her and give her back. I wish to buy her. Sell her to me. I'll pay whatever you ask. You have so many women, and all I ask is for this one. I want her, no matter what. No price is too high."

Chapter Twenty-four

Beth couldn't help it; she let out a little squeak of protest and began to raise her head. Jeeval gathered a fist full of her hair and let out a warning growl, making it clear she had nothing to do with his decision, and she'd better not embarrass him.

Maxwell stood stone still, ready to spring into action. If he had to fight their way out of there, then so be it. It was better to die trying to escape than to have Beth land in the hands of the likes of Palo. He prayed she would keep still and do nothing to anger Jeeval, or goad him into selling her.

"So you like my new pet enough to spend your silver on her do you? What else are you willing to bargain with? What price are you willing to pay? I suppose she could be had, but she wouldn't come cheap. My man has already taken considerable time breaking her, and I would of course lose the pleasure of having her myself.

"She is such a rare jewel is she not? Such hair and skin, spun gold and porcelain. And her eyes are like the most precious of emeralds. It would be hard for me to part with her. Perhaps it would be best if you wait until I tire of her and then have a go, though I was just telling Maxwell that will take a while."

Jeeval yanked Beth's head back so she was looking up and into his eyes as he stroked her cheek. "You must remember that the women that are given to my guests are only those who bore me or have done something to lose my favor. This one has enough fire to keep my bed warm for a long time. If you want her soon, you'll have to pay me well."

Beth's hands were fisted at her sides, her breath held, her heart pounding, her eyes squeezed shut as she waited to find out her fate. She willed them open and tried to glance at Maxwell but he was out of her view. What would they do if Jeeval consented to Palo's request?

As for Maxwell, he shifted subtly, placing more weight on his left foot so he could more easily make a grab for the blade that was concealed in the boot on his right. He carried two knives at all times, one in his boot which he planned to go for immediately, and one openly in a sheath on his belt like the other guards in the estate. Still, he knew one man armed with two knives had very poor odds against a small army of Jeeval's men, especially with Beth in tow.

"I agree she is a prize Jeeval, which is why I desire her. You have so many and have the talent for acquiring many more. I lack your resources but not the funds to pay for such a delightful creature. Have pity on me man, and sell me the girl. She stirs my blood like none I've ever seen."

Maxwell stared at Palo with undisguised disgust. The man was practically drooling.

"She isn't properly trained yet." The protest sprang from Maxwell's lips before he could stop himself. What was happening was insanity. "You can't very well sell him a woman who will give him trouble. I know Palo is an old friend and his wishes should be considered, but Beth will disappoint him if he takes her now. Think about it Jeeval, she won't be like the others he's had. I think perhaps when Beth's ready he... "

Jeeval again held up his hand, silencing Maxwell and his objections, and Maxwell knew if he said too much he would push Jeeval the wrong way. The man wasn't a fool. He knew Maxwell had a special fondness for Beth.

"I have no problem with training her myself. In fact it will make sure she's to my liking. A few days tied to my bed feeling the wrath of my cock and my lash should quench any rebellion she might still have inside. Properly applied pain can do wonders for the female attitude."

Palo raised the riding crop he was holding and tapped it against Beth's nipple for emphasis. To both Maxwell and Beth's dismay, Jeeval said nothing about the liberties he was daring to take. "Please my old friend, I simply must have her. What is her price?"

Jeeval stroked his chin thoughtfully. "You have a niece do you not? A pretty young thing, tiny and sweet."

Palo drew in his breath sharply. He was a man of few principles and enjoyed the women who were trained to be sex slaves, but Miriella was family. It wasn't that girls held great importance, but to have her brought to Jeeval's estate would be unsettling.

"Yes I do Jeeval, but she is just thirteen. Surely you aren't suggesting she come here as a trade for this one?

"Women are but playthings Palo. All women. It's never too young to begin their training. You said name my price and that's it. I don't want silver, I want blood. If you want Beth, then the price is your niece, Miriella. It's your choice. Take it or leave it."

He shrugged his shoulders casually, the repulsive nature of his suggestion not weighing on his conscious at all. Beth had to fight back the bile that was rising in her throat at his words. It was bad enough that she was here, but a child! He wanted a mere baby brought here for his depraved pleasure. Did he not have one shred of decency inside?

"Ah Jeeval, you drive a hard bargain but what's the girl to me really? She will be given to a man in an arranged marriage for my brother's profit, so better that I am the one who has something to gain right? As the eldest son it is within my rights to make the match I see fit. You must marry her though. I cannot abide by having her be a mere concubine. Marriage will quiet my brother's protests as well."

Palo laughed heartily at his decision and the ease at which he just sold his young niece. "Miriella is yours. I'll set the plan in motion and deliver her within a fortnight."

"You have yourself a deal Palo. Enjoy." Jeeval reached down, and unfastened Beth's leash, handing her over to a leering Palo. He took it in his sausage like fingers with glee.

"Ahhh, all mine. Come to your new Master pretty whore. I want to see the rest of you. If you're a good girl, I won't be too harsh tonight."

Beth looked up into his pig eyes and had to fight back a scream. He reached for her, intending to strip away the remainder of her sari and her fighting instinct kicked in. She didn't care what would happen anymore. There was no way she was going to be taken from the estate by this man. She'd rather die.

Beth lashed out at the grinning Palo, catching him by surprise and slashing her nails across his cheek. He hissed in outrage and lunged for her, but Beth kicked and flailed her arms, striking him and pushing him away. She spun wildly, looking for Maxwell, looking for help, but Maxwell was in a battle all his own. He'd gone into action the moment Beth had. The odds were stacked against them. The chances of them escaping were almost slim, but he was determined to get them out of the estate before any more harm came to his love.

As Beth fought off Palo, Maxwell turned, pulling the blade from his boot. He lunged at Jeeval but missed getting a clean hit, only grazing his side. A line of bright red blood appeared on Jeeval bronze skin and his eyes turned cold as steel.

"You would honestly betray me for this little whore?"

"I would and I am. She'll never be yours. We're leaving. This can be easy or hard, the choice is yours. Why not just let us go?"

"I told you Maxwell, she belongs to me, as does everything you have. You sold your soul when you came to work for me, traded it all for a chance to have all the women you ever dreamed of and live in splendor. In my eyes, I own you as much as I own her. You'll never be free of me. Even if you manage to get out of the estate, I'll hunt you down no matter where you go."

The two men faced off like predators in the jungle, silently eyeing each other, Maxwell holding the knife ready, looking for his chance. As of yet, no one had spied the scuffle on their side of the room. It was large and filled with the loud merriment of the other guests, and Jeeval had waved away the other women and guards when Palo approached him with his offer.

Beth was still clawing and striking out at Palo, but she wasn't gaining the upper hand. The man was easily twice her size. He quickly subdued her, grasping her wrist and twisting her arm behind her back before throwing her to the ground. In seconds he was on her, pinning her down, shaking her, slapping her across the face backward and forward in a rage. Beth knew she was going to lose consciousness soon if she didn't do something.

She spied a knife on the platter of food that had been brought to Maxwell and extended her hand, reaching, stretching, and praying she could get to it but it was too far away.

Palo slapped her again and she saw stars, then his wet greasy lips came down on her neck. Bile rose in Beth's throat and she gagged as he kissed and suckled her skin. His putrid breath filled her nostrils, the weight of him was crushing her, his hands and lips were everywhere. She clawed with all her fury at his back, but the man seemed immune to the pain. Beth reached again for the knife and touched the very tip with her fingertips, but she couldn't get a good grip on it so she began to struggle in earnest under her obese attacker.

She wiggled and rocked and squirmed and fought but it was no use, so finally in desperation, she closed her eyes and went limp. Palo stopped his assault, thinking she had lost consciousness, and rose up on his elbows.

In a flash Beth shifted, stretching and then wrapping her fingers around the knife handle. She brought it up and plunged it into Palo's side. He fell on her, hard, letting out a bellow that was smothered in her neck. Squeezing her eyes shut, fighting back her horror and revulsion, Beth pulled the knife free and then stabbed him again. She then flung her arm out and dropped the knife, stunned, terrified, sickened by her actions, unable to breath.

"Maxwell." The word was a whispered plea for help that went unheard. Maxwell was engaged in his own fight for their lives. Too shocked to move, too weak as to lift Palo, Beth lay where she was a watched Maxwell and Jeeval.

All the while Beth had been fighting with Palo; Maxwell had been circling the floor with Jeeval, doing his best to ignore what was happening to his love. Maxwell knew if he took his eyes off him for one second, their chance for escape would be over. Beth was being hurt and it filled him with rage, but she would die if he stopped to save her now. All he could do was pray that she stay strong. If his little tiger was ever going to use those claws, now was the time. When he saw her stab Palo he knew it was time to act. It was now or never.

Their activities wouldn't remain unnoticed for long. Their luck had to be wearing thin.

"Pull yourself free Beth and go to the far corner of the room behind me, the one behind the potted palms over there." Maxwell circled and circled with Jeeval, trying to find his chance. Watching his enemy, waiting, wondering when Jeeval would sound the alarm. It was a good thing the man liked to play games, and wished to do battle instead of calling his guards.

"I... can't... move him." Beth shoved and pushed at Palo dead weight, her hand slid in the growing pool of blood, making her retch and cry out. Maxwell heard her but knew he was helpless to act.

"Easy kitten, be strong for me. Do it Beth. Push him off and get to that corner." Circling, circling, circling with the enemy, males in a fight to the death for their female, time was running out. "Do it pigeon, do it now."

Tears streaming from her eyes, Beth shoved at the body of the man who had tried to rape her, with all her strength. A sense of panic finally filled her with adrenaline and she found the power to shift him enough to slide free. She stood, bloodied, bruised, bottom lip cracked and swollen, cheeks stained with tears, tugging her ruined sari up over her shoulders. Maxwell saw her from the corner of his eye and felt a rush of relief.

"That's a girl, now go! I'll be right there."

Beth turned and fled, and in the second Jeeval was distracted by her flight, Maxwell leapt forward and grabbed him around the neck, bringing his fist up into the man's stomach, knocking the wind out of him and turning him around. Maxwell then brought the knife to his throat before Jeeval could catch his breath and call for help.

"Now then, since I would like nothing better than to cut your throat, you're going to be our personal escort out of the estate."

"This is insane. I'll let every guard in here have a go at your precious Beth before I cut out both of your hearts. Release me you fool. Do not forget who I am. Do you really want to kill the Emperor's nephew for that whore? Is she truly worth the cost of running for the rest of your life? Unhand me now and you'll go free, as long as I get the bitch back."

"Um... don't think so. I like my idea better. Let's go."

Maxwell pressed the razor sharp blade to Jeeval's throat to show just how serious he was, and headed for the corner where Beth was waiting. She was staring in confusion at the smooth wall before her, stunned and on the verge of panic. He pushed his hand against the small of Jeeval's back, hurrying him on until they stood next to Beth. She turned, looking terrified, eyes huge welling with unshed tears.

"You okay kitten?" She tried her best to give him a small smile of encouragement. She wasn't after all, a simpering ninny.

"Open the passage Jeeval."

He didn't move and Maxwell pressed the tip of the knife blade into his throat, drawing a bead of blood. "Do it now, no funny stuff."

Jeeval did as he asked, stepping on an octagon shaped piece of tile in the floor, and one of the palaces many secret panels opened before them. Suddenly a cry of alarm rang out from the other side of the room. Their run of luck had come to an end.

"It looks like it's going to be rough going from here on out kitten, stay close. We've got Jeeval for insurance and they won't risk my slitting his throat, but they'll also do their best to make sure we never get out of here." That said the trio took off into the dark passageway.

Chapter Twenty-five

Beth rushed headlong into the darkness, terror nipping at her heels as the shouts of the guards rang in her ears.

"Wait kitten." She spun eyes wide with fear, brow creased in confusion. Wait? Why? Was he insane? Maxwell backed up into the panel, kicking back to push it shut, then crooked his head at Beth. "Come here luv."

"Maxwell, we have to run."

"No. Take the blade from my belt and break the spring latch on this side."

"But they'll just come another way! We have to go!" Beth was on the edge of panic. Maxwell could see her strength slipping away, but he could do nothing to hold her or comfort her, his hands were full with Jeeval.

"Damn it kitten, do as I say and do it now. Take my knife and jam it in the latch. It's there, four tiles from the wall on the left. Feel for the crack and drive the blade in. Wiggle it around until you hear it break."

The voices were closer now, closer and enraged. Beth reined in her terror and did as Maxwell said, taking his small dagger and dropping to her knees. She pressed her fingers to the floor then carefully followed the crack between the tiles until she counted off four. Just as she was driving the knife in, the sound of pounding boomed from the other side of the wall. Beth screamed and frantically worked the blade back and forth until she heard the ping of metal popping, then jumped back, still clutching the knife.

Again the pounding came, this time angrier and accompanied by shouts when the guards realized the panel was jammed.

"Leave us be or I'll slit his throat! Let us go in peace and no one will be hurt."

Maxwell once again pricked the skin on Jeeval's neck, drawing blood. Jeeval hissed at the sting of the knife and let out a growl of rage. "Don't listen to him fools. If you let them leave this estate every last one of you will be horse whipped. I want them taken alive, especially the whore."

"You are in no position to make demands or even open that foul mouth of yours, Jeeval. I suggest you shut up before I decide to cut your throat a bit deeper, or better yet, slice out your vile tongue. Beth, put your right hand on the wall for guidance and go where I tell you. Just keep moving and your eyes will start to adjust to the darkness. Trust me kitten. I'll get us out of here, I promise."

Before doing as Maxwell asked, Beth stepped forward towards Jeeval. He couldn't see the rage and disgust on her face, but she was determined to make him feel her wrath. She raised her hand and slapped him as hard as she possibly could. Once, twice, three times, then spit in his face even as her tears began to flow anew. Her voice was hoarse with emotion, but the sincerity of her words couldn't be in doubt.

"How's that for disrespect you depraved bastard? If you ever lay a hand on me again, I'll kill you and feed your corpse to the vultures. I'll tear you to shreds with that beloved whip of yours and leave you to bake in the sun. I'll... I'll..."

Beth bit back a sob, choking on the rush of raw hatred that flowed forth from her soul for the evil creature before her.

"Someday you'll burn in Hell where you belong, Jeeval, and it won't be soon enough for me." That said she stepped to the side and leaned in, kissing Maxwell quickly on the cheek. "I know you'll get us out of here Maxwell. I trust you with my life. I'm ready now. No more tears"

"That's my girl." With one arm held tight around Jeeval's waist and the other hand held a hair's breath away from slicing his throat with the razor sharp dagger, Maxwell began to direct Beth through the passageway, listening for the sound of pursuit.

They made their way through the darkness, tripping all the latches for the secret panels as they went.

Maxwell had a specific destination in mind, and he hoped to hell the guards would think it was the last place they'd go to seek escape. As of yet, his plan seemed to be working. They heard nothing as they went. Everyone must have been headed towards the entrances of the estate in order to intercept them. They knew Maxwell had Jeeval, and fighting in the open was safer for their boss. Accosting them in the narrow dark passage would be to risk hurting the wrong man.

Maxwell's plan was to get back to his chambers. Beth's English dress and shoes were hidden in the secret passageway right outside his rooms. There was no way he could take her into the outside world looking as she did. Her transparent sari and slave collar would give away her concubine status immediately. It was going to be next to impossible for them to hide as it was, not to mention if he ran down the street dragging an obvious slave with him.

Maxwell knew he needed to arm himself with more than one tiny knife as well. True Beth also had a dagger, but he would feel better if she had one to hold, and one secreted away. They also needed the bags of silver he had tucked away with her dress. It was a shame he would have to spend some of the money on clothes for them but they couldn't take the time to gather their things, and they certainly couldn't arrive at the ship without anything. It would raise too much suspicion in the already curious ship Captain.

"Okay kitten, turn left when this wall ends, then go four steps, and kneel down. They'll be a bundle on the floor. I bought you a dress and some underthings today while I was out. After you get changed we'll go in and get my pistol and another knife for you. Have to wash you up quick too luv. It will take time, but you're all bloody."

"She's a murderess and an owned concubine who will be returned to me for justice as soon as she's found. You are forgetting the laws of my country."

"I think you're forgetting the fact that she wasn't given to you by her family or in an arranged marriage, Jeeval. Beth was kidnaped. Last time I checked that is a criminal offense. You have an estate full of captive women. Your uncle might be able to protect you, but I doubt you want all eyes upon you and your cruel ways.

"Who snatched her off the streets, Maxwell? Who kept her locked up and forced himself on her? Who beat her? Who turned her into a sexual slave? I have hardly touched the girl."

"I wouldn't say a word against Maxwell, you bastard. Push me and I'll lie through my teeth to make certain you are arrested. You'll face the same firing squad. If Maxwell goes down, so will you."

Jeeval snorted and let out a cruel laugh. "You're a little fool. He's toyed with you and pleasured you so well between those thighs that you're willing to die for him. Stupid bitch, neither of you will leave the estate alive. We all have too many secrets to keep, and if you do manage to slip away I can assure you that one word to Palo's family will bring their wrath down upon your heads as well. It won't just be my men looking for you outside these walls. You'll never make it out of India."

"You underestimate us Jeeval, but none of that matters."

Maxwell dismissed Jeeval and refused further comment. He pressed his ear to the secret panel, listening for the guards, but heard nothing but silence. He told Beth how to spring the latch, then all three went quickly went into his chambers, each of them scanning for guards. Seeing it safe, Maxwell turned his attentions to Beth as she dressed.

"I see it fits kitten, you look lovely, though covering you up still pains me. Twist your hair up baby, all nice and proper. Have to have you looking like an English woman again. Make sure you pull the lace up over your metal collar."

After doing her best to hide the hideous collar, Beth quickly knelt at the side of the pool and scrubbed at her hands and face, sickened as the water turned pink before her. She knew she would carry the memory of killing Palo with her until the day she died. It had been self-defense, but the act still made her ill.

"You okay kitten?" She nodded. Yes, she was, she really was, they were going to get away from this estate of horrors. She could feel it. It didn't matter how and it didn't matter what had to be done to do it. They were going to be free and she was going to do everything in her power to make sure of it. Be free or die trying. Those were the only two options.

"I'm fine Maxwell. I can do this."

"Good girl. There is a chest under the bed. It has a pistol and two knives. Put one of the knives in your pocket, and keep the other for your hand. Put some of the bullets in the other pocket of your dress, and tie the bundles of silver in your under skirts then bring the other knife and the pistol to me."

Beth did as Maxwell asked as both men watched her, Jeeval's eyes full of hatred and rage. It was clear that he couldn't quite believe the situation he found himself in, and Beth found that amusing. A hysterical giggle began to rise up inside her at his plight, but she knew she couldn't give in to it. The sound that would come forth could very easy boarder on lunacy, and Beth knew she had to keep a tight rein on her emotions so they didn't overwhelm her. She couldn't help but meet his eyes and give him a smile though.

"How does it feel to be the one without control, Jeeval? To be the one whose helpless and at someone else's whim? To know your life belongs to us now? We decide if you live or die, and how much pain you have to suffer before you do."

"Hold your tongue, you little bitch. You're still inside the walls of my estate, and you're the one who will suffer unimaginable pain before the night is through."

Beth's hands itched to slap him again. To scratch his eyes out, to kick him where it would cripple him with pain, but she settled for merely smirking in his face. She knew her scorn and superiority would wound him as surely as his whip had hurt a thousand women.

"We shall see who suffers. Right now the way I see it, you've already lost. Your loyal friend has turned his back in disgust, and one of your slaves is speaking her mind and doing as she pleases. That has to gall you just a little. Listen to me Jeeval, a lowly woman, your so called possession, talking back and having the audacity to look you in the eye. How dare I?"

Beth began to laugh even as her hands fisted at her sides. Maxwell gave her a worried look, hearing the note of hysteria that was bubbling so close to the surface. Her hatred of Jeeval and the things she had suffered at his hands couldn't be wiped out in such a short time. Maxwell knew she would carry the scars of her ordeal for life, but right now Beth had to be strong so they could find freedom.

"That's right kitten, you're in charge here and he will pay, but not right now. Are you ready to go?"

Beth swallowed hard, regaining control of her runaway emotions. "I'm ready. Do you have a plan? I know this was a bit sudden."

"Of course, my lady." Maxwell said it with exaggeration and managed to get a true smile from Beth. Satisfied, he winked and pursed his lips in a kiss. Danger be damned, her sanity was important too.

"There are three secret escape tunnels leading from the palace. They will all be guarded, but with the men split up between those three exits, the perimeters of the estate, and the main doors, we should be able to take on our welcoming party is. It's gonna be rough kitten, but I know you can do it. Get out those claws, my little tiger. It's time to fight your way to freedom."

Chapter Twenty-six

Beth raised the knife and stared at Jeeval, her eyebrows coming together, determination written all over her face. "Oh I'm ready. No one will ever take me alive Jeeval. Ever."

Maxwell looked at his girl, saw her determination, and thought of what would happen to her if in fact he did fail and she was captured by Jeeval's men. He knew in his heart that he could never let that happen. Making a quick decision, he slipped the pistol out of the waistband of his breeches and held it out to her. It was the best way.

"Take it Beth. There are two bullets in the chamber. You have more in your pocket, but we don't have time to teach you how to reload. Shoot anyone who gets close to you, and save the other one for yourself. It's the only way if you are going to be captured. Do you understand kitten?"

Beth took it quickly so Maxwell could resume his hold on Jeeval, slipping the dagger she was holding into her pocket, but shook her head at his words. "No... I can reload. I can help fight Maxwell. I won't just kill myself and not help you."

"Damn it Beth you don't know how."

"I'm not an idiot." She hefted the pistol in her hands. It was heavy and awkward. She raised it, pointed it, then pulled it back down, fumbling until it opened and revealed the chamber for the bullets. Maxwell watched, knowing it would take too much time for her to reload, time she probably wouldn't have.

"Beth, please. You can't be recaptured pet."

"I won't be and either will you. I can do it."

"Ever the willful little bitch isn't she? It's not too late to wash your hands of her and come to your senses, Maxwell. I can forgive and forget. A bit of insanity caused by the longings of your cock. Every man can have a moment of weakness for a pretty bit of flesh. Deep inside you know she's a whore and not worth the trouble. They'll be others better than her."

Beth and Maxwell both made a growl of outrage. Maxwell would have gladly strangled Jeeval for daring to say such disparaging things about his girl, but all he could do was keep his hold on the man. Beth however, was not so constrained. She came forward in a flash, snapping the pistol shut and striking Jeeval on the side of his head. It was a savage blow that dazed him, as the gun sight gouged his cheek. Beth watch with morbid satisfaction as blood welled in the deep cut and flowed down his face. The brutality that now resided in her could have and would have sickened her, if she let herself think about it, but she pushed it from her mind. If she was acting like a vicious animal, it was because the man before her had made her that way.

"Shut up." The words were said between tightly clenched teeth as Beth fought to hold back the fury that threatened to unleash itself on Jeeval. Her fingers curled, breaths hissed in and out, eyes narrowed, as she struggled. She was better than him, and now wasn't the time. Finally Beth made a little sound of strangled rage and turned away, not able to look at Jeeval.

Maxwell felt a rumbling of laughter building in Jeeval's throat and scraped the dagger blade across his flesh.

"I suggest you keep your thoughts to yourself, Jeeval or I'll give Beth free rein whether we need you or not. Though I 'spose I could simply drag along your corpse for insurance instead. Guess they wouldn't know the difference till they were up close. If you think I'd choose loyalty to a demented sadistic bastard like you, over Beth's love, then you're sicker than I thought."

Jeeval's eyes gleamed with hated in the lamplight as he turned his head back to look at Maxwell. In response, Maxwell smirked in Jeeval's face, and made a three inch long shallow cut down the man's neck. Jeeval hissed in surprise when he felt the bite of the knife.

"That's for daring to put your hands on my girl and saying things to upset her. Show some respect or die."

The words weren't a request, and both men knew it. Jeeval held Maxwell's gaze, his eyes black as the river Styx, full of a fury so intense it bordered on madness, and then finally looked away in defeat. Jeeval knew he was trapped for now, but he also was determined that Maxwell and his treasured whore would pay for every insult.

Maxwell jerked Jeeval up harshly, and took off after Beth who was headed back towards the secret passage. "Hold on kitten. I'll lead the way. Just follow and stay close. Eyes and ears open."

Beth followed Maxwell, holding on to his shirt with one hand and clutching the pistol with the other. She was fully prepared to shoot anyone who threatened them. She was also determined not to use the second bullet in the chamber on herself. It would be used to fight their way free, not die a coward's death. If a guard killed her, so be it, but she was not going to use one of their best defenses to save her own skin. Death could be had by the knife if necessary.

The passage was quiet, eerily quiet. Where was everyone? Down they went, winding to and fro until the walls and the floor beneath their feet began to change. They became rougher, the smooth marble replaced by brick and dirt.

"We're almost out kitten. I know there'll be a welcoming party somewhere nearby. Be ready." Just as

Maxwell said the words, a faint glow appeared in the distance, they had reached the mouth of the tunnel. "Here we go."

As they neared, shadowy figures began to emerge from the gloom. One, two, and then three guards. Maxwell tensed, knife pressing into Jeeval's neck, ready for anything.

"Stay back Beth. Knife in one hand, pistol in the other." She inched in close behind him, pistol partly raised as Maxwell called out to the guards that blocked their way. "Let us by or I slit his throat to make the blood start flowing good and hard. We don't want trouble, but we'll give it if you make us."

Closer, then closer still they went towards danger, but it was the only way out. The guards backed up, out of the mouth of the tunnel. Were they giving way or simply giving themselves more space in which to fight?

Beth's heart was pounding so hard the echo in her head drowned out almost everything else, everything that was, except Maxwell's voice. She fought to calm herself as adrenaline raced through her veins. The fight or flight instinct was raging a battle inside her.

As if he could read her mind and feel her panic, Maxwell chanced a quick glance back and winked like he didn't have a care in the world. "Hold steady, kitten."

They reached the mouth of the tunnel and proceeded out into the night. The guards formed a cautious circle around them, not too close, but far too close for comfort. Beth turned so her back was to Maxwell's and pressed against him as they moved as one. The guards tightened the circle their movements mirroring Maxwell and Beth's. She raised the gun, and waved the knife back and forth, daring any of them to come near.

"You just let us pass and we'll find a nice safe spot to tie up Jeeval so you can fetch him later. That way we both win. If you want to keep him alive, keep your distance. One move against us, and he dies."

"What are you waiting for fools? Take them. She's harmless enough, and I can take care of myself. Just remember that I want the girl alive." Maxwell cut Jeeval's already bloody throat even more, but he didn't react in front of his men.

"Do it!" Commanded Jeeval and they did.

The two men closest to Beth came at her at once. She fired the pistol and hit one in the chest, killing him, but the explosion from the gun knocked her back into Maxwell hard enough to make him lose his balance. They both stumbled, Beth backward, Maxwell forward.

The second guard that had turned towards Beth lunged, and grabbed the wrist of the hand that held the knife. She pivoted and brought the gun up, firing again, but this one went wide. The man grinned at her failure and began to squeeze, ready to crush the delicate bones beneath his fingers in an effort to get her to drop the dagger.

When Jeeval felt Maxwell become off balance, he bent his knees and leaned forward, making Maxwell stumble further, and causing his knife hand to slip away from its position at the Jeeval's throat.

When he felt the blade slip, Jeeval tore himself from Maxwell's arms and gained his freedom. The man, who wasn't trying to deal with Beth, moved in for the kill when he saw Jeeval was safe, but Jeeval held up his hand to stop him. He wiped at the blood dripping down his neck and turned to face Maxwell, arm outstretched toward the guard, eyes locked on his enemy.

"No, he's mine. Give me your sword and help subdue the whore."

Maxwell had heard the two shots fired, and knew Beth didn't have any bullets left in the gun. She had to be protected at all costs, Jeeval could wait. He wasn't going to let her be taken. Turning, he threw his knife at the back of the man who'd just turned to go after Beth.

Surprise was on his side. The guard went down with a grunt. Maxwell rushed forward, jumping over the body to get near Beth so they were again back to back. Beth dropped the gun and pulled the other knife from her pocket slashing at the hand crushing her wrist, making the guard yelp in pain. She lashed out at him again, but missed. Back to back, she and Maxwell stood as the one remaining guard and Jeeval closed in.

Jeeval raised the sword as Maxwell slid his other knife from his boot, their eyes locked, both ready to be the victor in this fight to the death. Beth's eyes shifted back and forth as the guard with the bloody hand danced from side to side on his feet, ready to spring at her. He held a large dagger and was smiling as he waved it before her.

"Jeeval is going to slice your man to ribbons, whore. He's going to kill Maxwell and then we'll get you. Jeeval knows how to make a woman hurt, and he's going to make you beg for mercy. I bet he gives me a taste of you too. How loud can you scream little one?"

Beth moved side to side, her moves shadowing her adversaries, causing her toe to touch the gun. Should she go for it? If she tried to reload, he would be on her in a flash, but her skill with the knife was pitiful at best. Oh how she wished all those hours spent on needlepoint in the parlor had been offset by military training! Bending low, keeping her eyes on the guard, keeping her knife held before her, Beth picked up the gun.

"Kitten... no."

It was their undoing. The man lunged forward and grabbed Beth. Maxwell immediately spun and went after him. Beth lashed out with the knife but only grazed the guard's arm. He tried to pull her in front of him, to put her in the same position Jeeval had been in with Maxwell, but Maxwell was faster. He yanked Beth away and flung her aside with enough force to get her clear of their deadly battle and the fight was on.

Beth sprang to her feet, forgetting Jeeval in her panic over Maxwell, but Jeeval had not forgotten her. He sheathed his sword in one fluid motion, not wanting to hurt her, and was on her in an instant, but the second his hands touched her skin, Beth turned into a wild animal. Rage, loathing, fear, disgust, and pain filled her at the mere brush of Jeeval's fingers, and Beth went at him with all she had. Her fingers curled as she brought her hands up, nails becoming claws, needing to shed this man's blood.

An inhuman shriek tore from her throat as she kicked and scratched and twisted and fought. Jeeval tried to get a hand on her, to subdue her, but he was used to docile women, and Beth was a spinning dervish out for blood. Every time Jeeval gained the upper hand, Beth twisted away, her strength pumped by adrenaline and insane fury. She raked her claws over his eyes, blinding him and drove her knife in his side.

Stunned, Jeeval fell to his knees, but Beth's rage was not yet spent, not even close. She pulled Jeeval's coiled whip from his belt and raised it over her head, bringing it down on the shoulders of the man who had defiled and tormented her. She shrieked and cursed and cried out her pain as she whipped him over and over. Finally, exhausted from the emotions pouring through her and her mad fight, she fell to her knees and wrapped the wicked black coil around Jeeval's neck, tightening the makeshift noose.

As they knelt, Jeeval's hand came up in a desperate effort to stop his death. He clawed at the whip to no avail then looked over at his guard and Maxwell, and his eyes brightened briefly.

Maxwell was on the ground wounded, scarlet staining his shirt in a growing bloom. The guard was moving in for the kill. Turning back to Beth, his voice a hoarse whisper he taunted her even in the throes of death.

"You may think you have bested me, but Maxwell will not be with you to celebrate your victory, whore."

Turning, Beth cried out at the sight before her. When she was distracted Jeeval tried once more to make a move, to hold her and overpower her, but he had little strength. Nothing could keep Beth from Maxwell. She kicked Jeeval away and grabbed the knife in his side, twisting brutally, with finality, and then raced over to her man, picking the gun up as she went. She frantically opened it and dug in her pocket for bullets, screaming Maxwell's name, taking the time to load only one bullet in the chamber before snapping the gun closed, praying it was ready.

The guard heard her and looked from Beth to Maxwell then back to Beth, who raised the gun and fired. The unmistakable click of the hammer striking filled the air and he grinned. She pulled the trigger again and this time the blast resounded through the night, killing the guard, wiping the smile from his face.

"Maxwell! Oh God, Maxwell." She rushed forward, pulling him into her arms, cradling his head, as tears poured down her cheeks. "You have to be okay. Please. You have to be okay." Beth tore open his shirt and looked at the knife wound in Maxwell's side. She pressed her fingers to it, assessing the damage, and he groaned. It was long, maybe three inches, but the blood was just seeping out, not flowing heavily. Beth had no medical training, and Maxwell was unconscious, so she didn't know what to think. Was he dying?

"Oh, please, please, Wake up Maxwell. We're safe now, they're dead but we have to get out of here. Please wake up. I love you. I need you. Oh God, I don't know where to go. I don't know where we can hide."

She looked around in desperation. They were still near the estate and close to the lush gardens that surrounded Jeeval's estate, but they couldn't hide in the bushes. They would be found all too soon if they didn't get away from here. Her tears fell on his cheeks like a hot rain of anguish, and Maxwell's eyes fluttered open.

"Kitten?"

"I'm here. I'm right here my love. Wake up, Jeeval's dead. They're all dead."

"My head." His head? Beth ran her fingers over Maxwell's scalp and felt a large knot growing towards the back. He had struck it when he went down.

"Oh thank God. It's not you side. You're not going to die. Oh Maxwell. Can you sit up? I know it hurts."

Maxwell struggled to sit up, his eyes wide, then blinking furiously as he tried to focus. From the distance came voices. They were on the other end of the estate grounds, but coming closer. The shots had been heard. They had to get away, and they had to do it now, no matter what shape Maxwell was in.

"Help me up Kitten. Let's go. We have to get into the city and hide." Beth helped Maxwell to his feet and they went off into the darkness as quickly as they could, him leaning heavily on her as his head spun and pounded, and blood flowed down his side.

Chapter Twenty-seven

Neither knew how much time had passed as they made their way to the docks. Maxwell's head had cleared, and although his side burned with white-hot pain, he was able to walk mostly on his own. They couldn't board the ship for longer than Maxwell cared to think about, but the type of people who they encountered on the wharf were less apt to ask questions, so it was a good place to try and hide. Still, Maxwell knew they had to hurry. Jeeval and Palo had been slain by Beth. That meant they would be pursued day-and-night by both families until they were served up for justice. Jeeval was the nephew to the Emperor, and all of India would be hunting them.

It was going to take a lot more silver to grease the palm of the ship's captain now that they would be publicly sought. That was if they were lucky, and the man wasn't bought outright by those who hunted them before it was time to set sail. Guards of the state would be crawling all over the city, and leaving India was their only hope. A hearing in English court would give them a chance, being captured here meant certain pain and death. Maxwell prayed their luck would hold and they could still board the ship. Some English held a deep dislike for the people of India, though the shipping of their goods brought them riches. Maxwell hoped the Captain was a prejudiced man.

It was growing late and both of them were running on pure fear, but Maxwell pushed them onward. Wherever they hid, it had to be just right. They wound through the streets and alleys, ones which Beth had never seen, deeper and deeper into the maze of ramshackle building that surrounded the docks. Beth shivered in the night, and Maxwell didn't know if it was from fear or the mist that hung just over the ground.

"Almost kitten, just hold on."

He began to stop in front of the buildings with boarded up windows, twisting the doorknobs to see if they could gain entry. One opened but the scurry of rats could be heard, and Maxwell withdrew quickly. The next had a floor so rotted they would plunge right through. Finally he found a place that wasn't too bad. It didn't smell rotten, and there was no pitter patter of scurrying feet. Maxwell suspected the place hadn't been vacant for long, but the boards on the windows meant it was now empty and would suit their needs.

"Come on, kitten. There's no place like home." They entered cautiously but it was clear they were alone and soon let their guard down. Maxwell spied a lamp on the table and decided it couldn't hurt, the windows were boarded up, no one could see. He lit a match and a soft glow filled their humble abode.

"Stay close, Beth."

They walked through the buildings three rooms to inspect their new dwelling. It appeared to have been some type of office. There was nothing much of use. No food, no blankets, but there was an old cot in the corner of the back room.

"Guess someone liked to take naps at work. Come here kitten. Are you holding up alright?"

Beth went into his arms gratefully, whispering his name, laying her head against his heart and slipping her arms around his waist.

"I should ask you that question. I'm tired, dirty, hungry, and I ache all over, but Maxwell, you're the one who's injured."

Maxwell put her from him and brushed at a smudge of dirt on her cheek.

"My poor kitten. I'll get you right as rain in the morning, I promise. It's not going to be like this for us. I'll give you a good life somewhere quiet Beth. A place as wonderful as you deserve, a happy house, full of babies. No shacks, no desperate flights for our lives. We aren't always going to have to run. I won't do that to you."

"You won't do that to me? Maxwell, I killed three men! All you did was quit your job."

Maxwell couldn't help but chuckle at her simplistic description of his activities of the night, but he soon sobered.

"No luv, I spent a long time taking women off the streets and delivering them to that devil. And I killed a man tonight too. Murder, kidnaping, and well... rape as well, baby." His voice dropped to a whisper. "You can't forget what I am Beth, and if it ever gets to be too much, I'll understand."

"I can forget who you were Maxwell and forgive what you've done. You're a changed man. Look at where we are. Your heart has changed and you saved me, no matter what the cost was to yourself. You could have been killed. Your way of life is over. You're a wanted man because you chose to save me. You could have turned your back and delivered me into hell Maxwell, but you didn't."

"I would have died without you Beth, broken hearted over delivering you into such a fate. I love you, kitten. You're my life, and I promise I will spend it making all of this up to you. All the pain and humiliation you suffered. Kitten I... "

Beth reached up and placed her fingers to his lips, hushing him, and then brushed her lips over his. His arms slipped around her, pulling her close, his mouth brushing gently, seeking, soft and sweet. She opened and their kiss deepened as did their embrace and soon they were clinging to each other for dear life. All of the pain and terror of the night came rushing forth. They stood as one, lost yet at home, terrified, yet strangely calm and safe. Beth held Maxwell, and Maxwell held Beth, even as destiny held them in its deadly grasp.

Maxwell broke the kiss to look down into Beth's eyes. They were full of love and trust. How could they be? How? After all he'd done, after the things she had suffered because of his actions? How? But there it was. The feelings shining in her eyes were undeniable. He brought his mouth down for another soft kiss, barely moving his lips over hers, brushing gently, teasingly. God he loved her with his whole heart and soul.

An overwhelming rush of joy filled him despite their situation, and Maxwell lifted Beth off her toes, intent on swinging her around but his side had other ideas. He winced, bending forward, pain knifing through him. Beth cried out and stepped back, dismay replacing her look of love at Maxwell's obvious pain.

"We need to get you fixed up. Onto the cot with you Maxwell, and don't argue with me."

"Don't boss me woman. It's not that bad. Just a bit of a cut, I'll live."

"Damn it Maxwell. I know you don't like being told what to do, but if we don't clean and dress that wound it could fester. I need you whole. What will happen on the ship if you get sick from that bit of a cut? Do you want me to be left alone?"

Maxwell scowled at her. Of course she was right, but he certainly wasn't used to taking orders from a woman, not even Beth. Unfortunately he and Jeeval had lived with the same distorted views for a number of years.

Maxwell grumbled under his breath about bossy women, then pulled her in for a hard, possessive, 'I'm in charge here but I'll let you be the boss just this once' kiss, then lay on the cot.

The feel of the cool canvas on his back was wonderful, and he let out a sigh. He was so damn weary. It would be so easy to close his eyes and succumb to the exhaustion that was fighting to overtake him, but that wouldn't do. He watched as Beth rummaged through the last of the cabinets then heard her give a little exclamation of triumph when her search produced a bottle of whiskey.

She returned to his side and Maxwell reached for the bottle.

"Hold on you. Some is to drink, and some is for the wound. There isn't much in the bottle."

"Just a sip, pet, I don't need much. Don't think you have to sew me up, just want to numb up a bit before you go splashing this on my side."

Beth held up his head and gave Maxwell two mouthfuls of the potent liquor then lay him back down.

"Now you just close your eyes. I'll do my best to be gentle." Beth unbuttoned and removed his shirt then looked down at Maxwell with worried eyes. She'd never played nursemaid in her life and the thought of hurting him pained her. Her hands shook, and Maxwell reached up to gather them in his.

"Easy luv." Beth gave him a small smile and moved the lamp closer. She tore some strips of cloth from her petticoat and quickly splashed some of the whiskey on Maxwell's knife wound. He hissed but didn't say a word. Then carefully, Beth soaked a cloth in whiskey and wiped at the cut, cleaning the edges and doing her best to gauge the depth to be sure she didn't need to stitch him up. To her relief she didn't think so. He would have a scar from that particular battle, but it should heal on its own.

Beth made a folded pad of cloth then tied strips of her underskirt around Maxwell's abdomen until she was satisfied that the wound was properly dressed and would stay clean. She quickly stood and stripped to her chemise and bloomers, then pulled off his boots and pants. He would rest better, and she needed to feel all of him against her. She picked up Maxwell's shirt, and crawled onto the cot next to him, covering them up and turning the lamp down low.

Maxwell turned and immediately folded her up in his arms. She nuzzled into his hard, warm, chest, and let herself relax. His body offered comfort, security, safety, and love. The terror of the past few days melted away as he held her, if only for a while. Both needed rest desperately, and though Maxwell was wounded and they weren't truly safe while Jeeval's men continued to hunt them, the simple nearness of each other chased away their fears, allowing for the much needed sleep that was to come.

"My sweet baby." Maxwell whispered against her temple as he stroked her side and pulled her even closer. "Sweet, sweet girl, gonna sail away and be safe forever."

Beth heard him and opened her eyes. In them he saw questions and fear. Her eyes were full of what ifs and how's. Maxwell knew he didn't have any answers.

"I don't know kitten."

Her smile turned sad for a moment as she brought her hand up to trace the curve of his cheek. She rubbed her thumb over his lips and he opened his mouth, trying to nip it, but she pulled back fast, smiling at the return of his antics.

"I don't know either, but I know we will. We'll be together and that's what matters." That said Beth stifled a yawn. The exhausting day had taken its toll.

He kissed her eyes shut, her nose, her lips, and Beth smiled, relaxing in the haven of Maxwell's arms, drifting off to sleep amid the turmoil of their life. Maxwell soon followed. Sleep could be fought no more. Tomorrow and all its woes would come soon enough.

~~~~~~~~~~~~~~~~~~~~

Even as Beth and Maxwell were finally drifting off to sleep in the ramshackle building by the docks, Jeeval was being frantically tended to by the palace physician. His neck was inflamed from the many cuts and near strangulation, his throat almost swollen closed. The knife wound in his side could still very well be fatal. He'd lost a lot of blood. Another group of guards had found him just in time.

His loyal staff surrounded him as Jeeval lay pale and lifeless. Only two words were clear as he drifted in and out of consciousness.

"Get them."

Chapter Twenty-eight

Though they were exhausted, both Maxwell and Beth had woken only a short time after they fell asleep. At first Maxwell was tense, listening, waiting, wondering what had roused them at the same time, but then he relaxed as he realized it was nothing but their desperate need for each other. Their bodies, hearts, and minds were in sync, so much so that when one needed something, the other instinctively knew it. It could have been because their lives were in jeopardy, it could have been because of the terror they had suffered together, most likely it was because of the bond their love had created.

Beth had known almost at once that things were fine as she woke, recognizing their mutual need by their harmonized rapid heartbeats and quickened breath. As Maxwell lay wary and listening, she had begun to dance her tiny fingers up and down his chest, stroking, tickling, teasing him, but it was only when he was sure they were safe that he let his guard down completely. He turned to capture her lips with his, and grab her wandering hand, pushing it downward towards his rising cock as a moan rose from deep inside him.

Her hand encircled his shaft and she felt the power of his need encased in the silken skin, but she also felt the power that was suddenly hers. He needed her and he needed her now. She stroked his cock gently. Up and down, squeezing and releasing just as Maxwell liked, then made little rings around the head with just her fingertip.

"Don't tease woman." He grasped her hand but Beth giggled and pulled away completely. "Beth…"

"Oh hush. I have something else in mind." Maxwell looked down into her eyes and saw a teasing glint that was soon followed by a hint of innocence as she bit her bottom lip, blushed in that way he loved so very much, and slowly nodded. "Something new." She whispered.

"I happen to love new things, pet."

"Do you?" Back to being coy as her hand again trailed up and down his abdomen. "Really truly?" Up and down, lower and lower, back to stroking his shaft and teasing the tip. Her tongue darted out, wetting her lush lips, and she gave him a wicked smile.

"Promise kitten. I love new things. In fact I absolutely adore them." Maxwell pulled her tight against him and began to nibble her neck as he molded her body to his then his mouth was at her ear. "What exactly do you have in mind luv?"

"I'm not telling. Lie back and close your eyes. You're wounded, and I need to kiss it and make it better."

"I have something that's not wounded in the least that's dying for attention too, sweet."

"Why, I believe you are absolutely wicked, Maxwell!"

Maxwell let out a hardy laugh and lay back as she had requested. He did his best to stifle a grimace of pain as the knife wound in his side was jarred by the movement.

"I'll make it better. Promise."

Feeling both bold and shy, Beth welcomed the darkness. There was a hint of moonlight coming through the cracks between the boards on the windows, but it didn't add much light. She pushed Maxwell's hands up over his head, leaning forward as she straddled him low, so as not to hurt his side, and kissed the inside of each wrist. "You leave those hands right there."

"I'm happy to oblige, kitten."

Beth kissed from his wrist to shoulder, drawing her tongue along the sensitive skin of his inner arm and making him shiver. Maxwell bucked his hips up, pressing his hard cock into her moist folds but Beth let out a little scolding noise at his antics, so he forced himself to be still. She in turn gave him a little taste of what he needed and slid up and down his shaft, her dew making the journey slippery and incredibly arousing for them both as she gave his fingertips one last kiss, pressing her hardened nipples against his strong chest.

"Oh God luv."

"Ummmmm... like that?"

"Love that."

"Which part?"

"All of it Beth. Don't stop."

She danced her fingers down his arms and kissed her way along his neck, stopping to suck on the pulse point and lap at the ticklish spot behind his ear. Nibbling, kissing, lapping, then licking with the flat of her tongue, Beth then began her journey south. She reached his taunt stomach and was awed by its sculptured beauty. Rippled muscles that were hard as rock, lay under soft hot skin. Oh Lord, he was sexy, this man of hers. More kisses and licks; she couldn't get enough of him.

His skin was slightly salty, as they'd had such a hard journey that day, and Beth lapped at him as a kitten would, not to cleanse really, but to soothe the aching muscles underneath. Kisses and licks and nibbles until Maxwell's knuckles were pure white as he gripped the side of the cot in order to keep his promise not to move his hands.

Now to the spot between his hips, the lovely spot between the base of his shaft and his bellybutton. The muscles were as taut as the rest of him, and his cock rose proudly. Beth kissed the skin on each side of where Maxwell's cock lay and he hissed, his shaft jumping with need. She then placed a hand on each hip, careful so as not to touch his wound, and place the most delicate of kisses on the tip of his cock.

They both drew in a breath simultaneously. His drawn in because her mouth was so incredibly hot and her lips so ready to close around where he needed it, hers because the velvety softness of his skin pleased her so very much. To the touch of her hand, his cock was silk and steel, to her mouth it was pure velvet and marble.

A drop of precum beaded on the tip and Beth whisked it away with her tongue, making Maxwell growl with need. More kisses from tip to base, right along the pulsing vein. Her hair fell forward and lay like silk along his thigh, and Maxwell knew if she didn't take him into her mouth soon he would go mad. Just as he was about to beg, Beth's hand grasped him around the base of his cock and she lowered her mouth over the soft bulbous tip.

His hands flew from their spot at the top of the cot and fisted in her hair, not forcing her down, just winding his fingers in her silken tresses as she took him in inch by inch. God she was hot, molten wetness, silky smooth heat. She sucked in her cheeks and Maxwell groaned.

"Oh kitten, yes Beth. That's it luv."

Beth lowered her head and took in more of him. In the picture she had seen, the woman seemed to have swallowed the man whole. Down, down, sucking, then she gagged. She pulled up, embarrassed and Maxwell stroked her head.

"It's okay pigeon, easy now. It's all heaven love. Do what you can or stop if you want."

"No, I want to please you."

"Baby, anything you do pleases me."

"I mean this way."

Who was Maxwell to argue? "Use your tongue too kitten. Don't worry about taking all of me."

She kissed and licked his stomach, starting over, regaining her confidence, then reached down to gently cup his balls, occasionally giving the underside of his shaft a little flick of her tongue.

"That's it baby."

Beth grasped his shaft in one hand as she gently cradled his balls in the other, squeezing them as she took him in again. Up and down her head moved slowly as she ran her tongue along his shaft. Maxwell watched her for a moment and then rolled his eyes up into his head with a little whimper. He was in heaven. She increased her pace, her cheeks hollowing, sucking him as hard as she could while pumping her hand at the base of his cock and Maxwell moaned. Who the hell cared if she wasn't taking all of him? What she was doing was pure bliss.

In response to his moan, Beth looked up at him. She paused, eyes questioning, tongue licking her lips. "Is it okay?" Maxwell simply groaned and nodded. That little pink tongue needed to be wrapped around his cock.

She slipped an arm around his waist and held him tight as she lowered her mouth once again. Her mouth felt like hot velvet and Maxwell knew he was lost. One hand slid up and down his cock as her mouth made an aggressive descent time and time again. Her tongue swirled around the tip, her cheeks sucked in and out, velvety heat, molten and flowing. Beth laid the flat of her tongue across the head of his cock and lapped at him over and over, then once again ran the tip along the underside of the head. Doing with her tongue as she had done with her fingers, judging his pleasure by the spasms in his belly and the moans escaping through Maxwell's clenched teeth.

"Beth, oh God luv, oh so good, suck me kitten, suck me hard, so good. That's my Beth." His hips bucked wildly as he cried out her name. His muscles clenching and relaxed in time to her movements, his cock spasming with every lash of her tongue, and the hollowing of her cheeks. Maxwell didn't think he could take much more, but it was a hell of a way to go.

In the last second before he came Maxwell realized Beth was about to have a nasty surprise. She knew what happened when he climaxed of course, but she had no idea how it tasted or felt in her mouth.

"Beth, baby... Oh god. Baby wait."

She paused for a second and it was the longest moment in Maxwell's life. The loss of her hot mouth was agony.

"Do it Maxwell." Her whispered words filled him with relief even as her mouth resumed its work, and in mere seconds Maxwell was spinning out of control. Her heat and liquid fire were too much. He came hard and long, and Beth took him in as deeply as possible and drank every drop. It was part of him, and she loved him.

As his climax ended, Beth gently licked and kissed his cock, taking him in, easing him back to earth. She held his shaft and pumped slowly as it pulsed with the aftershock of his orgasm. Letting go, placing his shaft on his belly, she rested her head on his thigh and licked his cock from the base to the tip, pausing to circle the head and then licking down again over and over. His stomach muscles clenched at her movements and his cock stirred again. Beth's eyes widened but then she yawned. She couldn't help it. It had been a long day to say the least.

Maxwell reached down and pulled her up into his arms. "Better stop that kitten, you need your rest. Although I could ..." He gave her a wicked grin, but Beth shook her head.

"I am tired. Um... so tired, but I am going to hold you to that little offer in the morning." She nuzzled in close and closed her eyes as Maxwell's arms tightened around her, enveloping her in a cocoon of safety.

Maxwell thought he would follow Beth quickly into sleep but there was something tugging at his conscience. He knew it was stupid, knew he should let her rest, but just as the rhythm of her breathing had settled into the slow cadence of sleep, Maxwell whispered her name.

"Beth."

"Ummmmmmmmm?"

"Kitten, are you happy now? I mean, well, God pet, I don't want you to wake up one morning and realize you hate me for everything I did to you. I stole your life away."

"Maxwell I've never been happier. I love you. My 'life' before all this consisted of an attempt to force me into marriage with a man three times my age, and when I refused, being packed off to a strange country to live with a bunch of overbearing missionaries who were preparing me to live my life trying to bring religion to women trapped in the harems. I was lonely and miserable."

Beth could see the doubt that filled Maxwell's eyes even in the faint moonlight. She stroked the side of his head and furrowed her brow, scowling at him.

"But you were free."

"Listen to me. I'm glad you kidnaped me. I mean I know that sounds silly but... Okay, so you could have come up and asked if you could call on me. Maybe brought me flowers or come and try to talk to me in the market, but it didn't happen that way, and its all water under the bridge."

"Water under the bridge! Beth we're running for our lives. You were abused by Jeeval, Palo touched..."

"Maxwell stop. Yes, all that happened, and is happening, but I'm with you. I love you. Now hold me close and go to sleep."

"Bossy wench." Maxwell was smiling broadly behind his gruff words, his heart at ease. He kissed her soundly and gathered her close, rocking her slightly as they both drifted off for some much needed rest.

Maxwell awoke only once more during the night of their wild escape, Beth not at all. Both were exhausted. He smiled down at her and gently kissed her forehead, heart swelling with intense feelings that were still foreign and a bit unsettling, but oh so welcome. He slowly adjusted her knickers, tying the waist ribbon with quick, practiced fingers, and pulling them closed between her thighs, then lowering her camisole over her breasts.

Maxwell loved it when she looked like his golden wanton beauty, but knew his self-control could only be stretched so far. He longed to suckle and kiss those delectable buds and stroke Beth between her silky thighs, but Maxwell reined in his rising need and decidedly wicked thoughts, knowing they both needed the rest. Finally, he retrieved his shirt which had slipped to the floor, and covered them both, then settled in beside his girl, sliding his arms securely around her.

"Love you kitten." Beth made a sweet cooing sound and nuzzled closer to his chest, her lips making the cutest little smacking sound, before deep sleep overtook her again. Maxwell sighed, content despite their surroundings and perilous situation, and closed his eyes as sleep overtook him too, moments later.

Chapter Twenty-nine

All through the night hours and into the dawn as Maxwell and Beth slept hidden away in the abandoned wharf building, Jeeval and Palo's men scoured the docks searching for the fugitives. They questioned everyone they came upon. Lining palms with silver, loosening the tongues of those who had seen them, and making others slippery with lies. Facts and fantasies became jumbled in search of riches, and that was the only thing that boded well for Beth and Maxwell.

Some claimed to have seen them boarding a ship, some as they went past in the night. The guards were smart enough to garner truth from fiction for the most part, but checked out every lead, forcing their way onto ships, peering into every cabin and hold, paying each captain to keep his eye out for the pair, promising untold wealth for their capture.

From the multitude of tales they garnered Maxwell was wounded. Many claimed to have had seen a young blonde pair fitting Maxwell and Beth's description. Sources told of Maxwell holding onto Beth, their gait slightly shuffled as he pressed his palm to his side. Both were disheveled. This information pleased the guards immensely. Perhaps Maxwell had a fatal wound and they would find the bitch alone and cowering amid the rats in some warehouse.

The people also described Beth to a tee. Petite, flawless skin, strikingly beautiful, golden hair plaited and bound up. Just her presence on the seedy wharf had drawn attention and curiosity, though they hadn't spoken to a soul and had moved quickly. She was completely out of place on the docks. The plain dress Maxwell had bought did nothing to hide her natural genteel demeanor.

Most everyone spoke volumes as Jeeval and Palo's men laid silver in their palms or threatened bodily harm to any who dared to give aid. Most everyone that is, but there was one who turned away. She slid back into the shadows, her scarred cheek and milky blind eye hidden in the darkness. She had no desire to talk with anyone from the estates. Her business was here, her home was here, and had been for many years now. Nothing mattered but her next meal, that and keeping her own skin safe. She looked out for herself, kept to herself mostly, and scorned the likes of them.

"Whoever they be, I hope they slip from your grasp. Nothing but devils in fancy clothes you are."

Mattie muttered at the men searching the docks, and then pulled her shawl tightly around her shoulders as she began to follow them at a safe distance. She kept back in the shadows as they searched and questioned, questioned and searched, smiling as the night wore on and they came up empty handed. It was a small victory over those she despised, but a victory none-the-less. An hour after dawn she tired of her game and decided to go about her business, and headed to the place she called home.

Shuffling down the dirt alleys, Mattie hummed to herself and let her mind drift back to the time life had been kind and she was happy. It had been so long ago, but the memories were vivid. They were the only ones that didn't fill her heart with pain.

She'd a young girl, barely sixteen, just married and starting her life. It had been an arranged marriage, but she'd loved her husband dearly, having known him all her life. Their families were close. When she was a child, he was like an older brother, and when she grew older, Mattie fell in love. His family was in the import business and did well. The marriage was profitable for both.

Happiness filled their household for the short time fate allowed it. Her husband's family had given him his own small office, their home was cozy and full of love, she never wanted for attention, but destiny never seems to allow us much time for bliss. It comes in short fleeting bursts so we can recognize how exquisite it is, and then steals it away so we spend our lives yearning for it to come back. One afternoon, three weeks into her marriage, fate destroyed Mattie's new found happiness in the blink of an eye as surely as it had smiled on her only the day before.

She remembered walking down the main road, sun kissing her bronze cheeks, dark eyes twinkling, humming in much the same way she was now as she headed for the market. Her mind focused on the supper she'd planned for her husband, but that supper had never been put on the table. She had been kidnaped that day much in the same way Beth had, taken for a rich man's harem. Stolen from her life and love, her heart shattered.

Though her captors and done their best to beat her into submission, Mattie had a fierce will, and would not accept her fate. She'd fought them time and time again, and was nothing but trouble. She endured all they did to her, and had finally given up on her despite her beauty. First she had been tossed to the estate guards for their pleasure, and when that didn't break her troublesome spirit, Mattie was given to the kitchen staff for whatever use they saw fit.

She'd been made a scullery slave, working over the hot coals, preparing feasts for those she loathed, wishing she could poison the lot of them. Each night she cried into the straw that was her bed, as she marked off the days of her captivity with a small cut to her forearm.

One slit for each driving blade of sorrow into her heart. Weeks past, then a month, then two, and then the accident happened.

Mattie was squatting over the coal grate, stirring them up when a passing someone pushed her. She flung her arms out and managed to avoid falling face first into the burner, but her arm swept some coals out of the grate as she sprawled upon the stone floor, flinging them against the skin of her beautiful face, burning her cheek, blinding her eye, disfiguring her for life.

She had been tossed from the estate then, left to die from her wounds on the docks where no one cared. Disoriented, feverish, weak, utterly lost and alone, she stumbled into an abandoned building much like Beth and Maxwell had, and curled up to either mend or die.

She lay near death as fever swept through her body. At times not caring what happened to her. She had no life to return to and nowhere to go. She'd found the freedom she'd longed for, but was trapped by the circumstances fate had heaped upon her. Returning to her family and husband would bring shame upon them because she had been raped, and her disfigurement would bring only pity. She couldn't return to those she loved and bring them so much sorrow. Death was perhaps a kinder fate than a life full of loneliness and despair.

After a week of teetering on the brink of death, fate stepped in again, and pulled her through. Like it or not, Mattie's spirit kicked in, and it lit a small spark inside her that urged her onward. She was not meek enough to simply curl up and die. A small flicker of hope danced alongside of the flame that was her spirit, telling her that maybe she would be forgiven and loved despite everything destiny had cast her way.

When she was strong enough to leave the building, Mattie went home, only to find a burned out shell. The house she grew up in was the same, as were the homes of her husband's family. All traces of those she loved had been erased; leaving her with nothing, everyone she loved was gone.

In the end, Mattie had sunk to her knees in disbelief. Guilt and despair lay heavy on her shoulders as she accepted the fact that she would never find them. Her family wasn't the lowest of the castes but they weren't mighty and rich either, and in the end they were at the mercy of those above them. She couldn't be certain that the fires and disappearance of her loved ones was the result of her defiance and rebellion at the estate, but suspected what had befallen them may have been ordered by the one who held her in twisted act of revenge for the trouble she had caused in his household.

Her mind was pulled away from its haunting memories as she reached her destination. It was the place she now called home, a least for a little while. It was nothing but a boarded up building just like all the others she'd lived in for a time, and she'd claim it as her own until chased out by those stronger than her.

For twenty years she had lived this life, becoming a poor beggar on the streets and moving from place to place. Eating scraps and pleading for coins, resting at night in shacks or hovels, unable to find work as a servant or a washer woman because of her disfigurement, and too hideously ugly to even be a prostitute. Her life was a day to day struggle to survive, but the spark of her spirit kept her fighting to live no matter what kind of life it was. The spark was fueled by the need for revenge. It was all she had, but it had kept her going day to day.

Mattie swiped the back of her hand over her eyes as she turned the doorknob of the place she called home. Her bones were weary from following the guards all night, and seeing them had brought back things better left buried. She stepped in, and she froze. Something wasn't right. Listening, she heard the sound of a faint but very distinct snore coming from the back room. Some beggar or urchin child had crawled in and taken shelter during the night. Well whoever it was had to go. This was her place and she'd fight tooth and nail for it.

Walking softly so she could secretly observe the intruder, Mattie silently made her way to the room with the old cot. She stepped into the doorway and her eyes widened in shock. This was no street beggar. It was them, the pair fleeing from the estate. It had to be. Any doubt in her mind was chased away by the brass slave collar around Beth's neck. They were the runaways to be sure, but what should she do? They spelled trouble. On the other hand, they needed help and the hatred that still burned in her soul for those who had destroyed her life made Mattie's fear and gruff indifference melt away.

Noting the scattered clothing and the out of reach weapons, Mattie grasped a nearby chair and noisily dragged it closer, sitting down heavily even as Maxwell bolted straight up in bed. His head whipped from side to side, eyes widening as he saw Mattie, cursing and searching for a knife.

"Here now, I mean you no harm. Besides, I'm just an old woman. You have no need of that."

Mattie gestured towards one of the knives. "I'll go in the other room so you and the lady can dress, and then we'll talk. I know who you are and I know who's looking for you, but you have nothing to fear. They're the ones who did this to me." She gestured to her disfigured face, "Stole my life away. I'll not give you up to the likes of them."

Maxwell looked her over from head to toe. She was older, but he couldn't guess her age, her face and hands were weathered, her clothing rags. Maxwell had no doubt she lived a life full of struggle. The harshness of her life was written in the lines of sorrow upon her face. If anyone could benefit from Jeeval's money, he guessed the woman before him could. The beggar woman probably hadn't seen a silver coin in years. Why the hell hadn't he heard her come in? He was supposed to be protecting them.

"Maxwell?"

"It's okay kitten. Stay behind me and get dressed."

Beth had woken at the same time he had. She sat behind him now, body pressed close, fingers gripping his shoulders. She backed away a little, hand tugging uselessly at the neckline of her low cut camisole, trying to pull it up over her slave collar.

"Don't fret over that Missy. I already saw it. Wore one myself a long time ago. Hateful things they are. That's why my word's the truth. I'll not give you over to them devils from hell. You dress yourselves and I'll be waiting."

Mattie left and Maxwell felt Beth relax at the old woman's words. "Don't be conned so easily pet. Look at her. A pocket of silver would make her life easier."

Maxwell rose and began to pull on his breeches, his distrustful blue eyes meeting Beth's as he retrieved one of the knives and slipped it in his belt. He was full of skepticism. He'd slipped and not heard the woman come in, but now no one would make him let his guard down.

"No Maxwell, you look at her. Didn't you see her face? She said she'd been a harem slave, but we both know she didn't look like that then. Whatever happened, they were responsible, and she hates them as much as we do. I can feel it."

"You think with your heart kitten. I won't allow your pity for those who've suffered the same as you put us in jeopardy. Think about Siri. She loves Jeeval."

"You don't know that!" Her voice was incredulous. How could he say such a thing? "She may have wanted to be free as much as I did Maxwell. You can't know how she felt inside."

"We know nothing about her Beth. I want you to just sit quietly and let me do the talking."

Beth snorted, eyes flashing. "You must be joking! I'm not some simpering little thing who will sit back and let you take charge. You knew I had spirit when you decided to go on this little adventure, so don't expect me to roll over and be obedient now. Don't be so pig headed."

"Beth" Maxwell's voice was a low growl as he advanced on her, but Beth squared her shoulders and puffed up her chest, determined to make her five foot frame formidable. Her lower lip stuck out and her eyes flashed with indignation at his overbearing attitude, and Maxwell's simmering anger began to boil. He wasn't far removed from the days of docile, submissive women, and a fiery Beth, while being a thing of beauty, still tried his temper.

"I mean it Maxwell. Don't expect me to allow you to make all the decisions. I like her and think we can trust her."

"Damn it kitten, you don't know her." He wanted to shake her. Hell, he wanted to paddle her lovely bum until it was bright red and she was willing to see reason. No, that was a bad thought. Even now, thoughts like that made his lower region stir. Bloody hell this woman had possessed him body and soul.

They stood, chest to chest, Beth's chin tipped up in defiance, daring him, taking a stand, drawing the line on how things would be between them, but Maxwell was determined as well. He loved her spunk. Savored her fire, but there were limits, and she had to know that. Not that he would ever try to dominate her completely, but in some things she had to listen to him.

Quick as lightening, Maxwell spun Beth sideways and delivered five hard fast swats to her backside. When he was done, Maxwell pulled Beth up tight against him, gripping her arms fiercely, possessively, as he growled in her ear. "We will talk to the beggar woman, Beth and we will ask her questions, but if I get one hint of danger and tell you to move or run, you are to do it in an instant do you understand?"

That said his tongue darted out and skimmed across the shell of her ear, then gave her a little nip sending a shiver down Beth's back as she sagged against Maxwell's hard chest, nodding her assent.

Growly masterful Maxwell brought up her ire, but along with her anger was undeniable passion. She should be angry but all her fury had fled with his harsh whispered words and rough possessiveness. He was trying to protect her, them, in the only way he knew how. She'd told him he'd known who and what she was when they gotten into this, well the same held true for her. Beth knew of Maxwell's powerful dominant streak from day one, and there was no denying it. She would do as he asked.

Maxwell felt her melt into his arms and knew he'd won this battle. "Thank you, kitten. Love you."

"Ummmmmmmm. You're an insufferable beast."

Maxwell chuckled and gave her another playful swat, kissing her hard. Beth welcomed his claiming and opened her lips eagerly as his tongue darted in to dance across hers. His fingers entwined in her hair and he deepened the kiss, taking her completely as the world fell away if only for a moment. Even now, the strength of their desire and the flame of their love couldn't be diminished. With a groan, Maxwell broke it off and set a dazed Beth away from him.

"Remember, I don't mind the talking, sweet, but if I sense danger and tell you to run, you listen. Understand."

"I will Maxwell, but I'm telling you she's safe."

Maxwell sighed, slightly exasperated but also amused. "As long as you do what I say if I think she's up to something."

Beth rolled her eyes and huffed at him, shaking her head as she strode past, not looking back to see if he was following, which of course he was, right at her heels. They arrived to find Mattie siting at the large wooden desk. She'd pulled up chairs for them while listening to their little spat and chuckling to herself. Oh yes, this pair was in love. She hoped they made it. Fate had to be kind to someone.

They sat across from her, Beth leaning back relaxed, Maxwell on the edge of the chair, as Mattie told them what she'd told no other living soul. Maxwell began to relax and Beth began to quietly cry as she talked. It seemed Mattie's words opened a dam deep inside, and the feelings of despair and hurt both women had suffered came rushing out.

"Here now, honey. I didn't mean to upset you. Been through a lot haven't you? It'll be all right. I'll help you."

Mattie rose and came around the desk towards Beth, but Maxwell sprang to his feet, quickly barring her way. Mattie sighed, not really fazed or surprised by

Maxwell's attitude. He'd been through a lot too, and it was clear he loved the woman beside him.

"I'm not going to hurt her, but you don't know that for sure yet, do you? Care to tell me a bit more about yourselves? I've heard the talk. You killed a very rich man and some estate guards while escaping from an estate. From what I hear he's offered up a huge reward to have you back, and he wants you very much alive."

"Jeeval didn't die?" Beth stood her voice incredulous. "How?" She'd twisted the blade in his guts, felt his blood gush over her hands. Yes, and then she'd been distracted by the sight of Maxwell lying lifeless on the ground.

"It's the Emperor's nephew you're running from?" Mattie's eyes grew wide and her determination to help them grew. The whispered rumors of the depraved activities that took place in the estate of Jeeval had reached even her ears while Mattie had begged on the street. He was the worst of all those in power.

"Yes, it was Jeeval. I thought I killed him. I tried to."

"They say he lives. He's alive and furious, and determined to find the two of you. You were a pretty bauble my dear, and you both betrayed him."

"She never was his to have."

Mattie could almost see Maxwell's protectiveness for Beth. It emanated from his very being, surrounding them both like a shield. He spread his arms and back into her body, keeping her far from Mattie. Beth scowled at her watch dog but sat back down. Maxwell was just doing what was in his heart.

"Maxwell, it's okay. Please sit down." Maxwell did, but he pulled his chair so it touched Beth's, and took her hand.

"It truly is okay. I admire your loyalty to your lady. Please believe me when I say I'd like nothing better than to best those bastards by helping the two of you. Do you have a plan to get out of India? What about food and clothes? You can't go about like you are. Everyone is looking for you."

"We do have a plan, or we did anyway. Hopefully it's still in place. Can we still get on the ship Maxwell?"

Maxwell sighed. He was outnumbered, and Mattie did seem genuine in her desire to help them. Poor woman had been served up a life of hell by men just like those who were hunting them. He shook his head and looked from Mattie to Beth, then back again.

"All right, I give in, you two win. I'll tell you everything, and maybe between the three of us we can find a way to keep Beth safe."

"What?! "

"Down kitten. I simply meant..."

"I know what you meant, and you can get that noble idea out of your head this minute. We are in this together, not for just me. I won't go anywhere without you. Don't even think about putting me on a ship alone."

"Whoa, easy love. I couldn't live without you if I wanted to baby, and I certainly don't want to. Now hush up and let me fill Mattie in."

Beth glowered and scrunched her nose at Maxwell for a moment, then pursed her lips in a little kiss. Maxwell thought she was just too damn adorable and got lost for just an instant before shaking himself and turning back to the matter at hand.

"Yes we have a ship, least we did. Can't say what the Captain will do with us now." Maxwell went on to fill in Mattie as Beth listened and interjected at times, until their entire story was on the table. Mattie nodded silently, scowled, and shook her head, becoming more determined with every second to help her new found friends. When the tale was told, Maxwell agreed to give Mattie some of their money. They needed help, and help had arrived in the form of the woman before them.

First she would buy decent clothing for herself in an effort to taker her from beggar woman to servant. She'd been on the streets for a long time and unfortunately, her face would still be recognizable, but she was the best bet they had. Once she had clothing, Mattie would discretely buy food, clothing for them, and other needed things. It had to be done carefully, and Mattie knew of a few merchants who wouldn't tell tales. As for the rest, she'd been invisible to most of the folks on the wharf for years, folks tend to stop seeing what's right in front of their face day in and day out, especially if it's something that makes you want to look away. Hopefully no one would notice her now.

Beth simply had to have some dresses and a trunk, and Maxwell at least a change of clothes. When they arrived at the ship they couldn't be empty handed. They were a British couple from the mission going home to tend Beth's mum, not runaway fugitives, at least that's what everyone simply had to believe in order for them to survive.

Chapter Thirty

Captain Trammell watched as a group of Jeeval's guards headed back to the dock. They had asked about a British couple, and Trammell was certain the blonde man he'd met the day before had to be part of the pair. Escaped fugitives they said, him a murderer and thief, and her, an escaped concubine with blood on her hands too. There was a huge reward for their capture, but the good captain had held his tongue. He had riches and a ship to bring in more, what he didn't have, was a beautiful woman of his own.

He hated the rich men of power who had it all and held no respect for the British who now governed their country. They had umpteen wives and concubines, estates full of gold, armies to do their bidding. They disgusted him. He also hated this country with its sticky heat that made you gasp for breath and sun that beat down mercilessly day after day. He did business here only because it was so lucrative.

Maybe if the woman was to his tastes, and she had to be beautiful if she'd been in a palace, he'd find a way to get rid of the 'husband' and keep her for himself. Once they set sail, his word was law, and none of his men would go against him. He'd keep her on the ship until she saw things his way, then find a place somewhere to keep her and never sail for this Godforsaken country again. Keeping her was risky, but he had an idea she would be worth it. Besides, there were other places to do trade besides this God forsaken land.

One of Trammell's men came up behind him and watched them go. "What did they want?" The word 'they' was said with much scorn. Marcus hated the Indian people as much as he did. Both were bigots through and through, but bigotry ran rampant, and there was no love lost between the two countries.

They're asking about a British couple. Seems they escaped from one of the estates. There's a big reward for anyone who knows where they are."

"Think it's the ones who'll be sailing with us?"

"I know they are. Something was off with the man who came to buy passage."

"Did you tell them?"

"Nope, not gonna either. We'll get them out of India if they still come to the ship. You have any problems with that Marcus?"

"None Captain."

"That's good Marcus, very good. I need a man I can count on. Could be you'll see gain from the undertaking too."

Captain Trammell twisted the end of his dark mustache as he gazed off into the distance, watching the estate guards until they were lost in the crowd on the docks. He wet his lips, thinking of the girl, and hoped she wouldn't be found until she and her 'husband' made it safely to his ship.

~~~~~~~~~~

After securing decent clothing for herself then buying and hiding the other needed things, Mattie headed for where the tall ships were docked. Maxwell had mentioned the name of the one they were sailing on, "The Talisman" and she had a little idea in mind to help ensure the couples safety. This was definitely not in the plan, and Maxwell would probably be mad as hell that she was here, but someone had to do a little scouting to find out of the ship's captain was a decent man or if they'd be walking into a trap.

She stood tall in her new clothes. Proper maid's outfit it was. Navy blue dress with a starched white apron and cap, no sari for her, she was a ladies maid out to do an errand for her employers. There were many English couples who had hired native women to work in their homes, even at the mission there were servants. It was seen as a way to spread the word of their God. She just hoped she could convince the good captain that she was what she claimed.

Ah... there it was, "The Talisman", a fine looking ship. Mattie started up the gangway but was immediately headed off by a young sailor.

"Here now, what do you think you're doing? We've no need for a maid on board." The men behind him working on the deck chuckled, and Mattie squared her shoulders, intent on looking like she was on a mission, which in a sense she was. Nothing would sway her from helping Beth and Maxwell.

"I have business with the captain. My Mister and Missus sent me. They'll sailing with you at dawn."

The man knew of their passengers and decided he'd better go get Captain Trammell, though he couldn't for the life of him figure out who would hire a woman as ugly as the one before him. "Aye, you wait here. He don't like women on the ship."

Mattie's eyebrows rose at that. He didn't, did he? Where did that leave Beth? Apparently money came before superstition. "Fine. I'll wait, but my Master is waiting too."

The man headed below, and soon reappeared with Captain Trammell. The Captain walked slowly down the gangway, eyeing up Mattie, as she did the same to him, both wondering if the other worked for the side of Jeeval and Palo. He knew in his gut the 'married couple' coming on board from the mission were really the ones being sought, and therefore the chances of them having a maid were slim to none, but he'd play along for a while.

"What can I do for you?"

"My Master sent me. He spoke to you and booked passage. He and the Misses wish for me to accompany them on their voyage. She's so very distraught over her mum and he doesn't want her to be without another woman's companionship. He's a good man, and hates to see her tears."

"One woman on board is too many. Two is out of the question."

"I have silver." Mattie held out her little purse and gave it a jangle.

Captain Trammell was still suspicious. "Why didn't he come back to book your passage? I don't do business with women."

"Like I said, the Misses is distraught. He didn't want to leave her. I've been with them now for going on six years and she's very dear to me, poor thing. She needs a woman's touch during the long journey. The Master, he's good with her, but I can soothe her better over time."

"That's all I need. Two women! Especially one who needs coddling. I haven't the room, and their cabin won't fit you."

I don't need a cabin. A pallet anywhere will be enough for me. I imagine the Mister will spend most of his days on deck and I'll tend to my Miss in her cabin. We won't be a bother."

"You're another mouth to feed."

"And you'll be paid well for it. Same as what you got for the Mister and Misses. All of it British silver."

Captain Trammell didn't want the burden of this ugly woman, but on the other hand, he wasn't one to pass up such a large amount of money either. Another bag of silver would ease the bother this one would be, and he could always toss her overboard. Besides, she certainly wouldn't be a temptation to his men with that face; in fact she might scare away the storm gods.

"You do your share to cook meals, especially for your employers."

"Yes Captain. I will. I'll do everything they need."

"Fine. See the three of you are here at dawn. We'll set sail with or without you, silver or no."

"Thank you kindly Captain. The Master and Misses will be much obliged."

Mattie nodded her head in goodbye and turned away, satisfied that the Captain had no intentions of turning Beth and Maxwell in. He seemed a bit underhanded. His shifty eyes, and that pencil thin mustache over those fleshy lips made him look sneaky as a rat, and with beady eyes to boot. But his greed and desire for money seemed to be working in their favor, so she would simply keep her own eyes on him and let him get Beth and Maxwell out of the country. Now all she had to do was tell Maxwell she was going to be on the ship too.

Chapter Thirty-one

"You did what?!" Maxwell stared at Mattie in shock; eyes open wide, eyebrows reaching up nearly to his blond curls.

"I went to see the captain. It's okay Maxwell. It's all set. He's not planning on turning you in."

"Oh well that's good to know!" The sarcasm and anger in Maxwell's voice made Mattie cringe, but she pushed her shoulders back and raised her chin, fixing a fierce look of determination on her face.

"I'd say it's a damn fine thing to know. He's a greedy one, but the ship's safe. We sail at dawn."

Maxwell abruptly stopped the pacing he'd been doing and turned, gripping the back of a chair with white knuckles. It was quite evident he was about to explode, but his next question came out in a sinister whisper all the same.

"We?"

Mattie huffed and set her jaw, staring Maxwell down. Well trying to anyway. It wasn't an easy task, especially when he was this angry.

"Yes we. I'm going too. As Beth's maid."

Maxwell opened his mouth to protest but Mattie rushed on. "You need me. Three's better than two if there's trouble. I told him Beth's not well, that she's missing her mum and all. She needs extra attention. Think about it Maxwell. What if there is trouble. The three of us can do better than you two alone. I'm certain that captain isn't about to turn you over to Jeeval, but he seems sly all the same. I mean we need to risk passage because it's the only way out, but you're going to need help onboard. He wants that silver enough to risk his hide, but what's to say he won't cause trouble once we set sail? With me along, Beth will never be alone, and I'll be places on the ship as a servant where you wouldn't be able to go without raising eyebrows. I'll hear talk you won't be privy to."

"Oh and I suppose you were quite liberal with my money when buying your passage. You just said yourself there might be danger. I bloody well don't need to worry about you as well as Beth if there is. You're not coming."

"Maxwell."

"No Beth, Mattie stays here. I don't want to have to protect both of you. I'll not risk more than our lives. It's us they want. Mattie doesn't need to be pulled into this. Three may be better than two in trouble, but maybe not either. Two are harder to take care of than one."

Both women let out indignant shrieks and turned on him, shouting the same exact thing in unison. "I don't need taking care of!" The perfect timing of their declarations would have been amusing if not for the very real anger behind their words. Maxwell was in for it now.

"How dare you Maxwell? After everything I did to help get us out of that estate. I fought and I killed ..."

"Beth. I'm sorry. I didn't mean ..."

"And I've been looking after myself since you were in nappies Maxwell! Don't talk about me as if I'm some helpless old ..."

"Mattie"

"Don't you Mattie me. I can look after myself and do a damn fine job of looking out for the two of you to boot. There will be times when you have to be on deck. It will be expected. Most men don't hover over their wives. If you do, you'll appear weak and foolish. That means Beth will be below by herself sometimes, and that's not good. This way we can play up the troubled Misses act so she's never alone."

Mattie quickly turned to Beth who was beginning to feel as if both people in the room thought she was feeble. "And before you get your ire up love, all's I'm saying is that there is safety in being together. You're a very pretty woman honey, and you'll be alone on a ship of men who are gonna get real lonely before our journey's done. I'm coming on that ship Maxwell, like it or not. Besides, if you show up without me now, it will raise questions. Just accept the fact that you need me."

Beth had to hide her smile. Oh Maxwell had met his match with Mattie. Her own anger had slipped away at the stricken look on Maxwell's face as his head snapped back and forth between them. He was so protective of her and it really was sweet, as long as he remembered that she wasn't going to always agree with him or do what he said.

"Maxwell, I want her to come. We need her to come." She walked up behind Maxwell and slid her hands onto his shoulders, squeezing gently, pressing her forehead to his back at the feel of tension inside him. Poor Maxwell, taking on the weight of the world; he'd traded a life of luxury for one of being a fugitive, and he'd done it all for her.

"She's a good friend, and we are in very short supply of those. Besides, it's only natural that I would want my maid with me. Her presence helps add to our disguise."

"Were there really maids at the mission, Beth? I'd have thought it would be seen as a frivolous excess. Against God and all that."

"There are serving girls and maids. It was seen as a chance to better their lives and spread the word of our faith. No one had their personal maid, but there are native women working at the mission. Mattie... well Mattie would have been welcomed in as an act of charity." Beth immediately turned towards her new friend with a mournful look, her eyes apologizing for her words.

"You aren't saying anything but the truth, Beth. My face has made life hard. I am scorned, shunned, and feared. No one would employ me. Who wants to look at a monster day in and day out?"

"Oh bloody hell, how am I supposed to argue with the both of you? I'm telling you two right now that if she comes, things are not going to be like this on the ship. I'm not spending all my days at sea being ordered about. I make the decisions, and you both will listen to me. Is that understood?"

Beth scooted around so she was in front of Maxwell, her hands sliding from his shoulders as she wrapped her arms around his neck and smiled her brightest smile. "So she can come?"

"Woman if you think you're going to get away with not answering my question you're wrong." Maxwell did his best to scowl at her, but had to look away. She was too damn cute standing there, batting her eyes; still, he didn't give in.

Beth looked at Mattie to find the woman smiling at her. Mattie winked her good eye and nodded.

"Okay, okay, we promise. No ordering. You're the boss. We'll do what you say Maxwell. Thank you, my love. You'll see, you'll be glad Mattie's with us."

Maxwell just shook his head and sighed, marveling again at the effect Beth had on him. Never in his life had he met a woman who could charm him with such ease. She made his heart pound like great booms of thunder and his brains melt like butter in the sun, all with just a pout and the blinking of those brilliant green eyes. Oh he did he plan to hold her to her promise, but he also knew that he'd be doing his share of giving in too. Thing was, it didn't seem to matter so much anymore. Not as long as she was safe and loved him.

~~~~~~~~~~~~~~~~~~

They left for the ship before dawn, preferring to travel in darkness. Jeeval's guards were sure to be hunting for them on the docks and Maxwell wanted them on and below deck before first light. Mattie had been given money to hire a carriage after it was agreed that was the best course of action. A British couple wouldn't travel any other way, and those searching for them would be looking for two people, not three.

Beth had suggested she cut her hair in order to change her appearance, but Maxwell wouldn't hear of it, telling her he had other ways of making her look different. Instead, she had pinned it up securely under a large bonnet, doing her best to hide it. When she was done, Maxwell had her bind her breasts to try and change her figure. An extra, loosened corset and all her petticoats were also added in an effort to increase the size of her hips and waist. His hope was to make her less appealing if that were possible. The added underclothes made her dresses tight, but it wasn't too obvious.

They sat in the carriage, Mattie in her maid outfit, Maxwell in an Englishman's coat and breeches, Beth in a proper, high neck gown that covered her slave collar. All of them were feeling very vulnerable, and rode to the ship in silence. Each lost in thought and each scanning the road for estate guards. Luckily the only group of guards they did encounter gave them a quick once over and turned away.

Mattie wanted to elbow Maxwell with glee. She knew they hadn't been given a serious inspection because the men were searching for two people fleeing, most likely on foot, not three riding plain as day in a carriage, but she simply smiled in the darkness. Maxwell saw her but said nothing. She was right after all, her presence added to their disguise. They arrived without incident, much to everyone's relief, and Maxwell led their small procession up the gangway.

One of the ship's men heard them coming, and called out to Captain Trammell. He came to greet his passengers, eager to get his first look at Beth. As they boarded the ship, Captain Trammell quickly stepped forward to help Beth onto the deck, before Maxwell could turn and assist her. This, of course, did not sit well with Maxwell. He didn't want a hand laid on his woman, not even one single finger, and it didn't matter that it was done as a polite gesture. He grimaced and took Beth's elbow, moving her quickly, away from the captain's helping hand, to the point of being obviously rude.

Beth's eyes widened but she held her tongue. She was all set to be meek and heartsick in the eyes of everyone on board. She gave the captain a slight, polite nod, and stepped to the side, pressing against Maxwell and lowering her eyes.

"Welcome aboard the Talisman. It's a pleasure to meet you Ma'am."

Captain Trammell tried to take Beth's hand again, but she folded hers together, mumbling a quiet thank you. Maxwell glared at the man openly and thought Mattie had been right in her assessment that the good captain was a shifty character. He'd been all bluster and gruff, complaining about passengers and such when Maxwell spoke to him, and now here he was, all polite like, just so he could touch Beth. Well Maxwell wasn't about to let him think he'd be putting his hands on his woman.

"My wife is feeling poorly Captain. If you would be so kind as to have our baggage brought aboard and show us to our cabin, it would be much appreciated."

Their eyes met and each stared at the other with an open challenge. Maxwell telling of a world of pain if the Captain laid a finger on Beth, Captain Trammell making it clear that he knew they were running and felt he had the upper hand, all he needed was time.

Beth, seeing the direction things were headed, swayed on her feet and made a little noise of distress in an effort to stop all out warfare. Both men reacted at once, Maxwell scooping Beth up into his arms before Captain Trammell could steady her with his outstretched hand. Beth, thoroughly embarrassed by Maxwell's overreaction, turned her face into his chest to hide the scarlet flush of her cheeks.

"As I said, my wife is feeling poorly and needs to rest. If you'll simply show us to our cabin, we'll be out of your way."

The captain was clearly irritated, but couldn't very well do otherwise with Beth practically swooning in Maxwell's arms. He'd keep up the charade for now.

"Very well, I haven't decided where she'll sleep yet." Captain Trammell gestured towards Mattie. "We're still filling the hold. She'll have to stay with you till we sail."

"Oh don't worry about me. I'll be bedding down on a pallet right outside the Misses' cabin. Be able to hear her if she needs me. There's nothing these ears don't hear."

Now Beth had to hide a smile as well as her blushing cheeks. Mattie had sure taken care of him. Captain Trammel's wasn't going to get rid of her 'maid' that easy. Not only would the woman be in a position to hear Beth if she called, anyone entering the cabin would have to get past her first!

Chapter Thirty-two

After they were shown their cabin, Beth asked Mattie to see about their things, since it would be expected.

"I need to have a few words alone with Maxwell."

Mattie looked from one to the other and nodded, giving Maxwell just the tiniest of smirks. Beth was going to flay him alive for that performance on deck. She knew sparks were going to fly over Maxwell's attitude. Mattie quietly left the cabin, closing the door behind her. When she was gone, Beth rose from the chair Maxwell had set her in, locking it. Turning, she put her hands on her hips and narrowed her eyes at Maxwell.

"What exactly do you think you were doing up there?"

"What?"

"Oh you know what. You were puffed up like some insanely jealous peacock, and being very rude. He didn't even do anything! You could have gotten us thrown off the ship Maxwell."

"He touched you!"

"He touched me?! He touched me? Captain Trammell helped me onto the ship and then offered me his hand in a greeting. It is customary in civilized society you know. He wasn't acting like a barbarian, unlike you."

"Beth the man looked you over as if you were on the auction block, and I'm telling you, he liked what he saw. I'll not have him putting his hands all over you."

"You'll not have it? Well I have a say in it, and I say we act like normal people. Normal, Maxwell, polite and dignified. I can play up my distress over my mother as much as possible, but we don't want to make him suspicious."

"He already knows Beth. Didn't you see the way he looked at me? He knows, and he has something up his sleeve. He'll bide his time and wait. You're not leaving the cabin."

"Now I know you're insane! I can't stay in here for the entire voyage."

"Kitten don't."

"Don't you dare, kitten me."

"Fine, I'll compromise. You'll go out, but it will be rarely, and it will only be with me. I don't even want you going on deck with Mattie. You're a beautiful temptation luv, and I'll not have every man on board gawking at you."

Beth stamped her foot in irritation, eyes flashing at Maxwell's domineering attitude. "We aren't in the estate any more Maxwell. Don't treat me like we are."

"You would be wise not to push me on this Beth. I won't back down when it comes to your safety. "

He was already judging how much noise the men were making as they loaded the ship, and whether a sound spanking to Beth's backside would be heard. He didn't think so. His palm smacking her bottom couldn't outdo the rolling of the barrels and the hauling of crates over the deck above.

"You're being impossible and insanely jealous."

"And I'm never going to stop, pet. You knew that from the start. I love you, you belong to me, and I will make you see reason no matter what it takes. I'll do anything to be sure you don't put yourself in danger."

His voice had dropped to a low menacing whisper, and it simply ignited Beth's temper even more. She turned away from him, intending to storm out of the now confining cabin, her anger erasing all sensibilities. Maxwell saw her intent and leapt forward, knocking over a chair and grabbing her shoulders as she fumbled with the lock.

"No, leave me alone."

"Never." He took both her wrists in one hand and righted the chair with the other, sitting down and pulling her over his lap with practiced ease. Quick as lightening, her skirts were flipped over her back. Beth suddenly felt like she was drowning in a sea of petticoats. He pulled her knickers apart to bare her bottom and brought his hand down with a resounding crack.

"Noooooooooooooooooo!"

"Oh yes luv. I told you that I wouldn't hesitate to punish you if you were going to put yourself in harm's way. I find your fire and stubbornness charming, but only to an extent. You will do as I say woman. You were ready to walk out that door even though I forbid it. That was a very bad choice, Beth."

Again his hand came down, leaving a scarlet print on her creamy bottom. He brushed it lightly with his fingertips as she squirmed on his lap, and then fell to work, raining stinging slaps upon Beth's upturned bum, turning it crimson. The heat of her skin under his hand and the feel of her warmth pressing against his manhood began to put Maxwell in a state he didn't care to be in at the moment. Determined to ignore his need and deliver the punishment he felt Beth so justly deserved, he spanked her harder, causing her to howl in outrage.

"I suggest you silence your tongue little one, before I find something to do it for you. You are going to get every bit of what's coming to you Beth. I'll not have my wishes defied. Do you understand?"

"Maxwell I'm sorry. I was angry."

"That wasn't the question Beth. Will you obey me in this?"

"Maxwell........... "

Beth wailed his name but most of the sound was trapped in the sea of petticoats that covered her head. Every ounce of her wanted to defy him. How could he expect her to stay below the entire voyage? It was unreasonable. He was simply being jealous and possessive, reading things into nothing.

"Not the answer I needed, pet. You will do as I say. Is that understood?" His words were punctuated by spanks as she struggled on his lap.

In response Beth shook her head violently and began to beat Maxwell upon his legs. Her fists made little impact through the mounds of petticoats but they spoke of her continued defiance loud and clear.

Maxwell reached down and captured her wrists in one hand, bringing them up behind her back, and began to spank her bottom with all his might. Stinging blows back and forth, cheek to cheek, up to the top and down to the sensitive spot where her legs met the sweet curve of her bottom. She cried out again and he paused long enough to place a hand over her mouth, pulling her up, back arched, so he could hiss in her ear. Her sweet lover was gone, replaced by the man who had first abducted her.

"I'm warning you pet. Cry out again and you will find your little mouth full of petticoats, or perhaps I could silence you in a better way. Now take your punishment like a good girl and don't make me gag you, Beth. You've pissed me off good and proper and this lesson won't end until I'm sure you won't even think of going out that door alone."

Pushing her thighs apart, Maxwell slapped the tender inner skin, up and down the insides of her legs, in rapid fire little bursts, then began to rain blows on the cunny. These were lesser in intensity, designed to hurt, but also designed to stimulate. Beth gasped and twisted but Maxwell held her fast. He gave a little smile, one that if Beth had seen, would have outraged her to the point of no return, and began to alternate the cunny spanks with small caresses. There was more than one way to tame his tigress.

"Noooooooooooo. Maxwell no, not that. Please."

Her feet kicked and she tried to close her legs but Maxwell shoved them open roughly and growled that they'd better stay that way. He shifted her body so her bottom was high on his lap and her legs were spread wide, showing off all her charms and making her very, very, mortified and vulnerable, then proceeded to spank her some more, focusing on the area right over her cunny, which was becoming quite moist, in spite of her continued struggle.

"Will you do as I say? It's a simple question Beth."

"You're being unreasonable."

"And you're being stubborn!"

He rose suddenly, dumping her onto the floor in a heap, an angry scowl on his face. Maxwell scooped her up before she could get her clothes in order, and then tossed her on the bunk. With lightning speed, he flipped her face down, raised her skirts again, tore her knickers clean off, and used them to bind her wrists to the support beam of the bunk.

Beth tried frantically to twist in her bindings, wanting to see around all the fabric surrounding her face, but Maxwell pressed her cheek to the bed with a snarl. "Don't move."

He pulled her up onto her knees, preparing her bottom for another round of discipline. She heard him unfasten his belt, the leather sliding through the loops as he pulled it out in his fury, then snap it between his hands in preparation.

"Maxwell no. Please."

Maxwell took the leather belt and slid it slowly back and forth across her burning cheeks. It was cool and smooth, almost soothing, but Beth knew its bite wouldn't be. She gasped and Maxwell moved his hands, bringing the strap of leather between her legs, sliding over her cunny. Beth fought the sensations that began to build in her core, but it was no use. The edge of the belt rubbed her clit over and over, and finally she let out a moan she could suppress no more.

Maxwell pulled the belt away and slid two fingers into her wet passage, teasing her nubbin with his thumb while caressing her scorching skin with the other. He rubbed in just the right way, making all thoughts of future punishment flee from her mind. The stinging of her bottom combined with the delicate teasing of his fingers caused a pool of fire to form in her belly, and Beth began to move back and forth, needing his fingers deep inside her, needing him. She would fight him later, right now her body demanded release.

"That's right kitten, feels so nice doesn't it? My kitten is so hot and tight. So wet too. Do you want me luv? Do you want me to take you? Pain or pleasure Beth, which do you choose? Your body remembers what I can do for it pigeon. Nice things for good girls."

Beth made a little cry of defeat. He was horrid, but oh he did such nice things. Wickedly wonderful nice things. She wanted him; God, how she did. Her pride didn't, but her body ached with a hot, pulsing need. Part of her railed against the tide of burning lust, but the stroking of his fingers was making her insane. In and out, twisting inside, stroking her sweet spot and driving her headlong towards orgasm.

His other hand was kneading her poor punished cheeks in a way that made her whimper, as a reminder of what could and would be done again, but she didn't want him to stop that either. Pain and pleasure, pleasure and pain. He'd taught her body so well.

Maxwell leaned over her shoulder, hard as marble thighs and cock pressing against her tender backside. Both were aware that all it would take was a flick of his wrist to undo the lacings of his breeches, and he would be free to pleasure her. Pushing the folds of her petticoats away from her ear so he could whisper and hiss nasty things designed to make her surrender to his will, Maxwell continued his torment.

"Do you kitten? Do you want me to take you hard and long from behind? Do you want me to fill you full of my cock and pound you until your knees give out? I'll pump and grind into your sweet wet cunny Beth, until you quiver beneath me all limp and sated. Do you want me to make you cum Beth? I can kitten. You know I can. Sweet, sweet treats for good girls."

Pump, pump, twist, twist. Fingers moving in and out, thumb rubbing her clit in slow circles. Beth could hardly breathe. She was so close, so close. "Yes Maxwell. Yes, please. Take me Maxwell. Need you... need you."

At her words, Maxwell plunged deep inside her tight cunny and danced his finger across her sweet spot as he thrust in, once, twice, three times, leaving Beth mewling and shaking. He then withdrew and slapped her bottom hard, shocking her. Her body arched, tight, aching, so close. He spanked her again on her hypersensitive cunny and she quivered, almost exploding in climax.

"Then tell me what I want to hear."

Beth screamed in outrage but thankfully her cries were muffled by her petticoats and the fact that her face was pressed to the bed. She tried to rise, but Maxwell put a restraining hand on her back.

"Noooooooooo. Damn you. I'm not your whore to taunt. I'm not a slave to tease and torment!"

"No Beth, you're not my whore or my slave, you're my soon to be wife and I'll have you mind me in certain things. Answer me woman, or so help me you will regret it. You will learn to listen when I lay down the law. Now answer my question!"

"I won't. I won't do it." This wasn't about going up on deck anymore, it was about her pride and her right to have a say in her life.

Maxwell growled in rage. Never had he dealt with a female as stubborn as Beth. Well he knew a thing or two about handling headstrong women. All of Maxwell's old ways and emotions rushed to the forefront as he looked at Beth who was still struggling against her bonds and refusing to accept his dominance.

He loved her damn it, and he wouldn't allow her to put herself in harm's way. Her willfulness and defiance were intolerable. Latching on to the habits that had been ingrained so deeply inside him, determined to break her for her own good, Maxwell pick up the belt and brought it down across her already scarlet cheeks, leaving a wide welt.

Beth cried out in pain and outrage, horrified that he could treat her this way. Maxwell raised the belt again. His anger driving away all rational thought, but her next words stopped him cold.

"I hate you. Do you hear me? I hate you. You haven't changed. Leave me alone." Beth almost choked on the power of the emotions welling in her chest. She fought back a sob and fought harder to free herself.

Her words stopped him cold. He dropped the belt, stunned by what he'd done, letting out a cry of anguish. Beth twisted, turning even though it pulled her arms terribly. She dug her heals in the bed and backed up, arms caught behind her, a frightened look in her eyes.

"Beth. Oh God, kitten. Please don't say that. Don't say you hate me. I... I just wanted to make you listen."

"Just leave me alone Maxwell."

"Beth please. I needed you to obey, to keep you safe."

"You honestly think beating me and making me feel like a whore is the best way to do that?"

She spat out the words with as much viciousness as he had struck her with. There was no love to be found in her eyes, only anger, pain, and fear. It was the last one that cut him to the quick. She was afraid of him again.

After all they'd been through, after all she'd forgiven him for, she was afraid of him again. What the hell had he done? He didn't speak, only stared at her in shock.

"Making me feel like your whore and beating me was the way, Maxwell? Answer me? Now I'm the one who deserves an answer."

"I just ... No ... I lost control Beth. I... It's what I did for so long. How I was taught to react to willfulness. I know it's no excuse baby but it's the only way I know. I can change kitten and I will Beth, I am changing. It was just supposed to be a spanking, but I got so angry. The thought of you being hurt by Captain Trammell or his crew terrifies me. Beth that man wants to hurt you."

"You hurt me Maxwell. You. No one else."

"I know I hurt you and I'm sorry. I'm so sorry. Please kitten. I know you're not my whore, baby. You're a sweet, gentle, wonderful woman and I...I love you. You're the most precious thing on earth to me."

There were tears welling in Maxwell's eyes as he tried to sort out his feelings and gain her forgiveness. He didn't know how to make this right again. He'd never cared to make things right before.

"I have changed Beth, because of you. For you. I guess it will just take some time to get the old me to not react to your stubborn streak. Beth, I truly believe you'll be in danger if you go on deck without me, and that fear is what pushed me over the edge. I admit there's some of the old abusive Maxwell left inside me baby, and I admit I'm jealous as hell, but it's my fear for you that really drove me to do that. It won't happen again kitten. I swear."

Maxwell moved cautiously towards her, and Beth looked at him warily, not at all sure she was ready to be held. The fear she had felt, the loss of control that had filled her when he had gone from a lover who had spanked and pleasured her, to an abusive man, intent on truly whipping her into submission still had her reeling.

She shook her head slightly. "No Maxwell, don't." Maxwell's heart fell at her words, but he took a bit of solace in the fact that the fear had left her eyes.

"Let me untie you kitten. Your arms must be hurting. Then I'll leave you be. I'll send Mattie in, and the two of you can get settled."

He pulled his knife from his boot and knelt on the bed, quickly cutting the torn knickers that bound her wrists, and then looked deeply into her eyes, seeking forgiveness. His pleaded for understanding. He would be lost without her love. To hear her say she hated him..... well life wouldn't be worth living if Beth pushed him away. Better to simply take the blade to his heart right now.

"Beth luv, do you want me to have Mattie sleep in here with you and I'll take a pallet on the floor outside the door?" Maxwell held his breath, praying she wouldn't agree. He couldn't be denied the loving feel of her arms.

Seconds passed, heartbeats in which Maxwell felt his world slipping away. She was going to tell him yes, and he would do it because she asked it of him. He would do it, and take what little comfort there was in knowing she was close by and that he was protecting her, but it would tear his heart out all the same. Finally, Beth reached out and touched his cheek for just an instant.

"No. Your place is beside me. I love you, Maxwell. And I do understand you. You spent so many years forcing your ways on women. This is going to take time. I know that. I can live with that part of your nature because you were never truly like Jeeval. You always kept your heart. You kept your compassion and your ability to love, and that means you can change."

"I won't hurt you baby, ever."

Beth shook her head slightly. "No Maxwell, I can learn to accept a simple spanking if you think one is due. A woman is to obey her man as long as he is just." At this Beth blushed in that oh so charming way. "I know I can be stubborn, and you will be my husband soon. It's when the punishment turns into a violent forceful thing that ... well, then it's bad. That's the old Maxwell reacting, not the new Maxwell. That's not the man I love."

Maxwell leaned forward and brushed his lips across hers in the gentlest of kisses. When he pulled back, Beth saw more love in his eyes than she'd ever dreamed of finding, and she knew it was all for her, only for her.

"Thank you, kitten. I love you so very much. You'll not spend one day regretting your decision to love me. I swear it Beth, not one day. I'll give you everything your heart desires and more. I'll make you so happy, baby, you won't be able to see past the stars in your eyes."

He kissed her again, looking for all the world like a little boy who'd just gotten a puppy for Christmas. She giggled and nodded her head; happy things were going to be right between them. She knew they would be. Beth believed he meant every word, and she believed in him.

"You relax kitten, and I'll get Mattie. We're going to set sail soon, out of India and into our new life."

Chapter Thirty-three

They all breathed a sigh of relief when the ship moved from the Haldia River out into the open sea. The days passed slowly as they sailed towards freedom, but everyone settled into a comfortable routine. Maxwell escorted Beth around the deck twice a day so she was able to get fresh air and stave off the restlessness being confined to their tiny cabin caused. They would bundle her up, warm or cool, sun or rain, to prevent prying eyes from seeing her face, figure, and the hated slave collar that still adorned her neck.

Maxwell would glower at any deck hand that came near, making it clear he wanted his wife left alone. Beth played the part of the distressed wife to a tee, shuffling as she walked, mumbling in a voice that seemed shaky with tears when spoken to, and always keeping her head down and arms clutching Maxwell's.

Captain Trammell asked almost daily if they would join him for dinner, but Maxwell always declined, pulling Beth close and claiming her need for rest prohibited any socializing. The captain always accepted Maxwell's answer, but with a slight scowl. He would then, without fail, turn to Beth politely, and mumble some apology about her worries or his deep sadness regarding her mother's illness. The entire scene was played out with much decorum, but there were underlying tones in both the captain's and Maxwell's voices. The battle between them hadn't ended, but it seemed to be at a sort of truce.

At Captain Trammell's first invitation, Beth had told Maxwell she thought he was wrong to decline, when they had returned to their cabin, but one look at her lover's face made her change her mind. It wasn't a fear of him that made her concede to his wishes on this matter. It was the panic she had seen in Maxwell's eyes when she had suggested they dine with the captain, and that made her hold her tongue. Maxwell loved her dearly and didn't trust the captain, and he would move heaven and earth to keep them apart. It wasn't an easy task on a ship that size, and their short daily encounters had to be endured, but Beth was never, ever, alone with the man.

And so life went on, day after endless day. Maxwell taught Beth how to play chess and delighted in her quick mind and skill for the game. They took their strolls, read, made love in the tiny bunk night after night, and talked. Oh how they talked. Pasts were revealed, dreams were built, and bonds of the heart were formed. Words were whispered deep into the night until the need for each other claimed them again, and Maxwell would take Beth with a gentle rhythm as the ship rocked in time. Tender and sweet, and oh so loving. It was as close to heaven as either had been.

Mattie adjusted well to her life at sea. She relished being on deck, the wind on her face. Free. Gone were the dusty streets and filthy gutters. She no longer had to beg or hunt for scraps of food or was forced to accept the scorn of others. She did her job well, tending to Beth and Maxwell's every need so no one could complain, and she also won the hearts of many of the men by cooking up some delightful fare in the ship's galley. It wasn't long before some had developed a grudging respect for her, and she became accepted by them. Hers wasn't a face you fought over, so she could be a friend.

Captain Trammell was another story though. He didn't care for her one bit. He saw the way she watched him, especially when Beth was on deck, and the one time he'd tried to get near Beth and Maxwell's cabin when Maxwell was on deck, Mattie had practically thrown herself in front of the door, barring his way. She'd only slipped out for a moment, to get them both some tea, but sure enough, the sneaky bastard had tried to make a move, and Mattie had been even more vigilant ever since.

Now it was the morning of the big day. They had been at sea for eight weeks, but had docked at dawn and would spend the next two nights in Cape Town, taking on needed water and dry goods for the remaining trek home. Captain Trammell had given Maxwell strict instructions to keep Beth below until he gave word that they could go ashore. He didn't want her getting in the way or getting hurt. Mattie on the other hand, had been allowed to go ashore early when she had fussed about getting the freshest food for her employers before it was picked over. It was a mistake they would come to rue.

Maxwell watched Beth move around restlessly as they waited. He'd told her he would find a hotel for them, if there was one, so she could have a real bath when they were allowed to go ashore. The thought of being clean had her pacing around the tiny cabin like a caged beast in anticipation.

"Kitten come here and sit, you'll wear yourself out."

"I can't Maxwell. I'm excited. Oh I can't wait for a real bath. Can I have soaps and oils and lotions?"

"Yes, and powders and perfumes, and a great big bed." He gave a little growl and made a grab for her, but Beth giggled and scooted away. "Come here woman."

"Maxwell, we don't have time for that. Tonight, in that big bed, I promise." She gave him a look that took his breath away and sent a flood of heat to his lower region. Maxwell was just about to make another grab for her when there was a knock on the door. Beth clapped her hands, eyebrows shooting up as she spun to face the door.

"Ooh it's time."

Smiling at her happiness, Maxwell opened the door and was roughly shoved backwards as Captain Trammell and three uniform guards burst into the cabin. Beth screamed as one advanced on her, and then gave another terrified wail as the other two grabbed Maxwell. They turned him and shoved him hard against the bedframe face first. His head snapped against the support beam, stunning him, and they yanked his arms behind his back, securing his wrists with shackles.

"What are you doing? Noooo! Let him go. This is a mistake." Beth's head was reeling. This couldn't be happening.

"Maxwell Harrison you are under arrest for kidnaping and murder."

"No. He didn't kidnap me. Please. This isn't right. Maxwell is innocent. I want to be here."

"This man has kidnaped countless women and you certainly are one of them. You were held as a concubine were you not?"

Captain Trammell advanced on Beth and tore her dress, exposing her slave collar to all in the room. She shrieked and brought her hands up, ready to fight, to claw at him, hating him for turning them in, but the man closest to her grabbed her, pinning her arms to her sides in a bear hug.

"Can you deny he killed a man taking you out of the harem?"

"It wasn't like that. Jeeval, he's the one who..." Beth tried to twist in her captor's arms, to look at the guard. "Maxwell saved me."

"He murdered a man."

Beth faced Captain Trammell again, stunned by this turn of events. "Why? Why did you bring us all this way if you were only going to hand us over? Why? You could have simply gotten the reward in India."

"Oh I'm not turning you over, sweet. You will remain in my custody as a British citizen in need of protection. An unmarried woman can't very well go around unescorted, especially in this part of the world. It isn't safe. It also isn't proper. As the ship's captain I can place you under my protection as your guardian, as such. It's my duty to you as my passenger. You will remain with me, my dear and I will take you home."

"No! Take me too. You have to take me with Maxwell. I killed a man. I killed three of them. You can't leave me here with him."

"Ah she's gone feeble from the stress of it all. Just look at her. How could a little bit of a thing like that kill three men? You can leave her with me. I'll not let anyone harm her anymore."

"No. Let me go. He's lying. Please."

Captain Trammell moved forward. "Now, now, you are distraught over your ordeal. It will be alright now." He reached out to calm her, and then stroked Beth's cheek. She let out an indignant shriek and began to fight in earnest.

"Noooooooooooooooooo!"

Maxwell shook his head, clearing the cobwebs as he came to. He heard Beth screaming; Beth was screaming. Oh God, Beth was screaming! He tried to turn so he could see her but one of the guards punched him in the stomach. He doubled over and was struck with the butt of a pistol on the back of his head. Dazed, confused, unable to help himself or Beth, his world turned black. Beth began to sob hysterically when she saw him slump unconscious, and fought to reach him as Maxwell was dragged from the cabin.

Beth's shrieks increased tenfold. She fought the guard but it was no use. Turning in his grasp she pleaded with him to listen to her.

"This isn't as he says. Please. Maxwell rescued me. Please. We did everything for a reason. You have to take me too."

"I'm sorry Miss. Our orders were to apprehend Maxwell Harrison and to entrust your care to Captain Trammell, and that's what we are doing."

"At least tell me where he's being taken."

"To the jail. He'll be hung for murder at dawn."
Captain Trammell backed out the door and the guard
followed, still holding Beth. When he got to it, he
released her, flinging her towards the bunk, before
quickly slamming the door and locking it, leaving her
stunned and terrified.

Beth let out a wail of anguish but there was no one
left to hear her, no one that is except Mattie who was
hiding behind some crates that were stacked next to the
gangplank. She'd followed Captain Trammell the minute
he'd left the ship and had seen him fetch the guards.
She'd also seen them drag Maxwell away in chains. Now
the question was how the hell was she going to get them
out of this mess?

Mattie heard another faint, but distinct cry come
from the ship. "I'm coming honey. Mattie's coming as
soon as I can."

Chapter Thirty-four

Cape Town, South Africa

Maxwell came to, slowly, as the smell of rotten straw and filth filling his nostrils. His head was throbbing, bolts of pain shooting through his skull with every beat. It also felt as if it were stuffed with cotton. Thinking was a bit out of the question at the moment. His mouth was bone dry and every inch of him ached. What was going on? Fighting the comforting blackness that threatened to overtake him again, Maxwell forced his eyes open to assess his surroundings and try to make sense of his world.

Bare stone walls, wooden door, tiny window no man could get through, dirt floor covered with wet, filthy straw. Jail, he was in a jail cell. He was in a bloody jail. It all came back to him in a flash. The guards had come for them on the ship. They'd hit him in the head, and other places as well from the feel of it. The last thing he remembered was Beth screaming. His girl had been screaming and he hadn't been able to help her.

"Oh God, Beth." Where was Beth? Had they brought her here too? He had to find her. Maxwell tried to rise, but when he did, a sharp pain cut through his rib cage and nausea threatened to spill the contents of his stomach onto the already filthy straw. His entire body hurt, but the ribs were the worst.

"Bastards cracked a rib. Must have gotten in a few punches and kicks when I was out; cowards." Question was, what had been done to Beth, hell, what was being done as he lay here wasting time?

He grit his teeth against the pain, determined to stand and start pounding on the door until someone came to answer some questions. Digging his heels into the slippery straw, he pushed his back to the wall, and slowly rose. The room around him spun but he fought off the blackness as bile rose in his throat making him gag. He retched, pain knifing through his side as he vomited, then wiped his mouth with the back of his hand.

"Bloody hell." Maxwell took in a steadying breath, the pain of his cracked rib making him hiss, but at least his stomach was steady. At least the pain in his ribs was helping him stay conscious.

"Got to get to Beth."

He slowly made his way around the tiny cell, keeping to the wall for support, until he reached the door. It was thick and impenetrable, but it had a small window. Maxwell held onto the door latch, which of course wouldn't move, and curled his other fingers around the bars of the window. He rested his forehead against the rough wood for a moment, fighting the sea of nausea that tried to overtake him once again, then took a deep breath and looked out.

Nothing, just two other doors like his in a short dark hallway that opened into a room at the front. No one was about, the place was silent. There was light coming from the room, but no sign of movement. He didn't detect movement from the other cells either. Surely there'd be a scuffle or noise if Beth was being hurt. Rape was hardly a silent act. Though it was true, it offered little comfort. I was also true that she could very well be lying hurt and unconscious.

"Beth." No response. He tried again, a bit louder. "Beth. Are you here, kitten?"

Still he was met with silence. Part of him was glad she wasn't in this filthy place, but the other half was terrified. What had they done to his girl? He felt so incredibly helpless.

"Hey! Anyone here? Come talk to me. Someone tell me what the bloody hell is going on."

A man entered the hallway and moved towards Maxwell's cell. "I don't have to answer to the likes of you. Shut yer mouth and get away from that door."

"Where's Beth? What did they do to the woman I was with?"

"The pretty lady ain't none of your concern."

Maxwell let out a growl of rage and grabbed the window bars, shaking them in fury, but the solid door didn't so much as rattle. He hissed as pain knifed through his ribs, but it didn't do a thing to dampen his rage.

"Don't tell me she's none of my concern. She's my wife. Where did they take her? If anyone touches a single hair on her head they'll bloody well have to answer to me."

"Oh now that's a terrifying threat mate, seein' as how you're in there and I'm out here. There you'll stay too, least until you go to the gallows in the morning. You're gonna be swingin' by your neck come sunrise."

Maxwell closed his eyes. The gallows. They were going to hang him soon. He was locked up tight and they were going to hang him, and Beth would be at their mercy. Was she being taken back to Jeeval? Did his influence reach all the way here? Maxwell doubted it. The lying bastard of a captain could have turned them in long ago. No, the man must have had other plans. Plans for Beth. That brought him back to the question of where she was. Where was his kitten? He decided to try and change tactics.

"Listen, I have money. Lots of British silver. I'll make it worth your while if you let me out. You can have every bit of it." The guard scoffed at his offer, laughing, and

Maxwell grit his teeth to maintain control. "Please. I have to get to Beth. She's in danger."

"From what I heard, you were the danger. She's with Captain Trammell. He's her guardian now, and is going take her home."

"No! Listen to me. That man has been waiting for a chance to get his hands on her since we got on board. This is a mistake. She's my wife. When do I get to talk to a magistrate? When does my side get heard? All he's telling is lies."

The guard laughed again and shook his head. "You're not in England man. That's not how we do things here. You've already been charged, convicted, and sentenced. All that's left is the hangin'. There is no trial. You're guilty by the word of Captain Trammell."

"He's a lying bastard."

"Bastard or no, he's friends with the law in this part of Cape Town. He's been doin' business here for years, and we don't know nothin' about you at all. There won't be any mercy shown for you. You hang at dawn. Now sit down and shut up. I haven't time for this, nor do I care what happens to the likes of you."

The guard turned away, dismissing Maxwell, and left him standing alone as his heart sunk. Maxwell tried to call him back but the man had no interest in hearing anything else. Slowly, trying to swallow down the panic that was threatening to choke him, Maxwell slid down the door and sat amid the filth of his new home.

He closed his eyes and prayed to a God whom he was sure wouldn't listen to the likes of him. Never-the-less, he begged for assistance, asking for protection for Beth. How could he have let this happen? He should have known Trammell was up to something when he'd told Maxwell to stay below. Why had he been so stupid? Why hadn't he insisted they leave with Mattie?

Mattie. A tiny flicker of hope filled his heart at the thought of the tough as nails woman. Where was Mattie? Had she returned to the ship? Could she do anything to protect Beth? He doubted it, but he knew she'd try.

Maxwell allowed his head to drop into his hands, hopelessness and terror filling him as he thought of Beth on that ship without him. He whispered to her, eyes clenched shut, trying to block out images of Captain Trammell raping her, images of Beth's face contorted in screams and wet with tears.

"Oh kitten, I let you down. I saved you from Jeeval just to hand you over to someone just as bad. Please forgive me Beth. I didn't mean it. I didn't mean it Beth. Oh baby, please be okay."

His words fell on deaf ears in the empty cell, haunting him. He looked around in desperation, searching for anything, anyway he might get free, but he knew there wasn't. He was a rat tapped in a cage, and he wasn't going to see the light of day until they were slipping a noose around his neck.

Chapter Thirty-five

Mattie crouched behind the crates, filled with indecision as another of Beth's cries reached her ears. Her heart called out to the poor girl, the need to comfort her was almost overwhelming, but her head told her to stay put. She heard a faint, but rapid hammering from within the ship, and guessed that Beth was pounding her fists against the cabin door with all her fury.

"Oh sweetie, you'll hurt yourself."

As she looked on, Captain Trammell and the last of the three guards came on deck. They walked to the gangway and Mattie ducked low, being seen was not an option. She hid as they went by her, unaware of her presence, and continued towards the dock, Captain Trammell swaggering all the way.

"Cocky bastard. Well you still have to deal with me."

From the bits of conversation she'd caught, Mattie gathered they were headed to one of the taverns to celebrate the recent turn of events. The guard had slapped Trammell on the back, congratulating him on his beautiful prize, saying it was time for some whiskey. It was clear the captain lined the pockets of the local law, and that they were as thick as thieves. It was also clear they were both quite confident Beth was secure under lock and key. Mattie knew it would be impossible for anyone on the wharf to hear her faint cries, and her captors knew it too. Beth was trapped, but Mattie knew Trammell's confidence might give her the chance she needed.

After they were out of sight, Mattie again looked over the ship. The deck appeared deserted, but she knew the ship wouldn't be left completely unattended. Somewhere there had to be a deck hand doing watch. No way would the slimy captain leave his valuable prize completely alone, locked up or not. To think that the men she had begun to think of as friends would go along with this, made her sick, but then again, she knew the captain's word was law, and if they wanted their jobs, the crew would do as he commanded.

As she sat undecided on her next course of action, Mattie saw Marcus walk from the behind some rigging and head to the bow of the ship. He looked towards the stairs leading to the cabins as Beth let out another cry, her plea for help floating on the air. His face filled with contempt when he heard her, and he quickly turned his back again, ignoring her screams. Mattie knew in an instant there would be no help found here.

It was such a pity that men could be influenced by the likes of Captain Trammell and the need for money. She'd come to think of Marcus as a friend, but it was obvious that her trust had been misplaced. On the other hand, the man had a family back home to feed. If he refused to obey Trammell, he'd be kicked off the ship, possibly tried for mutiny, and at the very least, never get his wages. Still... how could he ignore Beth's plight?

Well it didn't matter why, he had. There would be no help from Marcus. The man would put a stop to any attempts to free Beth, and raise the alarm.

"I'm sorry honey but I can't chance a rescue right now. You just sit tight and I'll see if I can find help."

Mattie knew a thing or two about the kind of people who inhabited certain areas of shipping ports. This one would be like all the rest, teaming with undesirables. Every town had a place where the dangerous men and low life's of society called home, and if that town had a wharf, it was usually the place.

Taverns and brothels would be plentiful to satisfy the visiting sailors. Her father had regaled them with tales of danger from the days when he was at sea, and she had been expressly forbidden to ever go near the tall ships or the surrounding area. The only women near the docks were the kind not welcome in the company of her father's family.

Cape Town had looked no different during her brief walk through that morning. Parts of the town appeared basically lawless, aside from the so called Police Captain who had ordered Maxwell's arrest. Mattie thought he'd probably appointed himself or bought his way in. She was sure he'd gotten the position because of money and associations with other not so nice but powerful people. Rich men and their rich friends always held the places of greatest power.

Well she had a pocket of Maxwell's silver, given to buy goods that were never bought, and Mattie was sure there'd be some who follow the trail of money no matter who had it. There was no loyalty in those who could be bought. Silver was silver, and that was an advantage Mattie planned on using to save both Maxwell and Beth.

"I'm going hunt every tavern on the wharf until I get some information and round up a few men who would rather be rich than be good citizens. It shouldn't be too hard in a place like this."

With her plan set firmly in her head, Mattie checked to make sure Marcus was nowhere around, and hurried back down the pier.

~~~~~~~~~~~~

Two hours later Mattie sat completely dejected, outside one of the noisy taverns. She'd shoved her way inside most of the seedy looking ones that lined the docks, avoiding the fancier, inland ones in fear of being seen by Captain Trammell, but had come up empty handed. Not to say there weren't those who were willing, they just hadn't fit the bill.

Time after time, she'd slipped silently into a dark corner of the room to listen to the men talk, coming out of hiding when she caught sight of a likely prospect. If that didn't work, and they saw her sneak in, Mattie went into her begging routine to try to size up the customers. The ones who were meanest were the ones she'd target, whispering she had money and a deal for them. Everything she did had to be done quickly, before the owner tossed her out. Whores were welcomed, old whores tolerated, ugly beggar women were not. It was not a pleasant afternoon.

So far, she'd had no luck finding anyone she felt she could trust. Oh she'd approached quite a few, found some who showed a hatred for the local law, but when she told of her plan to get Maxwell out of jail then slip aboard a ship and slit a few throats to save Beth, their eyes had either shone too brightly at the thought of the pretty young woman, or seemed too likely to slit her throat too after they got their silver. Good thing she'd had the presence of mind to hide her riches instead of carrying it around or it would most likely be gone.

So all told, her mission had been a dismal failure. She had no idea what she was going to do. It was getting late and Captain Trammell was likely to go back to the ship soon. He knew Beth was waiting there, alone and vulnerable. When he did make his way back to the ship, Beth would be in grave danger. He'd rape the poor girl for sure. Mattie also knew though, that her going back to the ship alone wasn't an option. There was nothing she could do there.

"Maybe I ought to see if I can get to Maxwell." She knew the chances of breaking him out were next to impossible, but the poor man had to be desperate. "I can at least see how he is and maybe talk to him."

She knew the location of the jail from following Captain Trammell on his early morning errand, and quickly made her way towards it. When she arrived, she shook her head as her heart sank. The small building looked impenetrable. Its thick walls had only tiny windows, and as she walked around its sides, she discovered that the front door was the only way in or out. There was no way she was getting Maxwell free. Not with brute strength anyway. Nor did she have a weapon to go in there and demand his release.

She stood for a moment, staying in the shadows, lost in thought. Night was falling quickly and darkness would be on her side if she did manage by some miracle to get Maxwell out of there. She tried to peer into one of the windows, but it was too high. Looking around, searching for anything that would let her get high enough to see in, Mattie came up empty handed. Nothing, nothing but dirt.

"What did I expect? A ladder?"

Shaking her head at her own poor excuse for a joke, she stood on her toes and called out softly under one of the window, crossing her fingers. "Maxwell. Are you in there?" Nothing. She called a little louder but was still met with silence, so she moved to another window.

"Maxwell, its Mattie. Can you hear me?"

Chapter Thirty-six

Maxwell jumped at the sound of his name. He'd been dosing, lost in a sea of misery. He forced himself to stand, ribs screaming in protest, and went to the window, heart pounding with excitement.

"Mattie. I'm here. Is Beth with you? Is she okay?"

Mattie winced. Poor man had to be suffering, worrying about his girl. What should she tell him? How much did he know? Hell she didn't know much.

"No. She's still at the ship."

Maxwell made a sound of anguish at the news, but Mattie rushed on before he could speak.

"It's okay for now, the Captain left, Maxwell. He went off to get drunk. Beth's alone and okay for now." Mattie didn't know that for sure, but there was nothing she could, do so why worry Maxwell.

"If that bastard touches her..."

"He hasn't, and that's all you can think about right now okay?"

Maxwell didn't answer. His silence made her want to weep. She could picture him, seething, tormented with horrid thoughts in the darkness of the cell, trying his best to maintain control. Mattie knew how incredibly protective he was of Beth, and this had to be tearing him apart.

"Listen to me. I know she's all you can think about, but I need you to tell me about the guards here. How many are there? Do you think they can be bought?"

"Well three came to the ship, but only one came back here when I started yelling for information. I don't know who's here now. It's been real quiet. No conversation from up front that I could hear. There might be only one, but he was a right bastard. The law is bought and paid for here. I don't think you'll get far."

"Well I'm going to try. I searched the docks for men who would be willing to get Beth off the ship, but they're a last resort. They're a very motley bunch, dangerous as hell. I didn't trust any of them to be around Beth. As for breaking you out, no one wanted to be a part of that. You sit tight, I'm coming in."

"Mattie, you'll just get yourself locked up."

"We'll see. I'm not just leaving you here to be hung."

"Mattie don't. Save yourself and get Beth off the ship." His plea was met with silence. "Mattie?" More silence. "Damn it! Bloody stubborn, willful woman."

Maxwell went to the door of his cell to listen, praying Mattie could pull off a miracle, and that the guard was a greedy man who could be bribed.

While he was calling out for her, Mattie walked to the front of the jail and squared her shoulders. She glanced down at her maid's outfit, not so crisp after eight weeks at sea, but still clean, and wondered if it would doom her mission before she started. She searched her mind for someone she could say she was, some possible person who might have business here, but then abandoned the idea. She was after all going to try and bribe the guard, who else would do that but a family member, friend, or servant?

She touched the bag of silver in her pocket, hoping it was enough, and fixed a determined look on her face, thinking of her scars, and wishing for her past beauty. There was no way she'd ever be able to charm any man now. It was the silver or nothing.

She pressed the door open a crack and peeked inside. There was one lone guard sitting at a desk, feet up, looking extremely bored. He'd heard the small creak the door had made, and looked up immediately, making Mattie's heart leap into her throat.

She stood, frozen in shock, unable to breathe, her world spinning. It was Kamal. The man before her was her Kamal. Time had changed him, his eyes were old and tired, his hair thinning, but there was no mistaking the face of her beloved husband. Questions leaped into her mind. How? When? Why was he here?

"Here now. Who is it? Come in and state your business." He pulled his feet off the desk and sat up straight, reaching for his pistol.

His gruff voice and sudden move for his gun, jerked her out of her shock and Mattie pushed the door wide. At first Kamal scowled at her, looking her up and down, taking in the English maid's outfit, and surmising who she was immediately, but then his eyes traveled back to her face and a look of confusion overcame him. He cocked his head slightly, and stared at her, unsure what it was that had him so disconcerted.

Mattie slowly raised her hand and covered up her blind eye and the disfigured part of her face, so only the smooth, unblemished skin was visible. He looked at her harder, studying her, brow furrowed, and she whispered his name.

"Kamal."

Stunned recognition hit. His eye flew open wide and Kamal leapt to his feet. "Matagi? Matagi is it really you?"

The sound of her given name on his lips was heaven. She had forgone it years ago, hating it and the past it stood for.

"Matagi?"

Mattie slowly nodded. "Yes Kamal, it's me."

He rushed forward and swept her into his arms, kissing her, as tears filled both their eyes. Mattie's heart soared. He was kissing her and loving her. He didn't care about her face. No man had kissed her or looked upon her with anything but fear and revulsion in years. Kamal still loved her and things would be all right. Everything was going to be all right now.

He let her go and moved his hands to her cheeks which were wet with tears, stroking them, running his thumb over her scar.

"Oh Matagi. What have they done? Oh my beautiful one. They have hurt you." To Mattie's shock, he leaned in and kissed her horrible face, then pulled her close once more.

She clung to him, sobbing, unable to speak.

"Why are you here, my love? How did you get here?"

Finally Mattie recovered enough to get a hold of her tongue and her senses. "I might ask you the same thing." She smiled at him and took his hand. "Sit, it's a long story. Is it safe to talk here? Will the others be back?"

He nodded quickly. "It's safe my love. They have gone. Patrolling, or so they claim. I know that's not what they really do. Matagi, these men have no honor in their work but I am different. I try and uphold the law in this part of Cape Town, but it isn't easy. My shift always starts just before dark so the others can go about their evil business."

"So you weren't the man who went to see Maxwell a while back?"

"Maxwell Harrison? The prisoner? Matagi, what business do you have with him? He's despicable. He's the same as the ones who stole you from me."

"No Kamal, he's not. He's a good man. It's your captain, and the captain of the ship I was on that is corrupt. Maxwell's innocent. You have to let him go."

"Matagi... What have you gotten involved in? I can't just release him."

"Please just sit and listen, Kamal. I know what I'm saying. You have to listen, and we have to hurry. Beth's in danger."

"Beth?"

"Yes Beth." Mattie began to fill him in as quickly as she could, praying he was still the good man he'd been. When she was through, she looked into his eyes, begging for help.

"So you see why we have to free Maxwell and save Beth? Kamal, that girl was suffering the same fate as me until Maxwell saved her. Yes men were killed, but they were evil men. Men like the ones who destroyed our families and stole our lives away. Men just like those who hurt me. Please Kamal."

"My ever courageous Matagi. You have a heart of gold, my love. Of course I shall help you. You are determined to be there for your friends, and I will never be anywhere but by your side, ever again. Let's go."

Kamal grabbed the key for Maxwell's cell and they hurried down the hall, Mattie damn near floating with happiness the whole way. She had her husband back, and Maxwell and Beth would be saved. Sometimes fate did smile on you. It truly did.

Chapter Thirty-seven

As Kamal and Mattie rushed to free Maxwell, Beth was frantically pacing the tiny cabin that had become her jail cell. She'd eyed everything at her disposal, carefully looking for anything that could be used as a weapon, but there was nothing. Two of the ship's crew had come and taken Maxwell's pistol and knives, even discovering the one kept hidden under the mattress in their search. She'd gone at them, full of teeth and temper, fighting the whole time, but it had been useless. In the end she'd simply gone mute with despair as her means for protecting herself were bundled together and taken from her.

Now, exhausted, frantic with worry, and heartsick over what was happening to Maxwell, she finally stopped her useless movement and flopped down on the bed, giving in to the urge to cry. She wanted to be strong, and knew she would be if the situation offered any hope. She'd fight to the death with her pitifully ineffective fists and feet, if given even the slightest chance for escape, but it all seemed so hopeless. So for now, if only for a little while, Beth let the feelings that were threatening to choke her come rushing out. Huge sobs shook her body as she buried her face in the pillow to smother the sounds of her cries, refusing to let anyone hear her pain.

After a while, Beth's sobs quieted and she drifted off into a troubled sleep, driven there by the overwhelming exhaustion brought on by her frantic fight and her terror for Maxwell. Had she known at that moment that her love was being set free, Beth's sleep would have been much more tranquil.

~~~~~~~~~~~~~~~~~

Maxwell slowly rose when he heard voices and footsteps headed in his direction. He'd been standing at the door, one hand wrapped around the bars in the window, the other clutching his side, for as long as he could, doing his best to hear how Mattie was faring with the guard. In the end though, the pain in his head and ribs won out. He'd slumped to the floor once again, waiting, wondering, and hoping for Mattie to perform some sort of miracle.

Now the wait was over. They were on their way. Had Mattie been successful in her quest to bribe the bastard out front, or was the guard dragging her down the hall to toss her in a cell as well?

Maxwell once more used the stone wall for leverage and pushed his way to his feet so he could peer through the window. To his surprise, the first thing that met his eyes was Mattie's beaming face. The woman wasn't just smiling, she looked bloody giddy. What was going on? He then looked at the guard, a different one from before, and the guard was smiling as well. This looked good. A happy guard was a good guard. His gaze went back to Mattie who was still grinning like a fool, eyebrows raised in question.

"Maxwell, it's okay now. Everything's okay. Kamal will get you out. We can save Beth from that nasty captain. Oh it's wonderful Maxwell, and it will all be okay. It will all work out because he's my husband. We don't have to worry about a thing. I don't have time to explain. Kamal will... Oh just get him out Kamal."

Mattie was too excited and too overwhelmed to get things said properly. Maxwell had never seen her like this. She was making little sense and her words were far from assuring. Her happiness despite their dire situation baffled him. Maxwell wanted answers, but this had to be done right. They had secrets that must be kept. Beth's life was at stake.

"Hold on Mattie, slow down. Don't say anything else." Had she already told this guard everything? What was she thinking? While the man might be greedy and willing to help because she'd greased his palm, he wasn't to be trusted and there certainly wasn't cause for such optimism, at least not yet.

Kamal unlocked the door and Maxwell took a step into the hall, clutching his side and bracing himself on the doorjamb for support as a wave of dizziness and pain swept through him. Kamal reached to steady him and Maxwell made a low snarl, making it clear he didn't trust the guard. Mattie quickly put her arm around his waist, hushing him and looking him over with a critical eye, not liking what she saw. The guards had worked him over good. Poor man was in a world of pain inside and out.

"Now you listen to me. I know you're hurting and you're terrified for Beth but I also know what I'm talking about. This man is Kamal. My Kamal. He's my husband, Maxwell. I... well I can hardly believe it, but it's true. We needed a miracle and here he is. Now you stopped your fussing and mistrust, and let him help. Let me get you out front so I can get a better look at you."

Maxwell's head had snapped up at Mattie's words. He winced, immediately regretting the sudden movement, but looked Kamal over critically. Mattie he trusted, trusted with his and Beth's lives, but Kamal? He may be Mattie's long lost husband, but he still worked with some very corrupt people.

Maxwell knew damn well that he deserved to be in this jail cell for his crimes, but no way would Beth had been left with the captain if things were on the up and up. She had killed too. These people were on the take from someone higher up, someone who was friends with Captain Trammell.

Mattie may have known Kamal, known him, loved him, and lived with him, but it was a lifetime ago. Twenty years was a long time. The man could have changed. Maxwell knew that greed could do horrid things to a man, look what it had done to him. On the other hand, he was outside the cell instead of lying in the filthy straw, panicking about Beth with no way to help her.

"Maxwell, he's my Kamal. He's a good man. I know you're worried, but what choice do you have? You're going to have to trust him."

"Matagi, or Mattie as you know her, speaks the truth. I am not corrupt like the others. I try to keep justice where none is found. This area of town, here by the docks, is dangerous. It is full of bad men and governed by the rich who come here to find their guilty pleasures. I stay to try and make a difference. I can't do much, but I try, and now I'm risking my life to help you and your Beth. I could just as easily take my sweet Matagi and leave you here."

"Well I don't know about that Kamal, I couldn't leave Maxwell and Beth to this fate, but I know the first part is true. And Maxwell, I know in my heart that Kamal is the man I fell in love with. I can feel it in here."

Mattie touched the place over her heart and looked at him beseechingly, willing him to understand, to believe as she did. "And I'm not just babbling with a mind clouded over by wishes and fairytales. I know it is a fact. I can sense character in people. You know I can. Now stop being so stubborn. Beth is waiting. Think of how frightened she is. The captain could come back at any time as well as the other guards. We must go now. Please."

Though the urge to try and overpower Kamal and escape on his own was still inside him, Maxwell nodded and allowed the man's arm to replace Mattie's around his waist. He would wait and watch. Right now they had to get to Beth. It was clear that Mattie trusted Kamal, and so far Mattie had been right about a hell of a lot of things. He just prayed her judgment hadn't been led astray by love.

"Fine, let's go, but if you betray... "

"Maxwell!"

"Aw Mattie, we're talking about Beth here. I have to be careful. You know that. I never was one to trust, was I?"

"No you weren't but it's time to start now. Let's go.

"All right, but we're not stopping for any doctoring. There isn't time."

Mattie grumbled and narrowed her eye in a glare that shot daggers, but yielded when Maxwell allowed Kamal to help him down the hall.

As they walked through the front of the jail, Kamal stopped to retrieve his hat, jacket, and pistol. He put them on, looking very official again. The actions renewed Maxwell's mistrust in Kamal's motives and he raised his eyebrows, worried. Was the man dressing up to look spiffy when he turned them over? Getting all proper like for whatever rich bastard was behind Beth's abduction?

"I see the doubt in your eyes. Please don't worry. I have an idea. I will need to convince anyone on the ship that I am there for official business."

They left the jail and made their way through the back alleys as quickly as Maxwell's condition allowed, trying to stay out of sight. Kamal filled them in on his plan as they went.

"You two will stay back, hidden on the docks and I will go onto the ship as if I'm on official business for the Captain of the Guard. I will tell whoever is watching your Beth that my captain has changed his mind and decided she must also be charged with murder, and that I am there to arrest her."

"No way I'm staying on the dock mate. Mattie should stay back, but I'm going too, at least as far as the gangplank. There might be trouble and you'll need me."

"The minute you are seen, our plan will be ruined!" He wanted to remind Maxwell that his injuries would prevent him from being much help as well, but knew the stubborn man would take serious offense if he pointed out the obvious. He held his tongue and repeated his request. "You must stay back or they will know."

"I won't be seen. I'm not a fool."

"Both of you stop this bickering at once. It's not getting us anywhere. Kamal, I'm not inclined to stay back at the dock either. Don't ever begin to think I'm helpless. Maxwell here can fill you in on how wrong that assumption is. The things I've seen and done to survive, well... let's just say I'm not your sweet Matagi anymore. Haven't you noticed that I talk like a gutter rat? I'm not all helpless and refined. Twenty years on the streets will change a person, and not for the better."

"Matagi, please do not say such things about yourself. You are still my beautiful wife. I don't care about your past."

Maxwell looked from Mattie's anguished face to Kamal who was struggling for the words to make Mattie see none of it mattered to him, and decided this simply wasn't the place or time for the soul searching reunion needed between the two. He cared about how Mattie felt, hell he loved the feisty woman, but Beth was alone and needed them now.

"Listen, I don't mean to sound like a cold bastard here, you've done so much for us Mattie, but Beth..."

One more look passed between the reunited lovers, and Kamal gently reached out and stroked her face. It was a simple gesture, but one full of promise. Mattie took his hand, smiling.

"Now then where was I? Oh yes, me going to the ship. I am going up to the ship." The fire in her eye left no doubt, and Kamal simply nodded in agreement.

"Maxwell and I will move into place one at a time, and when we're ready, you'll march onto that boat like you own the place and do your thing. That way we can watch, and Maxwell and I can be in position to ambush Captain Trammell if he comes back before you get Beth off safely."

"We've still got a problem though. Beth isn't going to trust Kamal any more than she'd trust another guard."

"My guess is that she'll be so relieved that she's being taken to where you are that she won't fight. Besides, if she goes without a struggle it won't look right."

"But she might get hurt if she fights back!"

Mattie looked at Maxwell and sighed. "You know very well that Beth can take care of herself. If anything, I should be worried about Kamal. I've seen Beth when she's mad. Now please Maxwell, just let Kamal go on that ship and get Beth. If she knows you're waiting, she's going to look too happy for a woman being hauled off to jail."

Maxwell grumbled, but finally nodded his head, then looked up at Kamal.

"Does she always win every argument?"

"As far as I know. That has been my experience." Even with the dire situation they were in, Maxwell couldn't help but grin and shake his head at Kamal's words.

"Just make sure you're careful with my girl, okay?"

"Like she was my own, Matagi. Beth will be safe."

One at a time, Maxwell then Mattie made their way along the dock and up the smaller plank way that led to the ship. They hid amid the cargo that was stacked there, waiting to be loaded when the crew got back from their shore leave. Once they were in place, Kamal walked briskly up to the ship and onto the gangway, shoulders squared, looking very official. He stepped on board, looking around for the man on watch, sure he couldn't be far, and he didn't have to search for long.

Their eyes met and the sailor immediately jumped to his feet. He'd been lazing on deck, almost dozing, not expecting any trouble, and was surprised by Kamal's appearance. He walked forward, wary, hand on the butt of his pistol, and Kamal did the same.

"Can I help you? There's no trouble on this ship. No need for you to be here."

"That's not quite true now is it? There has been plenty of trouble on board as you well know. Your Captain transported two fugitives here from India. We have the man in custody and I have been sent for the woman you are holding."

"Your Captain told mine she was to remain on board under his custody. She's a victim, innocent of any crime. Kidnaped by the man you hold."

"There is new evidence against her. The man we have, Maxwell Harrison, has implicated the woman. He has been very helpful in our investigation now that we have been able to persuade him. She is as guilty as he is. The royal family in India must be placated. Take me to her now."

"I think we'd better wait until Captain Trammell returns. He said the girl was to stay on board."

"Perhaps you would like to occupy a cell in our jail as well. We are the law when you are docked in our port. I repeat, she is a fugitive, and you are to take me to her now. I will not tell you again."

The sailor scanned the dock, searching for his captain, confused. If he let the girl go he would most likely be whipped to shreds once they were back at sea. On the other hand, if he didn't, he'd be in jail and most likely hung at dawn. Perhaps it was best to release Beth and jump ship. He'd wait until the Talisman left port and find work on another. When it came down to it, why should he risk his hide so Captain Trammell could have some fun with the woman?

"Very well. Follow me. I have to warn you that she's feisty." Kamal eyed a long scratch on the sailor's cheek and had to fight back a smile.

"Feisty does not do well when faced with a pistol. Take me to the woman."

In the back of his mind Kamal was wishing he had brought some irons for Beth's wrists. He didn't want to risk her struggling for the gun.

"Ah… but I am not one to shoot a woman. My Captain would be angry if she were injured. Perhaps you have something to secure her? It was a foolish mistake on my part."

The sailor cut a length of rope for Kamal and tossed it to him then took him below to Beth's cabin. He unlocked it quickly and shoved hard, knowing if Beth had been standing behind it, she would have been knocked clear. Kamal rushed past the sailor and grabbed a startled Beth who was rising from the bed, her nightmarish dream still fogging her brain.

"What? Let me go!"

"Miss, you are under arrest for murder, and must come with me. We can do this easy or hard. The choice is yours."

Beth looked at Kamal in shock. They were arresting her too? "I... I thought... Maxwell. Will I get to see Maxwell?"

"If you are referring to the man brought in earlier today, I suppose that it might be possible for you to catch a glimpse of him through the window of your cell door. Put your hands behind your back so I may secure them."

"Is he all right? Tell me please. Is Maxwell okay? Did they hurt him?"

Kamal didn't want to panic Beth, but if she thought Maxwell was seriously hurt she would come more easily. Besides, he wanted to convince the sailor he was as evil as the rest. "We have had a bit of sport yes, but he will live to see his hanging."

It was a bad bit of judgment on Kamal's part. Beth let out a screech that could clearly be heard by Maxwell and Mattie, and went at Kamal with everything she had, kicking, screaming, scratching, in a rage.

"How dare you hurt him? He did nothing. NOTHING!"

Kamal was in a quandary. He had a crazed woman on his hands and the situation was spinning out of control. He knew Captain Trammell could return at any time and be alerted by Beth's cries. He also knew Maxwell was hearing every scream, and was probably ready to rush to her aid.

Turning without warning, he landed a punch squarely on the sailor's jaw, and then hit him again, two more times until the man went down unconscious. Kamal then turned back to Beth who had stopped mid shriek, and stood there with her mouth hanging open in shock.

"My name is Kamal. I am Matagi's husband." At Beth's blank look Kamal realized his mistake. "Mattie. I'm Mattie's husband. She and Maxwell are waiting on the dock for us. Come with me now. We must hurry."

Beth took a step back, forehead creased, eyes narrowed. "How do I know you aren't lying to me?"

"What purpose do I have in beating your guard? Please, come with me now. We must hurry. Your Maxwell is injured, and we all need to get somewhere safe."

"Maxwell is hurt? Oh God. Maxwell."

"No, no, not too badly. He will live. Ribs, head, but not bad. Please come."

Beth nodded and started towards the door with Kamal at her heels. "Wait, I should tie him, hide him, and tie you too. If anyone sees us..."

Beth turned, eyes flashing. "Not on your life mister. Hurry up with him, then take me to Maxwell and Mattie."

Chapter Thirty-seven

The sight of Beth racing across the deck of the ship was one of the happiest visions Maxwell had ever seen. When she had begun screaming, Mattie had had to hold him back. His fury mounted with every cry, but his wounds prevented him from breaking her hold. He couldn't draw a deep breath without tremendous pain, and fast movements still made his head spin. Thank God she didn't look hurt. By the look on her face, she wasn't in shock either, just mad as hell. That was his girl.

He made his way from behind the crates, supported by Mattie, and held open his arms. Beth flung herself at him, and Maxwell hissed, but held her tight. Hearing his sound of pain she tried to back off, making a little sound of panic, but Maxwell would have none of it.

"Oh kitten, are you okay baby? Did that bastard hurt you? I swear if he touched one hair on your head I'll hunt him down. I'll string him up and flay him alive." He ran his thumbs over her cheeks which were stained with tears, but flushed with happiness.

"Maxwell I'm fine. I am. He didn't touch me. He left right after they took you away. What about you? Kamal said you were hurt. Oh Maxwell, they beat you."

This time Beth did push back so she could look at Maxwell, and her eyes welled with tears. He clutched his side, unable to stop himself, each breath felt like broken glass grating his insides. His face was bruised, and blood stained his collar from the gash in his head.

"Oh Maxwell. Just look at you."

"Never mind me, kitten. That's enough fussing. Kamal, do you have any idea where we can hide? It won't be long before Trammell realizes his prize has gone missing, and then the search will be on."

"Don't you pretend you don't need doctoring, Maxwell. Beth's right, you're in pretty bad shape. Kamal, where can we go? I need supplies. Bandages, hot water, that head might need a stitch."

"My friend, he is a ship's captain and is gone at sea. His house is empty. We are close and shared a bond, but happily I do not have being a widower in common with him any longer. I now have my Matagi back.

"His house is down the coast, away from the city. He hates it here, but the commerce is good. They will most likely look for me at my home, but I doubt if they would think of searching for us there. He has no caretaker. He is very much a recluse, but for me."

"How far is it? Maxwell can't..."

"Yes I can kitten. Whatever it takes, I can. Let's go. It's dark now and that's good. Better to hide. We can stay in the back alleys and..." Maxwell suddenly stopped and turned to Mattie, a frown of concern creasing his forehead.

"Mattie, listen to me. Maybe it's best if Beth and I head out on our own from now on. I mean here's Kamal who doesn't even know us risking his neck to save our hides. This isn't right. If you stay with us it will ruin your lives. You've done your share Mattie, been there through it all, and helped us more than we could ever repay you for. Maybe it's time to let go.

"Point us in the right direction and we'll be on our way. I can break in the place all nice and gentle like, and we'll leave it safe and sound. Go away with him Mattie and be happy. You deserve it."

"I'd kick you in the shins and box your ears for that if you weren't hurt already. You listen to me Maxwell, we're friends and friends stick together through the rough times. You helped me get out of India, gave me a chance despite my ugly face, and even got me out of the slums. You two gave me a reason for living. I'm not leaving you now. Besides, I like a little adventure in my life."

In a fraction of a second Mattie's scowl turned into a look of pure love as she turned from Maxwell to Kamal. "But as for you my darling. You didn't ask for any of this. I know you vowed to stay by my side but I don't think you knew what that meant when you said it. I'll understand if you don't want to help us. Your job, your life here, it's all ruined unless you go back and ..."

"And say what? The man on the ship will identify me as the one who beat him and took Beth. Besides, that doesn't matter one bit. It's not why I'm staying. We belong together, Matagi. You are my life. It has been empty since the day they stole you from me. We will go together, all of us, and it's time to leave right now. We'd better not risk a carriage. I don't want anyone to remember us. It will be a long journey on foot but it can be done. Come Maxwell. I shall help you. We can stop once we are out of town so Mattie can tie your ribs. It will help if you only take shallow breaths."

With a hiss of pain Maxwell went and leaned into Kamal, as Beth took up her place on his other side, then Mattie led the way as Kamal directed her, keeping a close watch for Captain Trammell or any of the guards as they began their journey to safety and freedom.

Chapter thirty-eight

The foursome made their way through the darkness, heads down, yearning to be invisible to all who passed. Few gave them a second look. Maxwell would let out a drunken laugh when anyone did glanced their way, stumbling a bit, clinging to Kamal, to hide his injuries, feigning a lack of coordination due to too much whiskey rather than the brutal beating he'd received. Mattie in turn would mumble a scolding, muttering about the chore of fetching drunken husbands, and Beth would shake her head in dismay.

Their ruse worked remarkably well, and they were able to leave the main of Cape Town behind them without incident. Once they were safely away from the busy port, surrounded only by darkness and the hum of insects, Kamal guided Maxwell to the side of the road so Mattie and Beth could tend to his wounds.

"I don't need to stop. As soon as Captain Trammell discovers Beth is gone, he'll sound the alarm."

"Hush you. This will only take a minute. Let me bind those ribs. Every breath must feel like ground glass."

"I said, don't fuss over me. Leave me alone, woman. I'm fine."

At odds with the stubborn Mattie once again, Maxwell pushed away from Kamal, moving to stand on his own. He managed, but couldn't hide the grunt of pain caused by his rash movement.

"Maxwell, please." Beth came forward to support him, hands squeezing his upper arms. As she did, the moon came out, shining directly on her face, and Maxwell was lost. Pure emotion poured forth. Love, tenderness, but now fear too. Such fear it killed him.

"Beth... kitten I'm all right. We have to get to safety."

"How can I go on knowing you're in agony? Don't ask it of me. You're everything... I love you. Do you know how much it pains me that I can't carry you? Please do as I ask."

Maxwell cocked his head to the side, and stared at his girl in wonderment. Oh those eyes of hers. They mesmerized, charmed, and overwhelmed him. He'd once heard that the eyes were the mirrors of the soul. If that were true, then Maxwell wanted to see himself through Beth's for the rest of his days. Love had blinded her to all his faults, his soul had been washed clean. If the world saw him as she did, then he would truly be redeemed.

"All right kitten, for you, but please hurry."

Kamal quickly helped Maxwell sit while Beth tugged one of her petticoats from under her dress. She began tearing it into strips while Mattie opened Maxwell's shirt and pressed her fingertips to the discolored flesh. Maxwell winced and shot her a fierce look.

"Here now! That's not necessary. Just bind me up and be done with it. Your prodding won't help and we don't have time."

"Do you want me to do it right or not? Maybe I should just bandage you up from chin to hips."

Maxwell grumbled but held his tongue while Mattie continued. She shook her head and muttered about thugs and evil men, but quickly took the strips of cloth Beth offered and bound Maxwell's ribs.

"There now. You can't bend or take such a deep breath. It'll help with the pain. What you need is rest. I imagine that head of yours needs tending too, thick as it is."

"Perhaps it can wait Matagi. I feel as if our luck is running out." His words made Beth look nervously back towards town. Time was not on their side tonight.

"He's right Mattie. As much as I hate to say it, we need to push on. Lean on me Maxwell. We can make it together."

"Wouldn't have it any other way, kitten."

On they went into the night, stopping once to lie silently in the ditch beside the road when a trio of men on horseback approached. After they passed, Beth looked up, her eyes widening when she recognized the uniforms of the Cape Town Police on all three.

"I think our secrets out. Best go as fast as we can now. How far is it, Kamal?"

"Just around the next bend, then through the brush. We'll go the back way."

As they approached the house, keeping low in the tall grasses, it became evident that lamps were lit within.

"I thought you said your captain friend was at sea." The frustration at this new turn of events made Maxwell's voice thick with emotion.

"He was to have left two days ago. I... I don't understand this."

No one said a word as they all stared at the house that was to be their refuge. The silence cut into Kamal's heart. He felt as if he'd betrayed his new friends and his love. Maxwell and Beth were good people, preyed upon by the very people he'd been trying to oppose since taking the job as a guard.

"Wait here."

Before anyone could say a word, Kamal dashed out of hiding and went towards the house in the clearing before them. As they watched Kamal making his way to the safe house, Maxwell felt Beth tugging frantically on his sleeve. He turned to her, and she gestured not to the man sneaking steadily to their place of refuge, but to the house itself. Maxwell watched closely and saw what had caused Beth's concern.

The house wasn't lit by lamps in each room; it was lit by three lanterns moving through it. The guards they had seen must be inside, searching room by room. What did that mean on the whereabouts of Kamal's friend, and better yet, what did that mean for Kamal who was at that very moment about to sneak into the place that was inhabited by the enemy?

Mattie had also noticed the movement of the lanterns, and knew what it meant. As she stood, intent on warning Kamal, a loud click rang out in the silence behind them.

"Don't move a muscle the lot of you, or I'll shoot you where you stand. I won't have your thieving kind on my property."

He jabbed the pistol in Maxwell's back. "You, hands up." Maxwell complied, unwilling to put Beth and Mattie in danger, praying he'd have a chance to reason with the man if they did as he asked.

"Good, now slowly walk towards the house."

Beth turned her head slightly, Mattie was frozen, staring off towards the spot where they had last seen Kamal, her face etched with terror, her usually sharp tongue silent. Beth knew it might be unwise to speak at this point, but she was also unwilling to give this man a reason to shoot Maxwell. The sooner he knew they meant no harm the better. She knew she had to try and explain.

"Please, we're friends of Kamal."

"Kamal doesn't have any friends but me."

"You must listen to me. He brought us here and is about to go into your house right now, but we have to stop him. The guards from the jail are in there, looking for us."

"More like he and the guards are looking for you. Hush your mouth wench." He jabbed Maxwell again, indicating he should get moving, and grabbed Beth's arm roughly.

Mattie was snapped from her trance by the man's actions. She looked from the man's hand, to the fire about to explode in Maxwell's eyes and knew she had to do something.

"Look, I know this all sounds fanciful, but I'm Matagi, Kamal's wife. He thought I was dead but we found each other today in that hell hole of a jail. He's helping my friends escape from those corrupt bastards, and now he's in trouble himself for doing it.

"Think about it. Would he be working with them to find prisoners who escaped? Especially women? No one held there is guilty of anything but going against the likes of them. If we don't stop him before he gets into that house there's gonna be a lot of bloodshed. If it winds up being his, you'll answer to me, pistol or no pistol."

The man's eyes narrowed with disbelief. "Matagi's dead. How could you be her?"

"We don't have time for the how's and all. We have to call him back."

Mattie tugged a silver medallion from under her dress and held it up in the moonlight. "Does this look familiar at all? He ever tell you about a pendant his mother gave me to welcome me into the family? One is made on the eve of the wedding and given to each new bride. It was all I had left of him. He had one just like it. Might still have, I don't know."

The man looked at the pendant then nodded. "So be it. I'll go ahead and catch him. If the guards see me, they have no reason to question my being in the gardens of my own home. You stay here." That said the man was gone.

Time passed slowly. Each silently watching as the lanterns moved throughout the house, waiting for a cry of discovery or the crack of a pistol shot, praying Kamal would return to their hiding place safely before that happened. Finally, he did, and Mattie threw her arms around his neck, pulling him down into the brush where they sat.

"Shhh... It's okay Matagi. I'm safe. We have to move now and quickly. Hameed went in through the back, acting as if he'd been walking in the gardens. He is now serving whiskey to the guards in the front parlor, and that will keep them well occupied. We shall go in the back entrance too, but then we will slip into a secret room. There is a bookshelf in the wall of his study that conceals it. He had the room built when the political uprisings were at their worst here. It's small but secure, as long as we make no noise.

"Are you sure we can trust him? I thought he was supposed to be at sea, and he seemed awfully trigger happy out here."

"He's a cautious man. We have seen too much corruption and pain in our lives. If you are on the side of good, then Hameed will do all he can to help. I didn't want to involve him but he wouldn't hear of doing anything but helping. As far as his being home, his ship needed unexpected repairs. He called it a good twist of fate."

"All right then, let's go. Beth love, take my hand, Kamal, lead the way."

They made their way out of the brush and through the small garden to the back door without a sound. Kamal led them inside, and everyone stopped a moment to let their eyes adjust. Even the dim moonlight outside was bright in comparison to the blackness of the deserted kitchen.

When they could make out the silhouettes of each other and the furniture around them, Kamal took them down several hallways and into a small study. He stood before a large bookcase and touched it in three places, causing it to swing wide without a sound. The passage to the secret room was kept well oiled. Two by two they entered, and when they were safely tucked away, Kamal closed the case up tight.

Wrapping his arms around Mattie, Maxwell, and Beth, Kamal said in the faintest of whispers. "No light, no talking, until Hameed comes for us."

All nodded in agreement and Beth helped Maxwell to the floor, curling up next to him, holding his hand like a vice. Kamal and Mattie huddled near the door, watching, waiting, barely breathing for fear of being heard.

Time passed slowly, while they listened to the voices of the guards become slurred with drink. Finally Hameed was able to bid them goodnight. Still he waited to come for them, going about the house, preparing it and himself for bed, following his routine, in case he was being watched. At last, his footsteps sounded outside the hidden room and the bookcase swung open.

"Greetings, my new friends. Forgive me for my earlier welcome, as one can never be too cautious these days in Cape Town. Come this way. You're in need of rest. We can talk in the morning."

Hameed led them to their rooms. The thick drapes had been pulled securely shut, a lamp lit, the wash bowl filled with hot water, and night clothes laid out.

"If you need anything else, let me know, otherwise I won't disturb you." That said, Hameed, Mattie, and Kamal left Beth and Maxwell at their door.

Chapter Thirty-nine

Beth helped Maxwell to the chair near the bed and began to unbutton his shirt. For once he didn't protest her fussing. She stripped it off him and rang out a cloth in the wash basin, lifting the hair at his brow to gently wipe at the crusted blood on his head. Maxwell grimaced but didn't speak. Every muscle in his body ached, and his ribs throbbed in time with the pounding of his head. Their wild journey had been hell on him.

He let Beth wipe the grime and sweat from his face, neck and chest, relishing in the tender touch of her soft hands. Reaching up, wincing in the process, he took one in his and turned it palm up, kissing it gently.

"Do you know how much I love you kitten? How proud of you I am? How incredibly brave I think you are? You're my angel, sent to redeem me and make my life worth living."

Beth had to blink back her tears at his words. "I'm not your angel, Maxwell. I'm just the woman whose heart you've captured completely. I do the things I do out of love. Now let me undress you and tuck you in that wonderful bed. See there? You promised me one just like it for tonight. You always live up to your promises."

"That's my girl, always finding the good in everything. Never mind the bed isn't in some fancy hotel like it was supposed to be, and never mind the ordeal we had to go through to get here. Come here for a kiss luv."

Beth leaned in and let her lips linger on his for just a moment then pulled back. Maxwell tried to protest but she held a finger to his lips and moved her hands to the button on his breeches.

"You, into that clean night shirt and under those sheets, now."

Elizabeth tugged off his boots and pants, slid the long shirt over his head, and then helped Maxwell stand. He swayed slightly but Beth steadied him and helped him to the bed. Maxwell couldn't help but sigh when he slid between the cool clean sheets.

"Feels heavenly, kitten. Come here."

"In a minute, you. Let me wash and change."

Maxwell's eyes never left his love as she stripped off her gown and wiped off the dirt of their ordeal. They sent a shiver down her spine as they traveled every inch of her in time with the cloth. Smiling, she slipped the other night shirt over her head, doing a little turn from side to side to show off her new outfit, giggling at how the material engulfed her small frame.

"Not the height of fashion or the least bit romantic but it's clean, and romance is out of the question anyway."

"You'll have lots of satins and lace soon luv, I promise. Now come here."

Beth slid into the big bed and turned to blow the lantern out. She then carefully snuggled up against Maxwell. He lay on his back and wrapped his arm around her as she nuzzled into his neck, hand held over his heart, body pressed close. Being safe in his arms had never felt so good.

"I love you Maxwell."

"Luv you too, pet." Both fell asleep within minutes, Maxwell gently stroking Beth's hair, each listening to the soothing sound of the others breathing, lost in the world of them.

~~~~~~~~~~~

Morning came and went as did most of the afternoon, and still the pair slept on. They slept the sleep of utter exhaustion, spirits and bodies mending with the badly needed rest. Finally Beth awoke. She tried to slip out of bed without waking Maxwell, but the mere absence of her body woke him at once. He opened one eye to see her standing at the side of the bed and reached out for her, pulling her back to him.

"Where you going, kitten?"

Beth gave Maxwell a fierce look at the hiss of pain his movement caused him, ready to scold him, but couldn't do it. He looked too adorable, with his sleepy eyes and tousled hair. Instead she gave in and lay in his arms, gazing up at him as he leaned in for a kiss. His lips were soft as they moved over hers, exploring, relishing the sweetness of her, showing her with exquisite tenderness just how much he loved her in that one simple action.

When he was done, Maxwell leaned back, eyes twinkling at the flush of her cheeks. "Morning kitten."

"Actually I think it's more like afternoon judging by the growling of my stomach. I was on my way downstairs to bring us something to eat."

She moved out of his grasp and got out of bed before Maxwell could catch her. He made a serious sound of displeasure and narrowed his eyes.

"You'll do no such thing. I'll not have you waitin' on me. I'm not an invalid. Besides, I want to talk to Hameed. I don't think we can stay here long. Help me up, kitten. We'll get dressed and go down together."

Beth knew there was no use arguing, besides, he had a point. They couldn't stay here and put Hameed at risk. "Okay, I give in, but don't get used to it Mister."

"Wouldn't dream of it pet, I like you feisty." He reached for her, intending to pull her down for a heated kiss, bad ribs be damned, but Beth dodged him.

"Oh no you don't." Beth stood out of reach tapping her foot in mock irritation, and all Maxwell could do was grin at her. God she was beautiful.

"You're impossible. Stop that smirking and get out of bed."

"Can't, bad ribs remember?"

"Maxwell..."

"What?"

"We both know you'd be up in a flash if you wanted to, and would refuse anyone else's help."

"No one else is as pretty as you."

"I repeat. You're impossible."

"And I'm all yours pet. Now come help me. I promise to be good. They really are still sore."

Beth shook her head and narrowed her eyes. She certainly didn't want him to injure himself further. Besides, how could she resist those gorgeous blue eyes and that puppy dog look, he was giving her?

"Okay, but no kisses until we're both dressed and ready to go downstairs."

Maxwell gave her his best pout, but agreed. He knew they needed to get moving. The problem was he couldn't help teasing her just a little too. "It's a deal luv. No kisses... for now."

Fifteen minutes and a dozen kisses later they were making their way towards the large kitchen at the back of the house where delicious aromas were wafting from. The sound of merry conversation drifted on the air. Arm in arm they entered the room to find Mattie, Kamal, and Hameed sitting around the big table with a veritable feast laid out upon it.

"Ah here you are. I was starting to think you'd sleep clear through the day and into the night." Mattie smiled and gestured for them to come in, as Hameed rose and pulled out a chair for Beth. "You must be as famished as we were. Hameed's a wonderful cook; I'll get you some coffee. We were just catching up."

Hameed began to pass various dishes as Mattie poured coffee. Beth smiled as she watched the way Kamal's eyes followed her every move. There was no doubt he was still very much in love with her. Time, and the pain of her ordeal, hadn't diminished her in his eyes one bit.

Everyone ate and made small talk, and after a while the conversation turned to the inevitable. What were they going to do? How were they going to get out of Africa? They couldn't just stroll back to the dock and get on board Hameed's ship.

Hameed listened to the conversation, filling his pipe, leaning back, mulling over various ideas. He was a quiet man, and very intelligent. The combination made most think of him as a brooding loner. The spark had gone out of him when he'd lost his family years ago, and he never much cared for the company of others after that.

Finally, after thinking long and hard about the country he'd come to call home, an idea came to him. It wouldn't be easy, but it might be possible. It depended on the strength of the people before him. Hameed sat up in his chair and nodded slowly, pulling his pipe from his mouth and rubbing his chin.

"I've thought of something, though I don't know if there's even half a chance it will work." Everyone sat waiting as Hameed thought over the plan once again.

"Well mate, don't keep us in suspense any longer. What's on your mind? We've already been through hell, a little more won't stop us."

"You'll walk out of here. You'll walk to Saldanha Bay and I will pick you up there. Once you're on board we'll sail to England or where ever it is you're bound. I'll load enough supplies that we won't need to stop, and take only the crew I know I can trust. It will only be a handful so Maxwell and Hameed, you'll have to pitch in, but I think we can do it."

Chapter Forty

"Saldanha Bay!" Kamal had risen to his feet but Mattie put a calming hand on his arm and pulled him back down. Still he looked at his old friend like he was insane.

"Hameed, the journey by ship doesn't worry me. It's the trek by land that's madness. It's well over a hundred kilometers, almost a hundred and a half. The terrain is rough, there's little water, the women..."

Both Mattie and Beth slapped their hands on the table at Kamal's last declaration making the dishes rattle.

"Do not add us to the list of reasons we can't do this, Kamal. Beth and I have overcome our fair share of hardships. That little bit of a woman has fought a damn good fight against some pretty big men to get this far. Don't misjudge her or me."

Maxwell knew if he'd been the one who'd made that comment; his tongue lashing from Mattie would have been less gentle. He was glad Kamal had been the one to bring it up. The women were a factor, but he was too. He wasn't a hundred percent right now. If anything, he'd be the one to slow them down.

"Let's hear him out. Tell us more."

"Saldanha lies to the west. It's a small coastal town. Used for whaling mostly. Not a lot of other trade there. There is no overland tract. People don't walk from Cape Town to Saldanha. There is nothing in between but the wilds. Brush, sand, animals. If you try to make it there, you would have to be heavily armed and carry a lot of supplies."

"What about horses?"

Both Kamal and Hameed shook their heads. Kamal spoke up first. There are too many predators. The horses would attract much unwanted attention from them, and the terrain is too rough. We'll have to carry packs. It will also be safest to move at night."

"I still think it's too far. As I said, people don't walk from Cape Town to Saldanha. It was folly to think of it."

Maxwell still wasn't ready to dismiss the idea. He was well aware that Kamal knew more about Africa than he did, but they hadn't come up with any other options.

"Maybe people don't, Kamal, but we can and will. It's not folly mate. It can't be. It's our only hope. Now I'm not sayin' it's best for you and Mattie, but Beth and I have to try."

"You're not gonna try it yourselves, Maxwell. If you go, Kamal and I go too. Safety in numbers and all that. Besides, we can't very well stay here, and neither of us wants to see India again. There's nothing left for us there."

"When then?" Kamal still wasn't sure about the whole plan, but he didn't see much choice. Mattie was right; they couldn't stay in Cape Town.

Mattie gave a small smile, glad that Kamal was coming around to their way of thinking. "That's up to Hameed. How long will it take to fix your ship, and how long do you think it might take for us to get there?"

"The ship will be ready in a day or so, as for the four of you, if you make it, and that's a big if, I'd say two, maybe three weeks, depends on the weather and how strong all of you really are. One thing's for sure. You have to leave soon. Winter's coming and we get some mighty fierce storms in this part of the world. No captain in his right mind sails near the Cape in winter."

"Then we leave, now."

"Maxwell, you can't, your ribs."

"Beth don't start mothering me. I just had a rest.'"

"I'm not mothering! I'm being practical. It wasn't a long enough rest. Not enough to help those ribs. You heard what Hameed said. We aren't going for a little stroll around the garden. This is serious. When we leave, you need to be strong. We all do. Give it two days. Please."

Maxwell turned away. He couldn't look Beth in the eye. Indecision and anger raged through him. He felt like a burden to all of them. Maxwell felt Beth's hand close over his.

"Maxwell please, two days to rest, and then we'll leave at dusk."

"What about Hameed? We can't stay here without putting him in danger."

"That's not a valid reason Maxwell. Those guards last night didn't suspect a thing. I talked with them long enough to know that. They are full of greed, not intelligence, and we'll take shifts keeping an eye out just in case. It won't take but a minute to get everyone in the secret room."

"They'll be signs of us here if they search again."

"Oh, you are so stubborn. Then we'll simply take turns sleeping in the hidden room and make sure we don't leave any messes. Now stop with the excuses. You need to rest. Isn't that right, Mattie?"

"Okay, okay. Don't get her involved. I know when I've lost, kitten."

Beth jumped up and threw her arms around him, kissing his face and whispering a multitude of thank you's. She knew it had been hard for him to give up the fight.

They settled back into conversation about supplies, making a list and talking about the terrain and animals they were likely to encounter. All of them knew it would be a very daunting task, but they also knew they had no choice. Where there was a will there was a way. When the fire died down and darkness filled the room, Hameed rose and stretched.

"Matagi and Kamal, you sleep in the hidden room. Beth and Maxwell take my bed. I'll keep watch. You're the ones who need to rest and recuperate. You have a long journey ahead."

When Maxwell began to protest anew about Hameed giving up his bed, the man held up his hand. "I won't hear of it. If one bed is slept in, they won't suspect anything, and you need a comfortable place to sleep in order to heal. I'll wake you at dawn for your watch."

Beth thanked Hameed, and took Maxwell's arm before he could come up with any more excuses not to take the man up on his generosity. Truth be told, even though she felt a little guilty for Mattie and Kamal, the thought of sleeping in a real bed again thrilled her.

"Come on you. We're off to bed. Good night everyone. Thank you Hameed."

They climbed the stairs and walked to the doorway of Hameed's room. Beth gave Maxwell a kiss on the cheek and a little push towards the bed. "You, bed, now. I'll be back in a minute."

"Hey now kitten, where do you think you're going?'

"I want to make the bed in the room we slept in, and make sure there are no signs we were there."

"I'll come with you."

"You'll do no such thing. I know those ribs have to be hurting you. Now get in that bed."

"You've become quite the sassy little chit now haven't you?"

Beth pursed out her lips. "Only when I have to. Besides, you like me feisty remember? Now I'll be right back. Then I promise I'll come right to bed."

She hurried down the hall and straightened the room they had occupied until no traces remained, then returned to Maxwell. He was waiting for her, lying on his side, head propped up by one arm, wearing a huge smile and nothing else.

Beth took one look at the gleam in his eyes and shook her head.

"Oh no you don't. I know that look. Put this on."

She tossed him the night shirt she'd brought from the other room then turned and quickly changed, keeping her back to Maxwell. Beth could feel the heat of his eyes on her skin, and knew that a glimpse of her bare backside was about as enticing as the front of her, but this way she didn't have to try quite as hard to resist the desire in his eyes.

"Aw kitten, are you making my blood heat up and telling me no? Come here and let me change your mind." His voice was a silken purr and Beth had to take a slow steadying breath to calm her own racing heart.

"Maxwell, we can't. If you won't be practical and listen to the pain in your body I will be the sensible one."

"I've got another more serious ache right now that needs tending, and I don't like this new sensible you."

Beth could picture that very serious ache. She could feel the hot velvety skin of his cock pressed against her belly and thrusting inside her, but she forced the images out of her head.

"No Maxwell. You have to heal. Two days isn't nearly enough time for those ribs to mend as it is. Making love is out of the question. Now do I have to sleep in the secret room with Kamal and Mattie?"

Maxwell let out a growl, his eyes flashing. "You'll do no such thing woman. Get in this bed. I won't be denied having you in my arms. Just remember you're due for a serious spanking and a good rough and tumble the minute these ribs are mended, pet. When I'm good as new, I won't be denied no matter what you say."

Beth knew Maxwell had reached his limit with being told what do to for the day, and slid between the sheets without a word. She cuddled up next to him, bringing her hand up to stroke his chest and looked up into his eyes.

"Don't be angry, Maxwell. If I were hurt, you'd be smothering me with your nursing. I'm really not trying to be a bossy chit." She kissed him quick and stroked his cheek, then rubbed gently behind his ear in the place that always made him purr.

"I know kitten, and you're right, but you're still getting that bottom warming."

"Will there be lots of kisses and cuddles afterwards?"

"Oh there will be kisses and cuddles, among other things, baby, among lots and lots of other things."

Maxwell pressed forward into her body and Beth could feel his desire hard against her belly. She stroked his back and kissed him gently. Oh how she wanted to please him with her hands and mouth, she really did, but the clenching of his stomach muscles when he found his release would cause him agony. Right now he wasn't thinking with his head.

"I love you Maxwell. I love you, and every part of me is full of desire for you but I am going to be strong for both of us."

Beth scooted back a few inches so their bodies weren't pressed together. She took his hands in hers and held them tight between them, up near their hearts. Leaning in, she captured his lips in a chaste kiss. "Soon my love, I promise. Now go to sleep."

"I have more willpower than that, and I need to feel you in my arms."

Maxwell pulled her close and threw a leg over her body, molding her to every inch of him, possessing her completely. "That's better. Now we can sleep. I love you too, kitten. Love you too."

Chapter Forty-one

Their two days of rest passed uneventfully, and once it was over, everyone eager to leave. Though Maxwell's ribs still pained him when he moved suddenly, he could take fairly deep breaths, and felt he could hold his own on their long journey.

Hameed had scouted the area around his house several times for signs they were being watched, and found none. A single rider had visited, but only to question him as to whether he'd seen anyone suspicious. Perhaps the guards felt Hameed and Kamal weren't that close after all, or perhaps they thought Kamal wouldn't endanger Hameed by enlisting his help. Whatever the reason, they'd been left alone.

They were sitting around the kitchen table, enjoying an early supper and conversation, set to leave as soon as the last traces of daylight left the sky, when Maxwell glanced over at Mattie and cocked his head. She in turn nodded and left the room, returning with two tiny velvet boxes.

Beth looked from Maxwell to Mattie, puzzled. Maxwell was grinning like a cat that'd swallowed a canary, and Mattie was beaming from ear to ear. Kamal and Hameed had knowing looks on their faces too. She seemed to be the only one finding the current turn of events a mystery.

"Maxwell what are those?"

"Hush now and wait. It's a surprise. Two surprises actually."

He rose and took both boxes from Mattie and knelt down before her, presenting her with just one. Beth's hands shook, her eyes getting misty, thinking she knew exactly what was in the tiny box. She slowly opened it and gasped.

"Is this..? How did you get it? Oh Maxwell is it really?"

Lying on a bed of satin inside the box was a tiny key, just like the one used to secure the hated concubine collar around her neck.

"It is kitten. Hameed here's been in shipping a long time. Africa has its own share of slave trade. He's given passage to many folks over the years, some of them men like Jeeval. He's also help women like you. Seems he managed to, shall we say, 'collect' a few keys here and there. He had them in a trunk in the attic. I think this one will fit. Your collar is unique, but if the key is the right size we should be able to at least loosen it. Hopefully it will come off easily."

Beth looked at Hammed, her lips parted, eyes welling with tears, unable to say the words of thanks.

The emotions she was feeling at the thought of really truly being free from Jeeval were too overwhelming. She held the box out to Maxwell, knowing she'd drop the key if she tried to pick it up, and took a shaky breath.

"Do it. Oh please, do it."

Maxwell gladly complied. He brushed back her hair and turned the collar so the tiny bolt that held it together was towards the front. Taking the key, he inserted it, and it fit like a charm. Turning it quickly, with nimble fingers, Maxwell removed the bolt and slowly pulled open the brass ring that had represented Jeeval's hold on Beth's freedom for these long months.

Maxwell looked up to see Beth's eyes squeezed shut. He slipped the collar from around her neck and held it before her face. "Open your eyes kitten."

"Oh! Oh it worked. Oh." She threw her arms around Maxwell and hugged him fiercely. Tears spilling down her cheeks, her heart soaring. "Thank you for this. Thank you so much." Maxwell rose, picking her up off her feet, despite the small jolt of pain it caused, spun her around kissing her, his own eyes getting a bit misty.

Beth finally turned and looked at Hameed, still stunned and overwhelmed by what he had given her. "I don't know what to say. How can I ever thank you?"

"No thanks are needed, Beth. Your happiness gives me great joy. Now if you'll turn back around, I believe there were two gifts. One is still waiting for you."

Beth whirled around back towards Maxwell. She'd forgotten the other box in her excitement. He took her hands and knelt before her again, presenting the second of the tiny boxes.

"Hameed had lots of interesting things in those old trunks of his kitten."

Beth opened the lid of the second box to find a simple, gold, wedding band.

"Marry me, Beth. I want to leave here with you as my wife. It seems a fitting way to start our new life. Will you have me?"

"Oh Maxwell, of course I will. I'll have you for two forevers. I love you too." She once more launched herself into Maxwell's waiting arms and rained kisses upon his face. Mattie began to clap and couldn't help but join in the hug.

"I've been waiting for this since Maxwell asked me to help him a couple of days ago. He's been itching to marry you proper for the longest time. Now take each other's hands and let Hameed get the job done. Sorry Beth, but we don't have time to do things up right. I'll get him to do you proper with flowers and silks when were settled somewhere honey."

Hameed moved before them, doing his best to look all official despite the wide smile on his face. "As Captain of the Merrimot, I am hereby authorized to unite this man and this woman in holy matrimony. Do you

Maxwell Harrison wish to take Elizabeth Thornton as your wife?

"I do."

"Then repeat after me. I Maxwell."

"I Maxwell."

"Take thee Elizabeth."

"Take my Beth."

Hameed gave a little shake of his head but let it pass. Maxwell had to do things his way. "To be my lawfully wedded wife."

"As my lovely, lawfully, wedded wife."

"Do you promise to care for her, cherish her, and protect her, forsaking all others for as long as you both shall live?"

"I do. I'm never gonna let her go."

"Elizabeth..."

"I do. I take Maxwell for my beloved husband. I promise to love him and cherish him, and to... honor him. I will always be by your side through whatever comes our way. Being with you brings me greater joy then I've ever known was possible. I love you Maxwell, with all my heart."

"I love you too Beth with all of mine."

"Well then, I guess that will do fine. Maxwell, place the ring on Beth's hand."

Maxwell gently held up Beth's hand and slipped the golden band on her finger. He then held both of her hands up and kissed them, looking deeply into her shimmering eyes.

"By the power invested in me, I now pronounce you man and wife. Maxwell you may kiss your bride."

Maxwell let out a whoop and crushed Beth to him, kissing her passionately. Both were filled with such an incredible feeling of joy. Yes they had been together for a long time, yes they had joined as lovers, but now they felt a special bond, a connection between heart, body and soul like nothing either had felt before. The kiss went on until both were out of breath. They finally broke away, Beth blushing when she remembered with a start, that the others were there. She had been totally and completely lost in her love for Maxwell and the joy that was soaring through her.

Kamal and Hameed slapped Maxwell on the back while Mattie hugged Beth, tears in her eyes. She swiped at them angrily, not normally one to show emotion, but Beth took Mattie's face in her hands and kissed her cheeks.

"You stop it. Tears are okay Mattie; especially now. Thank you so much for this. The wedding and ... and for helping to get that thing off me. I feel so free. Finally clean, like I belong to me again. I can't describe it."

"I know honey. I was there too, remember? That part of our lives is over. Come on now, time to get our packs. Are you ready for this?"

"I am. I'm more than ready. With Maxwell, you and Kamal by my side I can do anything. What's a little walk in the wilderness if it means we'll be able to go home? Besides, you and I are as tough as they come."

"That is the honest truth, honey. Give me another hug, and then let's get on our way."

"Mattie, can you and Kamal meet us out back in the brush? There's something I have to do."

"Sure honey. We'll get your packs."

Beth gave Mattie a quick hug, thanked Hameed again, and then took Maxwell by the hand.

"You're ready to go kitten?"

"Not quite. Mattie and Kamal are meeting us outside. Come on, there's one more thing that needs to be done before I leave this place."

Beth picked up the hated collar from the table and led Maxwell outside towards the cliff overlooking the ocean. She walked to the edge and stopped, gazing down at the waves crashing against the rocks, holding up the collar.

"What is it, luv? Not safe here so close."

"This thing represents all that was horrid in the past months."

Maxwell swallowed hard, becoming pale, as he felt a sharp stab of guilt inside. Beth quickly put her hand on his cheek, shaking her head. "No my love, don't feel like that. That's not what this is about. There was good with you, not bad. You are the reason I survived, the reason I found true love. This... this thing, represents that bastard Jeeval and all he did and tried to take from me."

"He deserves to be tortured. Deserves to be killed slowly for what he did to you, and what he may still be doing to other women. Our leaving, Beth, this running away is right, I know that, but part of me still needs to go back to India and finish what needs to be done. To get justice for you. I may have to go back someday, kitten."

"No Maxwell. We're not running away, we're going home. You have to let it go. This collar is my pain and my hurtful memories. In it are all the hateful things that were done to me. If I destroy it, they will be destroyed to."

With those words Beth flung the golden collar far out into the ocean. She knew it would take time, waves, and the rocks to batter down the brass, but in her heart, it had already been destroyed.

"I'm free Maxwell, were free." She gazed into his eyes and saw the lingering hurt, knowing the memories of his past and his part in what had been done to her, would be easier for him to deal with if he knew Jeeval were dead, but it just couldn't be. "Let it go Maxwell. Let your heart heal like mine has."

"But Beth, part of me will always have a need for revenge."

"Maxwell, some things are more important that revenge, more important than the past, more important than anything." Taking his hand, Beth gently placed it on her belly. "This is much more important Maxwell."

He looked at her in the twilight. The last crimson rays of the sunset barley lit her eyes, but in them Maxwell could see the truth of her actions. "A baby?"

Beth nodded as a single tear slid down her cheek. "Yes my love, a baby. A new life created out of the pain of our past. A child created by us who will forever give a joyous meaning to everything we went through. No matter what we endured Maxwell, it gave us a child."

Maxwell scooped her up in his arms, holding her lovingly, protectively, moving quickly away from the cliff. "A baby! Oh I love you. Oh Beth. You've given me the greatest gift a man could ask for. I'm going to be so careful with you. I'll carry you all the way. I'll..."

"You'll do none of that. We'll do it together, like we've always done, and we'll make it just fine, all three of us."

"Three. We're going to be a family. My kitten's going to have a baby. I'm going to be a father. I swear I'll be the best father, Beth. Oh, maybe it's a girl who'll be just like you, beautiful and smart and cheeky. Or maybe a boy..."

"He'll be stubborn and handsome and loving. Now kiss me quick and put me down. It's time to go home Maxwell."

"Yes luv. It's time to go home."

9 781481 038683